White Rain

(The Misadventures of
Max Bowman, Volume 4)

by Joel Canfield

Also by Joel Canfield

Dark Sky (The Misadventures of Max Bowman, Volume 1)

Blue Fire (The Misadventures of Max Bowman, Volume 2)

Red Earth (The Misadventures of Max Bowman, Volume 3)

What's Driving You???: How I Overcame Abuse and Learned to Lead in the NBA

(co-written with Lisa Canfield and Keyon Dooling)

Pill Mill: My Years of Money, Madness, Sex and Drugs

(co-written with Lisa Canfield and Christian Valdes)

226: How I Became the First Blind Person to Kayak the Grand Canyon

(co-written with Lonnie Bedwell)

"Where the Hell is Max Bowman?"

That's what people have been asking for almost a year. What no one knows is Max has been locked away in the Community — a "retirement" home for former CIA spooks with secrets too scary to share with the world.

But after engineering a daring and almost deadly escape, Max is back — or, at least, what's left of him. He's lost his love, his home, his money and most of his memories, while being haunted by a Russian Rat Pack that's out to kill him, a talking dog puppet that barks out apocalyptic warnings and a crooked lobbyist whose menace is almost as big as his stomach.

And then there's the matter of Max's dad — the man Max wants to make sure is dead.

Evil is pouring down in *White Rain,* the final chapter — and the final reckoning — in the Max Bowman saga.

Edited and abetted by Lisa Canfield

www.copycoachlisa.com

Cover illustration by A.J. Canfield

Audiobook version narrated by George Kuch

www.georgekuch.com

Find out more about the Max Bowman books at www.facebook.com/MaxBowmanBooks.

Table of Contents

Special thanks to Elisabeth "Sister Wife" Hinckley, Jeff "Rusty" Arch, Michael "Clintus" Camp, Dr. Sharon McCoy George, Beatrice Chestnut, Juan, Tania & Andrew Quintana, and Ethan, David & AJ Canfield.

And for all of you who have supported Max up until this final adventure. Even Bruce Kanin, even though he will never, ever, ever, ever post his Red Earth *review on* Amazon *because I made him leave that Mets game early.*

And most of all, for Lisa Canfield, who observes best practices at all times in all situations.

"You have to be born lucky in the sense that you have to have the right genes."

- Donald Trump

"You don't choose your family. They are God's gift to you, as you are to them."

- Desmond Tutu

"When his life was ruined, his family killed, his farm destroyed, Job knelt down on the ground and yelled up to the heavens, 'Why, God? Why me?' and the thundering voice of God answered, 'There's just something about you that pisses me off."

- Stephen King

Lady Blue Eyes

I like ice cream.

No, I really do. Chocolate is, of course, yummy, although somewhat overrated. It's what you expect. But butter pecan? Much more complex flavors, much more of an afterglow. My late father didn't pass on much to me that I could hang onto, but an appreciation for butter pecan is definitely something I inherited.

Strawberry, terrific, vanilla, good for a palate cleanser, and coffee? Surprisingly, coffee's a fave ice cream flavor even though I don't drink the stuff. I don't like bubble gum ice cream, by the way. Makes me slightly queasy. Maple? A little odd too. Let's face it, maple only belongs in syrup, nowhere else. So, food manufacturers, stop trying to combine things that don't belong together. It's annoying.

Then there's Neapolitan. You don't see that much anymore. Three flavors at once? You just want to shout at people eating it, "Just pick one! Not that hard!" I mean, where else does this happen? There's not Neapolitan meat. Nobody ever eats three vertical stripes of beef, chicken and pork packed in the same square. Maybe John Madden did back in the day, although he would have put the chicken inside the pig and then put the whole thing in a cow. Fun fact—in Ireland, instead of Neapolitan being made of vanilla, strawberry and chocolate, it's vanilla, strawberry and lemon. Weird. How did I know that? Think a field agent once told me. Maybe it was even dear old dad that clued me in. He traveled a lot when he was alive.

Dad. Why did I keep thinking about my father?

Anyway, I like ice cream. That's the great part about where I live. Every morning, exactly at 9:17 am, a nice woman in a Community uniform shows up at the door of my townhouse with a very small container of ice cream. I like to hold the container, because it's chilly, and anything chilly I encounter in this godforsaken steamy armpit of America is a very, very welcome commodity.

This nice woman, her name is Barbara, she always watches with an amused grin as I rip the plastic off the top of the container with eager anticipation.

You wouldn't think I would be all that excited.

After all, I already know what's in the container—one perfectly formed scoop of delicious ice cream, the best I've ever had in my whole sixty years of life—but what I *don't* know, what the wild card is in this otherwise very predictable process, is the exact *flavor* of ice cream that wondrous scoop contains.

As I said, Barbara is a nice woman, but she's not the prettiest one I've ever met. To be honest, she's a little on the homely side. Her nose is too big, not that I should talk, her hair is mousy and looks like she doesn't really do anything to it before she leaves for work, and there's some kind of giant blemish/birthmark thing on her cheek. I'd say she's pushing forty.

But the thing about Barbara is, she brings me the ice cream in the morning, and she always does it with a smile. She seems very happy to see me, increasingly so as time goes by. Plus, she has blue eyes. Frank Sinatra's wife was named Barbara. And her autobiography was titled *Lady Blue Eyes*. So that's what I call Barbara— "Lady Blue Eyes."

It always makes her blush a little.

She watches me closely as I try the first spoonful of ice cream. She's anxious to see how I'm going to react to the "Flavor of the Day," as we laughingly call it. (Oh, did I mention she also brings me a spoon with the scoop—a real metal spoon, not some plastic one that might snap in half? She does.) Sometimes I can tell what flavor it is just by looking at it—but many times, I can't, because I'm colorblind. It's another thing we laugh about (I should have a disabled license plate! But, of course, I can't because I don't even have a car!). Anyway, when I can't guess the flavor, she wonders, when I put that first spoonful in my mouth, am I going to be happy or disappointed? Sometimes I don't like the flavor, and she'll try to smooth things over, so I'm not left in a bad mood. But if I really like it…well, Barbara loves *that*.

She's always telling me how much she loves my smile!

She still talks about the day I sampled a spoonful of butter brickle. Holy cripes, butter brickle. It's like hitting the lottery. But better. Who needs money when you got butter brickle rolling around in your mouth? That gave me my "Smile of the Century," Barbara likes to say.

I'm pretty sure Barbara likes me. We have a thing going. But where can it go? Not very far. Little Max hasn't stood at attention for…well, I didn't really know. I'm not even sure how many days I've been here. I suppose I could count the number of flavors of ice cream I've consumed, but the monkey wrench in that plan is the fact that sometimes a flavor repeats. Barbara always apologizes when that happens, but I gotta admit there's not an infinite number of ice cream flavors in the universe. You have to work with reality.

So Barbara and I are stuck in that kind of Sam-and-Diane push-and-pull will-they-or-won't-they kind of relationship, except, in this case, they won't—because my penis doesn't work. Not that it bothers me. Nothing really bothers me these days. Not even when the ice cream is bubble gum, although I make a big show of pouting. It makes Barbara laugh and then she does something goofy to cheer me up, like stick out her tongue or give me a raspberry. I love our little fun.

Whatever the case, she stays until I eat the whole scoop. When I'm done, she takes the container and the spoon back from me and she says goodbye. After all, I'm not the only person in the Community who gets a morning ice cream delivery from Barbara and she has to be on her way, I get that. I only hope she likes delivering it to me more than she likes bringing it to the very old people that live around here.

Yes, I like ice cream. And after I have my scoop, I take a walk.

The DJ with the "Hey-Hey"

I like music.

And, when I take my morning walk around the Community, I hear a lot of it. They have thoughtfully placed speakers all around the neighborhood playing the biggest Top 40 hits from the '60's. Exclusively. That way, I hear the Beatles, but not Wings. Somebody made the right call. Can you get sillier than "Silly Love Songs?" I don't think so.

It's really great. At any given moment, you're liable to hear such forgotten great "rockers" as "Boogaloo Down Broadway," "Come a Little Bit Closer" or "Gitarzan." And what's really cool is that in between those classic tunes, you get to hear the hilarious patter of "Jumpin' Jack" Thompson, or, as he labels himself, "The DJ with the Hey-Hey." There's a good reason for the nickname—every time he starts one of his nonstop verbal barrages, he lets out with a loud "Hey-Hey" in a high, almost Jerry Lewis-like pitch.

At this moment, as I wander around the immaculately maintained walkways of the Community, the end of the Elvis hit, "Suspicious Minds," is beginning to fade out.

"I'm caught in a trap…I can't get out…"

But there's a trick involved with end of this song, a trick I know, because it was on the radio constantly when I was 13 years old. And I wonder how "The DJ with the Hey-Hey" is going to handle that trick. Because the job of every Top 40 DJ in the 60's was to talk right up until the second the singer started a song, and to begin bellowing on the back end of that song the second it started to fade away. The primary rule was NO DEAD AIR…and, pro that he is, "Jumpin' Jack" certainly subscribes to that law!

I'm already giggling to myself as the volume of Elvis' mighty voice slowly diminishes.

"...because I love you too much, baby..."

"HEY!" shrieks Jack, suddenly jumping in, *"That was Elvis singing his hugest hit of..."*

Oh! But now comes the trick! The engineers made it so that, just as you think the song is ending, suddenly, the volume comes up again! It's NOT the end of the song!

"Oh, hey hey HEY, I better get out of the way, because the King has not dismissed us!"

HA! That's a good one.

A minute later, when "Suspicious Minds" actually does fade out for good, "Jumpin' Jack" returns to make it clear he knew about the trick all along!

"HEY HEY! 'Course I knew that song did that, that was a dirty trick the RCA folks pulled on us back in the day, but it was a lotta fun, a lotta good fun, too bad Elvis would be dead in eight years, am I right? Such an American success story, from a two-room shotgun shack to the glory that was Graceland and we should all stop and appreciate the USA because whatever is done in the name of this great land is necessary and aligned with the life-affirming wishes of a great and benevolent God, which is why we don't play the records of Paul Revere and the Raiders here on the Big Top 40, after all, Paul Revere himself was a contentious objector during the Vietnam War and ended up as a cook in a mental institution while other brave men and women gave their lives for freedom, these colors don't run, am I right, folks?"

Wow. Who knew that about Paul Revere and the Raiders? That was part of what made "The DJ with the Hey-Hey" so fun to listen to. The trivia! Yet, some sadness with the fun. Guess I wouldn't be hearing the Raiders monster hit "Kicks" in the near future! Instead, "The DJ with the Hey-Hey" segues right into the opening licks of "Grazin' in the Grass" by...gee, I don't know. It's an instrumental. And I never understood the title until this very minute.

I think it's about marijuana!

I nod to myself and walk on. My mind is officially "blown." Far out!

As I continue forward, I follow the walkway, which winds around the various one and two-story townhouses occupied by the other residents of the Community. Even though I've been here for some time, I know very few of them. As a matter of fact, most of them never even leave their small, identical dwellings. The ones I do see out and about have one thing in common.

They are very, very old.

Yes, I'm 60 years old. And yes, many people might consider that old. But these other Community residents, who are almost all male, by the way, all look like they're at least 80. Some have walkers. Some get pushed around in wheelchairs by Community helpers. Others use the golf carts which we are all generously provided free of charge here in the Community.

These are very special golf carts—a new generation of golf carts. They drive themselves, and they follow spoken directions. Fun! You say "Straight," the cart goes straight. You say "Right" or "Left," the cart goes right or left. They also understand "Stop," "Start," "Faster," "Slower," "Forward," "Reverse," and "Park." They're even programmed to avoid collisions with anything they sense in front of them. Pretty remarkable!

But even though the carts are cool and amazing, I still walk. The exercise does me good. And I'm not alone in using my legs to get around. There are plenty of elderly gents here who—amazingly enough—still get around on their own power. There's one who's in his nineties!

It gives me hope.

As I approach the Community's town square, I spot several of my neighbors shuffling around on their daily walks, as well as others staring blankly into space as they sit near the clump of very tall palm trees that dominates the middle of the area. There was a time when I might have thought staring blankly into space might indicate a problem. Not now.

Now I understand peace at its deepest level.

Even though none of us really interact with each other, it's still comforting to see everyone out and about. This is the time of day most of us emerge for some welcome sunshine and fresh air. Since we are not allowed out after dark (our doors lock automatically—"The DJ with the Hey-Hey" always says it's for our own safety when he signs off at sunset), it's the coolest time the outdoors is available to us, when it's still a few hours before noon and the temperature is still relatively comfortable. The humidity is another story, of course, but I deal with it. Keep things positive, Lady Blue Eyes likes to say!

"HEY HEY," shrieks "Jumpin' Jack" as "Grazin' in the Grass" starts to fade away. *"Now it's time for 'The DJ with the Hey-Hey' to play one of his all-time favorites and I hope it's one of yours, it's amazing to think this was the NUMBER ONE single of 1966, a special moment in time before the public turned on the Vietnam War, when all people appreciated America's efforts, as they should, because whatever is done in the name of this great land is necessary and aligned with the life-affirming wishes of a great and benevolent God! Here, from American hero Sergeant Barry Sadler, comes, 'The Ballad of the Green Berets!'"*

Wow. It was Number One in 1966? The thing played constantly when I was a kid, but it was *that* popular?

As I listen to the lyrics about fighting soldiers from the sky and the fearless men who jump and die, I remember with shame that my cousin Rick and I would repeat that second line over and over, like we were paratroopers with brain problems. "Jump and die...jump and die...jump and die..." over and over, as if we were in a hypnotic trance, like know-nothing sheep dropping to our deaths. Maybe it was innocent fun. After all, we were children. But then again, these were American heroes.

I walk on...a little more slowly and a little more "woke," as the young people like to say now. Or did before I got here. How did I get here?

I reach the edge of the manmade lake, the Community Lake. And I finger the metal bracelet around my left wrist. Its power button glows as I draw near. The lake is a reminder that I can only go so far. If I get too close to its shorefront, that button will glow much brighter. And the pain will...

Well, I don't like to think about the pain.

It's the same with the edge of the woods on the other side of the Community. If I follow the path too far into the trees... I stop myself. I don't need to think about unpleasant outcomes. I don't really need to think about anything. I need to turn around, walk past my ancient, mottled neighbors and return to the comfort of my air-conditioned townhouse, where the refrigerator is restocked twice a week while I sleep, where I can take a shower (or bath) to wash away the thin layer of sweat the morning heat has sucked out of my skin...and then, for the rest of the day, enjoy some television.

Yes, it's a little boring. But that's okay. It's only about today.

Tomorrow will be different.

Tomorrow, Doug Daytona will come.

Doug Daytona

I remember the day Doug Daytona first visited me. I remember it very clearly.

I don't think it was too long after I first came to the Community. I still don't really know how I got here, but I do know that at first, I felt very restless about my situation. It was only over time that I learned to calm down, stop grappling with random negative thoughts and enjoy my new simple and carefree life here. As far as I know, this is the first time in my life that I have no problems. Absolutely none. And no worries. My every need is met.

It took time for me to realize how good this was for me. None of us ever get the chance to truly and fully relax in the outside world—there are always concerns about things like money, health, the people in our lives, what might happen tomorrow. I am lucky. All those uncertainties are gone. I have had many days to understand the advantages of my situation and embrace them.

Barbara, the lady who comes every morning with the ice cream, she saw the change in me happen gradually. And when she saw finally saw the serenity, real serenity, manifest itself in my eyes, she told me it was time.

"Time for what?" I asked.

She just gave me her Lady Blue Eyes smile and said nothing.

A few days later, when she came with the ice cream (I even remember it was a scoop of Cookies and Cream!), she told me I was going to have two very special guests later that afternoon. That in itself was notable because I had never had any unexpected visitors at the Community. Yes, a doctor came around once in a while to make sure I was healthy, but that man was all business. He took my pulse, listened to my chest while I breathed in and breathed out, maybe took a little blood (ouch!), then went on his way.

This was different.

According to Barbara, these new visitors were coming from far away to see me—and, she added, it was because I was such a *special person*. I had no idea why I was special or why anyone cared about me. Frankly, I remembered little from the past few years. But I trusted Barbara, her blue eyes always reassured me and I felt truth shining through them. I trusted her and sometimes looked at her legs and wished I could touch them. I told her that once and she turned bright red. At least, I assumed it was red, because, as I say, I'm colorblind. Reds and greens are hard, as are shades of blue and brown.

A few days later, it was definitely a while after lunch (they leave pre-wrapped sandwiches in my refrigerator so I don't have to do a thing!), a knock came on my door. I opened the door and two men stood there. One was tall, wearing a brown sports jacket and a button-up shirt and looked to be in his early forties. His big bouffy brown hair was parted down the middle and he had a big, welcoming smile on his face. He was carrying a simple brown briefcase.

"Max? Max Bowman?"

I smiled and nodded.

He extended a hand and I shook it casually. Maybe too casually, because he looked down at my hand to see if something was wrong with it.

"Hi, I'm Shawn Shepheard, we've actually met briefly a couple of times."

"Oh?" I said, because I didn't remember this fellow at all.

"Yes, at the Eddie di Pineda fundraiser last year? And the year before that, at the Keenan Van Zola event? I mean, neither of those ended particularly well..." he said, looking into my eyes to see if any glimmer of recognition appeared.

I shook my head. He actually seemed pleased that I couldn't remember. I guess they must *not* have ended well. Had I done something...?

"Can we come in?" he asked, snapping me out of my memory search. I nodded, and stepped back, so they could enter the townhouse. Then an odd thing happened. The other man, whose name I had yet to learn, actually rushed in past Shawn, pushing him to the side.

"Doug," said Shawn reprovingly.

"Hey man, sorry, but it's hot as heck out there," said the other man.

Now that he was inside, I could get a good look at him. He was short and energetic, wore thick black-framed glasses and had a lot of product in his short blonde hair. There was maybe more product than hair, to be truthful, with the result being small oily patches of it standing straight up into the air. He was a little chubby to be sure, but dressed smartly. He was wearing an expensive checkered shirt untucked over well-fitting pressed jeans, plus a pair of really hip cream-colored laced shoes. He was dressed to the nines!

"Hey man," he said to me, also pumping my relaxed hand in a shake. "Doug Daytona. Great to meet a legend like you, Max."

"I'm a legend?" I asked him guilelessly. I was unaware of that status! But Doug's pale round face nodded enthusiastically. He was very sure about this.

Shawn entered and closed the door behind him. "Maybe we can sit around the dining room table and talk a little?" he asked politely.

Talk. Most of the time I really didn't feel up to a talk. When Barbara came in the morning, I had the energy to keep up my end of a conversation. Late in the afternoon, that was when I began to droop. Sometimes I'd even nap. But I pushed myself. These gentlemen had come to see me for a special reason and I wanted to make sure they were happy with the results.

I sat down across from Shawn and Doug. Shawn put his briefcase flat on the tabletop and opened it up. He took out a couple of books. Both had large color pictures of Shawn's face on their front covers.

"Just as an introduction, Max, I thought I'd bring you a couple of my best-selling books. This one is called, *How to Talk Practically Anybody into Anything,* and the other one is called, *Sugar-Free Shawn.* It's about my battle with Type 1 Diabetes and how I overcame it to not only play hockey, but also become an internationally-known motivational speaker and author."

"Wow," I said, looking at the two tomes. "Books. We don't have books here."

"Well," said Shawn, in a special little confidential tone, "Then I guess you must be glad I showed up today!"

I looked at Doug questioningly.

"Hey man!" he said enthusiastically.

"And this is Doug Daytona," Shawn continued. "Doug published these books for me."

"Yeah, Max, I'm kind of a media guru. I have a consulting business in Atlanta. I've also authored best-selling books, I've written songs and, what's congruent to our conversation here is, I direct movies."

"Movies?" I said in awe.

"I've won five Emmys for my work, Max."

Shawn let out a little laugh. "Oh, you won them in Buttfuck, Georgia." Shawn turned to me. "He enters his little films in these very small television markets, where the only competition is some church lady demonstrating how to can peaches, and he wins. Now, he has a giant Emmy projected on the wall of his office, do you believe this guy? He's never won a *national* Emmy."

Doug stared at Shawn intently. "What are you doing here, man? Why are you saying that?"

"Calm down, Doug, it's just getting to be a little weird with you. I mean, you've got an Emmy charm bracelet now." I looked at Doug's wrist. He did indeed have a gold charm bracelet with five miniature Emmy awards dangling from it. "It's just getting a little terrifying, that's all."

Doug looked at me and pointed to Shawn, laughing. "You can't listen to him! He's Canadian!"

"I've applied for my citizenship, Martin Scorcrazy, so let's drop that subject."

I had no idea what was going on, but it was better than watching another *Bonanza* episode on the TV. Especially if it was one after Pernell Roberts left the show. Even worse if it was after Hoss died.

"What kind of movies do you make?" I asked. "Any I've heard of?"

"Probably not," answered Doug. "They're documentaries about notable people. That's why I'm here. To make a documentary about you."

"Why?"

Doug gave me an intent look. "Not for you, Max. And not for me. It's for your country. Are you ready to do something for your country? Are you ready to do something for America?"

I smiled. I knew the answer to this one. "Whatever is done in the name of this great land is necessary and aligned with the life-affirming wishes of a great and benevolent God."

They both looked at me in silent delight and amazement.

"Wow," said Shawn finally, "That is spooky. That was just what the nutjob on the speaker system was saying outside."

"He's not a nutjob, Shawn," Doug said, a little testily. He turned back to me again. "Max, I want to make my greatest film to date. I want to make a movie where you tell your story for the first time ever."

He looked at me expectantly. I was pretty sure I was furrowing my brow. If I wasn't, I should have been, because the plain fact was *I didn't know what my story was.*

"Max, you seem confused," said Shawn.

"I can't remember things," I answered. "At least recent things. I remember things from when I was a kid…and from when I worked for the Agency a little bit. And I remember stuff that's happened since I came to the Community. But other than that…"

I let the thought trail off. It was curious I didn't remember anything. But it didn't seem to really matter if I did or not. So…I let it go. Instead, I smiled at these two guys. It was kind of fun how they bickered with each other.

"That's the beauty of this, Max," Doug said. "When we do this movie, we can help you remember everything. That way, you can learn your own story through this process."

Huh.

"So *you* know my story?"

"Yes!" answered Doug. "And when we film, we'll tell you all about it. We just need to know you're up for doing this."

"Do I need to?" I asked. It sounded like a lot of work. What I really wanted to say was, "Why not leave well enough alone?" It was an attitude that came in handy around here. And I was suddenly feeling uncomfortable about dealing with stuff I didn't know. Something told me it was better I didn't know.

"Max, I really believe you have to do this," Doug went on (I could see he was a good salesman—this little guy didn't stop!). "What you just said about America. About doing what's necessary for your country. Well, this is necessary."

"How so?" I asked curiously.

"Because there are a lot of lies about you out there. People trying to smear our country and using you to do it."

"Really? What are they saying I did?" I was almost alarmed, but it was hard to get all the way there.

"It's complicated and I don't think you'll fully understand the importance of this project until we get into it. Now, I know this is impinging on your time and will require some effort, but I can guide you through it so it's as easy as possible. Best of all, we can get through it in just one day of shooting."

"All kidding aside," Shawn said, looking solemn, "Doug here is very talented and a great patriot. That's why I'm here, Max. I want you to know this is important, very important and it's something only you can do for the U.S.A."

Hmmm. I looked down at Shawn's books. I paged through them. He was an author. That meant he knew things.

I shrugged and smiled.

"Okay."

"Cool," said a very happy Doug. "This is gonna be killer!"

That was a while ago. I didn't know how many days had passed because there are no calendars here. But I knew that today, Doug Daytona would finally coming with his camera crew to film me. Last night, I had difficulty sleeping for the first time in months. I actually felt some anxiety. What was my story? Why were people using it to tear down America? What if I couldn't remember enough to make this film work? Would I be letting down my country?

I finally managed a few hours of sleep. But then I overslept. Barbara had to ring the doorbell several times before I heard it. I put on my bathrobe and hurried downstairs. Seeing her standing in the doorway, holding that bowl with that perfect scoop of ice cream, relaxed me instantly.

"Because it's a special day," she murmured, "you get Butter Brickle."

Whoa. I gobbled it down like there was no tomorrow.

Butter Brickle always makes me think everything is going to be okay. And, in a few hours, when Doug Daytona showed up with a sound guy and a camera guy and a few "grips and gaffers" as he called them, I felt like everything *would* be okay.

Now that the day is over—the filming only took one day, like Doug promised!—I realize that he was right. My story does need to get out. And now it seems like it will.

But now I'm tired. Now it's time to rest.

Faster

A small series of explosions are going off somewhere deep inside of me.

All night as I sleep, I wake up every so often with a jolt, only to find myself in a sweaty state of panic. Then, just when I manage to get back to sleep, there's another explosion, another jolt, more sweat.

I should have heeded my own advice. I should have left well enough alone. Hearing my story from Doug Daytona must have unlocked some kind of repressed shock. I'm upset. Something is wrong. I feel upside down in my own mind.

I wake up with the sun and think I might be able to get back to sleep and regain my cherished serenity. But instead, I just toss and turn some more. When Barbara rings the doorbell, I'm not dressed for the day as I usually am. Instead, I am in my bathrobe with nothing underneath it.

"Oh, my. Max," she says, seeing my condition.

I ask her to come in. I don't want her to stand in the doorway and watch me eat my ice cream. Today, I want her closer and I want the door shut to the outside world. She agrees.

She sits on the couch next to me as I eat my scoop. Chocolate Almond. It's good, but no Butter Brickle. As I finish, she puts her hand on my leg. It gives me goosebumps.

"I know you've been through a lot, Max. It was brave of you to do what you did. You'll regain your footing again, I promise."

Her hand feels good on my bare leg. I look at her. Really look at her.

"Sometimes I wish…" I said.

"What, Max?" Lady Blue Eyes whispers. "What do you wish?"

What could I say? I wish Little Max would spring to attention? I hand the bowl with spoon back to her without another word. She leaves. I think she knows the problem. Otherwise, she would have asked more questions. I'm disappointed she didn't.

Now, it's time to go outdoors, but I'm so tired and so rattled, I decide to use one of the hi-tech golf carts instead of walking. Luckily, I will still be able to hear the Top 40 tunes played by "The DJ with the Hey-Hey," because the audio feed plays through the cart's dashboard without me having to do anything.

As I turn on the cart and say, "Forward!", I hear the Wild One himself, Bobby Rydell, shout...

"Chicks! Kicks! Cats! Cool! School!"

Which can only mean I will be enjoying his rendition of 'Swingin' School" as I begin motoring around the Community. Actually, I think there is only his rendition to enjoy. I do not believe any other recording artists covered "Swingin' School." The only reason I knew the song at all is because my oldest brother Henry had the 45 single. I was a little young when it came out and mostly listening to my Huckleberry Hound story album at the time. When it came to the Pixie and Dixie adventure (they were two mice always pursued by this cat named Mr. Jinks), the duo always talked about how good cheese was and it always made me hungry for it. I would ask my mother for a slice of American cheese and it tasted delicious.

My childhood memory is disrupted as I hear a voice call from nearby. Is that voice calling my name? Maybe. But just in case...

"Faster," I said to the cart.

"HEY HEY," shrieks "Jumpin' Jack" as Bobby Rydell "whoa whoa's" his way to the end of the tune. *"That was Mr. Bobby Rydell with his 1960 hit, 'Swingin' School.' Bobby was one of a number of teen idols who suddenly fell off the charts when the four mop tops, John, Paul, George and Ringo came to America to play on the Ed Sullivan show, inaugurating the British Invasion and what a shame that was, that good clean-cut American rock n' roll was suddenly shown the door by drug-infested degenerates from a foreign land. It would be a few years until we could take our radio back and what a blessing it was when the King himself, Elvis Presley made his comeback in 1968, because whatever is done in the name of this great land is necessary and aligned with the life-affirming wishes of a great and benevolent God! Now, let's jump back to 1966 and celebrate another great American, Mr. Frank Sinatra. Get ready for some dynamite doobie-doobie-dooing as you listen to his landmark hit, 'Strangers in the Night"* ...

"Strangers in the Night." That summer for my birthday, I had gotten my first transistor radio and my first real earful of Sinatra. I loved that song. But I was afraid to tell anybody. It didn't seem very "cool" to like "Strangers in the Night." I felt like if I bought any Sinatra singles, my brothers would make fun of me. So, I didn't. Later, I bought all his albums.

My childhood memories are disrupted again—by that same voice. It is calling my name.

I don't want anyone to call my name. Not today.

"Faster," I say to the cart. Then, "Right." The cart takes the turn at the clump of palm trees and begins taking me out towards the lake.

The voice makes me afraid. I know it and I don't know why—but it feels connected to the small explosions that are still going off inside me. I really don't want that voice to catch up to me and cause me more restless sleep.

Just then, the cart brakes suddenly, abruptly. My head is thrown forward.

The person with the voice has run in front of the cart, causing the vehicle to automatically stop. It has that technology.

This man seems familiar, although I cannot place him. He resembles a bald rat covered in sweat. He is wearing a suit and tie on a day when the temperature is approaching 90 and the humidity is close behind it. I want no part of this. I want no part of suits and ties. I want to think about Pixie and Dixie and Frank Sinatra and American cheese.

"Forward," I say to the cart. It doesn't move. That's because the man isn't moving from his position directly in front of the path of the cart.

"Max," the man says, breathing hard from running. "What the *fuck*."

It comes to me. His name is Howard.

We sit on a bench near the lake. I want to go back to my air-conditioned townhouse, but he doesn't want to.

"Hey, I want to stop sweating fucking buckets as much as you do, but we have to talk here. There's got to be surveillance in your place, Max."

"Surveillance? But nothing ever happens."

"And that's the way they want to keep it. Jesus, I can't believe you're here. Are you all right? What the fuck did they do to you?"

I look at him a moment.

"Were we friends?" I ask.

"Depends on what day you're talking about," he says, with a little edge. "You know, everybody thinks you're dead."

"I just found out I'm lucky to be alive. Fighting for America is dangerous business."

"Fighting for America?"

"Yes. But whatever is done in the name of this great land is necessary and aligned with the life-affirming wishes of a great and benevolent God."

Howard sighs and looks up at the sky. I don't know why. There is nothing up there except a cloud once in a while.

"They turned your mind to fucking Jell-O. They finally fucking did it after two years of trying." He shakes his head and looks back towards the Community. "I always heard rumors about this place. Turns out they were true. The dumping ground for Agency old-timers who know too much and might talk. If you look hard enough, you can probably find the guys who really shot JFK *and* RFK. Shit, maybe I should move here. I'd feel young every day of the year next to one of these premature corpses."

"Why *are* you here?" I ask as pleasantly as possible, even though I really do not want to know the answer.

"I doubt if you'll understand a goddam word I'm saying, considering half of your brain has been turned to molten lava, but Senator Eddie di Penada asked me to come down here. My boss. You remember him?"

Eddie di Penada. Shawn, the man who came the first time with Doug Daytona, mentioned that name too. That I remembered.

"Anyway, he had me come down here looking for Andrew Wright, ironically enough. Nobody can find him either, so Eddie was thinking maybe the Agency mind-fucked him and dropped him here. You've gotta remember Andrew Wright?"

"Andrew Wright?"

"Yeah, the guy you apparently tried to kill? Well, actually, nobody knows what happened, there was an incident at a restaurant in Sedona, Arizona and then you both disappeared. I don't suppose you can shed any light on the situation?"

The little explosions inside me grew bigger.

"I can't remember anything…" My voice trails off. What is this man's name?

"Howard," he says insistently.

"…Howard," I repeat after his reminder.

He thinks a moment, then runs his hand over his sweaty fleshy forehead.

"Okay, I'm officially fucking melting, let's go back to your place."

Inside my townhouse, Howard picks up the TV remote and turns on the set. He starts flipping through the channels. We get about ten different ones here in the Community.

"The Beverly Hillbillies," Howard said, staring at the TV screen. Flip. *"Password."* Flip. *"Burke's Law."* Flip. *"The Mike Douglas Show."* Flip. *"High Chaparral.* At least that one's in fucking color."

"Yes, Howard, there's a channel with just comedies, one with just game shows, one with just action-adventure hours, one with talk shows, one with Westerns, one with movies, one with cartoons…"

"How much do you wanna bet they never show *The Prisoner?*"

"The Prisoner. Wasn't that an English show?"

Howard nodded, "They showed it on CBS every summer." He flipped through the channels a few more times. "Seems like none of these channels show anything produced after the Johnson Administration."

"The old shows are still good. I don't mind."

Howard looks at me. "In your condition, I don't think you'd mind if I hit you in the back of the head with a crowbar."

"Oh, that would hurt."

He rolls his eyes and looks around at the art on the walls of my living room area. There is a painting of an ocean wave that I really like. The one I like second best is of a boy getting his first haircut.

"Norman fucking Rockwell," Howard says while staring at it. "Figures." He turns to me. "Well, I guess you're set. You've reached Nirvana, Max. Nothing but music and TV from the 60's…you're flooded with all your ancient pop culture references 24/7. This is it. This is MaxLand, your own personal twisted theme park, all that's missing are the comic books. Maybe this was your destiny."

"They take good care of me, Howard. I get ice cream every morning."

"Ice cream? In the morning?"

"Yes, Barbara brings me a cold scoop every morning. And she watches me eat it and we talk. I really like her legs."

He looks at me thoughtfully a moment.

"Well, I'm not going to disturb your perfect life here, Max. Enjoy the peace and quiet. You've earned it."

I smile. Howard talks as though he is about to leave. That means nothing is going to change. Relief floods my heart and douses the explosions inside me. Howard is going to leave.

"But maybe you can drive me out to the gate in your super-techno-cart. They wouldn't let me bring my rental in here and it's a pretty good walk, especially in this fucking heat."

"Sure, Howard. I would be happy to."

We drive the cart towards the gate, which is at the end of a long paved path to the right of the Community. I never go down this way. The gate terrifies me. It's very tall and scary and manned by people in uniform with guns. Plus, when I get too close to it, the power button on the bracelet on my wrist begins to glow more brightly. Luckily, I know where to stop so I don't have to deal with the pain. I had to learn the hard way, but I learned.

As we ride along, Howard stares at me. He makes me uncomfortable. I am very glad he is leaving the Community.

"So you get ice cream every morning," he finally says. "And this woman…she watches you eat it. Does she wait until you eat it all?"

I nod. Why is he suddenly bringing up Barbara and the ice cream?

"And you think this woman is hot?" Howard asks.

"I like her legs."

Howard nods. "I get it. Any port in a storm."

"Storm?"

"Have you made a move on her?"

"I can't even masturbate, Howard."

Howard looks at me in disbelief.

"Faster," I say nervously to the cart.

"Wow. So, the dick is dead." He pauses. "How much would you like to fuck this chick?"

I don't like Howard talking about Lady Blue Eyes like that. But I want to hear what he has to say on the subject.

"A lot, Howard. I miss sex."

"Yeah, me too. I can only afford to buy some once a month or so."

He buys sex?

We get closer to the gate. I have to stop soon. I feel the growing vibrations from the bracelet. Soon, they will make my body hurt. But I will wait as long as I can, because I want Howard to say more, to give me a way to have sex with Barbara. But he's quiet and we're almost out of time.

"Stop," says Howard out of nowhere. The cart stops.

"Howard, I should leave you here anyway. I can't go further. The bracelet makes me feel too much pain."

He looks at the bracelet on my wrist and nods to himself. "That's how they keep you from straying. They must have an invisible fence around the perimeter, right?"

"Invisible fence?"

"Some kind of electrical field. This bracelet shocks you or something if you try to leave the area."

"I don't want to leave the area."

"I can see that. But if you ever did…"

"It doesn't shock me, Howard. It fills my entire body with pain. It really hurts."

Another pause. Why isn't he getting out and walking away? Instead, he looks at me. And looks at me.

"Listen, does this woman like you back?" he finally asks. Good. He has returned to the subject I want to discuss.

"I think very much."

"That makes sense, since you're the only one in that place who probably still has all his original organs. Okay, I'm going to try and help you out. And this may solve more than one problem."

"I don't have any other problems. But what do you think I should do, Howard?"

"Quit the ice cream."

"I don't understand."

"Just try and follow along, this isn't that complicated. I think the ice cream she's giving you isn't just ice cream. There's something in it that makes your dick not work. And maybe your brain too."

"Barbara wouldn't feed me something that would hurt me."

Howard gave me a nice, friendly and reassuring smile, like he was a dog owner talking to his beloved pet. It made me feel warm and relaxed.

"She probably doesn't know, Max," he said very slowly. "And that's why you have to talk to her about it. Start by asking her if she wants to be with you. Have you asked her that yet?"

"No."

"Then do it. And if she reeeeeeally likes you, she'll stop giving you the ice cream on her own. But you two have to be careful. Because a lot of people around here want you to eat the ice cream."

"Really?"

"I'm pretty sure of that. And one more thing. Talk about this with her outside. Not in your townhouse. Outside."

"The surveillance?"

"Yes, Max, good boy for remembering. And one more thing. Keep my name out of this. I have enough problems."

"Of course, you do. You live on the other side of the gate."

"Yes, I do. Nobody's bringing me ice cream every morning."

"It's really good ice cream. I like it."

Howard smiles and pats me on the shoulder. Then he gets out of the cart. "Good luck, Chauncey. You're going to need a shitload of it."

"My name is Max."

"Right now, as far as I'm concerned, it's Chauncey, Chauncey Gardner."

And then he starts walking away towards the gate.

I am almost sad to see him go. He seems to understand things in a way I don't. He even seems to understand me in a way I can't.

But the sadness is temporary. Now, I am too excited about the possibility of Barbara and me being together to hold on to anything that makes me feel bad.

Tomorrow morning, I will ask her.

Woke

"We have to go outside," I say to Barbara when she shows up the next morning.

"But…your ice cream."

"I will eat it outside."

We go out and I lead her back to the small grassy area between my townhouse and my neighbor's. She looks at me curiously. I see the scoop of ice cream is beginning to melt. It's already very hot out.

"Do you want to be with me?" I ask when we stop in the yard area.

Her eyes open wide with excitement. "Max…what are you saying…?"

"I would have asked sooner, but…my penis. It doesn't work."

"Oh," she says sadly, the excitement quickly leaving her face.

"But I think I know how to fix it."

The excitement comes back. "How?" she asks breathlessly.

I point to the bowl containing the melting scoop.

"No more ice cream," I whisper.

Now she is startled.

"You think it's the ice cream? Really? I…well, I shouldn't tell you this, but I know there's medication in it…"

Medication. Bingo! Howard, you *are* smart.

She continues. "But it's supposed to be helping you. Things do have side effects though, God knows the commercials let you know all about those…"

"I don't need any medication," I say. "And, Lady Blue Eyes, I think this will make it so we can…"

She blushes.

I gently take the bowl from her hand and dump the scoop behind a bush that grows by the edge of the townhouse. I don't even care what flavor it was. Some things are worth more than Butter Brickle.

"Every morning, we will pretend that I ate the ice cream. But I won't," I say quietly. "Do you understand? So, we will have to go outside to fool them."

"Why outside?"

"The surveillance," I whisper.

She laughs.

"Max, I *am* your surveillance. There aren't any cameras in your townhouse." She pauses. Then, finally, she asks with some disbelief, her hand moving up to her face to cover the blemish on her cheek, "You really want to be with me?"

"I love your legs," I say with a smile.

She looks away shyly. Lady Blue Eyes. She is a lady, all right.

I bring her close to me and kiss her. Nothing happens to my penis, but I know that soon it will. So, I kiss her again. She strokes my cheek.

"You have good jeans, I bet."

Jeans? I used to wear jeans. How did she know that?

It only takes a week.

One night, I dream that I'm rolling around with Elizabeth Montgomery from *Bewitched* and Barbara Eden from *I Dream of Jeannie* (I watched them on the comedy channel the night before). I wake up with an erection. And I successfully masturbate.

It feels good!

But, at the same time, the explosions inside me grow bigger. Images flood my mind. I see flaming buildings, lost dogs, samurai swords, an old man singing by a piano, a tiny little gun in my hand... They don't seem to make sense. But they haunt me because they seem so specific. I feel like they have something to do with the stories that Doug Daytona made me tell. I feel like they really happened.

I shake. I get headaches.

And I begin to wonder. How did I end up in the Community? Why was I put here? That opens up many other questions. My mind begins thinking about everything in a way it didn't before. This makes me sad, because it was finally at a place where it questioned nothing. It was blissful. Now, it's ravaged.

When Barbara comes in the morning, she notices my state of mind. We still melt the ice cream with hot water from the faucet in the kitchen sink and then pour it down the drain, as we did every day for the past week, but she is clearly worried about me.

I don't want her to worry. I take her back in the living room and we kiss some more. She is wearing a skirt, so I move my hand high up her leg, near the part I want to reach. I put my other hand on one of her breasts. It's like that time back in high school when Donna Frabotta (it sounds like a made-up name, but isn't!) let me do all that, but nothing else.

I feel a stirring between my legs, but I want to wait one more day. I want to make sure it goes right for me and Barbara. I tell her that, but she wants me to touch her more, because she says she needs "release."

But suddenly, I feel a very sharp pain in my head.

I see a dead woman lying on the sidewalk, I see her vividly, and I see another woman in a bathrobe and she kisses me too. I try not to let Barbara see that I am having these disturbing thoughts, because I don't want her to make me eat the ice cream tomorrow and ruin our plans. I ask her to wait just one more day.

But suddenly, I'm not so sure I like her anymore and I don't know why.

That afternoon, I watch an old episode of *The Rifleman* on the Western channel. It upsets me. I don't like looking at Chuck Connors. I get a feeling he wants to kill me. No...he actually *tried* to. Which is strange, because in the episode, he is kind to his son Mark and only trying to stop a man from hurting them both.

I tremble a little.

There has been a bottle of white wine in the refrigerator for quite some time. A long time ago, Barbara told me that it was okay to have a glass or two once in a while and that's why they put the bottle there. But I shouldn't have more than that glass or two, that's why they would never give me more than that one bottle at a time. That bottle has stayed corked since I came here. I never felt a need for it.

But tonight, I feel that need.

I drink all the wine, the entire bottle, while I try to make all the disturbing pictures in my head go away. I try to distract myself by watching the Jupiter 2 spaceship struggle through an asteroid storm on *Lost in Space,* but it does not work. Suddenly, I realize all these old TV shows and movies are boring. Most of them I've seen before and other ones, like *Judd for the Defense* and *Ozzie and Harriet,* I never liked in the first place. I wonder why we don't have any news channels. I wonder why there are no books to read, no internet to search, nothing to do except watch TV and listen to music that's fifty or sixty years old.

Because I have not had alcohol in a very long time, the wine quickly makes me sleepy and I pass out on the couch. It is not a very relaxing sleep, because I have more nightmares.

I wake up with a headache. It's morning. Today is supposed to be the day with Barbara and she will be here soon. I sweated a lot last night, so I need to take a shower quickly, before she gets here.

In the shower, I breathe in and out to clear my head. It does seem to be getting clearer every day, without me having to do anything. But, at the same time, I am feeling increasingly tense and nervous. I miss my serenity.

I touch my penis. It responds. I think this is going to work!

But then the shower door opens. Shocked, I turn abruptly to see who it is.

Oh. It's Barbara. And she's completely naked. Oh.

She kisses me as the steam from the water surrounds us. She touches my penis. Now it's really responding. Oh!

We're back on the bed and I'm inside her. She makes noises. Good noises, not bad ones.

But then something happens and I'm making bad noises. Very bad noises.

Because I see Jules' face where Barbara's had been. *Jules.* I remember her name. Angela. I remember *her* name.

The pain is suddenly overwhelming. I finish, but it's not a pleasant ending. I push Barbara off and roll away from her. I hold my head firmly between my two hands, pushing on it, trying to squeeze the pain out of my brain. And I fall on the floor.

What the fuck.

I'm not seeing so good, but I can make out this naked woman with a blotch on her cheek standing over me and she's plenty pissed.

"Tomorrow morning, you eat the ice cream again. This was a BAD IDEA!"

She picks up her clothes and leaves.

What the hell just happened?

The Forbidden Zone

I'd give my left ball for a Jack on the rocks. Maybe half of my right one too.

I was leaning against the side of the townhouse—hiding there, obscured by the bushes planted between my unit and my neighbors. It was night and I knew I wasn't supposed to be out, so I had been skulking around since before sunset. But it had turned pitch black and that meant I was going to have to make my move.

A lot had happened since Lady Blue Eyes left the building. First, I slept a little. Then I woke up in a panic. Maybe something about the sexual act, even though it hadn't exactly been completed, demolished what was left of the retaining wall that was holding back my former life. And that life started flooding my consciousness.

There were too many images to keep track of. A secret military compound. A lab where an incredibly hot woman with a lot of big knives injected me with drugs. A man with eyes that looked in two different directions, locked in an underground bunker. TV's *The Rifleman,* or at least someone who looked a lot like him, trying to kill me. And Howard…

Howard. Was Howard really here, in the Community?

It was hard to tell what was fact and what was fiction. But I knew one thing. When the sun came up, Barbara would be back to make me eat the ice cream again. If I refused, whoever she reported to would find someone a lot less friendly to make me eat it. I figured I was safe for the day, since she was probably more concerned with staying out of trouble herself. But if I didn't submit to the ice cream in the morning, I knew she'd have no choice but to turn me in.

I had to be gone by sunrise. Which meant I needed to leave that night. That gave me a few hours to get my shit—and by shit, I mean my head—together. Slowly, piece by piece, I put together the events that led to my forced retirement in the Community.

I remembered being plucked from obscurity by a man with a lazy eye to find a five-star general's missing son, and then uncovering a secret paramilitary operation.

I remembered being stalked by a psycho who for some unknown reason had plastic surgery to make himself look like *The Rifleman*. I remember blowing half his face off (or however he died, I forget).

I remembered finding out that said psycho was the son of Andrew Wright, America's King of the Spooks.

I remembered that was when the shit really hit the fan.

That was when Wright came after me again, poisoned my mind with a top-secret, designer drug and had my girlfriend murdered outside a Manhattan Starbucks. Which I assumed was just some twisted tit for tat over the death of his only son.

But it turned out there was more. I found out Andrew Wright had been part of my life since I was 10 years old, even though I never even met the guy until I was close to 60.

I remembered about the fucked-up ophthalmologist I used to see who was actually programming me become Andrew Wright's super-secret CIA weapon, which must have been a complete waste of time because my tenure at the Agency was not what I'd call super…

But why me? It didn't make sense.

That's when I remembered the most important part.

Andrew Wright was my father. That's why he'd been messing with me for so long. That's why I tried to kill him.

But did I? I couldn't remember. All I knew was, according to Howard, Wright and I both disappeared after our final encounter.

So that's why I wound up in the Community. It's where the CIA dumps their aging spooks-with-a-secret.

But what happened after that? That's where my memory went completely hazy. How long had I been a resident of the Community? How was I supposed to tell? There were no clocks, no calendars, not one piece of information to let a person know if it was Christmas or the Fourth of July. But none of that seemed to matter, as long as everybody ate their ice cream.

Howard must have figured that out, which means he really was in the Community, just to give my neutered mind the idea to stop eating the ice cream so I could get laid. You gotta give it to Howard, the man understands how to get through to even the most primitive male brain. And I was just beginning to realize how primitive my brain had become. I was motivated, it seemed, only by Butter Brickle and sex.

And I would be again in about 18 hours if I didn't get the hell out of Dodge.

Howard had been wrong about the surveillance and Barbara had been right, to the best of my knowledge. I went through my townhouse and found no trace of any security cameras. I even opened up the smoke alarm to make sure no video technology was lurking in there. When I went out for my usual afternoon walk, keeping up my routine to make sure nobody suspected I was in my right mind, I eyed all the streetlights and signage, not to mention the speakers blasting the mid-century mind fuck provided by "The DJ with the Hey-Hey." I couldn't spot any surveillance equipment out there either. It looked like the powers-that-be were so confident in their magic ice cream that they didn't really concern themselves with what the residents were up to. Especially since the overwhelming majority of said residents were older than dirt.

Of course, there was also the fact that we weren't going anywhere.

Looking around, I noticed for the first time that every single resident wore the exact same bracelet I did, in the exact same spot on their left wrist. The same bracelet I knew would shoot agonizing pain through my entire body if I happened to wander too close to the edge of the Community. In the early days, before I knew better, I used to try to test the bracelet's power, and it did not go well. I vividly remembered falling to my knees crying, crippled by the electric charge shooting through my bones while simultaneously hoping I didn't shit myself. Needless to say, I learned my lesson.

Unfortunately, even in my newly-lucid state, I could not find a way to get the damn thing off my wrist. I spent an hour in the late afternoon trying to pry it off, but it appeared to be grafted to my skin in some way. And even if I could have separated it from my epidermis, the bracelet was still way too small to pull over my hand. I don't know if they actually welded the thing onto my wrist or put it together through some other technology, but the upshot was that bracelet was staying put.

But I wasn't.

I had the beginnings of an idea of how to penetrate the Community perimeter despite the bracelet and despite the pain. All I had to do was survive it.

I waited a little longer by the side of my townhouse, because I knew what was next on the schedule. Every night at the same time, the Community workers would make the rounds to check and restock our refrigerators. Sometimes I would hear them come in at night from my bedroom, so I had an idea of when they would show up. Of course, it was just an idea, since I had no idea what time it was, ever.

Soon enough, however, I heard a golf cart stop in front of my place, followed by the footsteps of the worker bringing in some new goodies. I hoped the fact that I had consumed the entire bottle of white wine the previous evening wouldn't throw the worker into a tizzy. It didn't seem to be a problem, because, after a few minutes, the golf cart was on its way down the walkway to my neighbor's place. I made my way quietly to the front of the townhouse and watched for a few more minutes, as the lights of the cart continued down the path and turned right. As it disappeared around the corner, I looked up and down the dimly-lit walkway. I saw nothing else moving in the shadows.

I went in the opposite direction of the way the golf cart had gone, towards the woods.

It was a new moon, or close enough to it, so, luckily, the night sky was close to its darkest. I continued to walk past townhouse after townhouse, each identical to the one before, dark and silent as can be, like empty model homes. I lost track of how many there were. My formerly-fogged brain never realized just how many residents the Community had—I guess there was a never-ending supply of aging spies to dump there.

I must have walked a few miles before I finally reached the edge of the Community, because my legs were aching. I was also sweating profusely, because it was also still 80% humidity in the middle of the night. Usually when I made a trip this long I used the cart, but I thought I'd draw less attention if I went on foot.

I paused next to the very last townhouse in this particular neighborhood and peered out into the darkness. There was a walkway that continued winding from where I was standing into the trees, and about a football field of flat grass where I would be exposed until I made it to the cover of the woods. And once I reached those woods, the pain would kick in at full power.

But the woods were my best option. Actually, my *only* option. The lake wouldn't do. I didn't have any water wings on me and I didn't have gills last time I checked. There was also the possibility the bracelet might electrocute me or something. The gate side of the Community was, of course, out of the question, since it was manned by armed guards 24/7. But the woods looked doable. The path seemed to go deep enough into the woods to enable me to escape. I just had to make it that far.

It was time to get some wheels.

There was a cart parked next to this townhouse at the edge of the universe. I got in and realized my first problem – I didn't know what voice commands controlled the cart's headlights. None of us were allowed out at night, so lights had never been an issue. Now it was a big one. What if the cart had light-sensitive headlights that came on automatically when I started it? I could be a dead man by the time I figured out how to turn them off if any kind of security was watching.

I really didn't have a choice. I had to try.

"On," I said quietly.

And, of course, the headlights immediately lit up in high beam mode.

"Lights off!" I said, quickly, quietly and in a minor panic. Nothing.

"No lights!"

Nothing.

I looked around nervously. Jesus. I didn't see or hear anyone. But still.

"Dark!" I finally barked in way too loud a voice. That did it. Shit.

I sat there for a moment, hoping nobody would jump out of the bushes and force feed me ice cream. Nothing happened. And the cart's electric engine was so quiet, no one beyond where I was sitting would notice its low rumble.

Okay. Time to make like Charlton Heston and exit Ape Town. Meaning I had to go and see what lurked in the Forbidden Zone, just like old Chuck did in the original *Planet of the Apes*. If I found the remains of the Statue of Liberty? Well, then I'd just come back, gobble up some ice cream and watch *Burke's Law* reruns until the Apocalypse. For now, however…

"Forward," I said.

The cart jerked forward.

It was a straight shot into the woods, so that was the last direction the car needed to hear. It somehow knew to stay on the paved pathway. Still, I was nervous. I was out in the open. And even though I saw no lights and no sign of any guards or alarms, it was a frightening feeling to be so exposed.

"Faster," I said quietly.

The cart sped up.

"Faster."

The quiet motor whirred and the cart increased its velocity.

"Faster!"

The electric engine probably wasn't happy to hear that, but it seemed to have one more burst of energy in its mechanism. So I assumed that would be my speed. I couldn't risk overheating the thing and breaking down. How fast was it going? I had no idea. It didn't matter how fast it was going, I would still want it to go faster. Because my very, very desperate gamble was about to begin, even though I had no cards left to play.

I approached the edge of the woods. The power button on my bracelet began to glow brightly. The vibrations were beginning.

"Straight," I said again, to make sure the cart didn't change its mind about where it was headed.

The first pulses of pain hit me. I closed my eyes and steeled myself for what was to come.

"Faster," I murmured. But it would go no faster. I had been right. The cart was pumped up to the max.

Oh God. It was coming.

The pain.

It radiated through my entire body. It got bigger. And bigger and bigger.

I could say "Reverse." I could stop this whole thing right this second. In the moment, it was all I wanted. I had to remind myself why I was putting myself through hell. I had to stop myself from granting my body instant, wonderful relief.

I wrapped my arms around myself—because I felt like I had to do *something* to keep my body from splitting into a million pieces. So, I crossed my arms across my chest and held on tight, swaying uncertainly in the driver's seat. I had to stay upright. If I fell out, I would be right in the middle of the electric death perimeter, where there would be pain and only pain, and I knew it would be too much for me. I knew it would kill me.

Think about a thousand knives plunging into your body, think about a million watts of current surging through you, think about what it would feel like to be on fire and watch your skin be seared off. Now, put all those feelings together. You're still getting off a lot easier than I did.

The cart surged forward.

My eyes still firmly shut, I wept and moaned from the pain. I felt like I might pass out, but that meant I would fall out of the cart, which would mean even more agony. So I grabbed onto the dashboard with everything I had left. I grabbed on so hard, I thought either my fingers would break or the top of the control panel would snap off.

Jesus, Jesus, sweet Jesus, how much farther do I have to go to escape this? Is there even an escape? Or will the pain never leave me, even if I do get out of the Community?

I couldn't think anymore.

I couldn't.

I was going under, still terrified of where I would end up or what it would feel like when I woke up.

If I woke up.

Some Geek in Bangladesh Hates Me

Okay, so I woke up. But it wasn't easy.

I was lying on my side on the ground. At some point, my pain-plagued body had fallen out of the cart—probably because the cart's anti-collision feature had come to a sharp stop before it plowed into the giant tree ahead of it. What kind of tree was it? How the hell would I know? I could tell a pine from a palm, but not much else.

The important thing was I had gotten past the pain perimeter. My body, however, was still hanging on to the extreme trauma of what I had just put it through—I had a migraine the size of Cleveland and there was a little pool of vomit next to my mouth—but I had accomplished my mission. I had escaped the Community. I rolled over on my back to avoid adding to my throw-up puddle.

Then I winced and I flinched. There was a tightness in my chest and a lingering ache. I had been afraid of the pain giving me a stroke, a heart attack or God knows what, but all my organs seemed to be functional. Then again, I was sweating, I was aching, there was a tingling in my arms, and it was a little hard to breathe. All of those were heart attack danger signs, something I knew full well because Jules used to get on my ass about getting my heart checked out every other day. When I would tell her I lunched at a McDonalds, she had the charming habit of screaming such lovely sentiments as, "Why stop THERE, DOUCHEBAG? Why not just SHOVE A STICK OF BUTTER IN YOUR ARTERY and put out a FUCKING CLOSED FOR BUSINESS SIGN???"

Wow. Guess my memory was all the way back.

Then I noticed the searing pain in my left wrist.

That was where they (whoever "they" were) had attached the bracelet, the bracelet that was designed to flood my body with pain. I glanced down at it. It was actually charred and smoking…which meant God knows what was happening with my skin underneath it.

Jeeesus.

I tried to touch it, but the damned thing was too hot. This wasn't my idea of a good time, but I went ahead and spit on it to try and cool it down. This resulted in the horrifying sight of small wisps of steam rising off the bracelet where my saliva made contact. That didn't do my roasted wrist much good, so I rolled it around in the dew that collected in the leaves on the ground. That seemed to lower the temperature, but it still hurt like hell and I still had no way to get the metal monstrosity off of me.

Regardless, I didn't have any more time to try anything else. The first signs of morning light were appearing in the sky and soon, Lady Blue Eyes would discover I ran away from home.

So, I made myself move.

I slowly managed to get into a sitting position and took a moment to eye my surroundings. I had made it fairly deep into the woods. I couldn't see where the walkway had ended, but a primitive path had evidently carried on in its stead. That path took a sharp turn at this juncture, but I, being unconscious and all, couldn't direct the cart, so it stopped itself rather than smash into a tree. Eventually, it must have shut down on its own—there was still a small power light blinking, which meant the battery wasn't dead.

And that was good. It meant the cart just might have enough juice to get me to civilization—or, at the very least, some kind of highway where I could flag down a vehicle and maybe even find out where the fuck I was. I was pretty sure I had to be somewhere in the southern United States, maybe even Florida, judging by the sky-high humidity and heat as well as the vegetation I recognized from my years living in Miami. Florida. Of course. Where else would you build a retirement village for wayward spooks?

Leaning on the side of the cart with my right hand, I got to my feet and gingerly lowered myself into the driver's seat. All I wanted to do was close my eyes and collapse. But I had to move and move fast. Well, what was fast for me anyway.

"Reverse," I whispered. The cart backed up. I directed it around the tree and back on the path that continued through the woods. Every path had to go somewhere—so my best bet was to see where this one led.

After a few minutes, the path abruptly ended. I was on the other side of the woods, motoring my way through a seemingly-endless, open span of solid dirt. There was hardly any grass or bushes around. It seemed…unusual.

What was also unusual were the wicked holes in that dirt I had to keep steering the cart around. They were messy holes with messy sides, holes that looked like they had maybe been made by some kind of explosives.

Explosives? That wasn't a fun thought.

And that's when I heard the whirring.

The soft, mechanical sounds seemed to be coming from right above me. But this golf cart had a canopy cover, so I couldn't see what was up there. It wasn't loud enough to be an aircraft, but it sounded pretty close to it. It also sounded like it was getting a lot closer. I had an idea what it was, and I dearly hoped I was wrong.

"Right," I said quickly. The cart turned right. And it was a good thing it did, because…

…BOOM.

A small explosion blew a hole in the ground exactly where I would have been if I hadn't turned the cart. It was a messy hole that resembled all the other messy holes I had been steering around.

Then I saw it ahead of me, flying through the air—a large drone about four feet in diameter with three whirling blades holding it aloft, buzzing through the early morning sky and rapidly moving into position to drop another grenade on my head.

So, this is why nobody ever leaves the Community. I had discovered their final safeguard to make sure every Resident ended up a dead man who could tell no tales—drones. Maybe they outsourced their security, like everything else in America these days. Maybe some geek in Bangladesh was playing a video game that's sole purpose was to blow me up.

Maybe I needed to stop inventing ridiculous scenarios in my head and deal with the shit that was actually threatening to kill me.

"Left!"

BOOM.

That one came way too close. The cart rocked a little and my head didn't enjoy the movement. The whole "death from above" thing was getting to me. And it was about to get markedly more lethal. Because I suddenly heard a second whirring. I looked up to the right of the cart—then to the left. That's where I saw another drone, identical to the first as far as I could tell.

"Faster. Faster. FASTER!" I yelled at the cart like it was some chowderhead of a kid crossing the street with a bus bearing down on him. The cart responded as much as it could. And as it rocked and reeled over the uneven ground below, I looked ahead and saw relief staring me in the face. There was another wooded area a few hundred yards in front of me. Drones wouldn't work well in there. I just had to outrun the Community's flying death machines, lose myself in between the trees, and everything would be okeydokey.

"Left!" I shouted as I heard the whirring descend towards me.

BOOM.

This time dirt from that blast actually flew in my face. I grabbed the dashboard with my left hand to steady myself—not a good idea, because that wrist was still a hot mess. Some dirt had made its way into my eyes, so I also suddenly couldn't see so good. But I had to make some kind of move, because one of the drones was about to drop another kid off at the pool. I had to make a non-educated guess as to where that little rascal might hit.

"Right!"

BOOM!

It was the right guess, but it was also the closest blast yet. If it was a kid in Bangladesh working the controls, his joystick skills were growing by leaps and bounds.

My eyesight cleared and I could see the drones circling around to return for another round. "FASTER!" I yelled, but the cart was already on overdrive. I got a whiff of a burning smell. Was the thing about to flame out?

Then I heard a more whirring from above. Louder than the others.

I turned and looked up. The first two drones were hovering at the sides of my trajectory. And smack in the middle was Big Daddy Drone, about twice the size of the others and packing, I assumed, twice the punch.

"Left!" Then, just as soon as the cart had made the move, I yelled, "Right!" I was putting the cart through the best serpentine move it could muster, but the cart was not happy about it. I started to worry I might cause a rollover as the two smaller drones each dropped another bomb.

BOOM. BOOM.

"Right! Left!" I successfully evaded both of the gruesome twosome's payloads—but Big Daddy Drone was hovering behind, waiting for its moment. I had a sinking feeling it was the failsafe, designed to come in for the kill if the other two failed. I thought about the guy in Bangladesh, holding my life in his hands, or at least his joystick. The woods still seemed as far away as they were before.

What was it about human beings? I actually had a pretty sweet deal going in the Community. Classic TV, air-conditioning, and whatever was in that ice cream melting my mind into a pleasant lump of contentment. No worries. No stress. All I needed was as many laughs as an episode of the *Joey Bishop Show* yielded, which, from my experience (and contrary to the laugh track's opinion), was about two. Now, there I was, with a wrist burnt to the third degree and a body wracked with pain, trying to outrun Big Daddy Drone in a golf cart designed for ninety-year-olds. Vegging out in the Community versus being chased through a dirt field by bomb-wielding drones? Put those two options on either side of a scale and see which one gets flung up into the ceiling like a pencil in study hall.

Gripping the dashboard with my left hand, trying to ignore the searing pain in my wrist and the aching in my chest, I stood up as high as I could in the cart without knocking off the canopy top. Since I was 6'1", that involved some crouching.

It was an awkward position, one where I had to try and keep my balance, so I didn't fall out of the cart. When I stabilized myself about as much as I could, I reached up with my right arm to see if I could somehow push off that canopy top. I didn't have a lot of strength or leverage in my half-up half-down stance, but I still shoved that ragtop with everything I had—and, after a couple of tries it worked. The canopy ripped away from where it was attached and flapped away in the distance as the cart continued forward.

I quickly fell back down to a sitting position. I could finally see what was happening above my head. But what caught my eye wasn't above, but below my line of sight—because the words "LOW BATTERY" were blinking on the cart's little digital dashboard screen. The import of that message distracted me for a moment too long, because, as I stared at it, one of the little drones quickly positioned itself over my head.

"RIGHT!" I shouted, just in time. The cart swerved.

BOOM.

I think I got some dirt in my mouth that time. And my eyes too.

Then something new happened. Both of the little drones began to hang back as Big Daddy Drone surged forward, slowing as it approached the space directly above me. Then it began to slowly descend. Holy fuck. It was close enough that I could see it carried only one grenade, but it was a pretty substantial one.

However, by this point, I was very close to the woods. I just needed another minute or two to make it to safety. But it was obvious I didn't have that kind of time. The cart battery was pretty much drained. I felt it start to slow, just as I felt the breeze from Big Daddy Drone's propellers blowing through my hair. It actually felt slightly refreshing, even though it meant I was about to lose the top of my skull.

I looked up. It was only a few feet above my head, proceeding with obvious care and with precision. I had to admit, it was an impressive sight. Clearly Big Daddy did not intend to miss like the twins did.

It seemed like a good time to become religious.

"Our Father who art in heaven," I said quietly, *"hallowed be Thy name…"*

Then I threw myself out of the side of the cart.

"Thy Kingdom COME…"

I hit the ground. More pain. Just what I needed for breakfast.

"Thy will be done…" I whispered as I rolled away as far and as fast as I could, hoping that His will didn't involve blowing me to smithereens.

I had timed it just right. From my vantage point in the dirt, I saw Big Daddy Drone drop its payload right on the cart, which was immediately swallowed up by a vicious fireball about forty feet in front of where I had landed. The seat where my ass had been twenty seconds earlier landed about a foot from my head.

"…on earth as it is in heaven."

I got up as fast as I could. I had no doubt the two little drones were on their way to avenge their dead father, but I sure didn't have the time to turn and confirm that fact. No, I had barely time to make it into the woods and, luckily, I did.

But one of the baby drones didn't.

The kid in Bangladesh must have stopped to take a sip of his Coca-Cola, because the misfortunate drone bounced off a tree trunk, hit the ground, and promptly exploded. The other baby drone, however, was expertly, if slowly, whizzing between the trees. I kept going, dodging and ducking, until I found a big enough loose branch on the ground. Panting, dizzy and in pain, I picked it up and ran behind one of the bigger trees.

The baby drone approached. It couldn't see me, but, peeking out from behind the tree trunk, I sure as fuck saw it. When it got close enough, I came out and whacked that branch like I was Barry Bonds in all his steroid glory. The drone jerked back in an out-of-control spiral, got caught on a branch and ended up hanging there looking like a cheap piece of plastic shit some kid got from the discount rack at Wal Mart.

I fell down and landed on my back, and, just before I passed out again, I finished the Lord's Prayer.

I hated loose ends.

Truck Stop

My wrist was bad.

I had a feeling underneath what was left of the bracelet was skin resembling that weird, paper-thin meat product Arby's called roast beef. Or used to, at any rate. I hadn't been to an Arby's since the turn of the century. Had anybody?

The pain woke me up. Not just the pain emanating from my wrist, but also from my head, my chest, my legs…well, my fucking everything. This wasn't the kind of activity a 60-year-old should be engaging in. I raised my head off the ground and saw the baby drone, still hanging helplessly from the tree branch it flew into. I also saw it had one more small missile dangling from the bottom. I was lucky it didn't detonate and set the entire forest on fire. That was just what I needed, Smokey the Bear hunting me down with a sharpened shovel.

I got to my feet and looked over what was left of my clothes. My light blue Community uniform was covered in dark brown dirt. I was filthy, head to toe. I was also thirsty, hungry and exhausted, in addition to that whole being-in-a-world-of-hurt thing. But, again, I knew I had to keep moving. Something else would be coming after me sooner rather than later—and even if that wasn't true, there was still the possibility I might just collapse in a heap and end up as some animal's dinner. Whatever the case, I had to keep myself upright and keep putting one foot in front of the other until I got somewhere. So, I stumbled on through the wilderness.

Why couldn't I just have stayed and eaten the ice cream? Why?

After a while, I didn't know how long, I heard sounds. Sounds not associated with trees or animals or weather. I stopped and leaned on a nearby Sequoia. It probably wasn't a Sequoia, but, then again, I didn't know anything about trees. I listened closely. *It might be. Sweet Jesus, it might be.*

Vehicles. Cars, trucks… *all those good things that might take me far away from here.*

There was a small embankment ten or twenty yards to the right—the sounds seemed to be coming from the top of that embankment. I changed course and lurched in that direction. Somehow, I pulled what was left of me up the embankment.

And then, through a few more trees, I saw my salvation—a highway.

It was just a small two-lane state highway, but it would do. Unfortunately, at the moment, it was a highway without vehicles— apparently, I had just missed the traffic jam, because, at that moment, I couldn't see a car or truck coming in either direction. It was just bare endless asphalt and guardrails for miles. This was not only the middle of nowhere, it was the middle of the middle of nowhere.

I sat down on the shoulder and crossed my legs, looking like a roadside Buddha, like the statue that had been in Miss Yvonne's parlor. *Miss Yvonne, the so-called "psychic" who started me on my last futile quest...*

I was jolted by the memory. I guess it's hard to forget a woman who likes sheer clothing and doesn't like underwear. Which is how she was able to trick me into reliving my hellish past and deciding to track Daddy Andy down. Of course, she left out the part about being his girlfriend.

Ohhhh. My wrist.

I took a deep breath and tried not to fall apart. I had to wait it out. Somebody had to drive down this road at some point. I heard vehicles before, that's how I found the highway in the first place.

Finally, a car approached—an ancient white Toyota Corolla with numerous rust spots. I weakly waved my hand up in the air to try and get the driver's attention. It whizzed by. I thought to myself—*would I stop for a guy caked with dirt sitting on the side of the road?* Not likely.

But I had to find someone who would.

I got myself back on my feet. I had to be proactive. And as I swayed in the light breeze, I heard another car approaching.

I stuck out my thumb like a good hitchhiker should and waited. However, the black Nissan Rogue that resembled my car (if it was still my car – who knew?) ignored my thumb, as well as the rest of me.

Two strikes.

I couldn't keep this up much longer. Dark flashes were starting to interrupt my vision. I didn't want to end up as roadkill.

I heard another vehicle coming from the other direction. I turned to see a pick-up truck, an old grey beat-up Dodge, driving at maximum speed. With nothing to lose and next to nothing left in my tank, I ran out onto the highway directly in front of it to stop it. I heard the squeal of brakes, I smelled the skidding tires. And then I collapsed.

I opened my eyes a few moments later to see a skinny woman in her 50's hovering over me. She was wearing a pink sleeveless top, shorts and flip-flops.

"Jeez oh Pete, you okay? Let me call 911." She had her cell phone in her hand.

"No!" I yelled with what little energy had left.

She glanced at the phone. "No coverage here anyway, Murphy's Law." She turned back to me. "You really don't look so good…" She looked around, most likely wondering who else she could dump me on. But there were no prospects in sight.

"Can you just get me to a town?" I asked.

She considered me a moment. I probably didn't look all that trustworthy, I'd give her that.

"Mister, there ain't no town for sixty miles or so."

I wrinkled my nose. She smelled like tobacco. Lots of it. Chain smoker?

"Take me to where you're going. I'm not a criminal or anything. But people are after me."

She frowned. "Well, you ain't armed…and you sure don't look all that dangerous." A pause. "Can you make it into my truck?"

I nodded and she helped me up. I leaned on her as I hobbled over to the passenger's side. She helped me get in. As I sat there, part of me began to relax because it felt like I had made it to safety, but the other part of me had to be sure.

She got in the driver's seat and drove on, anxiously glancing at me to make sure I wasn't going to try to strangle her or something.

"I'm from Mayo, that's where I'm headed. It's gonna be about an hour to get there."

"Mayo?" I asked in disbelief. "There's a town named Mayo? Any other condiments nearby? Because it's not what I put on my sandwiches."

"You got enough strength to make jokes? You look half-dead!" Then she saw my wrist. "What the hell happened there?" she almost shrieked.

Sometimes, I felt the truth was best, even though it usually wasn't.

"I was being held in a secret government compound. The bracelet made me experience horrible pain if I tried to leave. I left."

Her eyes bugged out at me. "Who ARE you?"

"Max Bowman. And you…"

"Glenda Schmidt. Are you for real?" She giggled nervously.

Good question. She lit up a cigarette. A USA Menthol light, according to the box, whatever the hell that was. Were Winstons and Kents history? A few thousand old cigarette commercial jingles from before they were outlawed went through my head, and then she abruptly turned to me again.

"Wait…Max Bowman? THAT Max Bowman? Are you that guy? The one that went missin' last year?" She looked more closely at my face. "Holy moley, you are!"

"Yeah. I are."

"Oh Jesus. That was a big f-in' deal. You *really* him? You look like him, you gotta be. There was a *60 Minutes* thing about you just last week!"

"*60 Minutes?*" I asked with a start.

"Oh, yeah. There was a whole bunch of stuff about you on the internet after that."

"Huh." I took that in. "Did I get Lesley Stahl? Please tell me I didn't get Scott Pelley."

"Lara Logan, I think…?"

I shrugged. Whatever.

"I knew you looked familiar, it was the hair that threw me off!"

The hair…?

I glanced in the rearview mirror. What the hell. My hair had turned completely white.

For years I had prided myself on my Reaganesque head of hair. Like the late president, my hair color seemed to defy the aging process. It stayed brown with only flecks of grey popping up in my sideburns and my stubble when I didn't shave. It was that way when I left the Community. Now I looked like an Anderson Cooper that didn't exercise.

"But on the show, it said you were retired and on your own. It didn't say nuthin' about you bein' held captive. They even showed you talkin' about it. Actually, you looked kinda stoned or somethin'…." Another nervous giggle.

I turned back to her. "Was there somebody named Doug Daytona on this report?"

She thought. "Short guy, greasy blonde hair, big black glasses? Yeah, he said he was makin' a movie about you. He won a bunch of Emmys?"

I sighed. "Fuck me."

"What is all this?"

I told her about how I was drugged up, about how they got me to say what they wanted me to say. Doug Daytona was on a propaganda mission, and I was so busy doing my impression of Lenny from *Of Mice and Men* it was an easy one to pull off.

Why the hell was I spilling my secrets to a strange woman? I didn't know. Maybe because I hadn't talked to a normal person in so long. Maybe because I hadn't been in my right mind for so long. Maybe because I felt safe in a pick-up truck headed to Mayo driven by a woman smoking USA Menthol lights.

After I was done talking, Glenda Schmidt was quiet. She lit another cigarette. I could tell she was freaked the fuck out, because she suddenly turned into Little Miss Chatterbox. She started going on about how she was visiting her cousin Jody for the long weekend, Jody lived in Steinhatchee on the Gulf Coast, they liked to sit on the beach and finish off a few bottles of champagne, then she left in the middle of the night so she could get back in time for work today, she worked in the offices of the Lafayette school district, everybody was a freakin' moron and only she knew what she was doing, she wanted her husband Barry to come down to the beach with her, but he had this rock band (they played covers of Tom Petty songs) and didn't want to go and she's driving home and suddenly there's Max Bowman and she's in the middle of some kind of international incident…

I finally interrupted her with a question I very much needed to ask.

"What day is it?"

She gave me a look. "Huh? Jeez, it's Labor Day. Well, day after Labor Day, like I said, I gotta go back to work today…"

"Labor Day. 2017?"

"Yeah…?"

Ten months. I had been gone since last November. I turned 61 without even getting one Facebook birthday post. Shit.

Glenda Schmidt started going on again about her cousin Jody, she was a writer, freelance, wrote a couple of romance novels, maybe she could help tell my story, but she was a little weird, still…

I interrupted again. "Did the Republicans impeach President Clinton yet?"

She gave me another look. "Whoa, you really don't know what year it is, do ya? He's retired."

What? Then I figured out what she meant.

"No, no, not Bill. I meant Hillary. I assumed they wouldn't stop going after…"

She interrupted me with a big old laugh. "Hillary? Oh Jeez no. Trump won."

I stared at her in disbelief. I could not make words come out of my mouth. I didn't know where to even begin. Trump WON?

"Now it's all about the Russkies, you know anything about that deal? Hey, I shoulda asked, you want some water or somethin'? I got a couple bottles in the glove compartment…"

I was thirsty. But I was more tired than thirsty. And I was very overwhelmed. Ten months. I had lost ten months. That was around 12 years in dog years. Dog. My dog. *Where was my dog?*

"I think I have to close my eyes…for a while…"

And I did.

But, I don't know how much later, I woke up with another jolt.

PMA.

He'd been with me from the beginning, from when I first started searching for his poor, fucked-up uncle. I didn't even know if the kid was alive. He got shot in the chest and then Angela kicked me off the Davidson estate. *Angela.* Were she and I...who knew? But the kid...goddammit.

Glenda Schmidt noticed my eyes open. "Good you're awake, we're close to town. You were makin' all kinds of weird noises. Guess you've been through the mill," Glenda Schmidt said. "Anyways, we gotta get you to a doctor..."

I shook my head. "I need a veterinarian. And a jeweler. Jeweler first."

"Jeweler?"

"Yeah. They gotta have jewels somewhere in Mayo. After all, you had to come from somewhere..."

She gave me a smile.

"Awww..."

The Max Bowman charm. It still worked. Even with white hair.

Mayo

Mayo looked a lot like I expected. Only worse.

Maybe I was being unfair. After all, it was very small—about a thousand people in the metropolitan area, according to the city limits sign—and it had the honor of being the only municipality in Florida's Lafayette County, if you didn't count the Community and I doubt that they did. I guess I was just a little shell-shocked that this was the only place with a high school for a few light years around. I thought that shit only happened in Montana and Siberia, places that had a lot more in common than people knew.

It was around 10 a.m. when we hit the outside of town and I had no time to spare. Neither did Glenda Schmidt, who was already late for work. Now that she had cell coverage, she called the school district offices to tell them she was going to be even later than she had originally told them, then gave my wrist a worried glance.

"I really think a doctor…"

"Glenda," I said, "Jeweler first, then vet. I'm going to need to borrow some money for this stuff, I will pay you back. I'll get some money sent to me, but I have to take care of these other things ASAP. I also need a cheap cell phone too. Something basic."

She nodded. She had seen me on TV. People like Glenda didn't argue with people on TV. Plus all my talk about government kidnappings and pursuits had her completely freaked out. I had lured her over to my side, but it was a tenuous alliance at best.

"First, we're gonna stop by my place," she said, lighting up her 600th or so cigarette of the morning. "Ya look like the east end of a horse goin' west. Ya can't see people looking like a dirtbag. Barry has some clothes that'll fit you and he'll be at work by now, so I ain't gonna have to try and explain you right now, thank the Lord."

It was my turn not to argue. Besides, it would work to my favor to not look like an escaped convict.

After the stop and quick change at the Schmidt homestead, Glenda drove me to a jewelry repair shop in town. My face was now freshly scrubbed and my new outfit was a pair of old blue jeans and a plain dark blue t-shirt. I had passed on Barry's black tank top that featured a large eagle head on its front along with the words, "CAW CAW, MOTHER*UCKER."

Once inside the repair shop, I asked the guy behind the counter if he had a jeweler's saw. He said he did. I said good, I needed something removed. Then I held out my wrist and showed him the bracelet and the charred, bloody mess underneath it that used to be my skin.

He gasped and told me I needed to see a doctor. I said that was the next stop, but it wasn't going to do me a damn bit of good if that thing wasn't off and a jeweler's saw was the only way to do it. He still seemed rather reluctant, so I offered him an extra $50 of Glenda Schmidt's money to convince him. He said he wasn't going to be responsible for what happened. I said, "Good for you."

A couple minutes later, the bracelet was carefully cut off my wrist. And, as a bonus, the guy managed to do it without opening up an artery underneath. Kudos. What was left of the skin underneath it looked like three-month-old bologna, but I was pretty sure it would look a whole lot more palatable after it was cleaned up. My wrist still hurt like a son of a bitch, but the relief of having that evil piece of technology separated from my flesh was overwhelming. It had kept me prisoner for almost a year.

I took a deep breath and shoved the bracelet pieces in my—okay, Barry's—pants pocket, while the jeweler kept looking at me like I was an alien. As Glenda Schmidt paid him off, I resisted the urge to yell "BOO!" at him. I thought that might be counter-productive.

"I'll take you to see Kimmy, she's the vet I took our cat to. She was a big help when we had to put Chloe down last year, such a sweet girl!" Glenda Schmidt said as we got back in her pick-up. A few minutes later, after I had heard every single detail about her dead cat (Barry even cried a little), that pick-up was parked in the back lot of the Mayo Town & Country Animal Hospital and we were inside standing in front of a confused receptionist.

"I mean…Dr. Raymond doesn't see…humans," the receptionist said with a thousand invisible question marks swirling around her head. She then looked at Glenda for some kind of lifeline.

"Look, Eileen," Glenda said in a low voice, "This is kinda important. Can Kimmy squeeze him in quick? It's a situation."

Eileen, who was large but evidently not in charge, disappeared into the back. There was an urgent slice of whispering going on seconds later, but then it stopped and a pretty young thing in a white doctoring jacket came out to the front desk. This had to be Kimmy.

"How can I help you, Glenda?" she said, also eyeing me as if I were an alien. I was beginning to think I actually was.

"Kimmy, I'm not sure," Glenda said, "But just do me a favor if ya got the time? Just talk to this guy, he said he really needs the help of a vet."

"Only take a couple of minutes," I added helpfully.

"Well…my first appointment's not for ten minutes…." Kimmy looked me over again, because nobody's more suspicious than small town people, then she cocked her head and we followed her down the hallway.

Inside the exam room, I told Kimmy what I needed—I wanted her to scan me for a microchip. Having one of those little fuckers injected into me was usually SOP when people kidnapped me and if it happened again, I wanted that fucking chip out of me. Otherwise I knew they'd track me. I didn't explain all that, for fear everybody would hide under the examination table, I just asked for the scan.

"Why would you have a chip...?" she said uncertainly, looking at Glenda.

"You see *60 Minutes* last week?" Glenda asked her. I shot Glenda a look that screamed, "SHUT UP." She did.

It ended up not mattering, because Kimmy shook her head and explained she never watched news shows, she only watched the *Animal Planet* channel. Talk about taking your work home with you.

"Well, just trust me, this is real important," replied Glenda.

Kimmy gave a resigned shrug. What the hell would it hurt, right? She got her chip scanner, ran it up and down my body—and found nothing. I asked her to rinse and repeat, and she scanned me again. Nothing. I fingered the remains of the bracelet in my pocket. If there was tracking technology, it would have made sense to make it a part of that wicked little piece of jewelry. So maybe I was clean. That was good, because I didn't want to get carved up again trying to remove a chip—I had enough physical damage to deal with. Speaking of which...

"One more thing, doctor," I said.

"What's that?" Kimmy asked, still a little wary of me.

"Can you put something on this and wrap it up?" I showed her my left wrist and she gasped louder than the jeweler. "Just pretend I'm a Great Dane that stuck its paw in a grease fire."

That made Glenda Schmidt laugh in spite of herself.

"Where's the post office?" I asked Glenda as we left the animal hospital with my nicely-bandaged wrist.

"What're we doin' now? I really gotta get to work…" Then she started talking about how her supervisor always screwed things up and today they had to put together the next teacher planning day and if she wasn't there, they'd have to redo the whole thing because they always forgot about the district rules and what had to be on the agenda and…

"Just one last quick thing," I managed to interject when she finally had to come up for air.

At the post office, I put the bracelet pieces in a Priority Mail flat rate box, addressed it to the address of a Walgreens in Anchorage, Alaska that I looked up on Glenda's smart phone, and mailed it. If the tracking component was still working, that would keep whoever was after me busy. After that, we hit the local gas station, where an uncomfortable Glenda bought me my cheap cell phone.

My errands were done for the moment. As Glenda told me all about her brother Mick who worked in the sheriff's office in Cheyenne, Wyoming and had basset hounds and once met Dick Cheney and Lou Ferrigno, we headed back to her house, where she dropped me off. I intended to take a very long-awaited nap. And, even though my wrist still felt like it was on fire, sleep came almost immediately.

Casa de Schmidt

"WHERE THE FUCK ARE YOU?"

Turned out PMA was alive and well. Well, alive anyway. He didn't sound all that well. I mean, he sounded *physically* well, but mood-wise…well, not so well.

When I had finally woken up, it was dark. I had slept about ten hours or so and, when I did open my eyes, it felt like I could sleep another ten. Glenda Schmidt had put me in her son's old room—he was a choir director in Illinois somewhere—and she and husband Barry had left me undisturbed since then, which was much appreciated. From the aches and pains still pulsating through my body, I was sure I needed a lot more "west and wewaxation" (as Elmer Fudd had once famously said before Bugs Bunny fucked him over for the ten millionth time), but that would have to wait.

It was time to get a few balls rolling.

Most importantly, I had to know if the kid had survived last year's gunshot wound to the chest. It was the Big Horrible Thing that caused his mom (and my very temporary lover) Angela to throw me out of stately Davidson Manor and separate me from my beloved dog Eydie. It also caused me no end of intense soul-wrenching guilt…at least until I started eating the ice cream. After that I didn't feel guilty about anything. Ah, the good old days…

Hearing the way PMA yelled when he answered my call from my brand-new crappy cell phone, I realized I didn't need to feel guilty anymore. It seemed like he had fully recovered. Either that or his ghost was pretty damn good at shouting down the living.

"Your phone safe?" I asked after he shrieked at me.

"Max, after all we've been through, you need to ask me that? I'll never carry around an unencrypted phone again in my life, trust me."

"C'mon, kid, be nice. Isn't it a pleasure to know I'm still alive?"

"I know you're still alive, Max, the whole country does. They saw you on *60 Minutes*. Or at least some lobotomized version of you, what the hell was that?"

"Too much ice cream."

"Ice cream?"

"A long story. So, you're okay?"

"As okay as a person who took a bullet in the lung could be. How about you? Where were you? What did they do to you?"

I had no choice but to tell him that whole long story. So I told him about the Community, the ice cream and my escape courtesy of Lady Blue Eyes. He took that all in without saying much. I knew what he was thinking. We'd been through the worst and we'd both survived. But, even if Andrew Wright was dead, there were still plenty of horrible human beings out there who still thought I was worth containing. And now that I had gotten out from under their collective thumb, they wouldn't be very happy about me roaming around loose. Meaning there could be a forthcoming worst that would be even worse than the former worst. Which was the worst.

"So…Andrew Wright. Is he…?"

"Who knows," the kid answered. "Apparently he disappeared at the same time you did. Now, why is that, Max?"

I didn't tell him that Andrew Wright was my father. I didn't tell him that I tried to kill him and couldn't remember what had happened. I wasn't telling anyone that.

"I don't know, kid. I don't know."

The kid made some kind of noise. He knew I was holding something back, but he wasn't in the mood to pursue it. To be honest, the kid sounded down, very down. I asked a bunch of invasive questions, hoping to track down the source of his depression. Was he seeing anyone? What was up with his old CIA boyfriend, Kev? And what about his mom? And, most importantly, my dog?

"The stupid dog's fine," was all he said. And then he sighed. He was holding something back too. Not good, as our current Tweeter-in-chief might have tapped out on his phone. PMA didn't want to talk about anything personal, which meant everything in that arena was pretty fucked. Instead, he wanted to stay focused on whatever the hell had happened to me. And that meant asking who was this Doug Daytona freak and what was he up to?

I told him what I remembered from my ice-cream-addled existence in the Community—that Doug Daytona showed up and manipulated me into saying what he wanted me to say in front of a couple of cameras. I had no idea who he was or who sent him in after me. I just knew he won a bunch of Emmys (which were worthless according to Shawn Shepheard) and he had offices in Atlanta. But clearly he had ties to…well, something.

I finished up by asking the kid if he could wire a few thousand to me in Mayo. I spotted a Western Union outlet at the Fast Track, the local gas station/market where I bought the cell phone, that was probably the easiest and fastest way to do it. Lucky for me, PMA had some money in the bank from his trust fund, so he could do it without asking Mommy.

I started thinking out loud. I wanted to rent a car and drive up to meet the kid, but how the hell would I do that? I didn't have any form of ID on me and nobody was going to rent a Ford to a nameless drifter in my experience…

That's when the kid saved my life for the 18th or 19th time, I wasn't sure—I'd lost track. He reminded me that when I got my fake ID from the CIA, I left my real Max Bowman driver's license, as well as my credit cards, in the guest room at stately Davidson Manor, where I had been staying. He could Fed-X everything to me in Mayo.

That's when Glenda Schmidt opened the door. It was good timing.

"What's the address here?" I asked. She told me. I told the kid, I said my goodbyes and hung up.

I looked over my hostess. Glenda Schmidt was in some cat pajamas and a bathrobe and, for once, wasn't telling me a bunch of shit I didn't want to know about. As a matter of fact, she looked a little stressed.

"When'ja wake up?" she asked.

"Just a few minutes ago. Had to catch up with somebody. He's sending me money and my ID, so I'll be out of your hair in a day or two."

Suddenly, a guy appeared behind her. He had a blonde-grey moustache and what appeared to be a rapidly disappearing hairline to match. Unlike Glenda, he was still wearing day clothes and from his vibe, I realized why Glenda was a little closed-mouthed.

"I think you should maybe be out of our hair tomorrow a.m., pal."

"You must be Barry."

"Yeah, and I don't need any special spy force crashing in here and killin' us all to death."

"You're right. That would be the result of the killing. Death."

For some reason, I didn't get a laugh out of that bon mot. He made a move towards me, but Glenda held him back.

"Barry, you go microwave a couple hot dogs for Max, lemme talk to him."

Barry gave me a final scowl and vanished.

"Look," I said, "I'll be out of here well before anything bad happens. Besides, I don't see how anybody would know I was here."

"There were a lot of strange cars in town today," she said.

"Strange cars?"

"Most cars around here aren't in that great shape. So these kinda stuck out. You gettin' the money and the ID tomorrow?"

"Money, yes, but ID probably not until day after tomorrow. I'll stay in until then, so nobody spots me."

She turned and gave a look towards where Barry was apparently still standing. Guess he wasn't zapping those Oscar Meyers for me just yet.

"Thursday," she called to him in the tone of someone who had been married for a whole lot of years. "He'll go on Thursday. I think we'll fuckin' survive until Thursday." There was some muttering from beyond the doorway and then she turned back to me with an annoyed eyeroll.

"Thursday'll work."

"Thanks. You're a lifesaver."

"Yeah, I'm startin' to believe that."

I slept hard that night and most of the next day, Wednesday. Fortunately, I woke up in time to answer the door when the Fed-X package from PMA was delivered—somehow, he had gotten it to me the next day. Inside the package, as he had promised, was my driver's license and some of my old credit cards. Did they still work? Did I still have bank accounts? Did I still have my Roosevelt Island apartment and the car that was parked in the $200-a-month garage there?

Those last couple of questions remained unanswered, but I did the online banking thing on the Schmidt home computer and discovered that, yes, I still had bank accounts and enough in them to survive for a while. My credit cards were dead to me, since I hadn't made any payments on them for months, but my debit card would work.

Despite the return of at least some of my identity, I felt like a man whose life had been taken away from him. I was wearing Barry's clothes, eating Glenda's hot dogs, and sleeping in Michael's bed. I might as well have changed my name to Max Schmidt, I felt so disconnected from everything. I knew I would inevitably experience some kind of mental backlash after removing the comforting Community ice cream from my diet, but that knowledge did nothing to temper my rising level of anxiety. And that anxiety got a big lift from Glenda Schmidt's talk of strange cars. I may have been back in the so-called real world, but I was far from safe.

And, as it turned out, the real world had become incredibly unreal.

After 10 months in an ice-cream induced semi-coma, I decided to catch up on world events, and spent a few hours watching CNN. I was treated to a disturbing odyssey through the Trump Presidency, which I was amazed was still a thing. What happens when you elect a guy who brags about grabbing women's pussies, lies like other people breathe and has no trace of a conscience? "Well, let's find out," said the voters of America and lo, the Great Experiment was on. If I had to pick ten months of my life to spend as a drugged-up recluse watching black-and-white TV…well, the months I had just sat out would've definitely been contenders.

Of course I needed to know more, so I went on Glenda's home computer to research the horror show of an administration. According to everything I was reading, Trump was like a drunken airline pilot feverishly yanking out all the wires out of America's instrument panel when it was in mid-air. Whatever was functional about our federal government was rapidly being decimated and Republicans were just letting it happen. Then there were all the secret Russian meetings, the tacit endorsement of white supremacy, and the stupid babyman threats against foreign nations…and me, I'd been mindlessly eating ice cream through the whole thing. He actually refused to denounce Nazis until his staff forced him to. *Nazis.*

Nazis? That reminded me. I had to let my brother know I was alive.

Alan was the last person in my immediate family I had a relationship with. My parents had disowned me, my oldest brother had gone along with that agenda and Alan, my second oldest brother, was the only one who hadn't done me wrong in one way or another.

But he was a little weird about Nazis.

As a kid, he had a record album of Hitler speeches and marching songs from the Third Reich. I didn't know where he got it, but when I saw it, he told me not to tell our dad (who turned out not to be my dad, but I didn't know that at the time) about it. After all, the guy had fought in World War II—he wouldn't be too fond of my brother enjoying the soundtrack of the opposition. Actually, I didn't know if he "enjoyed it" per se. I played it once and didn't really see the appeal. Of course, I was only eight years old and didn't really have a firm grasp of the whole Nazi concept as of yet. It was around the time my parents took us to see *The Sound of Music,* which at first I thought was this charming musical tale of a rich guy hitting on his kids' babysitter, then the next thing I knew…well, Nazis.

Anyway, to me, the fascination with all things Nazi was just another facet of Alan's obsession with war as a kid. He watched *Combat!* every week and put his hundreds of miniature soldiers, which he treated with loving care, through complex maneuvers in our backyard. When I got a G.I. Joe for my birthday, it wasn't treated so lovingly, because Alan insisted we put him through boot camp. It was the rare recruit that could survive Alan's idea of training, since it consisted of such delights as getting shot up by a pellet gun, putting lit firecrackers down Joe's pants, burying him in the garden and leaving him there for two weeks on "bivouac," and finally, dousing his head with lighter fluid and setting it on fire. I ended up with a plastic double amputee with a ball of cotton for a skull.

Again, this was the brother who was good to me.

As a matter of fact, he had helped me track down the information that helped me figure out Andrew Wright was my father. Not that I had shared that final shocker with him, nor was I planning to any time soon. Instead, I just shot off a quick email to him explaining that I was alive and in my right mind, but to try and keep that to himself. I also added as a joke, ha ha, that I hoped he was staying away from the Nazi rallies that seemed to be popping up out of nowhere.

Nazi rallies. In America. In broad daylight. This was definitely a whole new era.

After a restless night of sleep, it was Thursday and time for me to depart Casa de Schmidt before Barry, at worst, called the authorities on me or, at best, knocked out a couple of my teeth after another one of my wisecracks. I was up early, even before the Schmidts left for work, because I needed to run an errand while it was still dark and strange cars wouldn't spot me. I hoofed it down to the Fast Track, where I picked up the Western Union money from PMA and excitedly went to purchase my first Coke Zero of 2017. Used to be I couldn't live without a Coke Zero—then, to my dismay, I found there wasn't a carbonated beverage to be had in all of the Community. But I was back in a Coca-Cola world, which meant I could finally partake of the nectar of the gods. I was so excited. It was going to be amazing.

Wait…

I furtively searched the refrigerated case of sodas for a Coke Zero. I saw no bottle that sported the black and white labelling of my daily substitute for coffee. I looked again. Nothing. Plenty of Diet Coke. Plenty of Coke. Plenty of Cherry Coke. But Coke Zero? MIA. Shit. Had the sales of Coke Zero been so catastrophic in my absence that they pulled the plug? I felt a wave of panic. I swear, a few beads of sweat popped out on my forehead.

That's when a young Fast Track employee noticed my desperation and asked if I needed help. I replied that what I needed was a Coke Zero and I wasn't seeing any. He reached in, instantly pulled out a bottle with a *red*, black and white label and handed it to me.

I read the label. "Coke Zero Sugar." Coke Zero *Sugar?* What the hell had happened to the world in the past ten months?

"They changed the name a few months ago," the Fast Track guy said. "It's good."

I quickly opened it and took a swig, even though I hadn't paid for it yet. That's the way I rolled. I swished it around in my mouth, as if I was sampling a fine Bordeaux, and swallowed. Interesting. It tasted more like both Diet Coke *and* regular Coke, but still sort of like Coke Zero. It would take some getting used to, but maybe…maybe…

I had to move on to more important matters. On my way to the counter to pay for my already-violated bottle, I saw a spinner rack of generic reading glasses. I picked out the plainest-looking pair I could find and handed them to the cashier with the soda. Between the specs and my newly-white hair, I wouldn't be so recognizable when strange cars drove past me.

The sun finally rose as I hurried back to Casa de Schmidt, where I peeled off a few hundred-dollar bills for Glenda and Barry, a lot more than I owed them. Suddenly, Barry was a lot more appreciative of my presence. I asked them where I could find the nearest car rental place and the answer was twenty miles to the north. Glenda offered to drive me before work, she'd just have to call in and say she'd be late, but even if she didn't call in, they'd be too dumb to notice she hadn't showed up because they wouldn't see a truck coming at their asses until they had the grill embedded in their f-in' foreheads.

I accepted her gracious offer.

When we got to the Alamo Rent-a-Car in Live Oak, the city north of Mayo, I felt like Glenda was actually sorry to see me go. I may have represented nothing but trouble to her husband, but I had a feeling Glenda needed a little trouble in her life. Unfortunately, I needed a little less cigarette smoke in my life, so I was ready to say my goodbyes.

"Y'all keep in touch," she said wistfully.

"Hope you can make my funeral," I said as brightly as I could.

You U!

Is this a good idea? Probably not. But here I am anyway.

I was standing in front of the building my new crappy cellphone told me housed the offices of Doug Daytona. To be more specific, it housed the business known as "You U!", whatever the hell that meant, which was apparently the name of Dougie's operation. It was a five-story professional building, the kind of place where you'd find a mid-level legal or dental practice.

So just what kind of practice did Dougie preside over?

It was mid-afternoon. Turned out it took only a little over four hours in my rented Nissan Sentra before I hit the notorious traffic that continually clogged the highways of Atlanta, Georgia. Technically speaking, I was north of Atlanta in the Buckhead district, one of the most prosperous areas of the city and one of the few communities named after the decapitated head of a deer.

Buckhead was an outlier. Pretty much everything else in Atlanta was named after fruits and plants, not dead animals. In particular, the word "Peachtree" was slapped on everything in sight. Limiting the discussion just to street names, you could find, without looking very hard, Peachtree Creek Road, Peachtree Lane, Peachtree Circle, Peachtree Plaza, Peachtree Way, Peachtree Walk, Peachtree Drive, Peachtree Park Drive, Peachtree Memorial Drive, Peachtree Parkway, Peachtree Valley Road, Peachtree Avenue, Peachtree Battle Avenue (named for a Civil War Battle that was fought (where else?) at Peachtree Creek), and Peachtree Road, the thoroughfare that had brought me to this particular parking lot. Peachtree Road was, let's say, the trunk of the Buckhead business district, where you'd find high-rise office buildings, hotels, condos and other upscale offerings.

This was the neighborhood where Doug Daytona had decided to plant his flag—where the money was.

Part of me was exhausted. Part of me was stressed. But a bigger part of me was pissed. This Emmy-award-winning freak hijacked my brain, put propaganda in my mouth and broadcast it to the world.

I had watched my *60 Minutes* segment on my phone—well, as much as I could without puking up a couple of the Schmidt hot dogs that were still working their way through my system. The density of deception perpetrated by Dougie on an unsuspecting American public was truly a marvel.

Anchorwoman Lara Logan kicked things off:

Over the past two years, a mystery man named Max Bowman has dominated many of the conspiracy theories that circulate continuously throughout the internet. These narratives portray Bowman, a former CIA analyst, as some sort of rogue warrior fighting against secret government operations designed to both dominate the world and control our minds. Standard kook stuff, right? Maybe not. Because there is some substance to these rumors.

It's well documented that, in 2015, Bowman singlehandedly exposed a criminal element within the private military company, Dark Sky, which briefly lost its government funding after one of its principles attempted to murder Bowman on New York City's Roosevelt Island. It's also documented that, the following year, Bowman was imprisoned by an experimental clinic on New York City's Upper East Side that was said to have CIA connections. That clinic went up in flames after his abduction. However, after that, the Max Bowman saga gets very murky. Bowman completely disappeared from sight for almost a year, further stoking online rumors that this Dark Knight of the digital age had been detained or even assassinated by our own government.

That wasn't so bad. I actually liked the "Dark Knight of the digital age" thing. I briefly considered having business cards printed up with that title.

Well, we're here to tell you Max Bowman is very much alive and well—and ready to quash any suggestion that he's at war with America's "Deep State." Emmy Award-winning producer and director Doug Daytona somehow found Bowman's hiding place—he won't say how—and obtained a surprising and revealing interview that will be the centerpiece of a new documentary to be released in the near future.

There was Dougie in the living room of my Community townhouse, asking me questions. And there was me. At least some version of me that had eyeballs resembling the googly eyes you'd find on a stuffed panda.

Doug: Max, a lot of people are wondering where you are…why you disappeared. So, what happened, man? Where'd you go?

Max: I went here. I was tired. I can relax here and watch "Bonanza."

WTF? I sounded like a very old baby. My speech was halting. The overall impression was that I should be planted out in the garden with the rest of the vegetables.

Lara Logan chimed in again.

Doug Daytona won't reveal where Bowman is. But he found a man who was anxious to set the record straight.

Max: I love this country. Nothing is wrong. There were bad people. They are gone. Everything is fine.

Doug: I'm glad to hear that, Max. Still, there are these rumors…all this fantastic stuff about secret government agencies trying to get you. You're now saying this wasn't the case?

Max: Bad people did bad things. But now everything is fine. They are gone.

Doug: And you still have faith in your country? You still believe in the U.S.A.?

Max: We should all stop and appreciate the USA because whatever is done in the name of this great land is necessary and aligned with the life-affirming wishes of a great and benevolent God.

Doug: (dripping with sincerity): Yeah. Yeah, man. I get it.

Oh, he got it, all right. The rest of the segment went on in the same vein, with me babbling half-coherent answers to Doug's questions in between b-roll featuring some of my greatest hits, like the time I vomited live on CNN. But there wasn't a lot of meat on the bones of Doug's big Max Bowman interview. Seemed like a lot of airtime was devoted to my analysis of *Bonanza* and how Adam, Hoss and Little Joe, the Cartwright brothers, all had different mothers and how I didn't know that before watching the entire series. And this was *after* editing my interview down? What was left on the cutting room floor, my musings on Hop Sing's cooking?

It almost made me feel relieved. How in the world did they expect this interview to quell any conspiracy rumors? It looked like I was sitting on the knee of a ventriloquist whose hand was shoved inside my ass to make my mouth move. Did Doug (and whoever had hired him) really think having me mouth kindergarten-level soundbites would be enough to quiet any suspicions that the government took me out? It looked more like they poured a barrel of kerosene on the inferno of conspiracy rumors still burning away in the heartland. I was not impressed.

But they did fuck with my head and put it on national television.

So I was going to fuck with *their* heads.

I took the elevator to the fifth floor of the building. Yes, the offices of Doug Daytona were at the very top, where he obviously thought he belonged. I exited the lift and saw a pair of double doors in front of me, double doors that sported a colorful red and yellow logo for "You U!" The "U" was huge and the "You" was nestled inside the "U." The exclamation mark was to the right of the "U." It looked like something that would have been too obnoxious for even the "Up with People!" organization to consider back in the day.

I opened the doors and entered a large lobby area that was unusual in two ways.

First of all, it was filled with the smell of freshly-popped popcorn. It was easy to determine where it was coming from—to the left of the large black reception desk was a popcorn machine. But not just any popcorn machine. This was a full-sized carnival popcorn machine cart, gaily decorated in red and white stripes, the kind of thing you'd find at a circus or a theme park.

Second of all, with the exception of the popcorn machine (that was lit up like the heavens for some unknown reason), the lobby was extremely dark. The walls were covered in some shiny black substance that glittered (the reception desk was covered with it too) and the lights were very low. But there was a very good reason for that. The room had to be a bit dim so you could fully appreciate the giant image of an Emmy statue that was projected on the back wall, just as Shawn Shepheard had described it to me back in the Community.

I looked around for a human face to ask, "What the fuck is going on here?" But there was no human face. No receptionist behind the desk, no sign of anyone, which was slightly unnerving.

Since nobody was in the vicinity, I took the opportunity to snoop around, and discovered everything I needed to know was contained in the framed photos and memorabilia that lined You U!'s hallowed walls. Each frame came complete with its own little pin light positioned to artfully illuminate whatever it displayed. There were photos of Doug Daytona with various clients, some of whom were holding their own Emmys. Most looked well-fed and well-off, and, while I had the feeling I was supposed to be impressed by some of them, judging by the size of the names on their frames, I had no idea who any of them were.

There were dozens of framed articles featuring Doug's appearances in various media—*Fox News, USA Today, Business Inc.* But upon closer inspection, I saw that they weren't real articles or interviews, they were paid advertisements designed to look like articles and interviews, published to portray Doug Daytona as the most creative and savvy individual ever to grace the field of marketing.

The framed materials also provided a look into just how Doug Daytona could afford a top-floor office in a pricey neighborhood named after a decapitated deer. Apparently his job consisted in talking well-off professionals—lawyers, doctors and the like—into paying him to get them their *own* fake articles and interviews in the very same high-profile media outlets Dougie appeared in. This didn't seem to have much to do with the central concept of "You U!," which positioned Dougie and company as some kind of institute of higher learning where you graduated with a degree in yourself, whatever that meant. The wall-materials seemed to indicate that once you invested in enough elaborate fake-media schemes, you could consider yourself a "rock-star celebrity," even if you were the only person who felt that way. Still, if you were a podiatrist from Columbus, Ohio, seeing yourself in the *Wall Street Journal* was probably a big fucking deal.

What did it mean to be a rock star celebrity in Doug Daytona's world? According to the wall-materials, it apparently meant winning a lot of awards. Frame after frame of photos showcased Dougie and his clients at various red-carpet ceremonies for awards I never heard of. Upon closer inspection, it became clear that these awards, like the articles and interviews in major publications, were also fake. Yes, Doug Daytona held his own awards ceremonies for his clients and, just like at the close of a season for a soccer team of five-year-olds, everybody apparently got a prize. Except with Dougie, it looked like even those prizes came at a price.

I never saw a single photo of an actual celebrity dodging flashbulbs in these photos. Just that same podiatrist from Columbus, thrusting his little golden You U! statuette in the air like he was Meryl Streep pumping an Oscar to the heavens.

Fake awards. Fake news. And apparently, fake books too. Bookshelves packed with row after row of books, all published by Doug Daytona, all with generic, success-themed titles. I picked one out at random called, *Your Success Starts with You!* Inside the book were chapters by various Doug Daytona clients, who clearly forked over more cold, hard cash to be part of this potential Pulitzer Prize winner. I leafed through it and discovered that, yep, there was a chapter by the podiatrist. It was called *At the Foot of Prosperity*. I got it.

So Doug Daytona made millions off of the egos and bank accounts of professionals with more money than sense—that was clear. What wasn't clear was what this had to do with me. How did I get pulled into Doug Daytona's world of bullshit? I didn't pay him to put me on *60 Minutes*. So who did? Who was paying for the documentary he was making about me? Who told him where I was? Who told him which words to put in my mouth? Obviously he had some connection to the fine folks who banished me to the Community, but who the hell were they?

The final framed item, the biggest piece of Doug Daytona trivia on the wall, provided another clue. Apparently, *Max Bowman: The Movie!* wasn't the only production in Dougie's pipeline. Also on the slate was an upcoming documentary profiling Senator Eddie di Pineda, Andrew Wright's personal political puppet. And what do you know, hovering in the background behind Eddie was none other than my old pal Howard.

As I took all that in (and it was quite a meal), I slowly became aware that someone was watching me. I glanced around the lobby. I couldn't see anyone.

"Maaaaax…" said a high, cartoony voice.

Okay, somebody *was* watching me. And finally I saw who it was. Or rather, *what* it was. It wasn't a person.

It was a puppet.

The plastic head of a dog appeared over the top of the reception desk. It had a white sleeve behind it, which presumably held the arm of whoever was working it, and not much else. The dog looked a little demonic. Its eyes didn't quite line up correctly and it had no arms or legs. It was clearly homemade by someone without a scintilla of artistic talent.

I slowly approached the makeshift puppet.

"Max Bowmaaaaaaan…" it said. It sounded a little like Vincent Price in those old Roger Corman horror movies, a little, high-pitched, elegant put-on voice.

"You're a dog," I replied, giving my best impression of my simpleton voice from my days in the Community.

"Yeeeeessss," it said. "My name is Morris the Dog. Hello, Max Bowman, so good to see you, my friend."

What the fuck.

"How do you know me?"

"We've met before, Maaaax."

"I don't remember a talking dog," I said, maintaining my Man-Child Max persona.

The puppet started laughing. It reared back its plastic head and opened its mouth wide to reveal some white Lego blocks glued to the bottom of that mouth which were meant to serve as teeth.

Just then, a woman emerged through a glass door I didn't notice was there. She was a skinny bag of bones in a crisp little Southern dress. She had a big nose and big red lips. Maybe 30. She smiled at me, but the smile didn't extend to her eyes. I don't trust people who don't smile with their whole face and I didn't trust whoever this was.

"Hi, I'm Leila Butz, may I help you?" she said in a chicken-and-biscuits accent.

"Leila. Butz. Hi, I want to see Doug," I said.

"Regarding what?"

"I want to see Doug," I repeated in a flat, childlike tone.

"He's Maaaaax Bowmaaaaaan!" Morris the dog cackled loudly. Was I in some kind of Samuel Beckett play? The one he never wrote because it was too crazy an idea even for him?

"Max Bowman?" Leila exclaimed in a shaky whisper. Her eyes appeared to bulge right out of her skinny little face as she slowly backed up a couple of steps in her stiletto heels before vanishing back into the bowels of the office.

Moments later (and I mean moments), Doug Daytona himself came running (and I do mean running) out the same hidden glass door Leila disappeared through. Dressed once again in what I could only assume he thought was "Hollywood casual," but was really what a dork who thought he was cool would wear to a PTA cocktail party, Dougie's big round face was sweaty from shock. No doubt he was wondering what I was doing there. Or doing anywhere, for that matter.

"Max?" he looked at me in bewilderment. "Ohmygosh. What…your hair…?"

"It's a different color," I said brightly. "It hurt bad when I left and then my hair turned this color."

He narrowed his eyes and looked at me.

"You're still…"

He stared at me another moment. I knew he wanted to say, "You're still brain dead" or words to that effect (okay, maybe "retarded," but that wasn't very PC anymore). But he said nothing.

"There's a puppet," I said pointing to Morris the dog, who was watching us closely.

"Yes, there's a puppet, I just thought it would be cool to do something new and different with the whole reception-desk thing, something fun and creative..." He stopped himself, remembering he was trying to explain esoteric concepts to a guy he thought was a drugged-up moron. "What are you doing here, Max?"

"I want to see my movie, Dougie."

"Your movie..."

"My movie, Dougie. I want to see my movie."

He licked his lips. The sight of me must have sucked all the saliva out of his mouth and left it in a Sahara-like state. Nobody was supposed to see me again, that was the whole idea, but apparently, that idea didn't have a long shelf life.

Dougie turned to the dog puppet as though it might have some useful advice, but it just laughed its Lego-teeth laugh again.

"Can you..." He turned back to me. "Can you just wait here a minute...? I...I really want to show you your movie, but...I have to...get things ready." He slowly backed away, back towards the invisible door where everyone apparently went to disappear.

"Okay, Dougie, I will wait."

"Great...great...don't move...." And then he vanished.

After a couple of seconds, I did likewise. I turned around and headed back to the elevator.

"Oh, Max," said Morris the dog puppet with disappointment. "You told Doug you would wait..."

I didn't answer. I just got the hell out. Because I knew Dougie disappeared through the invisible door to call someone to come and recapture me.

When the elevator made it down to the lobby, I quickly darted towards the double glass doors that would take me out of the building and back to the safety of my car. But as I approached those double doors, I saw three men approaching from the outside, walking from the parking lot. Three men that would definitely catch your attention.

They all wore matching suits—and I'm not talking 2017 Men's Warehouse suits. I'm talking suits circa 1960. The jackets were open and the ties were loose, like they were part of some kind of Vegas lounge act. The one in the middle wore a hat, the kind of hat Sinatra wore on his album covers, and he seemed to be the leader—the two guys on either side followed half a step behind him. The one on the left was a well-built, handsome gent who was slightly taller and oilier, and the one on his right was a way shorter, dark-skinned piece of ugly who looked like somebody had broken his nose somewhere along the way.

These guys weren't full of smiles, so, as I emerged from the professional building, I didn't waste time on pleasantries. Instead, I hurried past the threesome as fast as my feet would go without it looking like I was at full gallop. I had to take a little detour around the side of the short ugly one, because they weren't about to break up the act to let me through, but there was plenty of room on the sidewalk outside for me to make the maneuver. I felt them slowly turning and looking me over as I passed. But I didn't stop to confirm my sixth sense. Instead, I headed for my car like a heat-seeking missile.

A few feet from the rental, I heard footsteps running toward me along with the voice of Doug Daytona, who had evidently followed me down in the next elevator car and was yelling, I presumed, at the threesome.

"That's the guy! That's Max Bowman! Don't let him get away!"

I got in my car and started it up. In the rearview mirror, I saw the threesome walking towards me. I also saw them pull out—in synchronized movements—matching, long-barreled handguns, handguns that resembled the Buntline Special Wyatt Earp supposedly toted back in Dodge City or Tombstone or West Mifflin, Pennsylvania or…who the hell remembered where the fuck Wyatt Earp hung out? I shifted into drive.

"BACK IT UP RIGHT TO HERE, CHARLEY!" I heard the one with the Frank hat yell at my car in a thick Russian accent. The short one chimed in, "STOP OR IT WILL BE THAT BIG CASINO, BABY!" also in a Russian accent. "WATCH YOUR BIRD, PALLY," yelled the third…*also* in a Russian accent.

But they were too late to do any damage. I was already out of the lot and racing down Peachtree Whatever. I glanced at the rearview mirror and saw them standing back on the curb, watching me speed away out of range. They slowly put away their hardware as Doug joined them at the curb, gesturing and shouting wildly. That's when the one with the Frank hat slapped Doug but good.

That meant Dougie wasn't in charge. They were.

That's when it hit me. The three of them. One small and dark, one with a Frank hat, the other tall and good-looking in an oily sort of way, all dressed for a big night in 1960's Las Vegas.

They looked like Frank Sinatra, Dean Martin and Sammy Davis Jr. But they were Russian.

The Russian Ratpack?

Who was I? Joey Bishop?

The Return

I changed rental cars at an Alamo in Atlanta before I moved on up the road, just in case anybody from the Doug Daytona organization decided to try and track me down. I told the guy at the counter that the Sentra was making a funny noise, like if somebody put dentures into a blender and turned it on full blast. I don't know where the hell I came up with that one, but he seemed to think it sounded serious enough to warrant a switch-out.

A few minutes later, I was on my way in a Ford Whogivesashit heading up to Virginia Beach. It was time to reconnect with the kid—and, I hoped, with Eydie, my dog. I wasn't sure if I would get any kind of welcome from Angela, but, they say, time heals all wounds. Of course, "they" are usually full of shit.

In this case, I knew what happened wouldn't be easily dismissed. Angela warned me that I was going to get her son killed. She told me to leave him out of all the madness swirling around me, but PMA, bless his FBI-loving heart, persisted. He wanted in and, for that, he got a gunshot wound to the chest followed by a near-fatal infection. And while I made sure Mr. Barry Filer paid the price for that dastardly deed—I killed him and made sure it stuck—that couldn't undo the damage done. There was no doubt in my mind that stately Davidson Manor had been shaken to its core by all that had transpired.

All because of me.

After all, I was the one who stashed Filer in the Davidson's secret underground bomb shelter, ignoring PMA and Angela's warnings that it wasn't going to work out all that well. But I wasn't thinking about them. I was thinking about me and my need to even the score—for the kid, for Jules, for what remained of my sanity. Problem is, when you get into that mindset, you become as fucking amoral as the other side. You become a cold, hard creature and other people don't enter into your personal equation.

You become a complete dick.

So, I wasn't looking forward to going back to Virginia Beach to confront my sins. Not at all. But, at this stage in my life, I had nowhere else to go.

And they did have my dog.

I spent the night in a Super 8 Comfort Inn Embassy Suites in Charlotte, North Carolina, where I discovered just how exhausted I still was from my ordeal of the preceding few days. I conked out at 8 pm with no dinner in my stomach and woke up at 10 the next morning, without even getting up the usual two or three times typically required by my old man bladder.

Checkout time was at noon, so I decided to take my time waking up and switched on the TV. After ten minutes of watching insane freaks yell at Maury Povich about DNA tests and whose kid was whose (didn't really matter, from what I saw—the baby was doomed because all the potential parents were sociopaths), I realized I'd rather try to pull my lips over the top of my forehead than deal with daytime TV. I got myself up on my feet, out the door and into my car. I couldn't put it off any longer. Time to head north.

I got some breakfast from the McDonalds drive-through down the street, worrying as I idled in line that I'd miss the cut-off time. That's when I realized the most wonderful thing had happened while I was locked away in the Community—McDonalds was serving breakfast shit all day! Just when you think everything in this world is a complete loss, Mickey D steps up and hits a home run.

As I sipped my Coke Zero SUGAR in the parking lot, I texted the kid to ask if it was okay for me to drive up that day. He texted back that I should come after dark and that I should call him on his cell instead of ringing the buzzer at the gate. That meant Angela was definitely not rolling out the red carpet for me, unless the carpet's color was the result of my blood spilling all over it.

That meant I had a few hours to kill—otherwise I'd get there around dinner time, when the sun was still up. But that was okay, I had a good idea of how to ruthlessly murder that time. I had gotten a good whiff of Barry Schmidt's clothes, the ones I had been wearing for two days straight, and the smell was toxic. I googled to find the nearest Banana Republic, the official supplier of Max Bowman's road clothes, and headed there for some hardcore shopping. I needed a complete short-term wardrobe—shirts, jeans, socks, shoes, bathrobe, pajamas and so on—along with all the toiletries a minimally-groomed human like me required, such as toothpaste, toothbrush, razor, shaving cream (gel was cold and unapproachable), etc. All in all, it took a good bite out of the remaining funds in my bank account.

And there was one more thing I needed above all else—a new Mets cap. I had checked the USA Today sports page and saw this season was a disaster among disasters for Mr. Met and company. They had more injuries than I did, so I was lucky to have missed most of the rolling catastrophe that this bottom-dwelling line-up had served up to their fans. Still, I felt naked without my Mets cap, especially with my new, white-as-a-sheet mop of hair, so I was happy to find a sports swag outlet in the same strip mall as the Banana Republic.

I put the new cap on my head. I was whole again. I was complete.

Then I ended up picking up one final item that surprised even me. On the way out of the Atlanta area, I stopped at a 7-11 and bought a pack of USA Menthol Lights and a lighter. Yeah, I felt the need to start smoking. Maybe it was because the closer I got to stately Davidson Manor, the more I knew I would start hating myself.

With a trunk full of shopping bags, I pulled up to the Davidsons' security gate around 8 pm. The sun was down, so I had fulfilled my side of the bargain. I called the kid on my cellphone to see if he'd live up to his side.

"Max?" he asked, in a tentative voice.

"Yeah. How are we doing this?"

"Turn around and park down the access road a little. Walk back and text me when you get back to the gate, I'll buzz you in."

"Then what?"

"Come out to the shed in the backyard. You know what to do from there."

The kid hung up, while I stood there feeling very befuddled. Inside the shed was the elevator down to the underground shelter, the one where I stashed Mr. Barry Filer. Were things so bad with Angela that I was already being relegated to the Mr. Barry Filer Memorial Suite?

I drove my car back a little ways down the access road, parked it, walked back and got buzzed in by the kid. Then I headed out to the shed and punched in the old code from before. Shockingly, my brain still functioned well enough to remember it. Slightly less shockingly, it worked. The door unlocked.

I entered and had a quick look around. The video monitors that displayed what was happening in the three-room shelter below the shed were shut off. The interior of the shed was completely dark, except for a small red security light mounted in the ceiling. It all felt a little creepy, like I was walking into some kind of trap. Was the kid pissed off enough to sell me out?

I paused. Then I walked back outside and stared at the mansion. More than half the windows were lit up. That meant Angela was home, because she wasn't a fan of darkness. Which meant my dog, Eydie, was in there too, most likely. I hoped she had been okay without me. I had been the Master She Could Not Live Without. After all this time, I wondered if she'd even remember me. Maybe it was better if she never saw me again. Maybe the same went for Angela too.

I lit up another cigarette and took a few puffs. I noticed my hand was shaking.

Finally, after a minute or two, I threw the cig on the ground and ground it into the dirt with my heel. Then I took a deep breath, which made me wince. There was still a faint pain in my chest that I didn't like. It probably wasn't the best idea to be pulling cigarette smoke in there. "Would you like some cancer with your heart attack?" "Yes, please, and I'll have a side of stroke with that." "Very good, sir."

I shook off the death wish, went back into the shed and pushed the DOWN button.

When the elevator door opened way down in the shelter, the first thing that struck me was the smell. It stunk like a locker room that hadn't been cleaned in weeks, but there was an extra layer of stench on top of the stink. It took me a couple of seconds to figure out the additional bonus smell, but it finally hit me.

It was weed.

Which was weird. The kid had previously expressed disdain for drugs, preferring to keep his mind crystal clear, so he could make split-second decisions when facing down danger. But maybe after danger paid him back with a sucking chest wound, he felt differently about things.

I looked around in the shelter's living room/kitchenette area the elevator opened into. There were dirty clothes, dirty dishes and the occasional empty pizza box scattered all over the place. Wait, did I smell pepperoni? I lifted the pizza box lid. Yep, still plenty of pepperoni in there. But it didn't look like it was aging well. Kind of looked like my face first thing in the morning.

The kid stepped out of one of the bedrooms.

"Hey."

He leaned against the side of the doorway and looked away. He looked like hell. His eyes were glassy and his frame was flabby. He was wearing a random ratty t-shirt with the logo of a band I had never heard of and stained gym shorts. And he held some kind of pen in his hand that had a small glowing light on its side.

"Hey," I said. "Long time, no see."

I saw him eyeing the hair sticking out from the bottom of the Mets cap. I took it off so he could enjoy the complete view.

"Max—your hair. It's all white. What the hell?"

"Happened during my escape. The trauma did some damage, I guess."

PMA shook his head and let himself fall into a nearby chair. "Jesus, Max. How did all this happen?" He pressed a button on the side of the pen, then he put it in his mouth and sucked on it.

"What's that?" I asked, still standing.

"Vape pen."

"What?"

"You don't know about vaping?"

"I don't know about anything, kid, you should know that by now."

He explained that you didn't have to roll joints or smoke pipes anymore. You just had to buy a vape pen, which magically turned dope into mist, mist that was colorless and odorless.

"Odorless? Then how come I smell weed down here?"

"Well, I still have some of the old kind. In case I run out of cartridges for the vape."

"So, you're a full-blown stoner now?"

"It helped with the pain from the wound. Then I got used to it, I dunno."

I looked around at the mess.

"I know," he said tiredly. "I was going to pick up a little, but…" He shrugged.

I sat down across from him at the small table.

"PMA, what the hell happened to your PMA? Power, Mind, Action. You look like you're 0 for 3."

"Jesus, Max, I knew you'd be on me. Just lay off. You have no idea what it was like after you left. How long it took me to recover…and then my fuckin' mom on top of everything else…"

"Your fuckin' mom? What happened?"

He sucked on the pen again.

"Why you bunking down here?" I persisted. "Why aren't you in the house?"

He shook his head again. Then he shook his head again and again and again.

"That's not a place I want to be."

"What happened with your mom, kid?"

He sighed. He knew it was inevitable that he'd have to tell me and I knew the news was going to be of the horrifying variety just from how he was acting.

"She thought you were dead just like I did."

"And…"

"I mean, both of us…we didn't know what the fuck to do with ourselves. It was like the bad guys won and you were gone. I mean…" He actually started tearing up. "You had become kind of an important presence around here…"

"Kid," I said gently. "Just tell me."

He looked me straight in the eyes.

"She's married."

Duds

As I took the elevator back up to the surface world, I tried to process what I had just been told. I failed miserably.

Angela married? I had only been gone ten months and this had happened in addition to President Trump, vape pens and Coke Zero SUGAR? Sure, ten months was long enough to get married—and even give birth too, if she really pushed it. But she started this relationship from scratch, as far as I knew. Which meant this was more than a whirlwind romance, this was a rebound revved up until it broke the sound barrier.

Angela? *Married?*

The kid was sketchy on details, because he didn't like to think about it. The only thing he really knew about the lucky groom was that he was some kind of lobbyist. Other than that, all PMA could say about him was that he seemed like a slimy oily pig and PMA hated him more than painful bloody diarrhea. Angela tried to make peace, but PMA wasn't having it. He thought of the union as a tragic farce, the result of his mother having been emotionally traumatized by his wound and my disappearance. She was after some kind of security, according to the kid, because she desperately needed to have something to hang on to. I almost said it had to be hard to hang on to a slimy oily pig, but for once, I kept my mouth shut.

The kid went on to tell me the wedding had just happened a month or so ago—it was just a simple ceremony at a courthouse, so not many witnesses to the crime. PMA was not in attendance and he moved down into the shelter while they were on their honeymoon, which ended up just being a weekend at some Virginia resort. The lobbyist didn't have time for much more than that—he apparently was a workaholic.

Since the newlyweds' return, PMA had avoided all contact with them, aside from the occasional and unavoidable sightings. After all, everybody was on the same property, even it was a fucking big property.

We made plans to have lunch the next day at some location TBD off the compound. It was getting late, I was getting tired again, so I said I was going to go find a hotel for the night. I could tell the kid was disappointed, like he expected me to stay the night in his smelly dungeon so we could talk shit about the slimy oily pig until the wee small hours of the morning. But I just wanted to go anywhere but there, somewhere where I could crawl into a little ball and sleep for a month or so. My mission was to reconnect with the kid and it had been completed.

I exited the shed and lit up another cigarette, with every intention of smoking it down to where my fingers held it. With that objective in mind, I stood in the cool night air, taking the occasional puff and enjoying the quiet.

Then suddenly, I heard barking.

My heart stopped. Not literally, or I would have been dead, but that was the expression and I was stuck with it. I knew that bark and I couldn't believe the ice cream ever had the power to make me forget it for even a second.

I turned and saw her running towards me, barking her insane nasty bark, reserved for other dogs, cats, squirrels, the occasional bird and people she didn't trust. That meant she didn't recognize me yet.

Then she stopped a few yards from me. She seemed frozen, like a little doggy statue, staring at me with unblinking eyes, clearly not able to fully accept what she was seeing. Then her entire body began to vibrate with what I think was incredible emotion, not that I'd ever seen an animal's frame do that before.

And then she ran as fast as she could, heading straight for me.

I reflexively covered my groin, and good thing too, because Eydie had suddenly become an airborne and very dangerous projectile, with the target being my balls. She hit me hard, knocking the air out of my gut, and then, as she landed on all fours, she began crazily whining and barking all at once in a manic stream of doggy pain, joy and love—pain at me having been gone so long, joy at having me back, love at being reunited with her number one.

I sat down on the wet grass as the desperate terrier-mix attacked my entire face with her tongue. I cried as she whimpered. It would have been a great ending to a Lassie movie, but at the moment, it was the beginning of a whole new set of troubles for me. The idea had been to sneak out without the dog spotting me. But I couldn't leave her again, especially knowing I was still somehow the center of her universe.

I was so distracted by Eydie's loving and my own fretting that I didn't notice the immense figure heading my way. It wasn't until he stepped in front of the large, bright moon hanging in the night sky, transforming himself into a one-man lunar eclipse as he peered down at me, that I felt his presence.

"Bowman?" he asked in disbelief.

I didn't look up right away. That's because I was too busy staring straight ahead at his socks. Even in the darkness, I could tell they were two different colors, which instantly told me who he was. Before everything went haywire, Angela had told me about some lobbyist who dated her a couple of times—and that he was so fat he couldn't see his own feet.

This was the new Mr. Angela? I instinctively shifted my brain back into damaged mode. I knew I shouldn't trust the guy, so I went back to acting addled.

"I am Bowman. Max Bowman," I said, finally bringing myself to look up from the feet.

He gave me a funny look, since I had made the statement with the ice cream-inspired sing-song delivery I had perfected in the Community.

"I'm Dudley DeCosta. Call me 'Duds,' everybody else does."

They did?

He offered a hand. Eydie bared her teeth and growled at him. He withdrew the hand and backed up.

I got to my feet on my own. Then I picked up the dog and gave "Duds" a good look. Minus about 800 pounds, he wouldn't have been completely repulsive. He was wearing a dress shirt and suit pants, meaning he hadn't been home from work all that long. Of course, if he was still working in DC, he had a helluva commute from Virginia Beach. I know fat-shaming isn't politically correct these days, but this guy...well, he was FAT and it was a dirty lowdown shame I couldn't verbalize a few plus-sized jokes. Even so, a thousand Ralph Kramden interchanges from *The Honeymooners* shot through my head (Ralph: "Peanut? What am I gonna do with peanuts?" Alice: "Eat 'em. Like any other elephant!") as Eydie began growling at the big dark-haired man whose chin disappeared down into a flesh blob that completely entombed his neck.

"She hates me," he muttered in his low guttural voice, glowering at Eydie. "This dog is a menace. Been living here for three weeks and she still almost bit me when I took her out here for her bathroom break. Shitfuck." He gave me a look that had some suspicion creeping in. "What the hell are you doing here? Nobody knew where you were. People thought you were dead."

"I was gone. I couldn't get out. I watched *Bonanza*."

He gave me the once over again as Eydie licked me some more.

"Well," he said with some authority, "I don't know if you've heard…"

"You had a wedding. With Angela," I said brightly.

He paused, a little relieved he didn't have to break the news. "Yeah, I did." Another pause. "Wherever you were, somethin' happened to you. I saw that *60 Minutes* interview you did." He smiled with something resembling triumph. "You're not right in the head, are you?"

"I ate a lot of ice cream," I said by way of explanation.

"And here I was, worrying about you coming back," he said, as if he were talking to a child. "But I'm thinking all I need to distract you is a box of crayons and a root beer float, am I right?"

I was about to extol the many, many delights that a root beer float had to offer me, when suddenly, there was one more figure coming towards us in the night.

"Duds, go back inside!" shouted Angela, tramping her way through the grass in her slippers, which, of course, matched the color of her bathrobe.

Duds turned. "Hey, Angela, c'mon, I was only…"

"Just go back inside. Please," she said in a way that lacked any trace of politeness.

I was impressed, because he had mastered the harried husband look in less than a month. I used to be an expert on them. He took the look, turned around and headed back towards the house. That left Angela and me standing a few feet apart, rigid and unyielding in our positions, like Charles Bronson and Henry Fonda at the end of *Once Upon a Time in the West*. Which didn't end well, because it turned out Henry Fonda had hanged Charles Bronson's father while the guy was standing on the kid version of Charles Bronson's shoulders and…

"Where have you been?" she almost whispered, interrupting my welcome escape into Old Movie World.

"They took me away," I replied in my natural voice. I couldn't put on the act for Angela. I had done enough to her.

"Where, to some secret prison?"

"No, worse. Florida."

"Oh good, you're going to play games." The light seemed to go out of her eyes, like she had summoned all her energy just to get out there. "Look, I just took two Ambien and washed them down with three gin and tonics. So, let's skip the banter, just bring your stuff in the house."

"I can't do that."

"Max, the fuck, Eydie will lose her mind if you leave again. Take Jeremy's old room. Just…do it…"

"But…Dudley…Duds…"

"Don't bring up that name."

"Okay. But don't you have to?"

"Just…just bring your shit in the house."

She turned and stumbled away into the night, back towards the house. I watched her the whole way, just to make sure she didn't collapse in a heap and spend the night on the lawn.

I did my final tally for the night. There was a pothead in the ground, and a drunken pill-popper and a man who couldn't see his feet in the house. All about to be joined by an idiot in the guestroom.

Because I was dumb enough to actually do what she told me to do.

The Cook, The Thief, His Wife and Her Lover

My days of sleeping in were over, because I had my four-legged alarm clock back. Eydie was on me bright and early around 6:30, jumping up and down on my face with abandon. Yeah, I could have slept a lot longer, but having the pooch back was worth the sunrise wake-up. I almost forgot what it was like to be mortally afraid of one of her claws puncturing my eyeballs while I lay in bed.

I put on my new Banana Republic sweats and took Eydie down to the backyard for her morning bathroom break. As she did her business, I eyed the shed. I would have to break it to the kid that I was staying in the house. If Eydie hadn't seen me the night before, I had no doubt I would at that moment be sleeping in some sort of Holiday Inn Hilton Place Quality Suites Inn Express. But she had and I couldn't break her little puppy heart again.

When I got back inside, I went in the kitchen to see if there was any Coke Zero SUGAR in the fridge. Funny enough, there was still one can way in the back of the middle shelf, left over from my previous stay. Best of all, it was only Coke Zero, not Coke Zero SUGAR and that was glorious.

As I popped the top and listened to the wonderous sound of my old-school chemically-flavored fizz, Angela's chef entered all in a huff, anxious to get started on a dish, so anxious that he only gave me a minor glance before diving into the contents of the fridge. It took a couple more moments before it fully registered with him—Max Bowman was back and that was probably going to turn everything at stately Davidson Manor upside down.

"Max?" he said, as he broke a few eggs in a bowl. "OMG. We thought you were dead. And your hair…"

"White as your ass, Chef."

He giggled. "Max, you have no idea what color my ass is."

"Yeah, and it's not something I'm going to follow up on. What are you scurrying around for? It's Saturday."

"You remember when I complained that I didn't have anything to do?"

"Yeah. Back then, Angela never ate and the kid was never home."

"Well…there's a new sheriff in town."

And that's when the new sheriff came plodding in, "Duds" Dudley himself, in a very, very large brown bathrobe. He shot Chef an irritated look.

"Jesus, fry cook," Duds spit as he sat down at the table, "Where's the breakfast?"

"Sorry, got a late start."

"Well, I can't have a late start, my driver's due here in twenty minutes, so let's make things happen, all right?"

Chef went quiet and poured a cup of coffee for Duds, who was eyeing me as I stood and sipped my Coke Zero over by the Cuisinart. His tone was a lot different when Angela wasn't around.

"At least I didn't have to take the damn dog down this morning," he said. He gave Eydie, quietly laying at my feet, a dirty look. "You know how many times she's almost taken one of my fingers off?"

Chef beat the batter for whatever he was making with the motions of a madman.

"Why doesn't Angela take care of her? Eydie likes Angela," I said, returning to my idiot voice. Chef gave me a look, wondering why I was suddenly going all Gump, but let it go.

"Angela's on too many pills to take care of herself. Thought when I married the general's daughter, she'd be a tough broad. This one folds like a card table whenever a breeze hits her the wrong way."

"Oh no, Angela is very tough."

"She is, huh? Well, for the entire first three weeks of our marriage, she's been a pharma-zombie. Don't even know why she went through with the wedding."

Could have sworn I heard Chef mutter, "Me neither," but I let it alone. He was pouring the batter in the waffle iron and the resultant sizzling luckily masked his searing commentary. Duds shook his head and sipped his coffee.

"I heard you are a lobbyist," I finally said.

"No, I'm a fucking fundraiser," he said irritably. "She keeps telling everyone I'm a lobbyist, but I'm a fucking fundraiser, really not that hard to remember." Another pause for coffee. "I'm not out there trying to change people's minds about shit, I raise money for political candidates, really fucking simple. Democracy doesn't work without the dollars, I like to say."

"Does it work with them then?"

The Chef gave me a warning look, but Duds took it in stride.

"Hey Chef, throw some blueberries in that waffle if it ain't too late." Duds turned back to me. "Look, Retardo, it's the system, I help it along. Whaddya want from me?"

"You must be from New Jersey," I said with a big smile. "You talk like that."

"Yeah, me and The Boss," he said, putting himself on equal footing with Springsteen. Then he lowered his voice. "So...where you been, Max? Where'd they keep you? And what kinda shit did they put you on?" He chuckled again. "Must've been even stronger than what my wife takes, because you have definitely become a Class-A moron."

"Where did 'they' keep me? Who's 'they?'"

More chuckles. "C'mon, Max. I hear things. I mean, I hardly ever get the whole story, just a few whispers here and there. You probably know some shit yourself."

He eyed me closely. I took another sip of my Coke Zero, because it suddenly occurred to me—Duds knew a lot of people. I was suddenly glad I was putting on the act for him. Wouldn't do for "them" to find out my mind was still relatively healthy.

"Like maybe about that thing they're building," he added.

"They're building a thing?" I said.

Chef put the waffle on a plate and put the plate in front of Duds' mouth. Duds gave him another pissy look.

"Syrup? Butter?"

Chef scurried back to the fridge, while Duds looked at me as if we both agreed Chef was the biggest waste of human space on the continent.

"Yeah, the thing up in Montana. Lotta people excited about it. Big people."

"Montana?" Then I added, in a low fearful tone, "That's where Dark Sky is."

"Alls I know is Montana."

"And Andrew Wright. I don't like him."

He laughed as he poured a half gallon of syrup over the waffle, only after applying a pound of butter, of course. "Andrew Wright. Nobody's seen that cat since...well, since they last saw you. Am I right, Retardo?"

He shoved a big forkful of waffle in his face.

"My name is Max."

"I prefer 'Retardo," he said with a mouthful of food. He nodded and swallowed. "Look, you can talk to me about those clowns, tell me anything you want. I mean, I work for them, but I sure as fuck ain't one of them. But I do know you occupy an interesting place in their pantheon."

"I need a favor," I said.

Duds had already shoved another forkful in his face, so he gave me a surprised look as he pointed to himself. He swallowed and asked, "Me? What's the ask?"

"Please don't tell anyone I'm here. I wasn't supposed to leave where they had me. I think they want to find me again."

He chewed thoughtfully on another forkful. "Sure," he finally said, spitting out a little waffle with his answer. "I'll keep your secrets. As long as you keep mine."

More chuckling. More forkfuls. A final swallow.

"You know, Retardo, I think we can be useful to each other. You take care of me, I take care of you, capeesh?"

"Capeesh?"

He ignored me and looked out the window at the backyard, where the shed and the shelter were.

"You get along with that little shit, right?"

"Jeremy? He's under the ground."

"Yeah, and he can stay there. The little prince won't even give me the fucking time of day. So maybe you can help me with that. Put in a good word for me. I mean, you and me, we can have a conversation, right? That's all I ask from him. A conversation or two. I'm not expecting hugs and kisses from the loser. He just needs to move back in the house, make his mommy feel a little better about things. Maybe she'll cut down her pill intake to 3000 a day. I mean, I don't get the problem with Jeremy, it's not like we have to ass fuck or anything, right?" He saw me flinch. "Hey, I know which team he plays on, I could give a shit."

He finished the coffee, wiped his sticky mouth with a napkin, and checked his watch. "Oh, man, I gotta get going."

"Where? It's Saturday."

"Doesn't matter, there ain't no weekends in Washington. Anyway, Max, interesting meeting you. Don't worry. As far as I'm concerned, I never saw you. And when I tell you something like that, you can take it to the bank."

He rushed past me, patting me on the shoulder and triggering a growl from Eydie, who was still on the floor, and then he was gone. I heard him taking big beefy steps up the stairs and I heard Chef heaving a big sigh of relief. Then Chef gave me a look.

"Why were you talking like that? You were normal until he came in."

"Keep a secret, Chef. Everyone thinks I have brain damage."

"Huh. Well, if that's what he thinks, he wasn't very nice about it."

"Doesn't seem like he's very nice to you either."

"And this was a *good* morning." He shook his head as he cleared the table. "I don't know how much more of this I can take. I left the restaurant business so I didn't have to take shit anymore. But...maybe now that you're back..."

"Don't put all your eggs in my basket," I said and then I took the final swig in the Coke Zero can.

Chef looked out the doorway to make sure nobody else was in sight. Then he whispered to me, "I don't trust him. You shouldn't either."

"Don't worry about it," I replied. "That's not about to happen. Capeesh?"

"Oh, yes," Chef replied. "So much capeeshing."

Mary Tyrone

After Duds' departure, Chef made me an omelet despite my protestations. It wasn't that I didn't want it, I just didn't want to put the guy out. I wasn't good with servants because, quite frankly, I didn't think I was better than anybody else and it was difficult to elevate myself to the level necessary to boss others around. Then again, I had to admit I did think I was better than some people. Take Duds, for example.

Please.

After I ate the omelet, I took Eydie for a little stroll around the neighborhood to clear my head and give the pooch some much-needed exercise. She was looking a little thick since I'd last seen her and I didn't want to end up with a four-legged Duds. As I walked her, she kept looking up at me nervously, as if to make sure I was still there and holding the leash. I expected that was going to be happening for a while. She had spent about an hour licking my leg the night before while I was trying to sleep, that's how much she had missed the great taste of Max.

Finally, me and the mutt returned to stately Davidson Manor, where Chef was busily cleaning up the kitchen. I asked him if Angela was up yet and got a huge LOL out of the guy. Apparently, you had a better chance of spotting Bigfoot than you did of Angela any time before noon. What worried me was the possibility of a morning when she didn't wake up at all.

"Do you…ever check on her?" I asked carefully.

"Oh, she's fine, I'm sure," he said nonchalantly.

I paused a moment.

"How can you be so sure?"

"Trust me," he said confidently.

Two words I usually didn't like to lean on, but Chef was a straight-shooter, so I gave it a shot. Since it was still a couple of hours before noon, I went into Angela's home office and used the computer to check on my Facebook page for the first time since I escaped the Community. The most recent posts were filled with fear and desperation. The Trump presidency had thrown over half the country into paranoid panic and uncontrollable anger and I was one of the outlets for their pain. These people weren't buying the *60 Minutes* whitewash. They were sure the government had done something horrible to me and asked for a reassuring message from Max Bowman himself. Unfortunately, since I was still trying to fly under the radar, I couldn't really oblige them.

Then I had to get down to the business of the rest of my life, if there was anything left of it. And it turned out there wasn't. After I made a couple of calls on the landline, I quickly discovered my worst suspicions had come true. Not only had I been kicked out of my Roosevelt Island apartment, but they had sold off or threw out all my belongings. That was the management company's policy after three months and I had been gone for ten.

After I finished hearing all that unpleasantness, I felt a little light-headed and leaned back in the plush office chair, which suddenly felt about as comfortable as a throne of nails.

It was official—I had no home and everything I had ever owned in the world was gone. I had to think my Nissan Rogue had been repossessed as well. I had nothing, I lived nowhere and my credit rating was probably just below O.J. Simpson's. While it was true I had been something of a nomad for much of my adult life, at least since the divorce, stumbling into this immense void of nothingness was more than even I had ever bargained for. Try this fucking existential crisis on for size, Jean-Paul Sartre. No exit? Hell, not even an entrance for this boy.

"You all right?"

Angela was standing in the doorway in one of her designer bathrobes. This one had angels on it. I briefly prayed in my head for several of them to fly off the fabric and come to my rescue, but, not surprisingly, they stayed put. I eyed the time in the lower right of the computer screen. 11:58 am. Angela was up before noon. Okay, so maybe miracles were possible. Maybe I should have tried calling on the bathrobe angels again.

"You all right?" she asked a second time, watching me stare vacantly as I attempted to telepathically connect with her terrycloth cherubs.

"You know, I was afraid to come back here," I finally said. "I thought you might not ever want to see me again."

"Yeah. Then I didn't see you again," she said softly. "Hasn't exactly been a lot of fun and games around here."

"I heard. According to your husband, you're currently auditioning for the part of Mary Tyrone in *Long Day's Journey into Night.*"

"Max, let me ask you something. Do I look fucked up?"

I looked at her closely. Her eyes were relatively clear. All in all, she had the normal grogginess of someone who had just woken up. She gave a little cock of her head, which moved her delightfully unkempt hair to the side, and threw a sly little smile my way.

Came the dawn. Now I knew why Chef was so sure she was still breathing. He was in on it.

"You're faking," I said in disbelief.

"So are you. You certainly don't seem like the idiot boy Duds is convinced you are."

"Don't wise him up. I need to fly under the radar."

"Fly away, I don't tell him more than I have to."

"Apparently not. The way he described your condition, I was going to buy a stomach pump to keep on the premises."

"If I took as many pills as that water buffalo thought I was, I'd be seeing five of you. This way, I look passed out when he's coming and when he's going. Do you think I want that touching me?"

"Well, it's generally a part of the marriage contract. Of course, I don't know how you kids do things these days." I stood up. "Why did you do it, Angela? Why in hell did you marry a man named Duds?'"

She looked at the floor. "Because I *was* fucked up, Max. Very fucked up. Jeremy got better after the shooting, but, for a while, it looked like he might not. And you were…"

"Do not blame Duds on me."

She looked back up at me with that sly smile.

"Okay, I won't. But you *were* gone…and dead in most people's opinions. So, I drank too much. I took too many pills. I was a mess. 'So lonely,' as Mary Tyrone might put it," she said, giving me a pointed look.

"Should have known you were a Eugene O'Neill fan."

"You continue to surprise. I thought you only read comic books."

"I have to go outside the genre sometimes to experience the kind of hopelessness and despair that doesn't involve masks and tights."

"Anyway…the more I fell apart, the more frequent Dudley's visits became. It got to the point where every time I opened my eyes, which wasn't often I'll grant you, he was always there, taking care of me, helping to take care of Jeremy, keeping the household running. So, I got more than a little dependent on him. And I thought there was nothing else for me…"

"Some things are worse than nothing."

"Tell me about it. This one time, he tried to get on top…"

"Stop."

"He did after I screamed. Well, after Jeremy looked like he was all better, Duds asked me to marry him. I panicked at the thought of not having him around, at the pressure of trying to keep everything together all by myself...and I said yes. And instantly inside my head, it felt like a giant black hole had opened up and I was falling through it."

"Not a good omen."

"I'd go so far as to call it a bad one. It didn't take me long to figure out that this was going to be an even worse ride than my first marriage. And you know all about that one."

"Yeah. That guy paints fruit on women's tits."

"Thanks for the reminder. Anyway, I didn't know what to do. Jeremy moved down into the shelter and I found myself looking up on the internet how many pills I had to swallow to take a permanent nap."

"Jesus."

She paused, as if she was afraid to say the next part. But she did, even though she half-mumbled it.

"Then you popped up on *60 Minutes*..."

"...acting like one of the kids on the short bus."

"Yeah. That's when I found out that somewhere along the way, I had forgiven you and didn't even know it. Because suddenly, when I saw you were alive, I felt alive again, all the way alive, and I kept wondering if you were going to show up here—or anywhere. I didn't sleep for three nights..."

"Duds didn't notice?"

"By then, I had talked him into separate bedrooms. Wasn't hard. He was already disgusted with me. So, I was pretty free to do what I wanted at night. I started cutting down on the pharmaceuticals. And I googled your name every night just to see if anything would come up besides the usual nutjob conspiracy sites...nothing did. But then, last night on the lawn, I heard Eydie barking. And from the way she was barking...I knew you were back."

I played with a paper clip I had taken from the desk.

"But…you're normal," she said softly. "You did sound brain-damaged in the interview."

"I was at the time. They had me all doped up."

"But you seem just the same now."

"Seems like it. Just have a few memory glitches. But, again, keep all that to yourself. Safer for me that way."

A pause.

"So…what happens next?" she asked tentatively.

I bent the paper clip around my finger as she looked at me, waiting for me to say something.

"You hungry?" I finally asked.

"A little off-topic, but I guess I could eat a little something. Why?"

"Because I'd like to organize a lunch."

Family Meal

Angela said it wouldn't work, but I insisted on giving it a try. But first, I asked her to go upstairs and actually put clothes on, if she remembered how. In retaliation for that last verbal shot, she took a finger and flicked it right at my nose as she walked past me on her way to the stairs. Shit, that actually *hurt.*

Then I called the kid down in the bunker. PMA didn't want to come back in the house, of course. So, I wielded my immense clout and told him he'd fucking better. Somehow, it worked. He said he'd need to shower, it would take a half-hour. I told him he could have 25 minutes. He told me to go fuck myself. I loved our snappy repartee.

I went into the kitchen, where Chef was feeding Eydie some cheese. I told him to knock that shit off, as far as I was concerned, the pooch was on a diet. Then I requested lunch for three, if he was willing to cook something up, something light. He gave me a curious look but got right to work.

A few minutes later, the kid came in through the back door sporting a very tentative look. Chef spotted him and his eyes went wide as PMA ambled into the kitchen with his head down.

"Well, hello, stranger," said Chef. "Something to drink?"

"Beer," he said quietly. Chef pulled out a bottle of Molson, popped the top and sat it in front of him. He took a pull on it and looked at me defiantly. He hadn't shaved. Take that, Max Bowman, I'm unkempt!

"Let me ask you something that's been bothering me," I said.

"What?"

"How the hell do you get cell coverage down there? I can barely get a signal in the backyard sometimes."

He blinked. I think he expected a more emotionally complex question.

"We put in a fiber-optic line down to the shelter and I've got my phone set to receive calls through wi-fi."

"Oh. I think I understood half of that."

"So…what's this all about?"

And that's when Angela showed up looking mostly put together, wearing a simple yet elegant blue top and white cotton pants, plus a little lipstick as a bonus. She looked at the kid. The kid looked away from her and took another swig of Canadian gold.

"Please…" I said to her, gesturing to the empty chair between me and the kid. She sat down carefully.

"Coffee, Miss D?" Chef asked carefully.

"Shouldn't it be *Mrs.* D?" muttered the kid very uncarefully.

"If it's going to be like this," said Angela, "Then I'll take my lunch upstairs."

"Nobody's going anywhere," I said. "I didn't eat ice cream for ten months in a village full of corpses-in-waiting for this shit." I turned to the kid. "PMA, your mom had a minor nervous breakdown. She saw her only kid get shot in the chest and it was all the fault of the idiot she slept with—who then disappeared. That would be me. Give her a fucking break."

"Not as long as that whale lives here."

"Kid, nobody in the room wants that whale to live here. Unless Chef's grown fond of throwing scoops of raw fish in his mouth every morning."

Chef, who was preparing some kind of amazing niçoise salad, shook his head as though it were on fire, indicating he hadn't.

I turned to Angela. "You sign a pre-nup?"

The kid laughed. "Right. I'm surprised she was in her right mind enough to say, 'I do.'"

Angela shot a few daggers his way, then shook her head at me sadly.

"Okay, then it might get complicated if he's not willing to go along with a split. I remember that from my own experience getting divorced in this goddam state."

"Why wouldn't he?" asked Angela. "I mean, shit, what's he getting out of this arrangement?"

"What I suspect he wanted in the first place...a piece of the General Davidson legacy. In his business, that's power. And you don't give up power just like that, if you're Duds. He's very...transactional."

"Transactional?" asked the kid.

"Yeah. You wash his back, he washes yours. We had a conversation to that effect this morning."

"What did that fat fuck say?" the kid asked angrily, as Angela looked like she wanted to crawl under the table and die.

"Doesn't matter. I just want to know, can we get shit back to normal if I resolve this situation?"

"What are you going to do?" Angela asked in a slightly panicked tone.

"Not sure."

"Well, what should we do?" asked PMA. Angela shot the kid a hopeful look, because he had said the magic word, "we." And that, to her, sounded like the whale-ectomy was the only operation the family needed to regain its health.

"Nothing. Kid, you stay in the hole, Angela, you keep doing Mary Tyrone."

"Mary Tyrone?" the kid asked.

"Don't they teach you anything in college?"

"Maybe they would...if he'd actually go to class," said Angela sourly.

"Don't get on me about that!" the kid yelled, pointing a finger and everything. "I've been through a shitload and you haven't been there for me!"

"It's hard to be there when your son is living a mile under your FUCKING LAWN!"

"Okay, OKAY! Let it all GO!"

A moment of strained silence. I could see the family resemblance in both of their pissed-off glares. Lucky me.

"Just let me deal with Duds and we'll move on," I said emphatically.

Angela gave me a curious look. "He calls you 'Retardo.' How the hell are you going to negotiate anything with him?"

"I have the childlike innocence of Forrest Gump. And everybody loves Forrest Gump."

"Max," said Angela. "I honestly think Duds would kick Forrest Gump in the balls and laugh for an hour afterwards."

"Well…be that as it may…let me try."

Chef quietly handed us our plates of salad. And I turned to the kid to ask one more question I didn't want to have to ask.

"You still talking to Kev?"

CIA Al Fresco

I stared at my phone screen for a full minute. Because there were three words sitting on it that gave me an instant burst of nausea.

hes not dead

The text had come from an anonymous phone number. And, even though the "he's" was lacking an apostrophe, my gut told me it had to be referring to Daddy Andy Wright, who I apparently attempted to murder shortly before I woke up in the Community. This text was telling me that attempt failed.

But here was the scary part. Nobody had my phone number but the kid. I had just bought the phone a couple of days before and I didn't even entrust Glenda Schmidt with it.

I didn't need this. I didn't need another round of stalking from unknown quarters. And neither did my body, because, as I sat in the chair in Angela's home office, my chest ached a little, as it had been doing off and on since I drove the golf cart out of the Community. I didn't want to think about what that signified about my health. And I also didn't want to think about what that text meant and whether its message was true or false.

What I wanted was to restore calm. I had a plan to put the lives of the denizens of stately Davidson Manor back together again. It was only fair, since I was the one who had shattered those lives to bits. I wanted to rebuild, not destroy. And, for once, I wanted evil to travel down a path that didn't lead to my door. It had been over two years of this bullshit and I didn't know how much more I could take. My body was already warning me to sit the next round out.

But those three words were still sitting there on my phone screen.

hes not dead

I had spotted the text when I picked my store-bought cell up off the desk to call Kev, the kid's former boyfriend and current CIA operative. It hadn't ended well between them, since Kev had a wife and kids that probably wouldn't be all that receptive to hearing about his alternate sexual leanings. At lunch, the kid had confirmed they were still on the outs. Kev made some overtures while the kid was in the hospital, but PMA was done with him.

But I wasn't done with Kev.

The year before, I had learned I could actually trust the guy and that made him a rarer commodity than vibranium, the shit they made Captain America's shield out of. Yes, there was no such thing as vibranium except in Stan Lee's mind, but I needed something pleasantly unreal to think about while I tapped out Kev's number on the phone keyboard. Because I was just about to jump into things that were unpleasantly real.

"Germano," came the brisk and all-too-efficient voice on the other end.

"Long time, no talk."

Then came the pause that was becoming all too familiar to me. The pause was all about the other person realizing that I was alive and the subsequent panic incurred by the question of what the fuck did that mean to his or her life?

"Bowman."

"This a safe line? Okay to talk?"

"Where are you?"

"Where I usually stay when I'm in the area. I don't know if that's a problem for you, but…"

"Stay put."

I was worried. I didn't expect such immediate action. What if the kid was above-ground when Kevin came over? Would we have a *Days of Our Lives* type of emotional confrontation? Turned out I didn't need to worry. The kid had gone right back down in his hole—evidently he was serious about staying out of the house until Duds was history.

A little while later, the doorbell rang. I was up in my room and somehow Angela, still dressed from our family lunch and, more amazingly, still downstairs, made it to the door before I did. As I came down the stairs, she was opening that door and looking blankly at whoever was on the other side of it. That meant it wasn't Kevin. Angela knew Kevin. This person, not so much. I started to go back up the stairs when I heard a flat female voice ask for me by name.

That stopped me in my tracks.

"Max Bowman?" Angela asked, as if she had no idea where in the fucking world I might be. That was smart, because she knew there were plenty of people who shouldn't have had that information. However, the response from the other side of the door was unexpected. It was one of the weariest of all the world-weary sighs I had ever heard in my life.

"With all due respect, I know he's here. Kevin Germano sent me. I'm Patrice Plotkin."

Patrice Plotkin? Someone named their daughter that? God damn those parents to hell.

"I got this, Angela," I said as I approached from behind, desperate to see what a Patrice Plotkin actually looked like. Turned out to be pretty much what I thought. She was wearing a no-nonsense brown top and slacks, very sensible brown shoes, minimal make-up and barely-attended-to brown hair hanging down to just above her shoulders. Oh, and her eyes were brown too. She wasn't exactly unattractive, and she wasn't exactly plain either. What she was, was Patrice Plotkin.

Angela gave me a look, then retreated inside, leaving Patrice to me.

"Your hair is white," she said flatly, playing the color card before I could. Then she began rummaging through an overloaded and large purse-bag hanging over her shoulder. The bag was actually sky blue, which was somewhat of a surprise.

"So, you're CIA." I said.

"Maybe we could not talk about this on the porch?" she muttered, pulling out a file with my name on it.

We went out on the patio, just Patrice and I, and didn't really get into it until Chef had completed his iced tea service and returned to the great indoors of stately Davidson Manor. I watched as she put on her brown-framed glasses and paged through my file.

"So—Kevin couldn't make it?" I asked.

She kept her nose in my file. "Kevin can't make anything. Kevin lost his job."

"Why?"

"He picked sides. The other side won." She looked up at me over her glasses. "I think you were an integral part of the process."

"So—which side are you on?"

"Goodness and truth. That shit," she muttered as she continued to rifle through my papers.

"Is he still living around here with his family?"

"Family's here. He's not." She looked up. "Turned out he was gay. Boy, were his wife and kids surprised." She looked back down.

Kevin. Out of the marriage and out of the closet. Did I dare tell the kid?

She continued to show more interest in the files than me. "Look, he asked me to connect with you as a favor. This is not an official call. It's a pain in the ass is what it is, which is why I now have to get up to speed on whatever the hell your crazy ass story is."

"So why didn't Kevin send Tracey? She's familiar with my case. She helped me out in Sedona."

"Oh, where you killed a guy on a cliff and took a shot at Andrew Wright at a bar? Lucky her."

"What are you saying? She got fired too?"

"Reassigned." She looked up again. "Transferred to Uzbekistan, Kazakhstan, some stan. I don't know, I barely know her." She gave me a wicked look. "She was cute, wasn't she?"

Before I could get my mouth open to answer, she looked back down, scanned a page, turned to the next, and scanned it too.

"You're missing from this file for almost a year," she said. "Until you showed up on *60 Minutes* a couple of weeks ago."

"They put me in a place called the Community, where I was drugged so heavily, I actually enjoyed watching *Petticoat Junction* reruns."

She swatted a bug away from her nose. "I don't know what that means. What's the Community?"

"Where they apparently dump old spies to die. I managed to escape."

She looked at me as though I were insane. "There's no such place."

"Patrice, I was there."

She sighed and shook her head. "I can't deal with all this. There's too much. I don't know if you noticed, but we have a batshit president who seems to delight in blowing everything up while he sits tweeting on his golden toilet. So, you've become a very low priority due to the dumpster fire that's currently burning out of control in Langley. I only came here as a favor to Kevin, but if they find out I'm even meeting with you, I'll be the next one jetting to Uzbekistan." Yet another epic sigh. "I just want to move to Canada and open a Tim Horton's."

"A what?"

She sighed. "They're like Starbucks, only Canadian."

"Oh."

"I have relatives in Winnipeg. I shouldn't even be here. I had to sneak out of the office to make this trip, they think I have an emergency dentist appointment."

"In other words, I can't count on much support from the Agency."

"Does anybody know you're here?" she asked without answering my question.

"You. Angela Davidson, Jeremy Davidson. The chef."

She scanned her records. "Angela abuses prescription medication and drinks like a fish, married Dudley DeCosta, who's dirtier than mud. Jeremy was shot in the chest trying to help you. He's a stand-up guy, also gay, Kevin's boytoy for a bit."

"You make Joe Friday look like a wild drunk, you know that?"

She gave me a hard look. "Now, your state of mind. Our records show that TV interview indicated it was questionable..."

"Yeah, as I said, I was drugged heavily. And I'm still playing that hand. So, with most people, I'm playing the special needs card. That way, they think I'm no threat and maybe they'll leave me alone."

Another hard look from a woman with the empathy of a snail. "You think you're that important."

"I'm just experienced in this arena, Patrice. By the way, is there a Mr. Plotkin?"

"For about six months. He said breakfast with me was too hard, and I still don't know what the hell he was talking about."

"Sorry, maybe you two should have just skipped right to lunch. Here's a more important question. Is Andrew Wright alive?"

"I really can't talk about any of this. There's a huge crackdown on leaks. I didn't even bring my cell phone with me, in case they're tracking me." She paused. "What do you remember? From that night in Sedona?"

"Not much. I keep trying. And I only get as far as pulling into the parking lot of that restaurant…"

"Mulligan's," said she said, referring to her paperwork.

"Yeah. I park…I get out…and it's a blank."

"That was while Agent Pearce…"

"Agent Pearce?"

"Tracey." She gave me a knowing flash of a grin. "You did think she was cute, didn'tcha? Anyway, she was busy cleaning up your murder scene up on Cathedral Rock…"

"I prefer to call it a self-defense scene," I said.

"Sure, fine, whatever." Back to the file. "When Agent Pearce finally arrived at Mulligans, she found your car sitting there in the parking lot, but no sign of you, or anyone else for that matter. Then she was called away from the scene, told that other agents were coming in to handle things."

"And what did those agents do?"

She gave me a flat look. "Redacted." She held up a piece of paper with only about five words that weren't covered in solid black bars. Most of them were of the "the" "and" and "what" variety.

"Look, there must be something from that night…" I said, desperate to understand what happened.

She paused again. She was uncomfortable. She had something, but she was afraid to tell me.

"Patrice, you've gotta be on the good side. This is important. If you have something, tell me."

"A piano player," Patrice Plotkin finally said quietly. "A wounded piano player."

"Wounded piano player?"

"The next morning, Agent Pearce was still worried about what had happened to you. So…she made a few anonymous calls to hospitals, looking for you, also asking if they had any unusual patients. She found out that a piano player by the name of Michael Blum was treated for a gunshot wound in the arm that morning at a local emergency room not long after dawn. Said he was hiking, some asshole was taking target practice and he got winged. But he refused to say where he was hiking, what asshole shot him, etc. etc. Only information on him that turned up was he was from New York City."

"A long way from home."

"We all are," she said again. "I don't know what's happening with this country."

"We should all stop and appreciate the USA because whatever is done in the name of this great land is necessary and aligned with the life-affirming wishes of a great and benevolent God."

She blinked. "Whaaaaaaaat?" she finally asked.

"Sorry, I…I can't help it, they kinda drilled it into me. Somebody's always planting shit in my brain. I'm the Manchurian Candidate who keeps being renominated."

She gave me another no-nonsense look. "A little dramatic."

"I'm beginning to understand your husband and breakfast."

She drove right past that wreck on the highway. "The truth is I don't know whether Wright's dead or not. I don't know what happened to you after Sedona. None of that is in the database. If you have anything for me to follow up on, maybe I can help in my spare time. You should know I don't have any spare time."

"Maybe you could check on Dudley DeCosta. He's hinting he knows things."

"Wait—he knows you're here too?"

I nodded.

"That's a big name to leave out of the mix," she said as she made a note of it.

"He was talking about something that was being built out in Montana. Something secret."

"Helpfully vague." She took a sip of her iced tea. "So, look, I'll be honest."

"That's not surprising."

"I can't do much. Nobody at my level can. Just lay low and maybe they'll forget about you is my best advice."

"Not if Andrew Wright's alive."

"Then don't lie low." She started stuffing her papers back into her giant purse-bag. "It's your funeral."

"If it is, please give the eulogy if you're available."

She almost cracked a smile.

"Can I have your number?" I asked politely. The smile faded. "For strictly professional reasons," I added. "I don't think our breakfasts would work out either."

She ignored the swipe and looked me over. "You know, your color isn't good. My father had that color. Then he died."

"I appreciate the kind words."

"They weren't kind," she said matter-of-factly.

The Art of the Deal

"Duds wants to see you outside."

Angela was leaning against my doorway and not looking happy about delivering that message. I wasn't that happy to get it. I had just brought the dog in from her nightly piss n' shit and was ready for bed, the same bed I was currently sitting on. As a matter of fact, I had already put on my brand-new Banana Republic pajama bottoms. They had colored rectangles at goofy angles on them. They were swell.

"Outside?" I said. "Why outside?"

"Because he's a freak. I told him you wanted to talk to him, like you said, and that's what he said. Outside, in ten minutes, in the backyard."

I petted Eydie on the head absently.

"And leave her in here," Angela added. "He hates the dog."

"Yeah. I heard she's overly attracted to his rich and delicious meaty fingers."

She didn't laugh, which was an indication of just how nervous she was about this impromptu summit.

"I just want him to go away," she whispered.

"That's why we're talking. Does he know that?"

"Seemed to think something big was up."

"Okay. Well, look, how about you let me go ahead and put my pants on and we can get this party started."

She smiled ruefully. "Used to be our parties started when you took off your pants."

"Okay, one thing at a time."

She turned to go. "Tonight, I think I'm going to take all the pills he thinks I'm taking…" she said as she disappeared down the hall.

I stepped outside and noticed it was raining. Okay, not exactly raining, but it was misty, and it left the driveway sparkling with moisture in the moonlight. Luckily, I had my Mets cap to at least keep my head dry. It was also dark, very dark, but then again, it was 10 p.m.

I walked out on the circular driveway and looked around. Not a Duds in sight. So I started walking around the back of the mansion, mentally going through what I was going to say. I finally gave up on the internal scripting, because I realized most of what I said was going to depend on his mood and his responses. I had to wing this one. And I finally let myself realize how nervous I was about it. You didn't often negotiate with a guy to leave his wife unless you were a lawyer. And, because I had been involved with Angela before I disappeared…well, it only made it more awkward. At least my braindead act might actually keep him calm.

As I came around the corner and into the backyard, I saw him standing alone not too far from the shed. He was in a shirt and tie and suit pants, no jacket. And I could tell from his defiant posture that the encounter wasn't going to be easy.

"Duds!" I said happily, just loud enough to be heard as I approached.

He wheeled his enormous girth my way. I saw from his face that my assessment was correct, he was not in a good mood. There would be none of the jovial conviviality we had enjoyed that morning.

"Retardo. I heard you wanted to talk to me."

The mist was collecting on his face. He made no move to wipe it off.

"Maybe we can go inside?" I asked in my idiot voice. "There's rain. I'm getting wet."

"No. Because I have a hunch what this is about. And I think we need some room for that kind of discussion."

"Room?" I asked as I finally stopped and stood there, face-to-face with him.

I never saw it coming. His big hammy fist moved at me a lot faster than I thought it ever possibly could and clipped me in the jaw. I fell down on my ass on the wet lawn and my new Mets cap went rolling off in the grass.

"You already fucking her again?" he bellowed over my prone figure. "Didn't think you had it in you, Retardo."

I got myself up on my elbows and shook my head, to clear away the stars circling it.

"C'mon, get up. I boxed in college, cocksucker, how about you?"

I felt my jaw. I was surprised it was still there.

"Fat slob. That's what you thought I was. An easy target, huh, Max Blowman?"

Max Blowman. Clever.

"Now get the fuck up, you piece of shit douchebag," he snarled.

"I just want to talk, Duds, with no hitting" I said with an innocent expression as I laid on the ground. And that's when his left Florsheim came flying at my forehead. I rolled out of the way and stopped on my belly.

"Okay, we'll try some kicking then. You wanna talk? Get-the-fuck-UP!"

I worked my way back to my feet, grabbing my Mets cap on the way. It, my clothes and I were soaked.

"Whatsamatter, Blowman? You all wet?"

"Please, Duds," I said, out of breath, "Angela feels bad, she says she married you when she didn't feel right. I said I would talk to you…"

"So, she wants me to just walk away, that it?"

"Yes, I think she…"

That's when another big hammy fist caught me square in the solar plexus and all the air I had just put back in my system got slammed back out. I somehow managed to stay on my feet. He moved in towards me until his groin was uncomfortably close to my head, because I was still bent over from the impact.

"Listen to me, Blowman," he said down to the top of my head. "Take in as much of this as what's left of your mind can comprehend. I've been working Angela Davidson for a couple of years now. Her on my arm makes a big difference to my business. She's the gold standard in my group, got it? I don't give a shit if she's happy. Look, I was there for her when her queer boy got it in the chest and her brain went to pieces, I kept this fucking place together, not because I gave a shit about her and certainly not because I gave a shit about her son the ass-fucker. No, I went through all that crap so I could cash in on this relationship. And maybe shove my dick in her once in a while, it's not like she's hard to look at, I'm sure you agree."

Holy shit. This guy was a monster too gruesome for Chiller Theatre. I slowly straightened up. My heart was racing. I wanted to kick him in the balls and run. But I had to ride this out for Angela. And I had to still act stupid, which wasn't so hard when cartoon stars were spinning around my head.

"I just want to help everybody..." I said, straightening up.

"YOU don't talk," he said, taking another couple of steps into my personal space and violently jabbing his meaty finger into my chest. "I talk. If this is gonna happen, it's on *my* fucking terms, not yours, Retardo." And then he put another fist into my belly that put me down on my knees and caused me to make a sound that resembled a balloon losing all its air in half an instant.

"You want to resolve this?" he went on when it looked like I was capable of listening again. "It's pretty simple. I lose something like Angela Davidson, I get something in return. Something big. Something that makes it worth losing her, you understand, Blowman?"

I nodded, before he tried to insert his size 12 loafer into my head again.

"What…do you want, Duds?" I asked when I could finally make words again.

"Get up," he said.

My head was reeling as I made it back up on my feet one more time. "What do you want?" I asked again weakly.

That's when he grabbed me by the shirt and pulled me close, so close I could smell the onions that garnished whatever giant slice of cow he ate for dinner. Then he belched in my face. Jesus. It was the loudest smelliest burp I had ever encountered. Now I was nauseous in addition to being racked with pain.

He let go of my shirt and pushed me away. I stumbled back a few steps.

"I want *you*, Blowman."

"Me?"

"Yeah. I'm going to own your ass for a few weeks. You want me to split with Angela, you have to agree to do something for me. And you have to do it fuckin' right and you have to do it fuckin' well."

"What do you want me to do, Duds?" I asked, expecting the worst.

"You're going to help campaign for Senator Eddie di Pineda."

Di Pineda. Andrew Wright's political puppet. Oh hells no.

"I just signed on with Eddie a few weeks ago and I need to make my mark. If I deliver you, I'm a hero."

"But I'm not good at talking anymore, Duds. You said so. People laugh at the way I talk now. So why do you want me to talk, Duds?"

"Because there's too many questions about him. All this internet conspiracy bullshit and you're a big part of it. You can put some of that to rest, if you show up to vouch for him. Just a minute or two. Straight, simple sentences. That much you can do."

Just then, there was a noise from the shed, which was ten or twenty yards away. We both turned to see PMA emerge from his underground lair. Barefoot, wearing athletic shorts and a Washington Nationals t-shirt, he burst out of the shed, looking angry enough to kill.

"No…" I said. But he wasn't looking at me and he wasn't going to talk to me. His attention was all on Duds. He marched relentlessly towards him.

"Mom called me. She saw what you were doing to Max from the window, you fat fuck, and it's going to stop now."

"Kid…"

The kid pulled back his fist to strike, but Duds (he boxed in college) went low and got him in the gut just like he did with me. Then, in a vicious uppercut, his other fist came flying up and got the kid under the jaw. PMA went down for the count.

I was shocked. The year before, I watched the kid decimate two guys at once. He had really gone to seed. Too much dope and Netflix.

"STOP!" screamed Angela from her bedroom window. "LEAVE HIM ALONE!"

"GOOD TO SEE YOU CONSCIOUS, BITCH!" Duds screamed right back at her. Then he turned back to me, while also keeping an eye on the kid on the ground.

"So, Blowman, here's the deal." He turned to the kid. "You, you little shit, listen up too because I don't know how much Retardo here is actually processing." Back to me. "You appear at five fundraising events for Eddie. Five—over the next three months. You do that, I pack my stuff tonight and move to a nice five-star hotel where people will actually treat me like I deserve to be treated. She'll get the bill, of course," he said, shooting his thumb in Angela's general direction. "But I don't agree to any divorce until you've done all five events. And you don't talk shit about me to anyone and neither does she and neither does he," he finished, pointing to the kid on the ground.

The kid looked up at me with shock, relief, disgust and pain. A very complicated look. Then he turned to Duds. "How do we know you're going to go through with your end?" he asked.

Duds turned back to the kid. "Like I told Retardo this morning…when I tell you something, you can take it to the bank. That's how I operate. Look, Sleeping Beauty can go ahead and get the divorce paperwork ready, I'll sign it when Blowman's done doing what I want him to do. Then you can all go to hell for all I care."

The kid looked at me. I nodded. Do the fucking deal.

A little smile played on Duds' lips as he saw he was going to get his way. And when a guy like that senses a win, he grabs as much as he can. "And one more thing…" he said to the kid. "You come along for the ride."

"Come along?" The kid was confused.

"Yeah, you be his handler," said Duds, thinking it through as he said it. "In his condition, he needs somebody to make sure he doesn't walk out into traffic. You intro him at the events and say a nice word about Eddie. I still get a little of the Davidson magic. Win-win, right?"

"Three fundraisers then," the kid said. Smart move. "Not five. Three. I got college going on."

Duds actually shrugged agreeably. "Sure. Three. That'll work. And we're done here."

"Yeah," said the kid. I breathed a sigh of relief. Maybe the nightmare was over. But then PMA had to add, "Yeah, we're done. And I wish you were too."

Duds turned bright red. "Fuck you, you spoiled little shit! I grew up the son of a dockworker, without a pot to piss in, I made it on my own. You got everything handed to you. But you'll see. A whole new world's comin' and punks like you ain't about to fit in."

And then he spat the "f" word at him. No, I don't mean "fuck," I don't have a problem with that word obviously. No, it was the "f" word that was designed to hit PMA right where he lived.

I grabbed the kid's arm as Duds lurched back to the house.

"Max," the kid whispered. "We don't have to go through with this. We have him. We can get him on assault. I saw him attack you and so did my mom."

"The assault thing is shaky," I said. "Your mom watching in the dark all the way from her bedroom window? Any attorney would rip that story to shreds. And yours isn't so hot either, you've got every reason to lie and you missed most of the beatdown."

"I want to take him apart."

"This isn't about you. It's about your mom and getting his fat ass out of here, as clean and simple as possible."

"One day, I'm going to kick that fat ass from here to China," he muttered.

"Maybe," I replied, feeling his flabby arm a little more rigorously. "But you better get back in shape first."

Arrangements

"He's gone…" Angela said with more than a trace of mystification. "He just threw everything in his suitcase and left. Didn't say a word."

She was standing at the top of the stairs in her bathrobe, looking down on me as I dragged what was left of my ass up towards her.

"Didn't even say goodbye?" I asked.

"Well, he called me a worthless whore."

"Yeah, he also called your kid something else. Rhymes with 'maggot,' which actually would have been preferable." Her eyes flashed. "Don't worry, he's gone. And he's not coming back. Also, the kid's moving back in. He's just getting his stuff out of the shelter."

I got to the top of the stairs and she instantly grabbed at me like I was a foul ball at Yankee Stadium. I almost felt like a hero.

"How did you do all that?" she asked.

"Leave me a little room for breathing," I said gently as I put my arms around her. I still felt nauseous and the squeezing wasn't helping. "Anyway, your boy did some of the heavy lifting out there. Good little negotiator."

She loosened her grip and looked at my face, remembering what she had seen Duds do to me in the backyard. "Did he hurt you?" She gently touched my lower cheek, where I assumed he had left a mark.

"I'm beat in more ways than one. But no real damage. Of course, I'm filthy from spending most of the time on the ground."

She eyed the dirt on my clothes, half of which had been transferred to the angels on her bathrobe from hugging me.

Eydie came running out of Angela's room and jumped up on me. I petted her head, but when I bent over to do it, I suddenly felt dizzy and everything felt like it was about to go upside down on me again. I quickly straightened up.

"How did you get rid of him?" she asked.

I breathed in and my head cleared. "He's transactional. So I made a transaction. Unfortunately, your son's involved."

"What do you mean?"

"I mean, Jeremy and I have to put in an appearance at three Eddie di Pineda fundraisers. That's the deal. While we're doing those, you should get your lawyer in gear and get the divorce papers ready. Simple break-up. After we hold up our end of the bargain, he'll sign."

"You trust him."

"On this, yeah. He knew the marriage was going nowhere, now he's getting something out of it. Even if it's just me."

"But…di Pineda…?"

"You're not going to tell me anything about that weasel I don't already know. So, I help add a few coins to his war chest. It's not the end of the world."

She stared at me another few seconds. "You really don't look good," she said again.

"You're going to give me a complex. Look, I think I need to lie down."

I made a move towards my room, but she pulled me towards hers. I kept my feet planted, the way Eydie did when I tried to yank her away from some other dog's poop.

"I've got no objections…but at least let me shower and change."

She looked over my wet grass-stained wardrobe again, laughed a little and nodded her head.

A little while later, as I lay next to Angela, and believe me, laying there was all I could do, we both heard the kid bringing his shit back into stately Davidson Manor. I smiled and so did she. I had temporarily repaired the damage done by making a deal with the overweight devil. I had actually accomplished what I set out to do—and that occurred about as often as Halley's comet.

As shitty as I felt, I thought maybe that could be it. I could sleepwalk through the three fundraisers and then make a graceful exit from all this idiotic intrigue that had done its best to destroy every aspect of my life and the Davidsons'. If the folks in charge thought I was permanently brain-damaged from the Community, maybe they'd finally leave me alone. The only real threat was if Daddy Andy was still alive. Andrew Wright was obsessed with those who were fortunate enough to be composed of his blessed DNA and I was the only one left who filled that particular bill, so he might still try to find me. My only agenda was to make sure the old fuck was dead, so I could move on with my life.

Angela rolled over and her arm came over my chest. She smelled good. Maybe life could be as good as she smelled. Maybe stately Davidson Manor could be my home. Maybe.

Three fundraisers. And we would all be free.

A cloud had lifted. A really big, fat fucking cloud.

The next morning, we woke up to a new dawn, a non-Duds dawn. The kid was up early doing flying kicks in the backyard—and Angela, for her part, even got up before noon. Chef joyously served us candied bacon, raspberry crepe cakes and mimosas. We all were together and in one piece and it was almost too much happiness to bear.

Then a visitor came to remind us of what still had to be done.

It was 2 p.m. and I was napping, because that was about all I felt like doing at the time. Angela came in to wake me up.

"Max!"

I lifted my head. Which was Eydie's cue to leap out from between my legs, where she was also napping, and lunge at my face over and over in an attempt to lick it to nothingness.

"Jesus, what?" I muttered. My brain was in no mood to deal with the world.

"Howard's downstairs."

That got my attention.

"Duds sent him over to talk to you and Jeremy. About the fundraisers. Isn't he the awful man…"

"He's on-and-off awful. He actually helped get me out of the Community. He tricked me into getting off the ice cream with sex." She gave me a strange look. "The sex wasn't with him," I sighed. "Where's the kid?"

"In his bedroom."

I went down the hall to the kid's bedroom and told him that we both had to put on a good act for Howard. I had to pretend my brain was still fried and PMA had to act like my keeper. Sure, I might be able to trust Howard with the truth, but that had never really worked in my favor before and I didn't think it would now. He worked for Eddie's campaign and, like most people, his loyalty tended to lean towards wherever his paycheck was coming from.

The kid and I headed downstairs and found Howard in a suit and tie, his rat head shaved down to a dismal stubble as usual. He was sitting in a big chair in the living room, sipping on a cup of coffee. I put on my big dumb Community smile as the kid guided me over to the couch across from Howard, then sat down next to me. Howard, of course, immediately stared at my new hair color.

The kid jumped in. "We don't know what happened to Max's hair. Some kind of trauma, we're guessing."

"Jesus," whispered Howard.

Chef was kind enough to bring in a cold Coke Zero SUGAR for me. He had evidently made a point of buying some on his last grocery run. As I guzzled some down, Howard turned to the kid.

"Look, Jeremy, sorry about the things that happened last year. I wasn't exactly at my best…"

Truth was, back then Howard had just been fired from the CIA and thrown out of his house by his wife. He was broke and homeless, just like I was.

"And working for Eddie's campaign isn't my idea of a dream job. But I gotta pay the rent and the alimony. Just so you know, I'll make all this as easy as possible for you and Max."

"I appreciate that," said the kid without much conviction, since he knew how easily Howard cracked under pressure. But he had at least thrown Howard a crumb and Howard was glad to catch it.

Howard looked at me again, this time with a perplexed and heartbroken expression, then turned back to the kid.

"He any better?" he asked.

The kid shook his head sorrowfully.

"Max?" Howard asked me in a loud voice. "Do you remember me?"

I gave him a bright boy grin. "You helped make my dick work."

Howard smiled. "So, you did stop eating the ice cream. I was hoping to reboot a different one of your organs though—the one in your head."

"Organs are in churches," I said. As always, I was a convincing idiot.

"How the hell did you get out of there?"

"I rode a golf cart fast. It hurt but I rode it fast."

Howard turned back to the kid. "I can't stand this. I mean, Max was always kind of a jerk-off, but he was smart, he was funny….and to see him like this? I can't believe this is permanent, is there any cure? Have you taken him to a doctor?"

"Just a preliminary look." The kid then took a deep breath and leaned back against the couch. "But the doctor didn't offer a lot of hope." Shit, he was good at this.

"I got a guy," Howard said, "After we get through these fundraisers, I'll give you his name. My brother flew off his bike and bashed his head into a fire hydrant. Because of this guy, he now recognizes colors."

That wasn't a sentence you should laugh at, but I almost did.

"Anyway, I know you talked generally about the fundraisers with Duds, but the details are my end. So he sent me over to give you the info on the events where Max is supposed to appear. I guess you're going to be his…"

"His handler. I'll help him get there and do what he needs to do."

Howard nodded solemnly. Then he reached into the briefcase he had brought, pulled out a folder and handed it to the kid. "All the info on the fundraisers is in here. You'll see the first one is in three weeks in New York City at the Mandarin Oriental. Week after that, it's L.A., specifically Century City, and then finally, Palm Beach, Florida. Times, venues and everything else is in that folder. Duds said you'd take care of your own travel expenses, that right?"

"I guess," shrugged the kid in a pissy way.

"Well," said Howard, "that's what I was told. You gotta take it up with him if there's a problem."

"Are we going away?" I asked the kid. "When?"

Howard talked to me like I was two. "Max, you *are* going away. You and your friend Jeremy are going to come visit me in three different places. Isn't that nice?"

I nodded vigorously.

"Now, at these places, we want you to say some nice words about Senator Eddie di Pineda to some very, very important people. Do you think you can do that?"

"Is it for America?"

"Well…sort of…but…."

"Because whatever is done in the name of this great land is necessary and aligned with the life-affirming wishes of a great and benevolent God."

"That again." Howard rolled his eyes and sighed. "Well, at least it's the kind of shit the donors want to hear…great words about this land of ours."

I sat back with a satisfied big boy smile and, for some reason, shifted into Trump-speak. "I will say lots of GREAT words. The BEST words."

The kid shot me a "Don't overdo it" look.

Howard went back to the kid. "So how did they capture Max in the first place? What happened? Why did they put him away? You know?"

The kid shrugged. But Howard persisted.

"I've heard rumors. They say Max went after Andrew Wright. I mean, to kill him all by himself. Why the fuck would he do that?"

"I was shot. I don't know. I was in the hospital."

I said nothing. Still, Howard kept going. Obviously, this was eating at him.

"There's something weird here. Something between Max and Andrew Wright. I don't get it. It's like Max won't let go of Wright…Wright won't let go of Max…" He let his words trail off.

I saw the kid's expression change—like maybe Howard was making a point that PMA had never really considered.

"I don't know anything more than you," was all the kid said. Which was the truth.

"And there's no point asking *Regarding Henry* here, I guess," said Howard, gesturing in my direction. He got up, so the kid got up, so I got up. Howard handed the kid his card.

"If you have any questions, Jeremy, give me a call, on the cell, the number's on the card. I've prepared some brief remarks for Max to say at the fundraisers, they're in the folder, you can drill him on them a little maybe. They don't have to come out exactly as written…just get the idea out, if he can do that."

"Jeremy will help. He always helps," I helpfully added.

"So," said the kid to Howard, "You work with Duds?"

"Yeah, I do," Howard answered with some discomfort.

"You like working with him?"

"Um…I'll get back to you on that."

"DUDS IS A BIG FAT DICK!" I yelled.

Howard looked at the kid. "Maybe try and make sure he doesn't say that at the fundraisers." And with that, Howard saw himself out.

"Can you believe they're not paying our expenses for this shit?" the kid exploded.

"Duds is a big fat dick!" I replied.

"Max, c'mon," continued the kid. "Don't be cute. If you're too cute, they'll catch on to you and we're both dead."

"Relax. I can do this," I said, snapping back to normal.

The kid looked at me another moment.

"You know, Howard actually made some sense. I mean, what the hell *is* going on with you and Andrew Wright?"

"He shot you. I went to shoot him."

The kid nodded. But he knew there was more. He just didn't know how much more.

Respite

The kid and I talked over the travel expenses with Angela. The truth was they were out of my reach, considered my bank account was blinking on empty. Angela said she was happy to spring for them as her contribution to getting rid of Duds once and for all. I was fine with that. She had more than enough to go around, so some of it might as well go to me.

"I mean…there's not going to be any trouble, right?" she finally asked.

"We go, we talk, we leave," I said. "No trouble."

She nodded. I just wished I felt as good about doing it as I sounded. I knew what kind of people Eddie di Pineda was fronting for and I knew it was going to be hard for me to fake it through everything without snapping.

After a couple of days, I finally began to feel stronger and rested enough to do some longer walks with Eydie and get reacquainted with the mutt. I was also able to do more than just lay there next to Angela. You can tell when a woman misses you. They're much more energized, which, in turn, inspires you to hold up your end of the bargain. And it was good she was bringing a lot of vigor to the proceedings, because I was still lagging in that department. But it was good between us. Even easy. I was a hero again in her eyes. I liked that even more than she did.

Meanwhile, the kid continued to work hard at getting back in shape. He was afraid of what we would come up against on the road, so he was drilling himself in all his MMA moves out in the backyard. I told him I didn't expect any karate fights amongst the rich old bloated donors at Senator Eddie's soirees, but he clearly felt the need to return his body to its former glory. He too was energized, energized because he was out of his underground condo and back in the fresh air and sunshine—and, of course, out from under the very enormous shadow of Duds.

Angela regained her mental equilibrium. The kid regained his mojo. Me, I just recovered. I rested and I relaxed, and, even though there was an ever-present exhaustion that constantly threatened to pull me under, I tried to ignore it. The important thing to me was that, even though I had lost my apartment, my car and all my possessions, I still had a home. I still had a center. I still had some kind of family.

Those were three perfect weeks. You didn't get that kind of break often in life, at least I didn't. And the only fly in the ointment were the texts I kept getting on my phone, the weird texts from some anonymous number:

> *Rights a live*
>
> *he wants u max*
>
> *you are his*

"Wright's alive" was my translation of the first text. That confirmed who this freak was messaging me about. But it was the last text that felt the most ominous—because it represented my greatest fear, that Andrew Wright would try to reclaim his last remaining son, namely me. The rotten old asshole had not only presided over most of the batshit things America had been responsible for over the past half a century or so, he had also been fucking with my head one way or another since before I had pubic hair. Even at the Community, they were still trying to program shit in my brain. But what was the ultimate end game? Would I ever know? Should I even care?

The Wednesday before the first fundraiser, which was set for that coming Saturday night, the texts took a turn for the truly weird. And I had absolutely no fucking idea what the last one meant:

when the waters rise wite rain will poor down

I assumed, with the help of my internal grammar checker, that the message was supposed to read, "When the waters rise, white rain will pour down." But it still didn't make sense. Was this some kind of global warming message? And wasn't White Rain a shampoo?

I was in the kitchen staring at the newly-arrived words when the kid entered. I had avoided showing him any of the weird uncapitalized texts for three weeks, but, against my better judgment, I decided it was time to share. And the kid reacted to the texts just the way my better judgment indicated he would.

"Max, it's just some nut," he said, tossing the phone back to me.

"Some nut texting me about Andrew Wright. And again, how'd this nut get my number? This is a new phone, fresh from the Fast Track in Mayo, Florida."

"Max, I don't know. Unless you know something I don't, I don't know what to tell you."

The kid was avoiding. I didn't blame him and I said nothing.

"Look, who knows," the kid finally said, "Maybe we shouldn't go around kicking over rocks looking for snakes. Maybe we should just get through the fundraisers and avoid this kind of drama. We can get clear of all this if we stay focused. Focus is critical to goals."

"You been listening to self-help tapes again?"

"They help me…"

"…focus?"

He nodded. I looked at the texts again.

"We're leaving tomorrow," I said.

"Tomorrow's Thursday. We were planning on driving up Friday."

"Tomorrow, we drive. Friday, we go see someone, someone who might be able to answer my one remaining question."

The kid rolled his eyes. He was Michael Corleone and I was the Mafia. Just when he thought he was out...

Road Trip

Thursday morning. Eydie watched unhappily as I packed a suitcase—the luggage was a dead giveaway I was leaving again. Her tail was down and her ears were up, because she knew. The goddamn dog knew. Her eyes flickered with the fear of abandonment. After all, the last time I had left the compound, I didn't come back for many moons, as the Hollywood Native Americans used to say. She made a whimpering sound. She never did that unless shit was serious.

"We're not taking the fucking dog, Max." The kid was in the doorway of the bedroom examining the situation. He, like Eydie, knew what was up.

"I can't leave her. She'll be too afraid I won't come back."

"We're not taking her."

Angela came out of the bathroom in her freshly-laundered angelic bathrobe.

"Take the dog."

The kid gave her a look.

"If you take the dog," she said, "It improves the odds of you two not getting in any trouble." She looked at me. "You'll be too worried about Eydie."

"Fine," muttered the kid, who wandered away to finish his own packing.

I smiled at her. "It's good having a tiebreaker in the house."

She approached and put her arms around me. "You *are* going to stay out of trouble, aren't you, Max Bowman?"

"Call me 'Blowman.' Duds does."

"I don't do anything Duds does. I barely even did Duds. You, however..." She kissed me and I returned the favor.

"You sure you want to be my girlfriend? I'm broke and homeless, you know."

"There's enough home here for you."

"And the Mormon Tabernacle Choir."

She turned serious. "Just be careful."

"Always."

"Never."

But she kissed me again anyway.

"There was another Spider-Man movie???"

The kid was driving the same Jeep Patriot that he had before I disappeared. Guess his mom was too rattled to buy him a new set of wheels like she did every other year. We had been on the road about an hour and PMA was trying to catch me up on what I had missed in the ten months I was gone. Naturally, I had to find out what Marvel movies I had missed.

"Yes, Max, there was another Spider-Man movie. With a new guy playing Spider-Man. And Michael Keaton, he played the villain."

"I like Keaton. He could play me when they make a movie out of my life."

The kid gave me a look of disbelief.

"What?" I asked reasonably enough.

He shook his head and we rode on in silence for a few moments.

"God, I hope there's no shit," the kid finally said.

"What?"

"With these fundraisers. I mean, it's not even an election year, right? So what does Eddie di Pineda need money for?"

"His senate seat. Reelection next year. Then comes 2020…"

The kid looked at me. "You really think…?"

"Sure, he's gonna go for the White House. Trump is already a wounded animal. And Eddie's got a lot of powerful people behind him, seems like. So who knows? Could be our first President Eddie."

"All these people just give me the creeps. All that weird stuff Duds was saying…"

"What weird stuff?"

"That night in the yard. When he said there was a revolution coming."

"Everybody in politics thinks there's a revolution coming," I said, pulling out a cigarette. I kept trying to minimize everything. I was trying to fool myself as much as everybody around me.

"He sounded like it was something specific."

"Weren't you the one who said we shouldn't kick over rocks looking for snakes?" I lit the cigarette with my lighter and the kid took note as I brought down my side window down to let the fumes out. "Besides, Duds is a bullshit artist."

"You smoke?" the kid said in shock.

"Yeah, couple times a day, usually when I take the dog out. It's Glenda Schmidt's fault. I think her brand sucks too, but at least it's cheap."

"They'll kill you."

I looked at him. "You gonna tell me my color isn't good like everybody else?"

"Well…it's better than it was," he said.

"Thanks. Now, since you got into my business, let me get into yours. How's your love life?"

His eyes went right back on the road. "I don't have one."

"Look, Kevin wasn't the right guy for you. You need someone who doesn't have a stick up his ass, to make up for the giant one that's up yours."

The kid floored it, as if speeding up would spare him from this conversation.

"I also need a guy who doesn't have a wife and kids," he finally said.

"Well, apparently, that situation has been addressed." I said without thinking, because I was a big fucking idiot. Damn! It was a rock I didn't mean to kick over and now the kid was wrestling with the snake.

"What do you mean?" he asked quietly.

"Patrice Plotnik."

"Patrice Plotnik?"

"The CIA agent who was over the other day. She told me ol' Kev's getting divorced." And, before the kid could ask, I answered. "I don't know if he's with somebody else or what, that's all she told me."

The kid smoothed down his hair with one hand while he steered with the other. I winced at what was coming out of the radio.

"You mind if I change the station?" I finally asked. "I've had enough earnest alt-rock to last me the rest of my life. That may only encompass a couple of months or so, but still, I'd like to enjoy them without having to listen to millennials whining their way through grandiose themes of love and redemption…"

The kid just nodded. He probably didn't even hear what I said—his brain was too occupied with what I had told him about Kevin. So, I turned the dial to a hip-hop station. I needed some hardcore swearing to a beat. Meanwhile, in the back seat, the dog snored on top of the layer of hair she had already shed all over the kid's upholstery.

I took another drag on the cancer stick and thought about things. I knew the kid was hoping there wouldn't be any shit at the fundraisers, but I knew there would be. We just had to plow our way past it and make our way home. It didn't have to be an apocalyptic nightmare.

It didn't have to be.

Right?

I rested my noggin back against the headrest and threw the cigarette out the window, then watched it trail sparks on the highway behind us.

The Piano Player

Eydie was edgy.

The dog had barely been off the Davidson compound for almost a year, and now she was in a giant city filled with cars, people, skyscrapers and lots and lots of noise.

It was Friday morning and the kid and I were taking Eydie for a very long walk from our hotel near Columbus Circle all the way to Harlem, by cutting through Central Park. Yeah, it felt good to be back in the city, but the dog was doing her best to cut down on the enjoyment factor.

I had her on a tight leash, because she kept lunging at strangers she didn't trust and attacking dogs she didn't like, which, to be honest, was every last one of them. The kid tried to keep a few steps ahead of us to keep anyone from walking too close to Eydie, but, since the dog didn't like the kid either, she'd just go ahead and nip at one of his heels every once in a while. So, yeah, it was tricky.

It was a crisp day in early October, one of the great times to be walking in the city, and, fortunately, the park wasn't that crowded. But when we came out on the other side and into the Harlem area, the stakes rose considerably. That was when something I had long suspected about my beautiful blonde terrier-mix was confirmed and reconfirmed.

Eydie was a fucking racist.

Every black person we passed she either growled at or tried to go after. The kid kept stopping and insisting we take an Uber the rest of the way. I said it was only a few more blocks. The kid said that all three of us, men and dog, would end up being put to death for a hate crime. I told him to calm down. He didn't. The dog snapped at an elderly black woman with a cane.

We got an Uber.

We were heading to the apartment building of Michael Blum, the piano player that Patrice Plotkin had told me about. He was wounded under mysterious circumstances the night of whatever happened between me and Andrew Wright, the night we both disappeared from sight, and I was hoping he might be able to fill me in on the details, mostly about whether I had actually hit Wright with my single shot. The only problem was I still had to play dumb, meaning the kid would have to take the lead in asking questions. But, since I didn't have much of a memory about that night, it probably wouldn't make much difference. PMA usually knew how to handle things.

The Uber guy left us right out in front of Blum's apartment building, and we headed in. Even though it was a pretty modest complex, the entrance had a doorman and there was a security guard behind the reception desk to screen visitors, a common set-up in the city. Since Michael Blum didn't know us from Adam, I told the kid what to say to get us past the guard. It was a stab in the dark, but I thought it might work.

We walked up to the desk. Eydie saw the security guard was an African-American gentleman and lost her shit. I picked her up and took a few steps back as the guard eyed her warily. It was a good thing the mutt didn't know the n-word.

"How can I help you?" the guard asked, not taking his eye off the dog. I eyed his nametag, which read "Michael J. Hajduk."

"Hajduk," I said in my dumb voice, warming it up for my next performance.

"No," the guard said calmly. "It's pronounced 'Hy-dook."

"Where did the 'J' go?" I asked.

"We're here to see Michael Blum," said the kid, heading me off at the pass.

"Is he expecting you?" he asked, picking up the phone.

"We're friends of a friend of his…Julie Nelson, a singer? We wanted to talk to him about doing a…a gig." The kid had trouble saying "gig" in a natural way. It was like when a grown-up tried to say "groovy" when I was 12 years old and the word was already well past its expiration date. It was the "on fleek" of its time.

The guard called Blum's apartment and told him what the kid said. I took a deep breath. I had no idea if Blum actually knew my late lamented love, Jules. But I figured, if he had been playing piano for Andrew Wright, then he, just like Jules had, inhabited the world of retro New York cabaret performers, musicians who still revered the standards of Cole Porter, Jerome Kern, Gershwin and Rodgers & Hart, and didn't pay much attention to anything that happened musically after 1956. It was highly likely that Blum and Jules had crossed paths at one time or another. If they hadn't, then I had baited the hook with something no performer ever swam away from, and that bait rested in the word the kid had trouble saying—"gig." If we represented work, Blum should welcome us like long-lost relatives. I knew the performer mentality.

"Okay," said the guard as he hung up the phone, "You can go up."

Bingo. The power of the gig.

I carried Eydie to the elevator behind the kid. The guard never took his eyes off her and I didn't blame him one bit.

"You know, Max, I like this new arrangement," the kid said in the elevator. "Because I get to be in charge. I get to do all the talking. I think it's overdue, actually."

"Don't let it go to your head," I said, gently putting Eydie down on the floor as the elevator doors opened up.

A moment later, we were knocking on the front door of Unit 506, which had a mezuzah hanging on the doorframe. After another moment, a small wiry man, probably around my age, opened the door and peered up at us through his small rectangular glasses. He was wearing jeans and a black t-shirt that read "Shut Your..." and then it had a bar of music with four notes on it underneath. Since I had had piano lessons when I was a kid, I knew the notes spelled out F-A-C-E. But since I was supposed to be stupid, I just stared at the shirt and said, "Music!"

Michael Blum looked at me strangely and said, "C'mon in, guys."

And that's when Eydie erupted in a fit of savage barking and growling. Did she hate Jews too? Michael quickly backed away from her as the kid and I entered.

Actually, I knew what was behind this latest round of hound dog hostility, and it wasn't about anyone's religion. Eydie was always unnerved by anyone who was scared of her. If a stranger reacted to her with a panicked expression and was unsure of how to move in order to avoid a potential attack, she took it as a sign to go forth and nip. Michael Blum was that type of person. He was standing still and lurking, and if there was anything Eydie hated, it was lurking. I held her tight, but the spooked Blum backed himself up against a bookshelf of old dusty bestsellers from decades gone by (*Once Is Not Enough*, anybody?), knocking over a few knickknacks that were sitting on those shelves in the process.

The kid gave me a glare and then gave Blum a reassuring smile. "It's okay. He's got her."

I picked up the dog and sat down in a nearby chair that looked like it might have belonged to Blum's mother. Or his mother's mother, for that matter.

"Good," said a relieved Blum. "I hate animals and that includes agents."

We laughed politely. I looked around the small apartment, which looked like it had been furnished by an associate of Mamie Eisenhower, except for one glaring exception--a magnificent new baby grand piano sat where you would ordinarily have found a dining room table. This being a New York apartment, there wasn't room for both. Maybe he ate on the piano?

Blum noticed me staring at the magnificent instrument, with its beautiful polished wood exterior, and beamed with pride. "That, my dear sir, is an authentic Bechstein, my pride and joy. As opposed to my daughter, who's unemployed and living with her bitch mother."

The kid, who was still standing, nodded. "Impressive."

Blum, seeing I had a tight grip on the dog, relaxed a little and peeled his back off the bookshelf. "Yes, it is. If a Steinway is a Cadillac and if a Bosendorfer is a Porsche...then a Bechstein is a Lamborghini. You guys want a glass of water or something?"

The kid shook his head and sat down in the chair next to me. Blum settled down in a slightly-tattered love seat across from us. He looked at me again. "Do I know you? You seem familiar."

"You play piano!" I said brightly.

Blum gave the kid a questioning look.

"He's had some...some brain damage."

"Oh," said Blum with some dismay. "So, which one of you knew Jules? I did a few gigs with her. Great singer. Shame what happened."

"Well, Max and her...they were..."

The kid didn't finish the sentence. He didn't have to. Blum's face turned as white as my hair as he studied my face.

"That's who you are. The hair threw me off. You're Max Bowman. Max fucking Bowman!" He stood right back up, even though Eydie started snarling at him. "Okay, I don't know what this is about, but you two need to leave."

"You're not going to play piano?!" I asked.

"Max," the kid said. "Shhh."

"Seriously, you're in here under false pretenses. I will call the police…"

Eydie continued to snarl and wriggle in my grip.

"No, Eydie, no stop!" I said as I purposefully let her go. She charged Blum, who wasn't ready for it, and she went for his leg. Blum jumped up to a standing position on the love seat as the kid grabbed Eydie's leash and yanked the mutt back to our side of the room. Meanwhile, Blum rolled up his pants leg and saw that some skin had been broken. A little rivulet of blood was trickling down from the wound.

"I'm fuckin' bleeding! Listen, you assholes, now I *am* going to call the cops!"

The kid made a move like he was going to let go of the dog's leash. Michael gasped and stayed up on the love seat, but moved down to a crouch.

"You probably bled a lot more when you were shot in the arm last year, Mr. Blum. And you didn't talk to the cops then," said the kid.

Blum glared at PMA. "What are you talking about?"

"I mean, you were with Andrew Wright the night he disappeared. And the night that Max here disappeared. At a restaurant called Mulligans in Sedona, Arizona."

"How do you know all that? You CIA? A kid like you? That's ridiculous!"

"I'm not CIA, I'm a friend of Max's and I'm trying to find out what happened to him. That's all."

"BULLSHIT!"

Eydie growled again. Blum clammed up. Then he looked straight at me.

"It's all your fucking fault! You pulled out that gun and then all hell broke loose! I didn't even know if I'd ever play the piano again!"

"So," the kid asked, "Max accidentally shot you instead of Andrew Wright?"

"Oh no, oh no no no, he shot Andrew Wright all right—right in the damn head! But Wright always had security guys with him and that night, they were on both sides of the band. They heard the shot and they all started shooting and they got everybody except the guy they were supposed to get—HIM!" Blum pointed at Max.

"I fell on the floor…" I murmured. Because I remembered. I finally remembered. I shot at Wright with the one bullet left in my gun's chamber and then I threw myself on the floor, because I figured there would be return fire.

And there was. Plenty of it.

In the darkened confines of the restaurant, however, the security boys created a deadly crossfire, and everybody caught in the middle of it went down. I had wondered what happened to Yvonne, the self-proclaimed psychic who turned out to be Daddy Andy's squeeze. As the images of that moment flooded my consciousness, I saw her hit the floor next to me, with a neat little bullet hole in her throat. Blood quickly gushed out of it and she was dead in seconds. Around me, I saw other bodies fall off their chairs and onto the hardwood floor too. There was blood everywhere. Blood everywhere.

"Blood everywhere," I blurted out, traumatized by the images suddenly flooding me.

"You're fucking right there was blood everywhere," Blum said. "I ran out the back exit, blood gushing from my arm. Hid out in the wilderness all night. I ripped off the bottom of my pants and tied it around the wound and just stayed out there, shivering in the fucking cold, feeling scared shitless someone was going to come hunt me down. I was out there until sunrise. Arm still fucking aches, which is a helluva thing for a piano player."

Then he gave me a hard look.

"Why in HELL would you try something like that? With Andrew Wright? Jesus."

"Is Andrew Wright dead?" the kid asked.

"Who the fuck knows? A bullet to the head of a man who's as old as dirt…I'd say maybe the odds would fall that way, wouldn't you?"

"How did you know him in the first place?"

Blum took a breath, looked at Eydie, saw that I was holding her tight, and then slowly made his way back down to a sitting position.

"He liked the kind of music I played," Blum said quietly. "He was in New York a couple of years ago and happened into the bar where I was playing one night. He liked what I was doing, plenty of people do, you know, and then he kept coming in night after night, and every time he stuffed my tip jar full of twenties. Then one night, he said he was going to rent out a room and do a little singing for some friends of his—would I accompany him? When he told me how much he'd pay me, damn right I was going to. He couldn't hit a note to save his life, but the money was good, so who cared? And he kept on hiring me. I didn't know who he was, but word got around and then I was too scared to quit playing for him. He was an anti-Semitic cocksucker, I'll tell you that much."

"Anti-Semitic?"

"To be fair, anti-everything," Blum said, shaking his head. "He and his pals. Unspeakable conversations." He paused. "You know what he called me? The Jew Liberace!" He said it almost proudly.

Eydie growled and strained at the leash and Blum flinched again.

"Look, that's all I know, so maybe you could get little Cerberus out of here." He eyed his leg wound. "I could have that dog put away, you know, I could call the cops right now and…"

The kid looked at the Bechstein and proceeded to shut Blum up but good. "That looks pretty new," he said, still staring at the posh piano. "How'd you pay for it?"

"None of your business."

The kid let the leash out a little. Eydie got a little closer to Michael. She was better than waterboarding when it came to getting intel.

"Okay, the fuckers paid me off because I got shot! That's all."

"They?"

"The check came from something called The Eugene Group. That's all I know!"

"You keep saying that's all you know. But then you know more."

"Listen, you little pisher…"

More growling.

"THAT IS ALL THE FUCK I KNOW!"

"I want to leave," I said in my dumb voice. Because I truly did believe that was all the fuck he knew.

Fundraiser 1

"Well, your evil dog finally came in handy," said the kid.

We were in an Uber going back to the hotel. It was late afternoon and my energy was lagging. I nodded and held on to Eydie tightly, feeling a tad guilty for encouraging her to perform nefarious deeds. But the kid was right. Without the threat of my edgy terrier, Blum would've just thrown us out.

"And I did pretty good, pointing out the piano."

"You did. But that was a gimme," I said to the kid. "On the one hand, the guy's got sixty-year-old furniture that somebody's great-grandma threw out, and, on the other hand, he's got a brand-new fucking 40k piano. So yeah, somebody had just poured cash into his bank account, that was pretty obvious."

"Anyway, you've got a confirmed hit, Max. Andrew Wright in the head. So let it go."

"We don't have a confirmed corpse."

"Well, you must have at least taken him out of action. Anyway, what do you think he's going to do even if he is still alive? You escaped the Florida compound, big deal, as far as he knows, your brain is fried. I don't think we're in any danger, Max."

I didn't say anything. Instead, I took a peek at that text on my phone...the one that said, *when the waters rise*

"The Eugene Group," I said. "That's who paid Blum. We need to look into that."

"No. We. Don't." replied the kid. "Max, it's just a front name. Remember the Rosenbaum Foundation from the Blue Fire thing? This is probably like that—another bunch of evil creepy people doing evil creepy things with the help of a shell company. I'd rather not get shot in the chest again, so let's just do our time and let's move on, please? Maybe we can finally open that detective agency when this is over."

We rode quietly for a minute or two. I knew why I couldn't let it all go. I was too afraid Andrew Wright was still alive and planning his bad little boy's next punishment. But Daddy Andy was not on the kid's mind.

"He must be done with me," the kid finally said with a bitter edge.

"Kevin?" I asked.

"Yeah. If he finally had the balls to leave his wife…and he didn't contact me…"

"You're better off."

The kid nodded as he stared out the window.

That night we took in a movie and ate at a decent Mexican place. The next day, we took the dog for a good walk and ate outdoors at a decent pizza place. I realized I missed the city and all its food options, but maybe that was just the after effect of being stuck in a condo for ten months with only prewrapped sandwiches to eat.

Then came fundraiser time. There wasn't any discussion—we both knew we were leaving Eydie alone in the room for the night. We were going to have enough to navigate without having to worry about the mutt chomping on a donor or two. So, we put on our Sunday best and, when we were ready to go, we put Eydie in her crate so she wouldn't tear the place apart. She tended to like enclosed spaces anyway, so I didn't think it was a big deal.

We walked over to the fundraiser venue and we were both very quiet. Because we didn't know what we were walking into.

The fundraiser was at the Mandarin Oriental Hotel, a posh five-star wonder just a few blocks away from our humble digs. The event was being held in the hotel's huge and lavish ballroom, which was 6000 square feet and had 18-foot high walls of windows overlooking Central Park and the Manhattan skyline. I had no idea what the space cost to book for the night, but the number had to be close to some small nation's GDP.

We were told to be there an hour early, at 6 pm, and like the good boys we were, that's when we got there. I put on my dumb smile as the kid led the way into the venue. After we got through security and the metal detectors, we got a good look at the room. The ballroom was magnificent. It featured three immense crystal chandeliers and the views of the city were truly astounding. So, this was how the better half lived, I thought. Then I corrected myself—this was how the *rich* half lived. I wasn't so sure they were better, especially if they were backing the likes of Eddie di Pineda to run the country.

And speak of the devil...

Inside the ballroom, not far from the entrance where we were standing, there was Senator Eddie himself, going over some last-minute details with my old buddy Howard and big ol' Duds himself. All three were dressed in elegant tuxedos. Tuxedos? Really? Was this the donor prom?

Senator Eddie paused when he saw me and the kid, not sure how to react. After all, at the last Eddie fundraiser I attended, he had attempted to toss me out of the joint. He turned to Howard and Duds, both of whom, I could tell, were trying to reassure the Senator that I wasn't going to throw him into a nearby wall. They must have said the right things, because soon enough, the three men were headed our way.

As they approached, I saw all too clearly the smirk on Duds' face—and it made me want to instantly smash it in with the closest chair. It was obvious he liked making people do things they didn't want to do. He liked it way too much. It took all I had to keep my expression mindless and happy.

"Well, if it isn't the dynamic duo," Duds said. "Ready to help our man here get elected?"

Senator Eddie smiled uncomfortably at me.

Howard turned to me. "Max," he said, talking more loudly than he had to because people always assume the intellectually disabled are deaf too, "You remember the Senator?"

I nodded with a smile and stuck out my hand. "Eddie's going to be president!"

I said exactly the right thing. Eddie's smile shifted into high gear and he shook my hand with enthusiasm. "Well, I certainly hope so someday, Max! But right now, it's just about re-election!"

I returned his shake with a grip and movement so manic, it made one of Trump's batshit handshakes look wimpy by comparison. The kid pulled my hand apart from Eddie's and then the kid took his turn shaking it.

"Sorry, Senator. Max gets a little carried away."

"Quite all right," said Senator Eddie. "Glad you're aboard, Jeremy. Your grandfather was a hero of mine." Then he turned back to Max. "It's wonderful having both of you come out to help me tonight. Having you on my side is going to make a big difference both to my campaign and, ultimately, to the whole USA."

USA? Ah! My cue!

"We should all stop and appreciate the USA because whatever is done in the name of this great land is necessary and aligned with the life-affirming wishes of a great and benevolent God," I replied with a big happy grin.

Eddie looked at Howard questioningly. "It's something he says," Howard said a little weakly.

The senator's smile wilted a bit as he turned to Howard. "Howard, let's go over the program one more time." He put his hand on Howard's back and led him away. Duds remained, his eyes suddenly on fire.

"Listen, Dumb and Dumber, first of all, you're supposed to be wearing tuxes."

"Howard didn't tell us that," said the kid.

"Fuckin' moron, I'll deal with him later. But you two I'll deal with now. I don't want any playing around. You try to fuck this up, the deal's off, you got it? This thing is going to be livestreamed to donor parties all across the country. So, no surprises."

"I thought surprises were good," I said sadly. Then I turned to the kid. "Ask Duds about the Eugene Group. I want to meet Eugene."

Duds looked thrown. "Where'd you hear that name?" he whispered.

I shrugged. And suddenly he was poking me in the chest with his big fat finger again, after he first made sure no one in the room was looking.

"Listen, Retardo, what I did to you in the backyard a few weeks ago might be just the warm-up if you don't tow the fucking line around here. You are here to serve the Senator, that's all, don't forget it." Then he turned to the kid. "Keep your halfwit friend under control. Believe me, there aren't enough pills on the planet to help Mommy survive all the shit I'll drag her through if you don't."

Duds left us on that pleasant note. The kid was silently fuming.

"Where do you think he gets his clothes?" I asked. "Tarps R Us?"

That got a smile out of PMA. And that gave me an inspiration.

"Hey, we should start doing 'Duds so fat' jokes. You know, like 'Duds so fat, Everest had to climb him.'"

"Max," the kid said, shaking his head, still smiling.

"Duds so fat, his belly has its own zip code."

The kid burst out laughing. I kept going, even though I was running out of material.

"Duds so fat, his meals have meals."

The kid laughed again. "I don't even know what that means," he said.

"It means we better keep ourselves entertained or we're going to lose our minds. Let's go see what's going on."

Most of the set-up in the room had already been done. The place was filled with elegantly set tables, there were open bars on both sides of the ballroom, and, as we approached the head table at the back, I spotted the video crew, presumably the group responsible for livestreaming the event.

Leading that video crew was a very familiar face.

Doug Daytona's.

He wasn't hard to miss. His tuxedo was an ungodly shiny purple and gold floral concoction, something Lady Gaga would have turned down as too flashy. He was directing about a crew of about eight or ten people as they set up three video cameras; two to the side to catch shots of the crowd, one in the middle in between tables to catch the speechmakers.

As we moved towards the head table, he saw me. I quickly put my idiot face back on. I waved happily. "Hi, Dougie!"

Doug, about forty feet away, weakly waved back.

"That's the guy who interviewed you," said the kid quietly.

"Yeah. He's also doing a documentary on Senator Eddie and he's also livestreaming this monstrosity. He must be the propaganda arm of this operation."

"Max Bowman?"

I turned. Another familiar face. But this one was from a much longer time ago. Holy shit. How was this happening?

"How is your dog, Max Bowman?"

There he was, just fifteen or twenty feet away, wearing a "You U!" t-shirt and workpants and holding some cable in his hands. That meant he was actually part of Doug Daytona's crew. A chill went through me as he stared at me with a blank expression. The last time I had seen him, he was going to kill me. But to be fair, it was only because he wanted my dog.

The kid looked at him and looked back at me.

"Augustine Bravino," I whispered.

"Wasn't he that weird guy who kidnapped Eydie?"

"Yeah. His brain was melted by Blue Fire. We're soulmates."

Augustine Bravino slowly walked towards us and asked again, in the same flat monotone, "How is your dog?"

"My dog is good," I said. "She is very happy."

"Very good, my brother friend." And then his eyes shone with a strange light. "You know how much I like dogs. Dogs are magical. They are from another place where there is only love..." He reached into a deep pocket of his workpants and pulled out...a dog puppet. The same dog puppet that sat behind Doug Daytona's reception desk. The one that recognized me.

"Remember Morris?" he asked with a smile as he put the puppet on his hand.

"Uh...yes," I said. Where the hell was this going?

"This is the only dog they let me have. But that is okay. He is very real to me."

"Hellooooo Max," the puppet said to me in that eerie high-pitched Vincent Price voice that Augustine was apparently able to access at will. The kid took a step back. It was a reflexive action. I understood. Because the whole thing was fucking spooky.

Then Augustine's expression turned serious as the dog puppet continued to talk. "I've been waaaaarning you."

"Warning me?" I said to the puppet. Yes, to the puppet.

Augustine moved Morris closer to us. Then closer still. Its Lego-toothed mouth moved up and down again as the puppet let out an ominous whisper.

"He's still aliiiiiiive. He wants you."

I looked at Augustine. "Who wants me?"

Augustine kept quiet, but Morris the dog puppet was another story. "It's wrong," the puppet said. "All of it is so very wrong." The puppet looked around the room to make sure no one was within hearing distance. "They are waiting for the oceans to rise. They are waiting for the white rain to come down." Augustine brought Morris even closer until it was just a few inches from my face. "We must find a way to stop them. Won't you help? Won't you?"

Then the puppet tilted its head, as if waiting for an answer.

"Um…" I said.

"Soon…it will be too late," it said. And then Augustine walked away as he carefully removed the puppet from his arm and put it back in the pocket from whence it came.

PMA was stunned. I moved to go after Augustine to find out what exactly he (or his puppet) knew, but the kid regained his senses and held me back and I quickly saw why. Duds was a few tables away, giving us the evil eye as he bawled out Howard, presumably for not telling us the dress code for the night.

"Remember my mom, Max. This isn't the time or place," whispered the kid. "Besides, you're going to listen to a dog puppet? You told me Augustine's crazy."

"He's not crazy like that," was my reply. "I understand how he's crazy. Because that's the way I was crazy."

"I don't understand what you're saying. At all."

I guessed the kid wouldn't, because he had never been that kind of crazy. When you're that kind of crazy, you speak in weird truths. You can't help but speak in truths. And that was what Augustine was doing. The last time I had seen him, he wanted to kill me. This time, was he trying to save me?

I turned and saw Doug Daytona staring at us. There was fear in his eyes. But I didn't get the sense he was afraid of us. I got the sense that somewhere inside, he was silently begging for help.

A little after seven, the wealthy donors came parading in for the cocktail hour—*they* knew enough to wear tuxes. At first, we kept our distance. We took our seats at the head table, even though no one else had yet, so we were all by our lonesome on the dais. We had our reasons for staying away, but mostly it was because we didn't want to mingle with a bunch of rich entitled pricks who had views we presumed were diametrically opposed to ours. So we pretended we were enjoying the pretentious string quartet that was playing some classical bullshit in the corner.

But what I actually found interesting was the fact that even within that gathering of elites, there was still a pecking order. The front half of the room was roped off, to keep the low-rent donors away from the Senator. Evidently, you had to come up with the big bucks to have any personal contact with Senator Eddie, who was working the opposite corner of the room from the string quartet.

Still, the fact that in an hour or two I would have to extol the Senator's virtues to the crowd was weighing on me. I knew he was just a soulless political puppet, up for sale if the price was right and all his glad-handing made my soul want to vomit.

Finally, after a half-hour or so of sitting and watching this horror show, I couldn't stand it anymore. I had to have a drink. Or maybe eighteen of them. The kid offered to go get me one, but I said I needed to stretch my legs. So, we worked our way around the back of the table and over towards the bar, where the liquor was flowing more freely than ketchup at an Applebee's. I got a double Jack and the kid got a glass of white wine.

As we sipped our beverages, we became conscious that everyone was watching us. That was because everyone knew who we were—and what our history was with Senator Eddie di Pineda and company. The unspoken question was being shouted at us from all quarters. *How in the world were we now backing this guy?*

I didn't let on that there was any conflict, of course. I gave everyone my big idiot smile and they nodded at me as one would at a cute, harmless animal. Then they turned to each other and said things like, "Isn't it a shame?" and "He's not right, you know." And they said it within earshot of me, as if I wouldn't be able to process their patronizing pity. As a matter of fact, I was hearing bits and pieces of all sorts of tantalizing conversations. No one was concerned what they said in front of me, because of my "condition."

And that's then I realized I had the keys to the kingdom.

Since these fat cats thought I had brain damage, they didn't bother to censor themselves. Who knew what secrets they might spill in front of me? I looked over at the other end of the bar and saw PMA being chatted up by some handsome clean-cut guy in his late twenties wearing the most amazing tuxedo I had ever seen in my life. *Must be an entitled rich fuck. Good for the kid.* Since he was occupied, I went ahead on my own and crashed a group of corrupt old assholes who looked particularly venal.

"Hi, I like parties," I said to their amusement.

"Hello, Mr. Bowman," said one old fuck.

"Surprised to see you supporting *our* side, Mr. Bowman," said another.

"What happened to your hair?" asked another.

"Glad you're finally helping to take our country back," said another.

"I was in Florida for a long time," I said. "It's hot in Florida. But I had sex once."

They looked at each other, not sure how to respond to that. So they didn't. Instead, they completely ignored me and started talking amongst themselves as if I wasn't there.

"Not my choice," said one, eyeing Senator Eddie glad-handing folks nearby.

"He's necessary," said another. "We need one of them to get their votes. It's simple demographics."

I surveyed the crowd and immediately saw no other person in the Senator Eddie "demographic" within spitting distance, except for a few of the help. It was true. A big part of the reason they had anointed Senator Eddie as their savior-of-the-moment was because he was Puerto Rican and would appeal beyond their very, very white base.

They continued to talk as I continued to smile and drink. The Jack really helped.

"And he'll do what we want. Not like that maniac Trump."

"Trump will be gone soon. Then 2020…we hit the reset button. Besides, do you know how much we've gotten away with because Trump sucks up all the media oxygen? Nobody even notices anything else that's going on."

"What's going on?" I asked brightly. "I don't know!"

"Something very interesting, Mr. Bowman," one of them said with a laugh. "Perhaps you'll be included if you're helpful to the cause."

"Is it something in Montana? People talk about a big thing in Montana."

Their faces dropped. Maybe I wasn't supposed to know that. But it didn't matter, I wasn't going to hear anything else. Because a big fat hand was suddenly gripping my arm with a strength that I knew was going to leave a big fat bruise.

"Excuse us, gents," said Duds as he pulled me away. Then, when I was far enough away, he told me to go back to the head table and stay there. Don't talk to anyone else. Stop drinking. Behave. He sprinkled more than a few four-letter words on top of those orders.

And that's when the bomb went off.

Aftershock

True, I wasn't a big fan of string quartets. But not to the extent that I thought they should be blown up.

Unfortunately, that's exactly what happened in the ballroom. A small explosive had been placed in the corner right behind the musical group and it blew the Bach out of them. Since the musicians took the brunt of the blast, nobody else in the room was hurt, except for an aging social x-ray who was standing nearby, luxuriating in the cultural lift the chamber music was providing. She was thrown to the ground by the explosion and her wig went flying to the side, leaving what was underneath completely exposed. I was unfortunate enough to get a good look—the top of her head resembled Voyager 2's snapshots of the surface of Jupiter. Luckily, aside from the indignity of having her nearly bald pate exposed, it looked like she only suffered a few minor cuts and bruises.

The bomb was a small plastic explosive, which is how it evaded the metal detector. It was clearly meant to cause more shock and awe than actual damage. It also brought the fundraiser to a premature end— Senator Eddie said a few perfunctory words about how violence wasn't going to stop his "campaign of ideas" and asked everyone to remain calm and stay put until the police gave the go-ahead for all of us to leave.

That took a while, because, when the men and women in blue arrived, they announced their intention to search and question every single one of the guests and there were about 500 of us in the room.

Fortunately, they started with the VIPs at the head table, and that exclusive group included me and the kid. We were able to leave fairly quickly as a result, which was good, because I was concerned about Eydie, alone and caged back in the hotel room. We walked out past Duds, who was not looking happy about having his big, expensive event result in a minor catastrophe.

But there was one more injury to deal with that night.

When we finally got back to the room, it was after midnight, and a distraught Eydie had somehow bashed her way through the caged front of the crate I had put her in. She had a little cut on her forehead, but it wasn't too bad. She whined and jumped at me for about ten minutes until she finally calmed down. Meanwhile, the kid listened to all the voicemails left on the phone by the hotel management regarding complaints about the loud barking and whining. As usual, Eydie wasn't fit for civilized company, even when she only happened to be in the same building as that company.

I had a hunch she would be sitting out the next trip.

The next day, we drove back to Virginia Beach and the day after that, the kid and I were back on the patio of stately Davidson Manor, still feeling a little shell-shocked. We had been following the news carefully and they still hadn't found the mad bomber. Perhaps I should say enthusiastic bomber. Or disillusioned bomber. Who knew the person's mood?

"The cellist was killed, y'know," I said idly. "His name was Joshua James. He wrote screenplays on the side."

"Screenplays? What are you talking about?"

"It was on the internet. Thought it was an interesting factoid. Anyway, the other three are in critical condition."

"They were so close to the blast, I'm surprised any of them survived," the kid said. Then he glanced at his phone that was sitting on the table between us for the ten thousandth time. "I feel bad for them, but at least it didn't have anything to do with us for a change."

"Well, if somebody's targeting the campaign, it's gonna have something to do with us. They're not calling off the next two events, they're just beefing up security."

"They'll probably have bomb-sniffing dogs. That's good. It's their problem, not ours, Max." He glanced at the phone again.

"Augustine Bravino," I said almost to myself.

"What about him?"

"He's not too fond of the candidate. And he's crazy enough to do something about it. He could've easily sneaked in the explosive in one of those video equipment bags."

"He didn't strike me as the master planner type."

"Then maybe his puppet is the brains behind the operation."

The kid's phone began to buzz. He grabbed it quickly as I saw a text pop up on the screen, which was apparently what the kid was waiting so impatiently for. He read the text and laughed.

"Who's that? Your new friend?"

PMA gave me a look. "What friend?"

"I saw you talking to somebody for a long time in the ballroom the other night. He was a cutie."

The kid quickly texted back. "He's a nice guy, so what?"

"If he's so nice, why was he there supporting that weasel?"

"It's his parents. He goes because he thinks these things are hilarious."

"Oh dear God. Well, at least he must be rich. Of course, you are too. So fuck you both."

I heard the buzz of another text coming in on the kid's phone. Seconds later, the kid was tapping out his response.

"What's his name?" I asked.

"Colin Burian."

"Colin Bureau?"

"B-U-R-I-A-N. Burian."

More texting.

"Does he want to meet me?" I asked. "Many people do."

"He might be at the L.A. fundraiser too. So, if you do meet him, try not to be an asshole."

"I always try, but I don't always succeed."

The kid was no longer listening. He was in full texting mode. Love was in the air. Or lust. It was hard to tell the difference at his age.

I went inside as the kid was much more interested in his phone than me. There, I caught Angela heading for the door. She told me she was going shopping with a friend and that made me glad, as I didn't think she had been out and about much in recent months. She wasn't as upset about the bombing as I thought she might be. Maybe because it didn't seem to be about me for a change and no ugliness had followed us home. She and the kid were both of a mind that whatever crap was going on, we would all survive it as long as we kept our heads down.

I wasn't as sanguine about the situation.

I went into the home office and sat down at the desktop. Eydie curled up in a ball at my feet. I started scouring the internet to see if there was any new information. There wasn't, just a little more info about Joshua James's screenplays. One was about a private island where rich guys kept women prisoner so they could rape them at their leisure. Guess that one wouldn't be made into a Hallmark movie.

But there was much more important news out there in that beloved World Wide Web. In the aftermath of the bombing, Senator Eddie and his colleagues were beating the drum against the violent terrorists that were getting away with murder. It was a genius move. They were building on Trump's tirades against the so-called "Radical Left," but without having the messy downside of having to defend Nazis and the Klan. By refusing to cancel future events, Senator Eddie looked like a brave and noble culture warrior to the conservative media instead of a small and stupid nut like Trump. That boded well for his political future.

After catching up on Senator Eddie's world, I moved on to my own and checked my email, which I hadn't done since before the fundraiser. I didn't exactly have a lot of correspondence going, but my brother Alan and I had gone back and forth a few times since I let him know I was alive and kicking. He had a lot of time on his hands. He had retired sometime during the ten months I was gone and was spending his spare hours poking around in our family history. Sure enough, he had emailed again, passing on the results of his DNA test, which he had arranged through one of those ancestry websites that let you know if you had any black sheep...or yellow or red or brown ones...in your family tree.

Well, it turned out our lineage was so white, it gleamed.

Almost half of the DNA was Western European, with most of the remaining originating in Scandinavia. Now THAT was Caucasian overdrive. Even though I knew I had a different father than Alan, I had little doubt that my DNA was similar to his. Daddy Andy didn't strike me as having anything but pure white in his blood.

Alan had also traced the family back on our mother's side all the way back to a region in the Ukraine where, apparently, our great-grandfather had died in 1945. Alan went on to say that this particular region had been strongly pro-Germany during World War II and that the Russians had not been kind to its people after it ended. Apparently, there was a lot of slaughtering of the Friends of Adolph after der Fuhrer had split the scene, according to Alan, who went on to say people didn't know about the atrocities done to Germans in the postwar era.

Wait a second. His takeaway from that whole World War II thing was, he felt sorry for the *Germans?* I knew he was fascinated with the Nazis when he was a kid, but this was a little...odd. I knew people whose grandparents had to flee their homeland of Germany in the 1930's because senseless hatred had driven them out of their homes. My sympathy went more their way.

The rest of my emails were spam and garbage. So, I went and did some Googling on Duds, who I hadn't really bothered to check out until then. There wasn't much to find, except that he had always worked for extreme right-wing candidates and he was a rising star in that sphere. I could see why Senator Eddie was an important catch for him. Who didn't want to be attached to a potential President?

But I couldn't find out much about the man behind the walrus stomach, because Duds didn't seem to do any social media. I couldn't find a Twitter or Facebook account, so I couldn't dig out any fun personal facts. But those kinds of guys always want to spew their bullshit opinions on social media, or at least promote their candidates or causes.

So why the low profile?

I mentally shrugged and took on one last internet task. The bombing. Did anyone have a grip on what that had been all about, beyond the usual insane conspiracy theories? If they did, I couldn't find a word about it. The FBI was on the case, but so far, they didn't have anything. If they did, they weren't talking. That meant whoever did it was still out there. And what did that mean for the next fundraiser in L.A.?

I didn't have time to think about it. Because I was suddenly clutching my chest and gasping for air.

L.A.

Flying really sucks.

I'm not going to launch into a whole horrible stand-up routine about cramped airline seats giving me cramps (ha, ha) or about how checking baggage costs more than the flight (hee, hee), but, Jesus, airlines have really gone to the dark side over the past decade or so. Somewhere along the way, they figured out how to charge you for every single little thing except breathing…but, even then, I understand there are some talks going on about opening a premium oxygen section (chortle, chortle).

The kid and I were on our way to the Los Angeles fundraiser, which I couldn't believe was still a thing. After the New York bombing, I thought maybe Senator Eddie and his pals might take a little breather while law enforcement figured out who was trying to blow them up, but no, Howard gave the kid a call and let him know the event was going forward.

So, that morning before dawn, I kissed Angela and the dog goodbye in that order, and we headed for the Richmond airport. I had that foggy, pinched feeling in my head I always got when I didn't get enough sleep, but knew it would pass once I had a few Coke Zero SUGARS on the plane, providing they actually stocked that shit.

But I couldn't bitch too much about flight conditions or my semi-exhausted state. At least I was still breathing.

I was pretty sure what I had a few days before was either a mild heart attack or a warning sign that a bigger one was on the way. But I kept my mouth shut about it. That was why I stayed seated in the Davidson home office for about a half-hour after it hit, trying to hold it together and not let anyone know I was experiencing anything out of the ordinary. Yeah, anybody with any sense would have told me to hightail it to the doctor or even the Emergency Room. Sense, however, wasn't welcome in this particular situation.

The fact was, I had to come through on the fundraisers or Angela would never be rid of big fat Duds, the mountain who walked like a man. Any health issue, real or not, would be perceived by the dear boy as a scam to get out of my end of the deal. Besides, within a few minutes of the attack, the pain in my chest was gone and I was okay. So, as long as I could function, the doctors could wait. Who the hell knew what they would do with me if I showed up for an exam? They might send me right into surgery and that would fuck up my obligations to Duds.

I knew whatever was wrong had to be the result of the ordeal of getting out of the Community. After all, it changed my hair color. But I couldn't obsess about it. I had to take it easy and follow through on what I had to do. So not a word to Angela, the kid, even the dog. It was okay, I was good at not talking. The guy who I thought was my dad taught me how to never share feelings when I was just a lad. Well done, pretend pops.

A few hours later, we were circling LAX. I had been to Los Angeles a few times during my very non-storied CIA career. And three things always hit me about the sprawl that called itself a city—it was (1) sunny, (2) brown and (3) filled with freeways that were, in turn, filled with cars. Okay, so Joan Didion had a much more nuanced view of the place, but I hadn't spent enough time there to be a real authority on it.

"You ever been here before?" I asked the kid.

"When I was pretty young. With Mom."

"Disneyland?" I asked.

He nodded. "And that Berry Farm place. My dad loves theme parks."

"Especially ones with berries, I bet. There's a man who loves fruit." I sighed. "I'll be glad when these fucking fundraisers are over."

"Me too. Then maybe we can get back to having a normal life."

"Don't know what one of those are like," I replied. "And I have a hunch I never will."

"Jesus, Max, stop talking like you're about to die."

He was right. I had to stop talking like that. And I had to stop thinking like that. Most of all, I had to stop feeling like that.

This, the second of the three fundraisers, was happening at the Intercontinental Hotel in Century City. Century City was a made-up metropolis packed with high-rises and shops that butted up against the Fox movie studio. As a matter of fact, the land it was built on used to *be* the Fox movie studio—more specifically, the backlot, where producers could pretend they were filming everywhere from Amarillo to Asia. Then, starting in the mid-1950s, more and more moviegoers became captivated by that newfangled television technology, leaving the studios to crash and burn. Fox sold off its massive backlot to developers and lo, Century City was born.

I was reading up on the history of the place on my phone as the kid and I took an Uber to the hotel, where Howard had a room reserved for us. We, of course, just had to pay for it.

"Hey, did you know all this land used to belong to Tom Mix?" I asked.

The kid was too busy texting and receiving to pay attention. Every other second, his phone buzzed like a jammed doorbell.

"Who?" he finally said.

"Tom Mix," I said. "The silent movie cowboy star. He owned all this land and then Fox bought it from him."

PMA was already texting again.

"Who you writing to? Your new boyfriend? What's his name? Colin the Bureau?"

"Colin *Burian*," he said with a little snarl. "Yeah, he's gonna be at the thing tomorrow."

"What do we know about young Colin?" I asked.

"I already told you, his parents are bigtime donors to 'the cause.'"

"The cause?"

"That's what Colin calls it. He knows they're full of shit."

"And he thinks they're funny, right?"

"Yeah. He likes to Snapchat to his friends about all the horrible things everyone says."

"Living ironically then."

"Hey, that's what he calls it," he said to me with a pleased smile. "Living ironically." For a moment, I was worth something. For a moment, I was in sync with Colin the Bureau.

"Tom Mix lived a little ironically," I said. "The first larger-than-life cowboy hero. Played the part to the hilt. Did you know he was a pallbearer at Wyatt Earp's funeral?"

Too late. The kid was texting again. I was worthless again.

That night, I didn't see hide nor hair of the kid. He dressed up for a high-end dinner with Colin the Bureau while I dressed down for a room service burger, Jack from the mini-bar and some more real-life Donald Trump nightmares courtesy of CNN. Around 11 p.m. I finally gave up on PMA's return. So, I took a couple of Angela's Xanax that she loaned me and crashed in my queen bed, while his remained unoccupied.

The next morning, he texted me and said he would meet me that night at the fundraiser, which was downstairs in the hotel's Grand Salon Ballroom. I texted back that it couldn't work like that, I was supposed to be a mental case and he was supposed to be my handler. He returned fire with an unhappy emoji that resembled my face at that moment. Then he sent one more text a few minutes later, saying he'd come back to the room before the fundraiser and pick me up.

Then I got one more text. Only it wasn't from the kid. It was from Augustine Bravino, back to bedevil me with enigmatic warnings.

> *tonite will be bad b-ware*

I wrote back.

> *Beware of what?*

A few moments later...

> *the promised one wil be born & YOU arennt safe*

The promised one? What the hell. I texted back.

> *Will the promised one get wet from the white rain?*

It was a few more minutes before his reply arrived:

> *b-ware*

Well, that explained everything.

So it was, with hours to kill and no one to kill them with, that I found myself wandering around the Century City Mall, watching the well-to-do cart around their shopping bags full of whatever, wondering if Augustine Bravino's incoherent text-babbling added up to anything.

And that's when I turned a corner and came face to face with Kevin Germano.

"Bowman?" he said, eyeing the white pile of hair on top of my head. I didn't even explain. I was at the point where I wanted to tattoo the circumstances of my new hair color on my forehead, so everybody could read it for themselves.

"Kev," I said, looking him over. He was tan, rested and ready. But I wasn't sure for what. Maybe it had something to do with the guy he was with. Equally fit and in his thirties, this brown-haired brown-eyed hunk was Hollywood on two legs. Everything he wore was the finest casual wear available. Which meant I had to mentally question how casual it all really was.

"You're Max Bowman?" exclaimed the friend, who then turned to Kevin. "I have GOT to do his story."

Kev put a hand up to his companion. "Cool it, Robert." Back to me. "Max, this is Robert Thickle, he's a screenwriter."

"That means he's a waiter!" I said in my idiot voice. "On TV shows, that's a joke."

Robert gave me a puzzled look. Kev abruptly told him he needed a few minutes alone with me. Robert shuffled off feeling a bit abandoned, while Kev and I ended up at a back table in the food court. He had a latte, I had a Coke Zero SUGAR.

Kev, as usual, got right down to business. "You don't have to put on your simpleton act for me, Bowman. Patrice filled me in on what's going on."

I exhaled with relief. It was harder playing dumb than it should've been and I was glad I could relax.

"You do still care," I said. "By the way, Patrice Plotkin is a minor gem."

"A major gem, you can trust her."

"So, what are you doing here? I figured you for better than letting your mind melt in the California sun."

"It wasn't my idea to leave the Agency," he grumbled. "Now I'm getting overpaid to be an 'advisor' to bronzed bimbos like Robert."

"In other words," I pressed, "it's a professional association, not a personal one?"

"Never mind me," Kev said, ducking the question. "What the fuck are you doing helping out Eddie di Pineda?"

"It's a deal I made with Dudley DeCosta. You know Duds?"

"I know he's so deep in the shit it's coming out of his ears." Pause. "Jeremy here?"

"Yeah, he's busy with his own bimbo."

Kevin tried to appear happy for him. But it was clear he wasn't. "So many things went wrong..." he finally said.

"Find a thing that went right and I'll give you a dollar," I replied.

He grilled me about the Community. I told him what I knew and he took it in with a startling eagerness. Everything about that place was a level above his formerly sky-high security clearance, so being able to find out about something Agency-related that he didn't already know about was apparently a gift from the gods. More than anything, he was stunned to know the Community really existed and even more flummoxed by the fact that I had managed to get out.

It was my turn for questions. "So...you have any idea who bombed the fundraiser in New York?"

"Nope. And neither does anybody in the Agency who still talks to me. How about you?"

"I don't know. And I'd like to find out, because I have to survive two more of these things. And even though I really want to stay out of whatever insane bullshit is going on, I keep picking up bits and pieces of things."

"Like what?"

"Well, you know anything about something big they're building in Montana? Or an outfit called The Eugene Group?"

"The Eugene Group? No. But Montana…that's where Dark Sky is. You know that. And they're flush with government cash again. A lot of activity up there, but the CIA was walled off from all of it. Strictly a Pentagon deal. But I do know they're building and whatever it is, it's really expensive. Billions of dollars disappearing up there, just like that."

He snapped his fingers a little too close to my face.

"How about Andrew Wright? I'm told he's still among the living, even though I now distinctly remember shooting him in the face."

"Another thing they weren't talking to me about, Bowman. Ever since January 20th, they made sure I was out of the loop until I was finally pushed out the door. A lot of us were purged, most of us over the past few months." He gave me a look. "Your color doesn't look good, Bowman. You have a check-up since you got out?"

"It's the white hair. It makes the rest of me look pale. You enjoying Hollywood?"

"I enjoy being useful, Bowman. But I don't know what the hell use I am out here. Yeah, they pay me plenty, but all I do is hold the hands of fucking idiot writers. They've writing all these shows and movies about the CIA…and yet, they have absolutely no idea what they're talking about."

"Yeah, I know a guy like that."

Speaking of those guys, at the same second, we both spotted Robert Thickle the screenwriter lurking nearby. Kev waved him over. Then Robert started in on me again about wanting to write my story. He thought Michael Keaton would be perfect. Well, we agreed on that anyway. I said nothing, because I was back to playing dumb, then got up to go. Kev got up with me to shake my hand goodbye. There was a lot in that shake and a lot in his eyes. He had a bad feeling, I could see it. But neither of us acknowledged it.

I had a fundraiser to get to.

It was 45 minutes before we were due to get down to the ballroom. I was sitting all by myself in my underwear in the hotel room, enjoying a quick glass of Jack to calm my nerves, when PMA finally burst into the room.

"You're not even dressed?"

I looked up at him with more than mild surprise. "How can I compete with *that?*"

The kid was looking sharper than a new razor. He was wearing an amazing tuxedo that even I could tell was something special, and I was far from a fashionista. He held up his arm so I could see the gleam on the end of his sleeve.

"Diamond cufflinks. Awesome, right?" He was beaming with pride. "This is all Stefano Ricci," he added, spreading out his arms so I could take in all his sartorial splendor.

"Stefano Ricci? Doesn't he make frozen pizza?"

"No, Max, he doesn't. He's the guy who outfits Russian oligarchs, Middle Eastern oil billionaires…"

"Oh. Rich assholes."

"Yes, Max, okay, rich assholes. But Colin is the son of rich assholes and we're the same size, so he loaned me his spare tux."

"Spare tux? I don't even have a spare tire anymore, if you don't count my gut."

"Look at this. I'm wearing a $7500 tuxedo. And $3000 crocodile loafers."

I suddenly felt bad for the aquatic reptile whose afterlife consisted of covering the kid's stinky feet, the stench of which probably still permeated the underground shelter. "Wonderful. Now, let me put on my Men's Wearhouse tux, so I can look suitably pathetic next to you."

I went to put on my low-rent monkey suit, while the kid stayed standing and watched TV. I had a hunch that Colin the Bureau told him not to sit down and wrinkle the pants. After all, that was how Sinatra handled his tux before showtime.

I didn't know what to make of the Colin situation. On the one hand, I was happy the kid made a love connection. On the other hand, I didn't trust anybody. The NYC bombing was fresh in my brain, as I was sure it would be in everyone else's at that night's event.

I didn't mention to the kid that I saw Kev. I saw no reason to disrupt his ebullient mood. I saw no reason to disrupt anything at all, as a matter of fact.

I just wanted to get home to my girl and my dog.

Fundraiser 2

As the elevator took us down to the second floor where the ballrooms were located, I reminded the kid we weren't supposed to mingle. Duds had been insistent on that point last time around and I didn't want any trouble with him. So, I said, we should just make a beeline for the head table and avoid any conversation along the way. The kid nodded.

But there was one conversation we weren't going to avoid.

As the elevator doors opened, I spotted Kev, dressed in his own Men's Wearhouse suit-and-tie special, hanging out in the foyer. Disruption was inevitable. When the kid saw him, he blinked and froze in place like an elegant popsicle. I had to gently shove his well-dressed ass out of the elevator, because a very impatient couple behind us wanted to continue on down to the lobby. That's when Kevin saw us.

"Hey, Jeremy," he said quietly. The kid looked gobsmacked and sandbagged.

"Why are you here?" I asked, with more than a little panic.

Kevin turned to look at the steady stream of well-fed donors heading for the metal-detectors that were manned by many, many security personnel. Nobody was paying attention to us at the moment, so he led us to a quiet corner before somebody did.

"I'm just hanging around. In case."

"How did you know we were going to be here?" asked the kid, his voice trembling.

"Bowman didn't tell you? We ran into each other at the mall this afternoon."

The kid gave me an irritated glance and turned back to Kevin. "What are you doing in L.A.?"

"I'm an advisor on some movie and TV projects. That's how I'm paying alimony and child support."

"Yeah. I heard about the break-up."

An awkward moment.

"Jeremy, I…"

"Look," I interjected, "Let's postpone the drama, we've got to get into the ballroom before Duds comes out looking for us. And Kev, I don't think you're really needed. As you can see, there's a small army outside the ballroom to handle threats. Might as well head back to your bronzed buddy."

"Bronzed buddy?" asked the kid. Oh no. Why did I have to be such a town gossip?

"When I saw Bowman, I was here with a screenwriter, talking through a plotline." Kev shot me a dirty look. "And he had a nice tan."

"Look, Kev," I insisted, "I'm serious. If someone recognizes you…"

"Nobody's going to recognize me, Bowman. If I just hang around out here, nobody'll suspect anything. There's another event in the smaller salon down the hall, so nobody's going to know who I'm with."

"That's a lot of nobodies, Kev," I said.

The kid spotted somebody else over Kev's shoulder. He broke into a little fuck-you smile as he waved. "Colin!"

Kev and I both turned to see Colin the Bureau coming out of the elevator. Colin saw all of us and smiled an amazing smile filled with gleaming teeth. His tuxedo was somehow even more impressive than the one he had lent the kid. Which made sense. After all, the kid was wearing the spare. PMA went off to join up with Colin and I turned to say goodbye to a crestfallen Kev.

"Why don't you go take in a movie, Kev," I said. "Maybe there's something with the Rock playing at the mall. We'll be fine."

"I'm going to make sure you two are fine, Bowman. It's the least I can do. And don't worry, I'm prepared."

He slowly opened his jacket to show me his shoulder holster.

"Steve McQueen is *Bullitt*," I nodded, completely giving up on changing his mind. "See you at the afterparty." I walked away towards the metal detectors.

Inside the Grand Salon Ballroom, there were a few hundred people milling about, many of whom I recognized from the New York event. For example, Doug Daytona had once again brought his video crew, which for some reason still included the batshit crazy Augustine Bravino. Our eyes met across the room, but not like in an old Cary Grant movie where man and woman instantly fall in love with a single glance. No, it was more like the original *Dracula*, when the Count met Renfield and knew he had found a man who would be content to eat flies for a living.

"Hey Retardo, where's your boyfriend?" Duds was looming large behind me with Howard following in his wake.

"He talks to Colin," I replied in my idiot voice.

Duds gave the evil eye to the kid and Colin the Bureau conversing a few tables away.

"I go to the big table," I added.

"Yeah," Duds said to me, "Good boy. You go to big table and you stay at big table. And Jeremy better be a good boy too." He turned to Howard. "C'mon, Senator Eddie's gonna be here any second."

Duds stomped off. Howard gave me a pitying look but followed his lord and master.

As I headed to the front of the room, where the big table was spectacularly set, I noticed that the music was a pre-recorded feed of soft jazz. Guess it was hard to recruit another string quartet after the last one got blown to bits. Besides, if there were any mad bombers around that day, the soft jazz would surely melt their brains before they could detonate any devices. Did I mention I hated soft jazz? To me, it sounded like if oatmeal was an audio file.

As I continued on my way, I saw, out of the corner of my eye, Augustine angling to cut me off, with Doug Daytona close on his heels to cut off Augustine.

"Max Bowman!" Augustine yelled. A few heads turned. Shit.

"I go to big table," I mumbled as I kept walking. But ignoring him wasn't going to do the job, because I could hear him scampering after me.

"I have more news," he whispered behind me. "The Promised One. He will usher in the new age. They speak of Him in awe."

"I go big table," I replied. But suddenly Doug Daytona was in front of me. It took me a moment to figure out he wasn't out to stop Augustine. No, Dougie was also after a piece of my time.

"Max," he hissed, looking around nervously.

"I go big table," I said again insistently. Why would no one let me go big table?

"Hey man," he said quietly with an edge of panic. "Please don't listen to Augustine. And please don't repeat anything he says."

"Are you afraid, Dougie?" I asked innocently. "Why you afraid?" I knew I was getting sloppy with how low my I.Q. was supposed to be. I was suddenly sounding like I was three years old. I had to get back up to at least six or seven.

"Look, man, just please. Don't repeat anything he says. This is very important, Max. Very important. Do you understand me?"

That's when Morris the dog puppet suddenly popped up in my face. "Don't listen to him, Max Bowman. So many lives at stake! So many!"

Doug ripped the puppet off Augustine's hand and shoved it in his pocket. "That's it, Augustine!" he seethed. "No more puppets! I'm not putting up with your shit anymore! This is your last gig with me! You're finished!"

Augustine shook his head vehemently. "No. Oh, no, no, Doug Daytona. You cannot fire me, they told you…"

"I don't care what they told me. This is my last gig for them too."

Oh boy. This was getting intense. And I was not getting in the middle of it.

"I go big table," I quickly said and then I finally went big table. The kid was already there, sitting where he was supposed to be sitting. Of course, they put us on the very end, since we were the wild cards Duds didn't want to be played. Which is why I saw his name printed on the card at the setting next to mine. He would be blocking us from contact with anybody important.

"Did Duds break up you and Colin the Bureau?" I asked, as I watched Senator Eddie arrive and begin to work the crowd, with Duds watching his every move.

The kid nodded. "We're going to hook up afterwards." A beat. "How come you didn't tell me you saw Kevin today?"

"Didn't have much time," I lied. "I had to get dressed, remember?"

"Well, I'm fine about it. You don't have to worry. I mean, the guy's a loser."

"Sure, kid, sure. Hey, where's Colin the Bureau's parents? Show me where they're sitting."

"Uh…no, haven't met them yet. I think he was going to introduce me, then that fat ball of shit…"

"You *think* he was going to introduce them? He didn't even point them out or anything?"

"No, they're probably not here yet."

I sighed. So much felt wrong that I didn't know what to pay attention to. Then Howard showed up in front of my face, standing on the other side of big table.

"Max, I just want to say I'm sorry. I know Duds is…well, he's Duds."

"Yes, and I'm Max."

"I know, Max," he said nodding sadly. "I know." Then he turned to the kid. "Jeremy, as you can see, we've got a strong security presence here. We even ran background checks on all the help and patted them all down. So I don't want you or Max to worry this time around."

The kid nodded quietly. After all we had been through with Howard, PMA trusted him about as much as he'd trust his mother with a bottle of fentanyl. But it was fine. Howard had run out of things to say, so he simply nodded back and walked away, but not before giving me one last look and one last pitying headshake. I didn't really enjoy pity, even when what I was being pitied for wasn't even real.

Unfortunately, most of the attendees were giving me that very same pitying look—they seemed to be taking turns wandering up towards the head table, stopping and peering at me as though I were some fucking three-legged gazelle hobbling around in a pen at the zoo. I couldn't take it, but there was nothing else to do during cocktail time, so I stopped staring back at the spectators and tried to see if there was anything else of interest going on in the ballroom.

And that's when I noticed the fidgety waiter.

Howard had just told the kid they had checked out all the help, but this guy's aura screamed "Prime Suspect" for any horrible crime that might be about to happen. Skinny, clean-shaven, maybe Indian, maybe something else, this twenty-something had a film of sweat covering his forehead and a shaky hand taking water glasses from a tray filled with them and placing them on tables. His hand was shaking so much I actually saw little splashes from the glasses hitting the linen tablecloths.

I was staring so intently that the kid turned to see what I was so fixated on. Being a gold star student of the Max Bowman School of Almost-Good Detectives, he too noticed the fidgety waiter and gave me a curious look. I returned it, then quickly turned back to the ongoing fidgety waiter drama, which had suddenly grown more interesting— because Colin the Bureau came out of nowhere to approach the sweaty server.

I squinted and bobbed and weaved. The room was growing so crowded and so many people were passing between me and the interaction I wanted to observe that I kept losing sight of it. And whoops, thanks to some doddering old donor who took a millennium to cross in front of them, I maybe missed something important— because Colin's hand was quickly retracting from the vicinity of the fidgety waiter's body. Colin himself then instantly turned on his heels and disappeared back into the moneyed and mingling throng.

"What was that?" I said quietly to the kid.

"What was what?"

"That fucking fidgety waiter and your friend. Something happened there."

"Max, I…I don't know what you're getting at. Colin saw the waiter, saw he was a freak, got spooked and just turned away from him. That's all."

I frowned. Maybe the kid was right.

More time went by, with each minute seeming like about 6000 hours. The undignified dignitaries, by which I mean Senator Eddie, his lovely blonde and blue-eyed wife, Duds and a few other political hacks, finally took their seats at big table. Duds plopped his huge ass down next to my comparatively microscopic one and gave me a look of disdain so piercing it was breathtaking. It punctured my soul and left it for dead.

After dinner, my nerves kicked in, not from any imminent danger— one of the senior serving staff members had finally escorted the fidgety waiter out of the ballroom after his attempt to refill a water glass from a pitcher resulted in a drowned piece of rubber chicken, so he was no longer a concern. No, my stress was about having to get up and address this loathsome crowd. I had to position myself properly on the brain-damaged scale and still sound incredibly pumped for Senator Eddie, and that balance was going to be tricky.

Duds was up first. He stepped up to the mike and lectern placed at the halfway point of the long table, made some jokes that would be offensive to just about everyone else in the world except for the people in this ballroom, then began bullshitting about how he appreciated everyone's support (i.e. money). Then, he began introducing someone else.

And that's when I saw the fidgety waiter burst through the double doors that led to the kitchen area.

I looked at the security personnel. They gave him a mild look of interest, but recognized him from before. So they didn't see any problem. After all, they had checked him out and searched him, according to Howard. No threat, right? Maybe he'd spill some more water. That was the hotel's bad, not theirs.

So suddenly, I was the only guy looking at him, because everyone else was paying attention to Duds as he droned on.

Which meant I was the only guy who saw Fidgety pull something out from behind him, presumably a something that was stashed in the waistband of his pants and covered by his server's jacket.

It was bright red. It looked like a toy. A toy gun.

He held it up and pointed it at the head table.

At Senator Eddie.

Those fine security folks were finally paying attention. But it was too late. The bright red toy gun fired in the direction of where Senator Eddie was seated. But Fidgety must have been fidgeting far too violently to shoot straight.

Because Senator Eddie's wife was suddenly screaming in pain as a big bloody stain began expanding across the chest of her lovely white formal gown.

Upside Down Anne Frank

Bedlam, of course, was the inevitable result of the shooting—pure, uncontainable bedlam.

The kid moved to get up. I stiff-armed him and kept him in his seat. First of all, if there was any more trouble, I didn't want him involved. Second of all, I wanted to be the calm *after* the storm—so I could keep my own stress under control and also watch what happened next.

And what happened next was that Fidgety ran back towards the double doors into the kitchen. And amazingly, security personnel couldn't get through the crowded table set-up quickly enough to take him down, so he actually made it through those doors without anyone getting anywhere close to stopping him.

There was noise from the kitchen. Then quiet.

Then a distant shot.

The kid wasn't going to sit still any longer. While the rest of the panicked crowd mingled in the ballroom, afraid to go anywhere where chaos might still be in play, he led me through a back emergency door that emptied out in a hallway. That hallway took us around the side of the ballroom to the reception area outside, near where the elevators were.

That's where we saw Kevin standing over Fidgety, who was writhing in pain. Kevin had his hands up, with pistol in one hand, and about fifteen security guys had their guns aimed at the two of them. One security guy took away Kevin's gun, while another one searched Fidgety.

"Holy shit. Kevin got him…" said the kid in awe. We moved closer.

"Plastic gun," said the one security officer, taking a weapon off Fidgety, who, I saw, had been shot in the leg by Kevin. Kevin was a pro. He knew if he only wounded the guy, you could get intel off him, even though, from what I could hear, Fidgety was just babbling about Senator Eddie being just a wee bit worse than the Anti-Christ. Kevin explained to the security guys that he was ex-CIA and he was meeting Jeremy Davidson there after the reception. He spotted the kid and waved him over.

I turned as some of the guests tried to exit the ballroom to see what had transpired, but the security guys kept them inside. In that clump of restrained humanity, I saw Colin the Bureau wearing a disapproving frown as he watched Kevin and the kid talking it up. Then he was herded back into the ballroom with the rest of the rich fucks.

I motioned to the kid, still with Kevin, still with all the other heroes with guns, that I was splitting. He gave me a quick nod of approval. I was close enough to the elevators to make it out without anyone raising a ruckus, I was tired and I wanted out. So, I got out.

Later, on the news, I watched as Mrs. Senator Eddie left too. With a sheet over her face.

Two fundraisers, two acts of violence, both committed with malevolent plastic. One person killed at each event. But the death of Mrs. Senator Eddie was going to cause a much bigger ripple in the political waters than that of a virtually unknown screenwriter-cellist. To me, it felt like war had just been declared.

And a couple of days later, back at stately Davidson Manor, the next skirmish occurred.

Augustine Bravino was running through the house, waving a gun and yelling for sanctuary.

I was on the computer in Angela's home office with Eydie in her usual spot by my feet, when I heard a ruckus and saw Augustine fly by with a pistol in his right hand. Even though he was running so fast he was almost a blur, he was still was easy to recognize. After all, Morris the dog was on his left arm.

I was momentarily stunned when he flew by the open office doorway—what now? What the hell now? But Eydie didn't take time to question. She was up and after him before I could stop her. Maybe she recognized her captor from the year before—or maybe she didn't. It didn't really matter, of course, since she hated everybody except me and Angela.

I got up and rushed into the hallway, bucking the tide of house staff coming at me, hurrying for the front door to get as far away from the mayhem as possible. Me, I hurried towards the mayhem, because I had to worry about my dog getting shot by a psycho puppet master. From down the hall, I heard growling and yelling and then another shot or two and then the sound of a ton of glass crashing. I raced in that direction, but when I finally got to the living room, the quiet was deafening.

I looked around the room until I saw the kid looking quizzically from the patio through what was left of the glass door—apparently he had been outside texting with Kev or Colin the Bureau or whoever was winning his heart that day. The bullet that had shattered the door was enough to finally divert him from his text-storm. He stepped in over the broken glass scattered all over the floor.

"What the hell?" he asked helplessly.

I put my finger up to my lips, aka STFU, and I looked around. No sign of the dog. No sign of Augustine. The kid and I met each other in the middle of the room and stood shoulder to shoulder as we scanned the immediate area.

"It's Augustine Bravino," I explained quietly to the kid. "And as you might have guessed, he's got a gun. The dog went after him...but..."

The kid shot me a look. "Is she...?"

I didn't want to think about the end of that question. We continued to search the room with our eyes.

And then a familiar face slowly emerged from behind the couch. But it wasn't an actual human face. It was the face of Morris the Dog, Augustine's homemade friend.

"Helllooooo..." Morris said.

"Are those Legos in his mouth?" the kid asked.

"Hello, Morris. Where is my dog?" I asked in my stupid voice that still had more than a hint of rage.

"Safe and secure, I would never harm my own kind, dear sir."

Morris cocked its head at us. The kid walked over and ripped the ungodly canine creation off Augustine's arm. Not the smartest move for the kid—and the results reflected it. Augustine jumped up on his feet and poked his gun directly into PMA's face. To do that, however, he had to let go of Eydie, who he had evidently captured and had been muzzling with his free hand. Not the smartest move for Augustine, as Eydie went after him with all the doggie fury she could muster—which distracted him long enough for the kid to take away his pistol.

I walked over and pulled Eydie off Augustine as he fell back to the floor, right beside his puppet's empty carcass. Eydie had broken some skin on the freak's arm, but nothing serious. The dog was more hat than cattle.

"You made a big mess in here, Augustine," I said. "Big mess."

"I...I had nowhere to go, friend Max. Nowhere. They were going to blame me. For the bomb. They were going to blame me."

He began to cry. The kid pulled him up on his feet, then yanked him over to a chair, where he let him fall into a sitting position. I thoughtfully picked up the puppet and tossed it on his lap.

"They?" I asked.

"The beasts of the past are alive again. They devoured my grandfather and now they will devour me."

I sat down on the couch across from him. The kid stayed standing.

"What are you talking about?" PMA asked.

"I've heard too much. The bomb that went off in New York, it was planted in an equipment bag I carried into the ballroom. They want to frame me."

"Augustine," I said, "I don't think they'd go to all that trouble. I think they'd just kill you if they wanted to get rid of you. They don't get that complicated."

Augustine lowered his head and began to weep as the kid looked at me in shock.

"You're supposed to be dumb," PMA said accusingly.

"I'm tired of keeping up the act for this clown," I said to the kid. "He probably didn't even know I was acting. He's in his own little world most of the time."

As if to prove my point, Augustine didn't seem to hear our exchange. He wiped away his tears and looked back up at us.

"They chased my grandfather all through Poland."

"Poland? What, was it a pogrom?" I asked in confusion. "'Bravino' doesn't sound all that Jewish."

"My mother's side. They chased her father...now they will chase me all over America!" he shrieked.

Eydie barked. I shushed her.

"They're after Jews?" the kid asked.

"Augustine, my friend Howard works for Eddie. And he's a Jew."

"Oh, it isn't just Jews," Augustine said casually. "It's everybody."

"Even Methodists?" I asked.

"The joke will not be funny when the punchline arrives, my friend."

The kid and I exchanged skeptical looks.

"Augustine," I said, "Let's get into specifics. You were texting me all this shit about Andrew Wright and waters rising and white rain…. how about you give me a little more than catchphrases?"

"I will not say more. There is no safe place for me. As it has ever been, there is no safe place," he continued to whine.

"Tell you what. You give up what you know, and I'll make a safe space for you. Just needs a little clean-up."

"No, Max," the kid sighed. "We're not putting him down in the shelter."

"We are. It's Anne Frank upside down. Instead of going up in the attic, the Jew goes down in the ground."

"The Jew goes down in the ground?' Jesus, Max."

"Jesus is not with me…" muttered Augustine.

"Look," I said to the kid, "Just get a couple of your mother's million-person staff down to the shelter to clean and Febreze the place," I said to the kid. "Or maybe get the whole million. It'll take a lot to get your stink out of there."

"Max…"

"C'mon, kid. He's harmless. Unlike the last psycho we put down there."

The kid shook his head and left, presumably to fulfill my request. I turned back to Augustine.

"Let me clarify a few things. First of all, how the hell did you get my cell phone number?"

"You rented a car before you came to Doug Daytona's office. You left your phone number there. They got it from their system."

Fucking Alamo Rent-A-Car. Davy Crockett died for their sins.

"Okay, so 'they' got my phone number, which means you got it from 'them.' Which means you're with 'them,' so why the hell are you so scared you ran here? I know they thought you might have done the bombing, but clearly, you didn't do the shooting. So what gives?"

Augustine shook his head. "I know what they want to do. And I know that they will do it."

"Do *what?*"

"You just have to know that they are going to do it, friend Max." He looked somewhere into the air. "The vibrations are obvious. And I'm not the only one who is scared. Doug Daytona. He is very scared because he has learned the truth as it exists. The fear walks with us. It is our eternal companion."

"Daytona looked spooked the other night, you're right about that. But again...*what are they going to do?*"

"Doug Daytona thought they would make him big. Famous. Doing documentaries. Getting on *60 Minutes.* Then he heard too much. We heard too much." He paused. And then finally, he said dreamily, "When the waters rise..."

Okay. This conversation wasn't going anywhere. I had to remind myself that I was trying to talk sense with a man who made a dog puppet with Lego teeth. Maybe if we put him down in the shelter, he'd calm down and start making things a little clearer.

Maybe.

I Did Nazi That Coming

Augustine was down in the shelter when Angela finally returned with a few hundred shopping bags. I exaggerate, but not by much—it had been a long time between mall visits. She gave me a kiss and went upstairs to put away her new wardrobe. I went outside with the dog for a smoke as I wondered if I should tell her about her new boarder. The kid came with me.

"We've put ourselves right back in the middle of the shit, Max. This isn't good."

I nodded as I blew out a cloud of smoke. "Should we let your mom in on this?"

"I don't know how she'd feel about hiding Jews," he said with an almost-laugh.

I gave him a look. "Come again?"

He shrugged it off. "Oh, my grandpa would go off on Jews once in a while. I think a little of it trickled down on her."

"Really? I don't get it," I said shaking my head violently. "I really don't get it. Why Jews? Why the hell do so many people hate them?"

"Hey, it's not me…"

"Seriously, what, that they're all about money? Shit, like no Christians are? I bet there are even a few money-grubbing Buddhists out there. I. Don't. Fucking. Get it."

"Grandpa was old school. You know, we'd be watching TV and he'd say, 'Why do so many blacks have shows now?'"

"Let's go for full disclosure. Did he use the word 'blacks' or perhaps a different term that's frowned upon in this day and age?"

The kid was quiet.

"Well," I sighed. "I guess he did hang out with Andrew Wright."

A pause.

"Is that it?" the kid asked.

"Is what it?"

"Andrew Wright. Is that why we've got a guy who talks through a dog puppet in the shelter?"

I took another drag on my cancer stick.

"Max, I need to know everything if this is going to work. C'mon."

"Have you heard anything from Duds or Howard? I mean, I assume the third fundraiser is going to be cancelled, since Mrs. Senator Eddie is dead."

"I've heard nothing."

"How about Kev?"

"Max, never mind about Kevin. This isn't about Kevin. This is about Andrew Wright. This is about your weird...weird thing with him. If I'm going to work with you on this shit, it's time you told me whatever it is you're not telling me."

I thought about it another moment. Then I decided it was time.

"Andrew Wright is my father."

Then I looked out past the trees in the backyard at the Atlantic Ocean and briefly wished I was at the bottom of it. I could feel PMA's eyes burning a hole in me. I bent down and let Eydie off her leash for a run around the yard.

"That's why he had your grandfather hire me in the first place, for the Dark Sky thing," I went on. "To see how I would do. He knew he was losing one son..."

"Herman..."

"So...he wanted to test me. And then maybe recruit me."

"I don't understand. How the hell can he be your father?"

"He put his penis in my mother's vagina, and eventually, through the process of friction, it stimulated his…"

"STOP. Max. This is fucking serious. Your father was a CIA agent, I thought…"

"The guy I thought was my father, yeah, he was. Look, I don't know exactly what happened…"

"When did you find this out?"

"On the way to Sedona, after you got shot. That's why I tried to kill him. He's obsessed with having a successor, someone who shares his magical DNA. If he's still alive, he's not going to leave me alone. It's why the shit keeps following me. He's the shit. And I'm still smelling his stink in the air."

I tossed away what was left of the cig. The kid looked lost, very lost.

"Blum. The piano player. He said you shot him in the head."

"But where in the head? Did it kill him? We don't know any of that, do we? Because Blum ran out into the night to save his own ass. Not that I blame him."

A beat. The earth turned a few degrees.

"What are we supposed to do?" PMA finally asked. "I've been texting Kevin…"

"Oh, you have?"

"I could tell him about this."

"He's in California and out of the agency, not much help. So I'm calling Patrice Plotkin."

"Who?"

"Patrice Plotkin. I told you about her, Kev sent her over when I tried to get his help before. She's not supposed to stick her neck out for me, nobody is, but maybe she'll have an idea about what to do with our puppet master down in the ground. Look, I don't want the shit to come to this house again. Not after last year. I'm gonna try to do everything I can to protect you and your mom."

The kid nodded. "Thanks, Max."

And then he hugged me. I stood there stiff as a board.

"You're not good at this, are you?" he asked.

"I was raised by wolves, kid. I was raised by wolves."

We went back into the house, where Angela was standing in the living room in a gorgeous new casual outfit, staring daggers at the busted patio door.

"Max!"

"Sorry, Angie. We had a visitor," I said. "Now you've got a Jew in the ground."

"WHAT?"

The kid jumped in. "Mom, it's this guy from the Eddie di Pineda fundraiser. He came here to hide out, so we put him in the shelter. But don't worry, Max is going to call the CIA to come get him."

"Was there a reason you called him a Jew?" she said to me.

"Because he is one. And he fears his own personal holocaust."

"Oh, Jesus," she immediately blurted out, "They always think somebody wants to kill them."

I looked at the kid. The kid winced.

"Well," she said defensively, "They do have a persecution complex."

"Must be from all the persecuting," I answered. "Look, he's scared and there is weird shit going on. I mean, the bombing, the shooting…"

"You're going to call the CIA. That's all I care about."

"I'm going to call the CIA."

She stared at the smashed patio door. "Everything gets messy. Everything."

"Patrice…it's Max Bowman."

There was a very light groan from the other side.

"I've got a Jew in the ground," I went on.

"A *what?*"

"A Jew in the ground."

"You know I'm Jewish, right?"

"Plotkin? Had a hunch. But I needed to get your attention, so I thought that opening line might do it."

"What is this about, Max? I don't have time."

"A man fled the di Pineda campaign and showed up here, afraid for his life. Says bad shit's going on over there."

"Bad shit? Do tell. Just a bombing and a shooting…"

"And maybe some anti-Semitism—this guy is afraid they're after him. We put him down in the bomb shelter here."

"At the Davidson property."

"Yes. This is the guy who insists Andrew Wright is alive. He works for Doug Daytona, remember, I told you about him, the guy who did the *60 Minutes* interview with me? But before that, he worked for the Blue Fire crew. Kidnapped my dog. Tried to kill me."

It's not often you can hear someone losing interest over the phone. But that's how intense the apathy was on the other end.

"He just sounds insane, Max. Even Jews can be insane, did you know that? He's probably got some kind of PTSD from what's been going on. Get him to a head doctor."

Awkward pause.

"So…I couldn't interest you into taking him into custody…or at least talking to him…getting his story…"

Another awkward pause.

"I mean, he's a Jew…you're a Jew…as for me, I wouldn't mind converting, I'm not locked into anything specific when it comes to God…"

Another awkward pause.

"Send me an invite to your bar mitzvah," she finally said, before hanging up.

Fine People

"Very fine people on both sides?" I exclaimed.

I turned to the kid, who was sitting in one of the other chairs in the home office, texting away. He ignored me.

"Trump really said that about a racist rally? That some of the racists were fine people?"

PMA nodded and kept texting.

"But, but…" I sputtered, and I didn't sputter all that often, "…they were holding signs saying, 'Jews Will Not Replace Us.' There were Neo-Nazis and Klan members and various other sons of bitches and bastards…"

"You missed a lot while you were eating ice cream in Florida," the kid said.

Seemed like I had.

All this shit about anti-Semitism that Augustine was spouting had me a little alarmed, so I decided to go a-googling to see if this was a thing. Seemed like it was. It was less than a year into Donald Trump's presidency and already everyone was comparing the country to Germany before you-know-who took over. Hate crimes of all kinds were on the rise as were crazy right-wing conspiracies blaming victims for victimizing those who victimized. While Trump was trying to make everybody afraid of Mexicans and Muslims, more and more very unpleasant white people were popping up and proving that perhaps Caucasians were a little more of an ongoing problem—at least the ones who had been stuffed nonstop with rabid racist propaganda and were happy to believe it. And in more and more cases, these folks accessorized with AR-15s, America's mass shooting weapon of choice.

"So maybe Augustine has a point?" I asked. "Or is it wrong to take the ravings of a man who talks to a dog puppet seriously?"

"Max, stop, I'm going back and forth with Kevin," the kid said impatiently. "Since that woman wouldn't help us...."

"Patrice Plotkin."

"Whatever, I'm trying to see if Kevin has any ideas."

"Does he?"

The kid put away his phone. "He's going to give it some thought."

"So, we're fucked."

"Kevin usually comes through," he said with a frown as he stared out the window.

"How is it between you two?"

"It's just business, Max."

I took a breath. "Okay, we don't need to talk about Kevin. But we need to talk about Colin the Bureau."

The kid turned back to me.

"I saw him and the waiter make contact. Right before the waiter shot Mrs. Senator Eddie."

"Make contact? What the hell does that mean?"

I reminded him about how I had seen them kind of bump into each other between donor tables and it looked like Colin had handed something off to him, but that I couldn't see clearly because of all the people and...

"Max, just stop. We talked about this at the time. You just don't like the guy and your brain is working overtime. They are not part of any plot."

"'They?' Who else are we talking about?"

The kid rolled his eyes, as if he let something slip he shouldn't have.

"Colin is gender-neutral," he said quietly. "They use 'they' for their pronoun."

"What?" I honestly had no idea what the hell he was talking about.

"Max, gender is more fluid now. You're cisgender, you identify with your birth sex."

"Um…yeah. And…?"

"Well, not everyone does. There are so-called men who identify as women and so-called women who identify as men. Then there are people like Colin who don't identify with either gender."

I wanted to look at a calendar. Seriously. I must have been in the Community for about 100 years if all this had just happened, along with vaping and Coke Zero SUGAR.

"So, he wants be called 'they.'"

"Some people use 'ze' and 'zir,'" the kid helpfully added.

"What and what?"

"Look, never mind…"

"No, wait, how do people know what pronoun to use? Do they wear signs around their necks? I didn't see one around Colin's."

"Max, I didn't expect you to get this. That's why I never brought it up."

"You're right, I don't get it. If I didn't feel like I was either gender, I would consider it a tie. The win would then go to whatever was between my legs. That would be my approach."

"Great, Max." The kid kept whatever torrent of abuse he wanted to unleash on me under wraps and looked out the window again. No wonder the country was so polarized. For God's sakes, everyone had a different reason just to hate me.

"Mom's worried," PMA finally said.

"I figured. She's probably afraid the Senator Eddie campaign's over for good. Which could mean Duds won't go through with the divorce."

The kid nodded. He was obviously worried too. But we had heard nothing from the di Pineda camp. Everyone there was too busy preparing to bury Senator Eddie's dead wife—when they weren't going on television to decry the violent element in this country that was determined to stop Senator Eddie's good and righteous campaign. They were transforming tragedy into opportunity, which gave me pause.

Actually, I had been given pause after the bombing at the first fundraiser. The cynical part of me thought maybe the campaign itself had planted the explosive, in order to victimize themselves and gain the sympathy of all those unpleasant white people I had been reading about minutes before. But this shooting went too far—a campaign doesn't usually try to assassinate its own candidate.

"One last fundraiser and this whole thing might have been over," said the kid. "Now, we've got a crazy man down in the shelter and who knows what that's going to bring our way..."

I thought a moment. And I realized something. "You know what? That freak shouldn't be our problem."

"I agree."

"Good. Because I want you to make a phone call."

The kid made the call. The handoff was scheduled for the next night.

The call was to Doug Daytona, who, according to the kid, was giddy with relief Augustine had turned up somewhere—so giddy that Doug himself was going to drive up personally, pick him up and take him back. He wanted to do the transport by car because he didn't want any electronic records of them flying back and forth—in other words, he didn't know who was watching what. The kid said he sounded paranoid as fuck. Daytona asked over and over what Augustine had said to us, and he wanted details. PMA played almost as dumb as I had been.

There was no need for complications. The kid and I both just wanted Augustine gone. We both just wanted trouble to pick a new destination.

Which is why I told the kid to call Dougie back. I wanted to give him a destination other than stately Davidson Manor.

I had a hard time looking at Angela all of a sudden.

All my life, I had made stupid, sick, racist jokes, I had to admit it to myself, and most of my friends did too. But they were jokes in our minds. Probably we shouldn't have made them, probably we were white entitled assholes—okay, strike the probably—but, in private, when I knew who I was dealing with, I said things designed to be offensively funny. And not just offensive to different races and religions, also to women, probably even to dwarves.

Of course, I wasn't shy about tearing myself apart in front of others either. My brain pled the Don Rickles defense—I was an equal opportunity offender. I made fun of everything and everybody, because, again, at least in my mind, I was kidding.

But Angela had not been kidding when she said what she said.

The kid explained it well enough—she was a product of her upbringing. But my childhood was far from the most enlightened as well. For instance, my father used to refer to FDR as "Franklin Delano Rosenfeld," which I never got until later on, when I discovered that was how Father Coughlin, the father of Hate Radio back in the 1930's and 40's, referred to the then-president. It was code for "He's not one of us—he's a dirty Jew." Even though he wasn't.

As far as my dad went, he seemed to think saying "Franklin Delano Rosenfeld" was funny. He treated it as a joke. Maybe he was doing some kidding of his own about the smear, I didn't know and I never would, because we didn't really talk about Jews in our house. Nor did we know any. In the small Maryland town I grew up in, there were Lutherans and there were Methodists and that's about as religiously conflicted as it got. But then again, my brother had the same upbringing and wanted to argue about who got treated worse in the 40's, Jews or Germans. Maybe I had poison in me too, maybe not. All I knew was that mankind as a whole had a seed of rot to it that we never seemed able to shake. And it kept finding new ways to manifest itself.

That night, it was a little awkward between Angela and me. And, truth be told, she was as irritated with me as I was with her—because of Augustine shooting up the house and shacking up down in the shelter. So it was a good thing that, the following night, we were taking Augustine off the property, hopefully for good.

It was time to visit Putt-Putt Acres.

Putt-Putt Acres

"You look tired."

The kid had just glanced at me, then went back to looking at the road, which was a good thing, since he was driving. I was riding shotgun in his Jeep Patriot sort-of-SUV and Augustine was in the back seat—he was being uncharacteristically quiet and so was Morris on his left hand. The sun had been down for about a half-hour.

"I'm all right," I answered. "Just get us there." I was lying. I looked tired because I felt tired—I had to guzzle a Coke Zero SUGAR before we left just to get a modicum of get-up-and-go into my gut. More and more, my energy level would plummet to the exhaustion mark late in the day for no apparent reason. Even Eydie had been looking at me with concern—and when the dog notices you're fucked up, you know you're in trouble.

"I could turn around and take you back home. I already told you I could handle this alone, Max."

"Not sitting this one out," I said. "Not leaving you out on a limb." Jesus Christ. I was too tired to say "I'm?"

I had decided the day before that having Dougie come to stately Davidson Manor to retrieve Augustine was a bad, bad, *bad* idea. Not that Dougie himself was dangerous, but he was traveling in some treacherous waters and I didn't want those waters washing up on Angela's doorstep. There were still bullet holes in the walls from Augustine's surprise visit and there was no reason to risk any more drywall being punctured. Or any more tension.

Our new makeshift family was already cracking around the edges, even though I had been back for just around a month and a half. Angela and I were only communicating grudgingly and the kid seemed to get more and more distant from me with each text he sent to Colin the Bureau. Maybe all that low-grade drama just meant we were something like a real family, because everyone in a real family can't help but drive each other nuts—it just didn't come with a laugh track like it used to on TV.

"Where are we driving?" Augustine asked quietly.

"To Jupiter or Mars," I answered. I turned to the kid. "You sure we can get in here?"

"She said she'd leave the gate unlocked. We're just about there."

Then I saw it up ahead on the side of the road—the huge sign with colorful kid-friendly lettering that read, "Putt-Putt Acres," adorned with a giant golf club whose length extended above and below the boundaries of the billboard. The sign wasn't lit up and neither was anything else beyond the fencing surrounding the entire family fun center.

Whenever the kid talked about when he was a real kid, instead of the 20-year-old almost-man he currently was, Putt-Putt Acres was invariably invoked in hushed and holy tones. The business was owned by someone named Chuck Riley, one of General Davidson's rich businessman friends in the area. When it was still a going concern, PMA had free access to whatever he wanted there. And there was a lot there—a sprawling miniature golf course, batting cages, a snack bar and even laser tag. The manager of the place would even give the kid a bag of tokens for the video arcade whenever he wanted. In short, it was his own personal playground and he could kill a whole weekend there with his friends without spending a penny of his own money.

But then the owner died. His widow Nancy didn't want to run it anymore because it was a huge pain in the ass and never made them all that much money anyway. So, she closed it down and put it up for sale. However, crotchety old Nance was asking an unrealistic price—and wasn't willing to entertain lower offers. In the meantime, the former fun zone was going to shit and, from how the kid talked, I think she was taking a special delight in watching it happen. She took a decent tax write-off from the place, so she didn't give a hot damn how long it stayed on the market, preferring to let it all rot in the hot Virginia sun while waiting for a buyer who would never show.

So, when I asked the kid if he knew a dark deserted private place with lots of space where we could hand off Augustine, he didn't hesitate. He immediately said, "Putt-Putt Acres." He called Mrs. Riley, told her some bullshit story about wanting to look around with a friend for "old times' sake" and she didn't blink, because, apparently, the kid's all-access pass was still good in her mind. She told him she'd have her maintenance guy leave the gated entrance open for the night. He just had to close up the padlock on the way out.

The kid texted Doug Daytona the address and told him to meet us on the mini-golf course around 8:30 pm or so, when it would be good and dark. The kid told him to go to the windmill hole and wait there. The windmill hole was, of course, PMA's favorite, because the windmill hole is always everyone's favorite when it comes to putt-putt.

We pulled in the massive driveway and the kid put the Patriot in park, leaving the motor running. He got out and wheeled open the 15-feet tall chicken-wire gates so we could drive in. And that's when Augustine showed his first sign of real stress, when he and I were alone in the car.

"You know they will just kill me, Max. And maybe you too." He paused. And then he raised his dog puppet up to my shoulder, so that it was presumably whispering in my ear. "Maaaaaax," Morris said in its high Vincent Price voice. "You cannot do this, Max. I will tell them of your secret. The secret is you are faking, Max. You are not stupid. You are still Maaaaaaax."

"And you're still a piece of shit puppet. How about I duct tape you to one of the front tires and drive over your head all the way home?"

"You caaaaaan't…" it replied. "You don't have any duct taaaaaape…"

Okay, that was more than enough. Anger trumped exhaustion, so I took a page out of the kid's playbook and grabbed the puppet by the head, then ripped it off Augustine's arm. Then I turned to confront him. Augustine, not the puppet.

"Look, Bravino, you want me to take you seriously, stop playing games. Stop talking in goofy weird riddles and tell me what you know. Is Andrew Wright still alive? What's White Rain? Who's the 'promised one?' Who's after the Jews, the blacks and the Latinos? Just. Fucking. Tell me."

Augustine leaned back against his seat and lowered his eyes.

"Take me away from here. I will tell you the everything of it all," he murmured, just as the kid opened the car door and got back in the driver's seat. He looked at Augustine and looked at me. And finally, of course, he looked at the puppet in my hand. It wasn't there for long— because I opened the glove compartment and shoved it in there like it was radioactive and I was Madame Curie already feeling a little dizzy from all the office uranium.

"What's going on?" the kid asked.

"Absolutely nothing," I said. "Drive in and let's get this over with." And then my whole body trembled for a moment, but just a moment. The kid never noticed. The kid was too busy driving us into Putt-Putt Acres.

He took us around back, away from the main parking lot and down the service road that led behind the main structures to the smaller employee lot, where the asphalt was already cracked across its entire span and foot-tall weeds were sprouting out of the fractures. The kid turned off the Patriot and we all sat quietly in the car in the dark—for about two seconds anyway, because that's how long it took for Augustine to ask, "What are we dooooooing?" in the voice of his puppet. Sloppy performance. He should have at least put his hand over his mouth to simulate the muffled tonal quality that Morris would have actually had, being in the glove compartment and all.

"Doug Daytona is going to text me when he gets to the windmill," I said. "Then we'll go make sure he's alone. And then we'll bring you to Doug and you two can be on your merry way."

"We should have brought a gun," said the kid. I sighed. We had already gone through all that at the house. Guns in the dark is never a good idea in my opinion.

"Not needed," I said. "If there's any sign of shit, we just leave. Besides, we have the advantage. You know this place, they don't. We'll be able to get out of here faster and easier than Dougie or anyone who might show up with him."

The kid pulled out his phone. There was a new text.

"Colin the Bureau?" I asked with obvious annoyance.

"Kevin. He wants to know what's going on."

"Tell him we solved the problem."

"He'll want to know how."

"Tell him how."

I closed my eyes to get some rest—for about two more seconds. Because that's when Augustine's puppet voice screeched, "I have to go to the baaaaaathrooooom!!!!"

"Don't piss in the glovebox," I muttered, as I drifted off to another land for a few minutes.

I woke up to the kid shaking my shoulder.

"Daytona's here. He texted."

It took me a few moments for my head to kick back into gear. The kid again asked me if I was all right. I answered by opening the car door and getting out. The kid got out on his side. Augustine stayed put, so the kid opened the back door and literally pulled him out by the arm. And when Augustine was all the way out, and when the kid had let go of him, Bravino dropped trou and started peeing in a solid stream about three inches from the back tire. Guess he did have to go to the bathroom.

"Jesus, dude!" the kid yelled. "It's splattering all over the car!"

Yes. Yes, it was.

Ocean's 3

There really was no other way to handle it.

I was the one who had to go meet up with Dougie at the windmill hole—and I had to do it alone. We didn't want him to know exactly where Augustine was, in case it was a set-up—he was the only power we had in the situation. That meant somebody had to stay in the shadows with the puppet master and that somebody had to be strong enough to make sure he didn't get away. That had to be the kid, since he was 40 years younger than me and I felt like I was 40 years older than I already was.

There was a perfect hiding place—Hole 18's giant eight-foot-tall sloped board, which had a giant clown face painted on it. The player was meant to hit the golf ball through the hole in the clown's big painted mouth, a hole that took the ball to a secret location that only management had access to. That way, the management made sure it got that golf ball back. This was always the ironclad purpose of a putt-putt Hole 18—*get the ball back under any circumstances.* On these types of sound business principles, putt-putt empires were built.

Anyway, PMA and Augustine stayed behind the large and incredibly ugly Hole 18, which provided a perfect clear view of Hole 16, which had the windmill feature, a 100-feet or so away. I carefully made my way over there—I say carefully, since there were plenty of those small thin cement canals running between the hole greens and the sidewalks, and, from the smell of the standing water in them, God knows how many diseases lurked in their depths.

I came down the large hill next to Hole 17 and ahead in the darkness, I saw the outline of the form of Doug Daytona, standing next to the five-foot-tall mock windmill, which had also suffered from years of neglect—the ends of four of its eight colorful plastic blades were broken off.

I took a breath and walked on.

Dougie seemed to be trying to look in all directions at once as I approached. And when he finally did spot me, he jumped a few inches off the ground like he was barefoot on a hot plate. Clearly, this was not a calm person. I got close enough to look him over. He was dressed southern cool, with a black sports jacket, nicely pressed white open-collar shirt and jeans, and, as usual, he had too much product in his short blonde stubby hair. The top of his head looked like the back of a porcupine that had its quills buzz-sawed down to a couple of inches.

"Max?" he said. "I thought Jeremy…"

I pushed my Mets cap back on my head a little. I was about to blow my cover, but I had no choice. Besides, Augustine already knew my dirty little secret.

"No, you're dealing with me first," I answered.

He blinked at my unchildlike-delivery.

"That's right, Dougie, I've been faking it. Safer that way. My brain actually works like it's supposed to."

His eyes opened wide. "OhmyGod." It came out in one word.

"But you don't tell anybody about me and I don't tell anybody about this."

He shook his head. "Notaword, notaword." He was speaking in hashtags. "I'm just gonna take Augustine home, man, and this ends right here." I scratched my neck and looked around as he kept on talking. "Kinda hard finding my way here in the dark, I used my iPhone flashlight, but it's almost out of power, so I had to stop, man, I was so stupid, I should have charged it in the car on the way down, but I…"

"So, you know, Augustine's been saying a lot of shit. Weird shit."

"Well, he *is* crazy, he's not faking it like you," Dougie chuckled nervously.

"So, Andrew Wright is not still alive?"

Dougie shook his head too fast. "I don't even know who that is."

"And everything else he's been saying. Means nothing?"

More rapid head-shaking and fake smiles. "Nothin,' man, nothin' at all. I mean, I should just say…well, look, like I told you at the fundraiser, he says things that don't make sense all the time and you just gotta ignore whatever crap he's spewing, I mean, the guy talks to a puppet all day, he's…you know."

"I saw you fire him at the fundraiser," I said. "So, I guess he's rehired now?"

"I lost my cool, man, I'd be the first to tell you that, and he freaked, plain and simple, freaked. I'm gonna hire him back, so I just want to take him home, that's all. Okay?"

I hesitated. Half of me wanted to try and get more information out of him, the other half wanted to stick to the plan of getting rid of Augustine and getting rid of trouble. But I was beginning to think trouble had already arrived. My hesitation was enough to cause a few beads of sweat to break out on Dougie's forehead, even though it was a cool late-autumn Virginia night. His eyes suddenly started darting around again even though I was standing right in front of him.

"Seriously," he whispered. "Just…just give him to me. Otherwise, we're all fucked." He hit "fucked" particularly hard.

That's when the first shot hit next to us.

I turned with a start. Where there had been four intact blades on the windmill, there were now only three. My legs turned a little rubbery.

"Just give me Augustine," Dougie hissed. "He's here, right?"

I thought quickly. Would the kid show himself to try and rescue me? If he was smart, he wouldn't. Whoever was shooting at us seemed to just be letting us know they were there. If they saw I had secret reinforcements lurking about, they might just gun us down and head for the hills. They obviously wanted Augustine—and, for the time being, they didn't know where Augustine was. They didn't even know if he was actually there. He was the only card we had to play.

Another shot. Another blade. Only two left. The value of the place just kept going down.

"Bring out the creep, baby!" a familiar, Russian-accented voice ordered out of the darkness. "Otherwise, say bye-bye at your bird!"

Oh, goody. It was my old pals the Russian Ratpack, the same fine folks who chased me out of Dougie's office week before. That was probably Frankovich Sinatrakov yelling.

"When I say, 'Go," I whispered to Dougie, "Run to your right with me."

"What? No, that's crazy…"

"Do it or they're going to kill us anyway."

"Max, just…"

"Go!"

I bolted, Dougie went along with me, and we headed in the opposite direction of where the kid and Augustine were hunkered down. I didn't want to lead the Ratpack to where they were or the whole game was done.

Whatever diseases were in the standing water were suddenly in my socks and Dougie's, because, in the rush to find a safe space, we didn't have time to even think about avoiding the cement water canals. We were lucky we didn't trip over one and bruise our faces on the fake greens.

Bullets were flying, but, as I had hoped, between the darkness and our movement, none of them took us down. We ducked behind some plastic tropical shrubbery on the border between the golf course and the batting cages and stayed down for a moment.

I was panting like there was no tomorrow, which, maybe there wouldn't be. I tried to slow my breathing as hyperactive Dougie spun his head around in every direction to see if they were coming after us.

"Who...are...those guys?" I finally whispered between breaths.

"Freaks. Russian mobsters. They listen to these old Frank Sinatra and Dean Martin nightclub concerts over and over..."

"Don't forget Sammy..."

"They think that's what being American is. They want to be those guys. They totally want to be those guys, they're insane."

"So, what are they doing hanging around you?"

Dougie grew uncomfortable. He didn't know how much he could tell me.

"Dougie, I think you're beyond the point of no return. Talk to me."

"This wasn't supposed to work this way. I won five Emmys."

"Yeah, in buttfuck Georgia, if I recall from the Community. Isn't that what Shawn Shepheard said...?"

"Fuck that guy, seriously, he's not even famous in *Canada*. No, I was on my way, I was sure of it, especially when the Di Pineda campaign came to me, wanting to work with me. And when my interview with you ended up on *60 Minutes*..."

I peeked up over the plastic palms. I wasn't seeing any movement. I took my phone out and texted the kid.

> *You okay?*

"I mean," Dougie continued, "that was *huge*. And then, doing all the videos for the Di Pineda organization..."

"Yeah," I said, as my lungs settled down to normal, "but why Frank, Dean and Sammy? Why Augustine for that matter?"

"Those were the two conditions if I wanted to work with them. I had to hire Augustine and keep him out of trouble…and I had to hire those three to hang around the office as my 'security.'"

"Who approached you?" I watched the phone.

"That fat fuck DeCosta. One of the lawyers I did a movie for, he told him about me."

I glanced at the phone. Nothing back from the kid. That wasn't good.

"Thought it was the greatest opportunity I ever got in my life. Worst mistake is what it was. Worst mistake. Worst absolute…"

"How did you find out what they were up to?"

"I don't…"

"Dougie, I know you heard something you shouldn't have. Because Augustine heard about it too and that's why we all just might end up bleeding red on the green here."

"I…well…we had DeCosta miked for an event. He went into another room with a couple of other guys. He forgot he was miked, he kept talking…the other guys talked…"

"Who were the other guys?"

"I don't know, nobody I'd recognize, di Pineda wasn't even in there. But I heard, Augustine heard, we were the ones by the equipment…and when DeCosta saw my face when he came back in…"

He stopped talking, because suddenly we were both blind.

Putt-Putt Acres was lit up, probably for the first time in five years, and one of the huge ultra-bright standing lights nearby was shining directly into our faces. I turned away and all my eyes saw for a few moments were rotating yellow splotches.

"C'mon out, losers! Let's not be the strangers in the night!" yelled Frankovich.

"Everybody, they shoot somebody sometime!" yelled Dean.

"Be cool and groovy, Jack!" yelled Sammy.

As our eyes adjusted to the lights, Doug turned to me. "Who's Jack?"

"A musical apparition. He hit the road once," I murmured, looking around, wondering where the threesome was. Then my phone buzzed in my hand. The kid was texting me back.

They got us.

Shit.

I had to assume one of them found PMA and Augustine and another one had found wherever the electrical center of Putt-Putt Acres was located. If so, they'd been plenty busy while Dougie and I had our little talk. Now the place was lit up like a fake Christmas tree. I didn't text back. I wasn't sure how to handle that situation. I just knew the Ratpack would use their hostages to get us out in the open.

It was only a matter of time.

Making sure no eyes were on us, I indicated to Dougie that we should run the rest of the way over to the batting cages and stay as low as possible as we did so. I could tell he wasn't sure this was a good idea, but, as he was about to shit his pants, I'm sure he wanted to keep on the move.

The batting cages were located against the boundary of one end of the fun center. Running over there meant we would be boxed in. But it gave us the only chance I thought we might have and it was quite a microscopic one. I led Dougie under the netting, the netting meant to stop the balls hit by the batters. The balls would then roll down the sloped floor, back to one of the individual pitching machines. The two of us crouched behind the side of one of those machines and, as I anxiously eyed it, I couldn't believe my luck.

It was still filled with balls.

My phone buzzed. "I bet that's them," said Dougie, by then breathing as hard as I was.

I answered and instantly said into the phone, "I once read that you ate breakfast off a naked hooker. That true?" I was talking about a rumor about the real Sinatra, but, again, I always liked to have a good opening line.

"What the fuck do you talk? Listen, we got your pallies," said Frankovich. "Give it up or they are a dead meat."

"Either way, I think we are all a dead meat."

"We are just wanting Daytona."

I made a pregnant pause, just to make it sound like I was reluctant.

"Okay. You'll just take him and leave?"

"What you think, we want a whole magilla here?"

"Okay. We're over by the batting cages. The kid knows where they are." I hung up. Doug looked at me.

"You're gonna let 'em take me?" he said, eyes wide open. "Why the fuck didn't you guys bring a gun?"

"My bad," I said.

A few minutes later, I saw the netting rise about forty feet away to the side of us. That meant they were holding it up to pass through. They were close. I motioned to Dougie to get down by the pitching machine and stay down.

Sammy and Dean came out in the open first—Sammy had a gun on the kid and Dean had one on Augustine. Both the kid and Augustine were holding their hands clasped together behind their heads. Then Frankovich emerged behind them, searching the cages with wary eyes. He, of course, couldn't be sure I didn't have a gun—which is why he was using PMA and Augustine as human shields.

"Okay, Charley!" Frankovich yelled. "Make yourself to be seen, dig?"

They were out in the middle of one of the batting lanes, still trying to find us.

"Over here!" I yelled, as Dougie tried to shush me. I waved a hand.

Frankovich turned with a start. He had assumed we were ahead, in one of the cages. Instead, we were behind them in the area they had just walked through. But that didn't bother him. After he saw my hand and realized we were there, a small smile slinked across his face.

"It's gonna be wee-wow-wheeeee," Sammy sang out as the very small gathering headed our way, finding their way to our lane.

And, as soon as they were front and center in that lane, I switched on the pitching machine, where I had dialed up the speed to the "Maximum" setting. A ball shot out of the opening and beaned Frankovich right in the noggin.

As he screamed in pain and went down on the asphalt, Dean and Sammy turned to see what the fuck happened. And, as I had hoped, because they were so distracted, the kid was able to make a move. He brought his hands down, spun around and took out both Dean and Sammy with the same kick, delivered at a ferocious speed. He still had his juice.

Unfortunately, Frankovich still had his gun.

Laying on the ground, he blindly started firing in a fury in all directions. To avoid dying, the kid pulled Augustine down to the ground, and I yanked Dougie around the back of the pitching machine. Which was still shooting balls. Which meant, when Frankovich got to his feet again, another ball hit him in the solar plexus.

And that made him REALLY pissed.

He aimed right at the machine itself and began marching straight towards it, shooting round after round, in a burning rage at a decrepit old pitching machine that had managed to get the best of him. After most of his shots ricocheted ineffectively off the machine's metal sides, one of his bullets finally hit something in the mechanism that finally stopped it cold.

That's when I noticed how depleted I felt. That's when I felt the chest pains coming back at me. That's when I looked up to see death strolling my way wearing a black fedora with a blue cloth grosgrain ribbon circling its width—the finest in 1960 haute couture.

It was Frankovich, of course, in a much-improved mood, because he saw that he and his comrades were going to win the day after all. He was grinning from ear-to-ear and whistling *My Way*—the beginning part with the lyrics, "And now the end is near..." Presumably that meant it was me who was facing the final curtain.

I heard a whimper from Dougie as Frankovich pulled out the clip from his smoking long-barreled handgun, threw it to the side, and pulled a new one out of his jacket pocket. Behind him, Sammy and Dean had their guns back on the kid and Augustine—all four were getting on their feet. The kid was neutralized. I had hoped he could get a gun off one of them and even the odds. That hope was gone.

"What do you want us to be doing, Frank?" asked Dean.

"After I blast these two, let 'em be having it."

From Russia with absolutely no love.

"Okay, baby," Frankovich said quietly towards me as he got within ten feet or so. "This time...it is the endsville."

He stopped and slid the new clip into place with a decisive click. He looked down at us, still flat on our backs on the ground, and aimed his gun at my head, then at Dougie's ...and then finally mine again. And there he left it.

"You I am not liking the most," he said, starting to walk the final few paces until his shoes reached mine.

"I'm honored," I muttered. I wasn't scared exactly. I just felt numb. After all I'd been through, I was going to die in Putt-Putt Acres at the hands of a Russian Sinatra impersonator. Regrets, I had a few.

And then I heard the shot.

But it hadn't come from Frankovich's gun. I glanced quickly at Dean and Sammy behind him. They were again looking around in confusion, because they didn't know where the shot had come from either.

I looked back at Frankovich. He was frozen in place, his gun still aimed at my head.

Then he fell to his knees.

And then he fell on his face.

A few more shots rang out. Dean and Sammy fell. They had literally been only inches from the kid and Augustine—this was some sharpshooter. The kid and Augustine were both completely freaked out. Dean and Sammy? They appeared to be in the endsville.

Dougie and I got up. Or, rather, Dougie got up, saw I was struggling, then helped me to my feet as well. I surveyed the area, trying to see where our savior had planted himself to make the kills. But who was it? It couldn't have been Kevin, he was on the west coast. Who the hell else could it have been? Who the hell else knew we were there?

Finally, I thought I saw something moving near the netting a couple lanes down from us. After a couple moments more, out came Patrice Plotkin, holding high-powered sniper rifle, whose barrel was still smoking, in her right hand.

"This is bullshit," she said in the tone of a dog-bit mail carrier.

And the Emmy Goes To...

Patrice Plotkin had a great big mess to clean up and she wasn't too happy about it.

When Kevin found out about our Putt-Putt plan from the kid's texts, he immediately called Patrice and harangued her into coming out to save our asses in case they needed saving. She was the one who had turned on the lights. She told us she had a special phone app that allowed her to download the blueprints for places like Putt-Putt Acres and quickly assess where that on/off switch would be located. And I thought to myself, of course she did. She's Patrice Plotkin.

"You know, if you had turned on the lights at the wrong moment, that might have gotten us killed," I offered.

"Well, it didn't," she answered with a pleased snap. She looked around at the dead Ratpack trio. "What the hell am I supposed to do about these guys? Who are they?"

"Russians," Dougie said. "They called themselves Frank, Dean and Sammy." Then he shrugged.

She gave Dougie a look I wouldn't give to a mass murderer.

"Russians," she repeated. "Great. If it's one thing the current administration loves, it's for us to investigate Russians."

"Can we help?" the kid asked. "I can call Kevin."

"Kevin doesn't work for the government anymore, remember?" she asked, slicing off his balls with one single swoop of her tongue. "I don't know how to explain this." A sigh. "I'll figure something out. Get out of here. All of you."

Dougie looked at me in amazement. He was off the hook? Meanwhile, Augustine was mumbling to his left hand, even though Morris was still in the glove compartment.

"What if somebody else comes after these two?" I asked. "Or, for that matter, us?"

"Then you're probably going to die. I'm really not responsible for whatever crap you boys are stepping into these days. Now, again…get out of here."

We complied.

When we got to the cars, I ran my hand under Dougie's shiny new Beamer and almost instantly found what I was looking for—a GPS tracking device the Russian Ratpack had obviously placed there so they could track him. I threw it in a nearby clump of bushes. How many of those GPS fuckers had almost gotten me killed? I'd probably have to count on my fingers and my toes to get to an appropriate total. Blow me, technology.

As the kid unlocked his Jeep Patriot, and an anxious Augustine waited behind him to retrieve his beloved dog puppet from the glove compartment, Dougie stood by, looking like a bewildered, lost child.

"What am I supposed to do?" he asked me. "Do you really think someone else will come after me?"

"I don't know, Dougie. Depends on how much you know. How much *do* you know, Dougie?"

"I just have to get out of this arrangement," he said under his breath. "I have to. I'm not gonna tell anybody anything. But I have to get out."

He walked to his car and yelled for Augustine, who was standing nearby, carefully examining one of the puppet's loose Lego teeth as if he were a certified DDS.

"Good luck," I said to the artificial dog head. It tilted its head—or, rather, Augustine tilted his wrist—as if it was taking everything in and choosing its next words carefully.

"Project M," the puppet said. "Look that one up, Maaaax."

"Jesus, dog," I replied, "Can't you just come out and tell me what something means for once?"

"AUGUSTINE!" yelled Dougie. "We have a long trip home!"

The kid and I watched as the two got in the car and drove off into the night. Then PMA gave me a hard look. "You know they're going to get killed, right?"

"Let's go home, kid. I'm bushed."

"And maybe us too," he said under his breath.

"Let's go home."

The undertow that had been tugging on my soul and my spirit finally dragged me down to the depths.

When we got back to stately Davidson Manor, Angela was downstairs with Eydie. She knew from the looks of us we had been up to no good. She started in on the kid about how she had gotten an angry call from Mrs. Riley about Putt-Putt Acres and how she had left it open for him and now there were police calling about things there and the government had sealed the place off and she didn't know what was going on, but what did Jeremy *do* there and...

I went upstairs without a word, the dog happily trailing behind me, and went into the guest room, not Angela's room, where I stripped down to my boxers and got into bed. And then I fell asleep for I don't know how long.

I was vaguely aware of the kid coming in, wanting to know if I was hungry, Angela coming in to take Eydie down to piss and shit, morning coming, afternoon coming, and darkness descending once again. Every few hours, being a man 61 years of age, I had to drag myself out of bed to pee, but, after I did my business, I simply crawled back into bed and fell back asleep in an instant. Occasionally, Eydie licked my face to bring me out of it—she had to be worried about me, dogs have that capacity—but it was no use, my energy was gone and so was I.

The dreams came and went and they were vivid. At one point I saw a fetus floating in outer space, like the end of *2001: A Space Odyssey,* and at another point, I saw Nazis playing gin rummy at a country club. Then I saw savage dogs ripping apart someone's flesh in an office. Then I dreamed I was in a room, a room that was much longer than it was wide, with chairs lining each wall. In two of those chairs sat my mother and my aunt, my father's sister, the relative who seemed to have the biggest heart and she got up and gave me a big hug while my mother watched and cried.

And then the next morning, I awoke to an unfamiliar male human staring down at me.

"I'm Dr. Hoffman, Max."

My eyes focused on the intruder as I mentally took stock of how much might be in my bladder at the moment—and I determined it was either half-full or half-empty, depending on your point of view. Anyway, this Dr. Hoffman was tall, thin, had white-blonde hair, maybe in his 50's, and had on a distinctly un-doctorly wardrobe.

"You're wearing sweats," I finally said.

"I was just out jogging when Angela called me."

I took that in.

"There's no stethoscope around your neck. What kind of doctor doesn't have a stethoscope around his neck?"

He held up his little black bag. "There's one in here."

Shit, he had me. Time to try the direct approach.

"I don't need a doctor."

"You've been asleep for over 36 hours."

"Jumbo-sized nap," was my reply.

The asshole opened up his little black bag.

My heart rate was elevated. My blood pressure likewise. He wanted me to go to the hospital for further screening. He had been told I had gone through some kind of trauma recently, a trauma so severe it had turned my hair white, and he wondered if I could fill him in on the details. I was going to tell him about the golf cart and the drones that dropped bombs and the pain that was so intense I passed out, but I was too tired for all that. And I damn well wasn't going to tell him about the recurring chest pains or the possibility that I had already had a mild heart attack, or he might have pulled some dumbshit move like calling an ambulance.

So that left us with very little to talk about.

Finally, with the appropriate tone of concern, he told me he would see me later that afternoon for more tests. He'd leave the information with Angela. He left me no room to turn down his kind offer.

I nodded and he left. And I went back to sleep.

A few hours later, I heard Eydie growling from the bottom of the bed. That meant the kid was in the room. I opened my eyes and saw him sitting by the bed, staring at me with empty eyes.

"They're dead, Max," he said in a whisper.

I got up on my elbows. Something hurt. I didn't think I had been down long enough to get bed sores, but something hurt.

"Who?" I asked.

The kid handed me his phone. On the screen was a news story from Atlanta, Georgia. Two brutal murders. Filmmaker Doug Daytona had been stabbed to death with his own Emmy Award statues.

How was that possible?

Well, someone had gone to the trouble of sharpening the ends of the wings on the back of the angel or whatever the fuck stood on the base of the award to razor-sharp points. Which meant somebody hated Doug Daytona even more than I did. One Emmy had been stuck in the front of his neck, one was stuck in the back of it, one was stuck in his chest, one was stuck in his groin…and one was literally shoved up his ass, as far as I could tell from reading between the report's much more polite description of events. Meanwhile, some other "unidentified male" had had a puppet of some kind shoved so far down his throat, he strangled on it. I guessed I would be getting no more unintelligible texts.

I continued to stare at the screen long after I had read all the words in the news report. Then I handed the phone back to PMA.

"There's more news," he said. "Howard's on his way over, so you better get dressed."

"Howard? Why?"

"The third fundraiser for Eddie di Pineda. It's back on."

A few minutes later, still half-conscious but dressed in a simple t-shirt and jeans, I came downstairs, Eydie trailing me the whole way again. I went into the kitchen. As I hadn't eaten in a day and a half, I was a little peckish, a word I had learned from *Monty Python* episodes forty years ago or so.

"You look like holy hell."

I turned to see Angela, staring at me in horror. She apparently had been directing Chef to make me a plate of something, as he was putting together a bunch of cheeses and meats in one of his artful arrangements. Chef turned to me, wondering if what Angela had just said was true. He quickly turned back to the plate, his expression confirming that I did, indeed, look like holy hell.

"Seriously, your skin color matches your hair color. Dr. Hoffman is expecting you in an hour," she said with no room for negotiation. "And the hospital's a half-hour away."

I sat at the kitchen table, because standing wasn't agreeing with me. "Can't make it. I have an appointment."

"Max, something is wrong with you, it's been obvious since you got here. I don't know what all you went through where you were, but..."

"I need to be here. Howard's coming here. We have to go to the last fundraiser in a couple of days, to get rid of Duds. I have to finish the job."

Her eyes narrowed. "Fundraiser. But the man's wife was just killed at the last one and it was what...a week ago? How can there be another one?"

Chef set the plate in front of me. "I'll get you a Coke Zero. That'll perk you back up."

I nodded. Angela sat across from me as I gobbled up some fresh cholesterol.

"Don't be angry with me, Max," she said in a quiet low voice. "I shouldn't have made those...remarks the other day. Sometimes, I don't think." She put her hand on mine. I let it stay there.

"We just have to get through this, Angie. We just have to get through this."

"Provided there is a 'through."

Chef put a cold Coke Zero SUGAR can in front of me. I popped the top and drank it down.

Franklin Delano Rosenfeld

Howard ran his finger down the side of his glass of ice water, making a line in the film of condensation on the exterior of the tumbler.

"So...we're sticking with the original date, which is two days away."

"How can there be a fundraiser in two days?" the kid asked, echoing Angela from a couple of hours ago. "The Senator just buried his wife yesterday."

"The Senator will not be attending," Howard said, as if he were at a press conference. "Dudley will be hosting the event. We've also pruned the guest list, so it will be strictly premium donors. No ballroom, maybe 75 people. It's going to be extremely low-key...and it will fulfill your obligation. I was told to tell you that, whatever that obligation might be."

"And this is the one in Palm Beach, Florida," said the kid.

"Yeah, the information all stays the same." Howard turned my way. "He looks worse."

The kid looked directly at me as he replied to Howard. "Sometimes it's hard to get an idiot to take care of himself."

Howard flinched. "That's...kinda harsh."

"I like Florida," I finally piped in. "Remember, Howard? We said hi in Florida."

Howard smiled too hard. "Yes! We said hi in Florida! You're right, Max!" Then he turned back to the kid. "Remember, after this fundraiser, I want you to take him to see my guy. Maybe he can fix him."

"I'm not broken, Howard!"

Howard got up and patted my knee. "Of course, you're not, Max."

"Colin's going," said the kid. We were in the home office again. As I was noodling around on the desktop, he was, as always, texting with Colin the Bureau. "To the fundraiser," he added.

"So, guess Colin's a premium donor then. One of the 'Super 75.'" I made that term up on the spot.

More texting. "They're going in place of their parents." They? Oh yeah, Colin wasn't a 'him.' "They're too scared."

"The imaginary parents?" I muttered.

"Max, knock it off."

I didn't like it, any of it. Doug and Augustine brutally murdered, us with an invitation to an event that wouldn't happen if anyone involved had a conscience or at least any sense of optics. But I couldn't figure out what anyone's end game was. The best outcome would be the kid and I getting out of the woods once we did our duty at the final fundraiser, and Angela getting her divorce. The worst outcome? The kid and I would end up like Doug and Augustine. But killing us would bring more very unwelcome publicity—after all, the kid was still a Davidson and I was still the hero of many a conspiracy theory. So, we were probably safe. But, just for fun, I decided to follow up on the final incomprehensible clue that Augustine had left me.

I frowned as I googled "Project M," one of the last things the dog puppet uttered to me, and the results were endless and confusing. I was confronted with page after page of articles and videos about video games. One article was entitled, "Project M Is Pretty Fun." I had a hunch that wasn't the Project M Augustine had been talking about. Maybe he said, "Project N" and I misheard. Or maybe I was as crazy as he was for even trying to find out if it made sense.

As I continued to study the search results, somewhere else on the first floor, I could hear Angela talking quietly on the phone. Then suddenly, her side of the conversation stopped and I heard her shouting towards me.

"Dr. Hoffman wants you at the hospital tomorrow at 2, Max!"

"No good. After I get back from the fundraiser!" I yelled back.

She yelled something nasty and went back to the phone call. I had prevailed.

The fact was my energy was back up and my color was back to something resembling a live human—apparently 36 hours of sleep can do a man good, after he gets past the shock of the initial wake-up. So, if I was doing all right, I sure as hell wasn't going in for any tests until the last leg of the fundraiser triathlon was completed. Finishing off the whole ugly obligation was still our best way out.

"Colin's making a lot of money on bitcoin," the kid said, still staring at his phone texts.

"Bitcoin. Just saw something about that. Digital currency. What could go wrong?"

"It is weird. I mean, it's not real money, but everyone treats it like it is."

"Kid, paper money isn't real either. We just all agreed that it's worth something. A potato, now that's worth something. You can mash it, broil it, or make French fries out of it."

"Hey, that's what Colin said. Not the stuff about the potato, but that our entire monetary system is based on imaginary value. So…it's just a matter of everyone making a mind shift. They say bitcoin is going to be the centerpiece of the next economy."

The kid was always looking for someone new to idolize. And he always chose badly. I mean, it was me for a while and how much lower could you get than that?

"Next economy?" I was still scrolling through the Project M results and was about ready to throw in the towel. "What next economy?"

"Max, the world's changing. This whole neighborhood will probably be underwater in another 70 years or so. Governments are going to fall…survival's going to be what it's all about."

I turned and looked at the kid.

"Where's all this coming from?"

"Climate change, Max, Colin's an expert on it. Let's face it. The waters are gonna rise and everything's going to be different."

That hit me in the gut like Duds' fist in the backyard a while back—because it brought to mind one of Augustine's most memorable babble-texts:

when the waters rise wite rain will poor down

I didn't say anything, but I had goose pimples on my goose pimples. I didn't trust Colin the Bureau and I didn't like the conversations "they" were/was having with the kid. But the more I pushed back, the harder the kid dug in. So, I kept my mouth shut. Besides…I had found the Project M I was looking for. I had accidentally zipped right by it. And, son of a bitch, it was all about Franklin Delano Rosenfeld.

"Project M," I said. "It was actually called 'The M Project.' Approved for funding by FDR himself."

The kid looked up.

"Summer of '42," I continued. "That's when it happened. Also happens to be the name of the first R-rated movie I ever saw. Jennifer O'Neill. Nice to look at. But she always spoiled things by trying to act. I mean, she was okay in *Rio Lobo*, but…"

"Max, for once, can we please stop talking about old shit?"

"But this *is* old shit. The shittiest. FDR had the documents socked away in a safe and nobody found them until after he had croaked. It was all about resettling the Jews after World War II. Making sure there weren't too many of them in one place."

"Jews. That was what Augustine was yelling about."

I kept reading and kept being completely disgusted. "Shit, it wasn't just about Jews, it was about all kinds of racial madness—it just started with Jews because Roosevelt was worried about where the ones leaving Germany would end up. But the M Project had an even bigger mandate—to find out which races were the *best* races."

"Huh?"

"Yeah, what I said. They wanted to create a kind of March Madness bracket, where different kinds of DNA faced off. FDR put some guy in charge who did intelligence work for him on the side. Listen to what Roosevelt wrote to him...'I know that you can carry out this project unofficially, exploratorially, ethnologically, racially, admixturally, miscegenationally, confidentially and, above all, budgetarily."

"Admix...what?"

"I don't know, that was a whole lot of adverbs, many of which I didn't know existed. Here's another good one—'Any person connected herewith whose name appears in the public print will suffer guillotinally.'"

"As in getting your head chopped off?"

I shrugged. I didn't think 'guillotinally' was a real word, but I had to assume decapitation was what Roosevelt was hinting at.

"What did Roosevelt think should be done with the Jews?"

I continued reading. "...survey the vacant places of the earth suitable for post-war settlement..."

"The vacant places of the earth."

"Yeah, looks like they were looking at Africa and South America. He wanted to determine, and I quote, 'the type of people who could live in those places.'" I skimmed a little further, where it got a little darker and weirder. "Here's another juicy tidbit. Roosevelt wanted the M Project to be led by this guy named..." I paused, intimidated by the letters in front of me.

"Named?" the kid asked impatiently.

"Um…Alex Hardlicker?"

"Now you're making shit up."

"You try to read this name. It doesn't have enough vowels, plus there's weird shit on top of some of the letters. Anyway, he was the curator of physical anthropology at the Smithsonian Museum of Natural History. And also, somebody who believed deeply in eugenics."

"Eugenics. That's like…racial breeding, right?"

"Right. Hardlicker was obsessed with the superiority of the white race. And Roosevelt was a fan. They were pen pals for over a decade. FDR wanted him to find 'opinions as to problems arising out of racial admixtures…'"

"There's that word again…"

I continued reading. "'…and to consider the scientific principles involved in the process of miscegenation as contrasted with the opposing policies of so-called 'racialism.'"

"I looked up admixtures. It just means interbreeding."

"Yeah. Like I said, this wasn't just about Jews. This was about everybody." I read another charming passage from FDR. "'Is the South Italian stock—say, Sicilian—as good as the North Italian stock—say, Milanese—if given equal economic and social opportunity? Thus, in a given case, where 10,000 Italians were to be offered settlement facilities, what proportion of the 10,000 should be Northern Italians and what Southern Italian?'"

"Holy shit."

"Nothing holy about this shit. Not when you're down to trying to decide which kinds of Italians should make the cut. You know, I appreciate the New Deal as much as anybody, but eugenics was the Nazis' thing. That was what we were supposedly fighting against."

"So, what happened with the project?"

"Scrapped by Truman when he moved into the White House after FDR died. Harry thought it was all bullshit—good for him. The State Department was handing over 10k a month to fund this thing up until he squashed it."

"Maybe Trump's starting it up again. I wouldn't doubt it. I saw some PBS thing. He's into eugenics."

"Yeah, always talking about his DNA. I don't know, this seems to be deep, deep underground shit. But everything I've read says eugenics used to be a huge thing in the early 1900s. Maybe that's why FDR latched on to it. Then World War II came along, and people weren't all that excited about racial cleansing anymore."

The kid shook his head. I thought a little more.

"I mean, I guess I see the point...we breed dogs to be better, why not people? Why not?" I asked.

"Are you serious? Because it's wrong!"

"Even if it wasn't, you just can't trust the human race to carry out anything with a sense of decency. You'd never find Boston Terriers putting poodles in death camps or anything like that. Of course, if we could lick our own balls like they do, maybe we wouldn't be such dicks."

"Max, what the hell is your point?"

"My point is we just happen to possess this wonderful seed of rot that always sprouts horrifying weeds of chaos and death." I paused. "Wow, I liked the way that last sentence came out. I should write that down."

"If this is about some kind of racial cleansing, how does Eddie di Pineda fit in?" mused the kid. "Isn't he the kind of guy they want out of the picture? Wouldn't they think he had 'inferior blood?'"

"I heard some donors talking. They're just using him, kid, to make people believe they're tolerant, although I don't know where Puerto Ricans rank on the Hardlicker scale." I stopped. "What am I saying? I don't think di Pineda has a chance at the presidency and I also don't think Hitler's coming back any time soon."

"You never know," mumbled the kid as he went back to his texting.

Yeah, you never did know. And all the talk about Adolf Schicklgruber made me think of my brother the Nazi apologist again. I turned back to the computer and closed the many racist tabs I had opened on the browser, then decided to check my email, which I hadn't looked at since the Putt-Putt shootout. Coincidentally, there, in the in-box, was an email from Alan he sent two days before. No subject heading. I opened it up.

And I got some news I wasn't expecting.

Buried Ashes

There we were, Kev, the kid and me, standing in the middle of Putt-Putt Acres at high noon. The kid had just finished filling Kev in on the events that had transpired there the other night. Kev's reaction?

"You're kidding me."

It was a miracle we had gotten back on the grounds at all. The widow Riley was still upset about the ruckus we had caused, but Angela called her and told her that we had been battling Communists, and that apparently made everything okay. Technically, it was maybe not a lie, since the three Russian assassins maybe *were* Communists as toddlers before Glasnost took root. I'd have to do the math on that later.

Kev was still taking in the kid's highly improbable but completely accurate narrative as I eyed the batting cage area carefully. I had to admit, whoever was in the CIA clean-up crew, they were experts. You never would have known anything had gone on there except batting practice. Sure, maybe there was a stray smidge or two of dried blood around the pitching machine, but you'd never know what it was if you didn't know what it was.

"You're kidding me," Kev repeated, in exactly the same tone.

"No joke," said the kid.

Mrs. Riley hadn't been the only person Angela had called the day before. She also called Kev, still in sunny California. And she made him an offer—she'd fly him back east and pay him a generous day rate to try and keep us all alive in the wake of the slaughter of Doug Daytona and Augustine Bravino. So, he flew in on the red eye and showed up bright and early that morning at stately Davidson Manor. The kid was the one who answered the door.

Shocked that Kev had returned, PMA had a brief flicker of hope that maybe he actually did care about him. But Kev quickly shot that theory down. He told PMA that Angela was paying him to be there. He only took the job because of what had happened to poor Patrice Plotkin (say that fast three times).

Even though it was easy to prove that the three Russians were (a) assassins and (b) in America under false pretenses, the political climate had completely changed with President Trump. The Agency was discouraged from kicking up any dust that contained any hint of Russian menace—and that's exactly what Patrice had done. So, she was put on unpaid leave for God knows how long, and, since Kev had gotten her into the whole clusterfuck, he wanted to make up for it. So, he told the kid, half of his fee from Angela would be going to Patrice.

Which brought us all to Putt-Putt Acres. And instead of saying, "You're kidding me" a third time, Kev threw his head back laughing in disbelief at the idea of a Russian Ratpack.

"Wait'll I tell Robert that one!" he bellowed. That's gonna make it into a movie, you can bet on that."

"Robert?" asked the kid.

"The screenwriter I'm working with," Kev said. "He says when he brings something like that in to a studio exec, he gets a deal. They love crazy shit like that."

"Crazy? It was fucking real," growled the kid, harshing Kev's mellow.

"I know that, Jeremy," Kev muttered.

"You know what else is real?" snapped the kid, who undoubtedly was still reeling from the existence of a Robert, "Tomorrow's the last fundraiser we're doing for Eddie di Pineda. And I'm just wondering if they're really going to let us walk after it's over."

"Well, Jeremy, obviously, I'm going with you guys. That's why your mom brought me out here."

"You're not going to do us any fucking good," I said with a growl of my own. "They won't let you anywhere near the event. It's going to be a small group, a small exclusive group of rich fat cats and security will be wound as tight as possible," I said. "Angela's wasting her money."

Kev gave me a pissy look, but I didn't care. The more I thought about the last fundraiser, the more alarm bells rang in my mind. I kept coming back to the fact that those three guys had been Russians. That Russia had fucked with our elections in 2016—and that Trump seemed to be involved. And then I remembered something else.

"Colin the Bureau."

The kid looked at me. "The name is Colin Burian."

"That's the guy you were with in L.A., right?" said Kev, with a hint of "right back atcha, chief."

The kid and Kev locked eyes. In L.A., they would probably say there was "energy" in the air between them. To me, it was bad shit, the worst kind of shit imaginable—unfinished relationship business. The shittiest shit of all the shit, what you might call nitroglycerin in a blender, waiting for someone to flip the "on" switch.

"What do they have to do with this, Max?" the kid asked wearily.

"You told me they got their clothes from somebody who supplied Russian oligarchs with their wardrobes."

"They?" asked Kev. "Who else besides Colin?"

"Stefano Ricci," said the kid, plowing on. "By the way, I also said Ricci sells to billionaire Middle East Arabs. You just hate Colin, Max, so let it alone. What, you think they're a Russian agent?"

I caught Kevin's questioning look. "Colin's gender queer," I said to him by way of explanation. "So, we have to murder the English language to accommodate them."

"Max, Jesus Christ, you fucking old white straight man!" the kid bellowed at me.

I nodded. I couldn't deny it. I was a fucking old white straight man.

"We should check him…them…out, Jeremy," said Kev quietly. "He…they may be trying to…"

"Oh, you too?" fumed the kid.

"It's just hard to…keep track?" Kev explained.

"Let's go back to the house."

The kid walked towards the Putt-Putt Acres exit, but Kev remained standing next to me. He asked me to spell Colin's last name and he tapped it into his phone. Then he looked back at me.

"I don't want to look like a douchebag to Jeremy, Bowman. You really feel like something's up with this guy…person? What do you call him…them?"

"I call them Colin the Bureau." I pulled out a cigarette. I still had half a pack in my jacket. I lit it up with my lighter that had some kind of beer logo on the side.

"You smoke now?"

As if in answer to his question, I took a long puff with a shaky hand. Things felt like they were catching up with me again. Mentally, physically, spiritually. It felt like my very core was under assault.

"Yeah," I finally said, answering his question before last. "Something definitely seems off with Colin." I took another puff. "There's one more thing you need to look into. Something called 'The Eugene Group.'"

"The Eugene Group?"

"Yeah. As in Eugene Levy or Eugene the Jeep or Eugene, Oregon. Eugene."

"As usual, I don't know what you're talking about. What's their deal?"

"I wish I knew. Just another bunch of fuckers doing fucked-up things," I snapped.

The Eugene Group had popped up in a very unlikely place, a very unlikely and personal place even the kid didn't know about. That's because I hadn't told him or Angela about what my brother had emailed me. I hadn't told anybody. I don't know why. Maybe because I was raised not to talk about anything. Maybe because I still felt guilty underneath it all. Maybe because the finality of her death just represented too much goddamn waste, a waste of a life devoted to a huge lie that kept threatening to suck my entire life into the sewer.

With all that racing through my head, there was little surprise that Kev was staring at me, wondering what twisted mental highway I was traveling down. There were shadows, deep, dark shadows flitting over my face. I turned away from him because I couldn't turn away from them.

"What's up, Bowman?"

What was up was my mother was dead.

Ellen Gladys Bowman had passed away from natural causes at the age of 92 about a week before. That was the news my brother Alan's email had delivered the previous day and the email was already a couple of days old when I finally looked at it. Not only that, but it had taken my oldest brother Henry (or as I liked to call him, "Fuckface") three days to let Alan know, which meant Mom had probably been dead for a week before I found out.

So, yeah, my mom was dead, but it was hard to cry about it. It was hard to feel anything about it.

All the love had been beaten out of her soul during her abusive childhood, which meant there was none of it left to offer her children. Abusive men ruled her life, from her abusive father to her abusive husband to the biggest abuser of all, Andrew Wright, my real daddy.

She allowed the man I had thought was my father to disown me and my brother Alan. She allowed Daddy Andy, possibly one of the vilest human beings put on this planet, to put little ol' me in her uterus. She was a victim who saw no choice but to perpetuate her own victimhood, leaving me with the eternal conflict of whether to blame her or let her off the hook because she couldn't help any of it. But I couldn't and wouldn't make that final call. It didn't seem like my right.

But others wanted more than my set-in-stone ambivalence.

One of my relatives had emailed me to ask if I was going to go to the funeral. When I told her I wouldn't be in attendance, she leaned on the shopworn sentiment, "But it's your mother!!!!" Biologically speaking, true, but, legally, she had relinquished that position. Now she was dead and most likely had joined Pretend Dad wherever he had gone. I didn't believe in Hell and Heaven, I believed in either going up or down a level or two depending on how things had gone. So, maybe they'd find themselves down a few floors in the afterlife elevator, which didn't seem all that horrible. Of course, who the hell was I to talk? I could end up rummaging around in the basement for all I knew.

And speaking about being below ground, Henry aka Fuckface had also told my cousin what the plans were for disposing of my mother, because she found it a bit weird. I, on the other hand, found it a *lot* weird.

Apparently, they were going to dig up my father's buried body, open the casket and throw my mother's ashes inside with what was left of him—then rebury the whole mess. Fuckface said that was what my mother had requested. When people say something turns their stomach, I usually think they're exaggerating. When I heard this, however, my stomach not only turned, it did a loop-de-loop around my other vital organs. This was done? Ashes were combined with a decomposing corpse exhumed from the ground? I'd like to shake the hand of whoever had that job, but only if I was wearing gloves.

"Your mother's dead?" Kev paused. "Jesus, I'm sorry. When's the funeral?"

I had blurted out the truth to Kev. I don't know why my unconscious brain had chosen him to be the first person I told. Maybe because I felt like he was the only grown-up in my circle at that moment. Maybe because I suddenly didn't feel like I could trust the kid because of Colin the Bureau. Maybe because it was time to tell Kev a few other things.

"I don't know when the funeral is. I'm not going. I was disowned years ago, along with my other brother Alan. My brother Fuckface is getting everything."

All those words put some furrows in Kev's brow. "Your brother Fuckface?"

"I guess half-brother would be the proper term. My mother slept with Andrew Wright. He's my real father."

The furrows disappeared as his eyebrows shot up to the sky.

"What the hell are you talking about, Bowman?"

I explained the whole thing. How Daddy Andy had lured me out of my Roosevelt Island exile after his "real" son started going off the rails to see how I would perform under fire. How he kept testing me, pulling me in, trying to get me to join his exclusive club of neofascist murderers who wanted the world all for themselves. How he saw me as the only way to carry on his poisoned bloodline, despite the fact that I had two daughters—apparently, girls didn't count in this equation. It had to be a man and that meant it had to be me. His obsession would only die when one of us did. Which is why I had tried to kill him and, unfortunately, failed.

Kev took it all in. For a moment, he had no idea what to say. Then, all he could come up with was this question…

"Does…uh…Fuckface know about this?"

I actually laughed and shook my head. "Fuckface doesn't know anything. He's an emotionally crippled hermit. I haven't talked to him in many, many years. Nobody knows about all this, except you…and the kid."

Speaking of PMA, he was looking at us from a distance, wondering why we hadn't followed him. I turned back to Kev.

"There's one more thing I need to tell you." I paused. "And I don't want you to tell the kid."

Playground of My Mind

Nobody would disagree that 1972 was a horrible year for pop music.

I was 16 years old then and radio was undergoing a radical revolution. All the "serious" rock music had been permanently relocated to FM radio at that point. Which meant that all that was left on the old AM Top 40 formats was the garbage that garbage would throw away, crap so crappy that everyday crap would find it offensive.

In many ways, the resulting music charts that year signaled the death throes of a generation.

In 1972, rock n' roll legend Chuck Berry had his last top 40 hit—with "My Ding-A-Ling." A goofy song about his penis. Somewhere Maybelline wept.

In 1972, Mr. Vegas himself, Wayne Newton, also had his last top 40 hit, the tenth most popular song of the year as a matter of fact— "Daddy, Don't You Walk So Fast." Unless, Daddy, you were headed to change the station if that fucking song was playing. Then run your ass off.

And finally, in 1972, Sammy Davis Jr. (not the Russian one) had *his* last top 40 hit, and the *fifth* most popular song of the year—"The Candy Man." It was a time when Sammy used to sign off his TV commercials for his old records by saying, "Peace, Love and Togetherness." But listening to "The Candy Man" was more likely to incite those who heard it to savage violence.

But another 1972 single, a tune more profane and excruciating than any of those cited above, was currently plaguing me. It had an iron grip on my brain and wouldn't let go. It was like a migraine with its own soundtrack.

It was the nightmare entitled "Playground of my Mind."

This was a song in which a grown man, when he was feeling oppressed by bell bottom jeans and leisure suits or whatever was bothering him in the seventies, reminisced about going to a playground as a child, where a little boy named Michael would sing about having a shiny nickel and a little girl named Cindy would sing about getting married and having babies. Talk about gender bias. Anyway, of all these diabetes-inducing lyrics were floated like a turd in a nauseating pool of background singers tasked with creating an unrelenting audio offensive by intoning "Ba Ba Ba, Ba BA BA Ba," over and over and over. And over.

Maybe my mind was summoning the sugary sweetness of this insipid tune to compensate for all the bitter dregs that were swirling around in my life. The current playground of my mind didn't feature cute kids running around singing cute songs. No, it was covered with broken glass and featured a merry-go-round that didn't stop until you projectile-vomited. There was a seesaw, that was true, but it didn't go up, it just stayed down. As for the swing set? It slammed you into a brick wall.

I had seen freedom. I had felt the hope of escape. I thought there was a way to free Angela from Duds and free myself from any more involvement in weird-ass conspiracy shit that followed me from disaster to disaster. But all that I had seen was a mocking mirage, that freedom was impossible, that every way out only led to a U-turn sending me right back into the shit.

The kid and I knew too much, and, at the same time, we knew too little. It was a whirlpool of Russian assassins, texts filled with equal parts gibberish and truth from the late Augustine and his dog puppet, and minor-league terrorism against Senator Eddie di Pineda's campaign. And somewhere behind all that lurked the specter of Daddy Andy. Even though we had a reliable source who said I had actually put a bullet into his diseased head, I suspected his evil, ancient heart was still beating somewhere, somehow and whatever was left of him was still up to no good.

As for the few people left who I confided in and trusted, somehow, they had all become minor nightmares of their own. I had a lover who was suspicious of Jews and a brother who loved Nazis. PMA, the person I had more faith in than anybody in the world, was suddenly untrustworthy because of Colin the Bureau—who I couldn't be sure was anything other than a slightly odd rich kid. But the kid's extreme defensiveness of him/them made me wary. It was like he knew something was off, but couldn't admit it.

Finally, there was the not-so-trivial fact that I was homeless. And that all my possessions were either for sale in various thrift shops across New York City or had been tossed into a garbage dumpster and barged out to sea.

I'm a guy who's well-acquainted with low points. But this was lower than the way my great-uncle Charlie Bowman played pinochle back in the day. He cheated so badly that my great-grandfather furiously threw a chair down the stairs of his house in protest—it was a family legend. Imagine getting that fucking mad about pinochle. Imagine a card game being the thing that made you have a breakdown. And there I was, trying to hold it together when everything in my life was once again being flipped and fried on a red-hot griddle.

All in all, it was a little hard to stay focused. It was extremely hard to stop smoking. And it was ridiculously hard to not feel like my place in this world was about as permanent as a bug crawling under a descending shoe.

But I still had a dog. And at that moment, she was licking my face.

"Eydie," I said to her as I lay on the bed. "If you had two legs, a working vagina and could talk, you and me just might hit the road together and never look back." She licked my face again and I briefly considered the peanut butter trick.

Then the door opened a crack and Angela looked in to see what was going on.

Before I knew it, we were both in her room and Eydie was locked out in the hallway—because the dog tended to growl and bark whenever Angie was on top of me. Maybe she thought Angela was trying to pummel me to death with her torso, which wouldn't be a bad way to go. All I know is we did it that night like we had never done it before, with a weird desperate energy that resulted in her seeing colors and me seeing stars. When we were done, when we were both naked, sweaty and sticky, I realized we might just have had break-up sex, the most potent sex of all, when two people know bonds are cracking and feel the need to wring the last few drops---okay, there were more than drops involved—out of the relationship. I didn't know what had just happened. I just knew I didn't trust anything to come out okay. I couldn't help putting a negative spin on everything around me.

After a few minutes, the dog whimpered. I put on my bathrobe and went back to the guest room and Angela didn't say boo about it. Maybe she secretly agreed with me about what had just happened or maybe she sensed my mood and was just giving me space. But the hard truth was neither of us knew what was about to happen. We just knew that the next day, the kid, Kev and I would be heading to Florida and the final fundraiser. And maybe Angela and I both knew on some level that I wouldn't be coming back.

Because at that final fundraiser, I had a feeling they would end up ripping the asphalt from the playground of my mind and exposing the boiling waters of the River Styx flowing underneath.

Hut-to-Peen

To say I was in a bad mood was to say maybe the Mets should've won a few more games last summer. Unfortunately, they finished 27 games back. And the thing is, the boys in blue (as well as orange and white) seemed to have it all going into the 2017 season—the pitching, the hitting, the willpower. Unfortunately, what they had more of than all that other stuff was injuries. So the Dodgers and the Astros (!) were playing in the World Series and Yoenis Céspedes was at home, counting the few body parts left that hadn't yet landed him on the DL.

Yeah, it was painful to think about the Mets, but it was less painful than any other subject at that moment. And that was saying something.

Our plane was coming down for a landing at the West Palm Beach Airport and Florida, as always, made whatever miserable mood I was in even worse. At least it was near the end of October, which meant the humidity in the Sunshine State was finally edging toward bearable. As the plane taxied to the terminal, I checked the time on my phone, which I had never turned off during the flight just to be ornery. 4:22 pm. In a little over three hours, I would be doing my last fundraiser star turn, with PMA's help.

Only problem was, the two of us were barely speaking. While we were airborne, I had suggested he stay close and avoid Colin the Bureau—at least until the fundraiser was over and we were hopefully free and clear of Duds as well as the whole dismal arrangement. The kid bristled at that and made it plain that he still resented my suspicions about his judgment and about Colin's trustworthiness. I reminded him that he was the one who had said the powers-that-be might not be willing to let us leave after this final obligation—so maybe he should try thinking with his brain instead of his groin for the next few hours.

That went over well.

So, conversation was pretty much shut down for the rest of the trip. The kid was too stubborn to admit I might have a point and I was too edgy to make nice. But my edginess was based in the reality of our situation. This time around, for this third and final fundraiser, we would be completely isolated. It was going to be held at the sprawling Hut-to-Peen Ocean Resort, right up the shoreline from Donald J. Trump's beloved Mar-a-Lago. The kid and I would be staying at the Hut-to-Peen, because there weren't a lot of other options in the area. This was the land of the rich, white Palm Beach crowd, which meant you wouldn't find many Motel 6's conveniently located in the vicinity. If anything went down, we would be more or less helpless.

Sure, Kev said he was going to be watching over us one way or another, but he also said he was going to make his own arrangements. He said not to try and contact him while we were there, in case they were picking up our calls somehow. He would stay in the shadows. Wonderful. But I didn't trust what I couldn't see and I was far from certain they wouldn't spot him and take him down, meaning I couldn't count on him either.

After we deplaned, we found a limo driver waiting for us at baggage claim, just as Howard had told us there would be. The kid and I rode in silence to the resort. We entered through the massive golden gates of the Hut-to-Peen and went into the main building to register.

Like Mar-a-Lago, Hut-to-Peen had pretensions of gauche grandiosity, swathed in faux-gold fabric and metalwork. Unlike Mar-a-Lago, it was much more affordable—especially since Trump had doubled the rates at his resort since his election and was not about to offer Senator di Pineda any kind of discount. That's because everyone knew di Pineda wanted the Oval Office all for himself in 2020—which is why Trump called him "Dummy di Pineda" whenever he targeted him in a tweet.

At any rate, the di Pineda campaign had upgraded us to our own two-bedroom bungalow, overlooking the golf course instead of the ocean, but I could give a shit. A staffer gave us a golf cart ride to the bungalow and, along the way, my reflexes made me shoot a look upward to see if there were any drones in the sky. After all, it was my first time in a golf cart since my escape from the Community.

After the staffer took our luggage inside our bungalow, and after the kid tipped him and he left, I went into my bedroom and crashed on my king-sized Serta, ready to start surfing the local TV channel line-up until it was time for the fundraiser. But that plan was rudely interrupted.

There was a knock at the door. I didn't like the sound of that knock. I got up and went out into the living room area to see who it was.

The kid had beaten me to the punch.

Standing there on our doorstep was Colin the Bureau, wearing something meant to be casual, but, at the same time, obviously and ridiculously expensive. It was how everybody dressed around there—pricey polo shirts tucked into pricey belted shorts, or, how to look old and stupid before your time.

"Colin," the kid said, a little flustered.

"Hey, Jeremy. Thought maybe you'd want to hang out a little before the thing."

"Hang what out?" I mumbled. The kid gave me a look.

"Oh, hello, Mr. Bowman," Colin said politely. "I hadn't noticed you there." "They" still thought I was brain dead, so anything I said would be excused. It wasn't a bad position to be in. "They" turned back to the kid. "This time, I've got my own room, I told my folks I wasn't coming unless I had my own space."

"I want to meet your folks!" I said with a bit of perk.

The kid turned to me. "Not today, Max. You can get by without me for a little bit, right?" he asked pleasantly through clenched teeth.

"I will watch the TV," I said. My insides told me I should try to block this particular cock, but I didn't know how to do it without creating a scene and making the kid completely disgusted with me. Besides, sometimes you had to let things play out, even when they shouldn't.

"Yeah, do that, Max, watch TV. I'll be back in an hour or so to help you get ready for the fundraiser."

And with that, the kid was gone, slamming the door behind him just to punctuate his general attitude towards me. In the kid's mind, I'm sure he thought he would be back in plenty of time to take me to the fundraiser. In the kid's mind, he was having a short romantic rendezvous and there would be no harm done.

Unfortunately, what happened in the kid's mind stayed in the kid's mind.

Ten minutes before the fundraiser was supposed to begin, he was still gone and not responding to my texts or calls. I tried calling Colin's room. They told me there was no one by the name of Colin Burian registered at the resort. Nor any other Burians. Maybe I should have been surprised, but I wasn't. I tried to bury my growing anxiety while I put on my monkey suit, hoping against hope PMA would show up.

Finally, there was a knock at the door. I ran and opened it before I came to a complete stop. But standing there wasn't the kid and it certainly wasn't Colin.

No, it was Howard.

"The kid's gone," I blurted out.

"Jeremy?" Howard patted me on the arm. "Max, I'm sure he's fine, let's just…"

"Don't fucking patronize me. There's some kind of bullshit going on here and you need to tell me what you know. NOW, Howard."

Howard blinked at me. I was trembling and my physical discomfort was probably obvious. He let himself in and shut the door behind him. And then he looked at me. Really looked at me.

"Yeah, I'm fine, Howard," I said, getting it over with as quickly as possible. "I've been faking it since I got out of the Community. I took your advice and got off the ice cream. The sex didn't go great, but my mind came back."

Howard fell back in a nearby chair and he continued to look up at me.

"You've been faking this whole fucking time?"

"Yeah, that's what I just said! Howard, I don't have time to deal with your shock and awe, I need information. This campaign's about more than the campaign. You've been along for the whole ride. What's going on?"

"Max...I...I..." He was having a hard time wrapping his mind around my mental clarity. Finally, he snapped out of it. "Look, I don't know. I mean, there's been some weird...undercurrents...but..."

Undercurrents. Undercurrents. I picked up the chair, the small delicate chair that came with the elegant aged beechwood desk and I threw it at the fucking TV, threw it with all I had in me at my age, which turned out to be more than enough to smash the Sony 50" flat screen on the dresser into the wall and crack the screen in a hundred different directions.

"What the fuck are you, the Who???" Howard screamed, gripping the arms of the chair. He finally came up with a pop culture reference almost as old as one of mine.

"Tell me about the Burians."

"Who?"

"The Burians. That's who the kid went with, their kid, Colin Burian. Supposedly, the parents are big-time donors."

"Burians? Max, I've been through the donor list a billion times, especially the list for this fundraiser, I never saw any Burians."

"I fucking knew it..." I kicked at a nearby dresser as hard as I could. And, upon contact, I screamed with pain on behalf of my foot. I fell back on the bed.

"Max, calm down," Howard said, getting to his feet.

I was sweaty and still shaking. "He's still alive, isn't he? Fucking Andrew Wright. I know the bastard's alive. What's the Eugene Group? What's White Rain?"

"Max, people throw words around, but I don't know anything about that shit, I just do my job. Yeah, I hear things, but I make it a point not to hear too much. You get it."

"Yeah. I remember that was how you worked it at the CIA. Which is how I almost got killed multiple times."

"Yeah, and I got fired without my fucking pension because of you! Which is why I have to work for these Nazis!"

"Nazis?" I asked, sitting down on the bed. "Tell me about the Nazis."

He glanced around the room nervously. "It doesn't mean anything, it's just something you call people!"

He thought the room was bugged. And I couldn't think of one reason he might be wrong.

"Look," he finally said. "I'll send a couple of our security guys to look for Jeremy. I mean, he is supposed to be at this event, so why would we do anything to the guy? But, in the meantime, I need to get your ass to the room. Or Dudley DeCosta will drag us both out to the fucking ocean and feed our asses to the sharks."

The chest pains were back. I was having trouble getting my breathing under control.

He stopped and stared at me. "Are you all right?"

The sweat was pouring off my forehead. I wiped off a bucketful and laid back on the bed. As usual, Howard was more sympathetic to his job than my condition.

"Max, seriously, I gotta get you to the fundraiser, with or without Jeremy. I'm sorry."

"I just want to know...what the hell...is going on...."

"Catch your breath. Then we have to go, Max."

The Last Boy Scouts

Howard waved away the golf cart and driver waiting outside the bungalow. For some reason, he wanted to go by foot to the event.

I didn't object. I thought the fresh air might do me some good. I had caught my breath and was doing okay again. But it still felt like a fragile recovery. The extra time would help, as long as Howard didn't try to power walk.

"So…you're okay?" he asked tentatively.

"More or less."

Howard nodded with some relief, then made a call on his cell to some security human and told them the kid was missing. He asked whoever was on the other end to search the property. Then he put his phone back in his pocket and walked on quietly.

"You should know. There's somebody around," I said in something close to a whisper.

"What's that supposed to mean?" He looked around furtively, like someone was about to rain hellfire on him.

"There's an ex-CIA guy who helped me and Jeremy out last year, probably here at the resort. His name's Kevin, Kevin Germano, he's got a buzzcut and more muscles than either of us combined ever thought of having on our best day. I just don't know where he's watching from."

"Wow. You're trusting me with this information?" Howard seemed almost touched.

"Sad to say, you're all I have left, Howard. Even though you alternate between saving my life and almost getting me killed. I'm hoping the former is in rotation at the moment."

We walked on without another word for a few more moments. It was completely dark, even though it was only approaching 7:30. Fall was in the air, at least as much of it as the Florida weather would allow.

"There is a lot of shit going on, Max," Howard finally said almost in a whisper. "And there's nobody I can talk to about it either." He stopped and looked around. "Really evil shit. I just hear bits and pieces. But I know if I go running off to tell anyone, I'll end up like Doug Daytona. That's why they ripped him apart that way, as an example, an example I don't want to emulate. It's not just that I can't afford to quit. It's that I know I won't survive it."

"I still don't get why they're having this fundraiser so soon after Senator Eddie's wife got killed."

"Because they're fundraising off the attacks on the campaign, that's why. Money is fucking pouring in."

"And Senator Eddie is okay with this? Making money off his wife's death?"

"Remember Doug's friend? The guy with the dog puppet...?"

"Augustine Bravino," I said.

"Yeah. Well, in this case, the senator is the dog puppet and has been from the beginning. I'm just not sure whose hand is inside his ass."

"What do you mean?"

"I mean, they're using a brown guy to show they don't hate brown guys. Just like they hired a Jew like me to prove they don't hate Jews."

We took another few steps.

"It's Andrew Wright. He's still alive. I know he is," I finally said.

"That I have no idea about. But what is it with you two, Max?" Howard finally asked. "Why did you go on a hunting expedition in Arizona to try and kill him? You're not exactly an expert assassin."

I stopped and pulled out a cigarette from my tuxedo pocket. I lit it with a shaky hand, then I took a few puffs.

"You're not answering my question," Howard observed.

I looked off at a bird on a trashcan. "Andrew Wright is my father, Howard. He fucked my mother and I think my dad let him."

Howard examined my face as though it was riddled with leprosy. "Jesus, Max, come the fuck on. You've gone over the deep end."

"Howard, I could give a shit if you believe me or not, it is what it is. As you might know, he's big on bloodlines. And I'm the tail end of his."

Howard sighed. "Bloodlines. There's a word I hear a lot lately."

I looked sharply at him. "How bad is this? Are these guys actual Nazis?"

"Nazis *and* Russians. I wish I had a nickel for every time I've heard a Russian name. Hardly ever see one, but they're always talking about some Ivanovich or Petrov or Kuryakin. Jesus, Max, when I signed on for this, I had no idea it would get this weird." He paused and shook his head. "Maybe it's true, you being his son, how should I know? I don't know anything. I don't know who I am, where I am, how I got here or where all this is going."

"I know how you feel," I said. "Trust me."

He laughed. "Sure was a lot simpler when you were in your ratty apartment on Roosevelt Island, huh? When I'd call you once in a while so you could go find somebody we really didn't care all that much about finding…"

"That's what I lived on, Howard, those stupid little jobs." I took another puff. "I do appreciate it."

"Yeah. I'm sorry I haven't…haven't always been there for you."

"You weren't in the best position."

"No, I wasn't. You never had to get your hands dirty like I did, you could just sit in your goddam apartment and play Boy Scout."

"Well, I was trustworthy, loyal, kind, clean, and reverent…um…"

"Wait. There's courteous, thrifty, clean…"

"I already said 'clean.'"

"The 12 points of being a Boy Scout," he laughed. "Who remembers all those words anymore? Nobody in charge that's for sure. I guess it doesn't matter. Neither of us is making it to Eagle Scout anytime soon." He stopped again. The main building of the resort, where I assumed the fundraiser would be happening, was up ahead.

"I made First Class," I said, staring ahead with him.

"I was short a merit badge or two," he sighed. Then he turned to me. "Look…this fundraiser…it's going to be…different."

"So…be prepared?"

"This one is just for the hardcore donors. The richest…and the most…"

"The most what?"

"Just the *most*. I'm not even allowed to stay in the room when Dudley makes the presentation."

"Duds is in charge?"

"Yeah. So, keep your cool. Keep playing stupid and you'll get out of there alive."

Howard still didn't make a move towards the building. He just stood there, staring at it. I looked around. Nobody was out on the resort grounds, except for a few of the staff zooming by in their golf carts. I checked my phone. Nothing from the kid, nothing from anybody.

"The Eugene Group is a shell company," Howard finally blurted out. "A lot of cash moves into the campaign from it. That's about all I know."

"Shell companies. A specialty of Andrew Wright. That's what was behind Blue Fire."

"Pretty much everybody involved with the Eugene Group is gonna be there tonight."

"Because they're all the *most*. Well, I guess it's appropriate that I'm there."

"You? Why?"

I squashed the end of the cigarette against a nearby wall and then tossed it into a trash can as we passed by.

"Apparently, I'm involved with the Eugene Group too."

"How?" asked Howard.

"They bought my parents' old house."

Fundraiser 3

This event took the "fun" out of "fundraiser."

First of all, there were a couple of armed security guys posted outside every exit door (all of which were closed) of the small ballroom where the fundraiser was being held. Secondly, there were only about thirty to forty people inside sitting around a few small tables, and all of them were old white men in tuxedos. No wives, no women of any kind— it looked like a reunion dinner for elderly headwaiters. And the closest anyone got to being a minority was a guy about two tables back who looked like he overslept on a tanning bed.

The kicker was the very rich and fattening dinner. The chef went overboard on the butter and cream to cater to this collection of moneyed Methuselahs and my stomach wasn't appreciating it.

I sat on one side of Duds. On the other side sat yet another armed security officer with a shaved head in some strange uniform I didn't recognize. However, I did recognize the 9mm Glock handgun in his holster on his hip. Duds, me, the guard and his gun comprised the entire head table of this evening's fundraiser. This was a barebones gathering, presumably because whatever was going to go down there was meant to be very, very confidential.

I sat mutely at the table throughout the entire drinks and dinner portion of the program. I wasn't out to poke any bears or kick up any dirt, especially since, every few minutes, Duds threw a glare my way to make sure I was staying in line. Finally, after coffee and dessert was served, Duds got up to address the group before their bones all turned to dust. As he did so, a lackey lowered a screen behind him. An image appeared on that screen of a beaming Eddie di Pineda.

Duds looked over the crowd. I had a hunch he was about to say some very interesting things.

"As you all know, Senator di Pineda could not be here tonight, due to his personal tragedy," Duds began. "While we're saddened by his loss, I will say that his absence will allow me to speak a little more candidly tonight."

Candidly. Yeah. This was going to be interesting, all right.

"This is a historic occasion, gentlemen," Duds went on. "The first time we've been together in one room—everyone at this level of involvement. Unfortunately, what's brought us together here tonight is unfortunate, but all too real. There's a war on us. A war we're going to win. We have the resources. We just need the *will* to win it."

If only I could have recorded everything. But we all had to leave our cell phones and any other electronic devices at the door for that very reason. That meant I had no way to find out if the kid turned up okay. I was stuck sitting there until the ordeal was over. And boy howdy, did I want it to be over.

"So, yes, we are going to talk candidly tonight. I'm going to update you on some things you already know about. And tell you some things you don't know about. We're at a critical turning point, gentlemen. Our society can easily go the wrong way. But we're determined that it go the *right* way."

When Howard and I arrived here, Howard tried to talk to Duds about the kid's disappearance. Duds' answer? A lot of bellowing about how we were late. Duds didn't care where the kid was, he said I was the only one they needed there anyway. Then he gave Howard the boot and told him to come back in a couple of hours. Until then, Howard was to wait out in the hallway and not leave the building until the event was over.

"It's funny how the media pits everyone against us and then they play the victim," Duds continued. "Then, when our bodies start piling up, they're suddenly pretty quiet. We're being attacked, people are dying, and yet, those bastards bury the story. Think about it. There's a full-blown terrorist operation going on against us. Joshua James, a fine musician, was blown apart. A very talented Emmy award-winning filmmaker, Doug Daytona, was brutally murdered. And Senator di Pineda...that poor man lost his beautiful and devoted wife."

I had only been half-listening up until that moment, because the cream-laden fettucine alfredo (served with extra cheese sauce on the side) that felt like a gloppy bowling ball rolling around in my stomach was preoccupying me. But it wasn't just my digestive system that kept me from paying close attention. It was also the fact that I didn't want to listen to whatever shit Duds was spewing. I just wanted my involvement with the whole sordid campaign to be over with and Angela to be free of that pig.

But as Duds detailed the deaths that had occurred, some very unpleasant thoughts entered my head. As unthinkable as it might be, it felt like the terrorist operation Duds was talking about just might have been masterminded by Duds himself.

After all, the cellist had been expendable. And I knew terrorists didn't kill Doug Daytona and Augustine, their murders were directly connected to someone at the campaign. The only thing I didn't get was that the last assassin tried to kill the Senator himself. How did that make sense? What was a campaign without a candidate?

Unless, of course, the idea was to make it look like Senator Eddie was the target.

Maybe it was supposed to seem like the guy was trying to kill Eddie…only to have him "accidentally" take out the wife instead. It made sense. It put more public sympathy on Senator Eddie's side and made the campaign look like it was really under siege. But I couldn't believe Senator Eddie would actually conspire to kill his own wife. If he hadn't, that would mean it had to have been planned out without Senator Eddie's knowledge.

Then again, didn't Howard describe him as a puppet with someone else's hand shoved up his ass? And didn't Howard *also* tell me money was flooding into the campaign because of the attacks? That was another great motive to fake some terrorist bullshit. It was sick and wrong to kill innocents to boost the bank account…but, then again, we were talking about Duds.

I looked over at the bloated sociopath as he continued his harangue. I flinched as I watched a couple wads of spit fly out of his mouth.

"I mean, they label people like us as Nazis. Nazis!" he said, raising his aggrieved voice. "Do you believe that shit? And what really makes it infuriating is that it's not like we're so fond of the Nazis either. Okay, maybe not for all the same reasons as a lot of other people. To be honest, my main problem with Hitler and his stooges? It's the fact that *they ruined it for us.*"

Um…what?

"Let me break it down. Eugenics isn't a word you hear much these days. Because it's automatically considered morally wrong to discuss genetic breeding when it comes to the human race. Because of the Germans, people hear eugenics, and automatically think you want to set up concentration camps and commit genocide. Now, I don't know about you guys, but I'm not real anxious to get into the Jew-killing business."

Some uncomfortable chuckles. At least they *sounded* uncomfortable. But sometimes I give people too much credit.

"Here's the thing. Before World War II, the situation was completely the opposite—eugenics was a respected science. And when you look at it objectively…it just makes sense. To get the best results, we breed animals and we engineer plants—but, for some reason, we can't even talk about doing the same thing for ourselves. For *people*. We are effectively prohibited from creating the best version of humanity. It's simply not allowed. We can do whatever it takes to make great hunting dogs, cows that produce more milk, crops that feed millions more people than they could in the past. Humans? Who gives a *shit* how they come out?"

His "shit" rang out across the dead quiet room. None of the elderly headwaiters said a word. All eyes were on Duds. He was preaching to the converted with a sermon they desperately wanted to hear.

"Now…how in holy hell is that our attitude? Why do we allow our species to be held back by political correctness? I mean, you go back and look at the facts, the history, you see a whole different picture. I don't know if you guys know this, but you know who started eugenics? Charles Darwin's cousin. That's right. Mr. Evolution, the guy we're forced to teach in the schools. Just how much do liberals love Charles Darwin, am I right?"

The elderly headwaiters nodded. Liberals. Charles Darwin.

"Anyway, when the cousin came up with this idea, people immediately went, hey, you know what? Why shouldn't we advance our own species? Why not? It's just common sense. And that's why, when eugenics popped up on the scene, scientists dived in to do the research. Eugenics began to be taught in the top-line colleges and universities all around the world. It got big funding from the likes of the Rockefellers and Andrew Carnegie. People were motivated to produce better people. Because better people would make a better world, right? That's why, by the early 20th century, eugenics was *mainstream thought* in America.

"How mainstream? Get this—there were Better Baby contests at state fairs. State fairs! Yeah, the mom who had engineered the best baby would win prizes, that actually used to happen. For God's sakes, eugenics was a major force in the rise of birth control. Birth control. Another liberal favorite."

The old men nodded again. Liberals. Birth control.

"Even FDR commissioned a study on eugenics. FDR. He wanted to know which race was superior. They pulled the plug before they got to finish the study…but, between you and me, I think I know which one would've won."

Duds winked at the old men and they wheezed with endless laughter. FDR was just the right button to push for this group, because they were probably still pissed off about the New Deal. My stomach gurgled as I struggled to take it all in. Jesus Christ, Howard was right. They were using a Latino and a Jew for window dressing, but the whole thing, whatever this thing was, was about white supremacy. It was as plain as what was left of the Bananas Foster sitting in front of me. Why the hell did I try to eat that fucking dessert? I could feel the butter and rum trying to creep back up my throat with the alfredo sauce posting a close second.

"So, again, let's review. Charles Darwin's cousin comes up with genetic engineering. It's embraced by the scientific community, by the business community, by the public. It's a huge movement. FDR was in on it. So, what happened?"

Duds took a pause and took in the room.

"What happened was the damn Nazis. They started slaughtering Jews, people with handicaps, blacks, whoever, to achieve their 'Final Solution.' The exact wrong way to get this done, using a goddam axe when you need a scalpel. End result? Eugenics becomes a bad thing, a terrible thing, a hated thing, all because some microbrain with a funny moustache went on a killing rampage. All legitimate science on this subject was suddenly thrown out the window—simply because the Nazis embraced it. That's the funny part, to me anyway. The Germans actually learned eugenics *from us.*"

Where the hell was this demented history lesson going? Where in hell was all of this going? This was all about the Nazis not being subtler about their racial cleansing?

"Okay, enough History Channel. Let's skip forward to today. Hitler's dead...but Donald J. Trump's alive. President Donald J. Trump, someone who would love to run the kind of operation Uncle Adolf did. You can tell he's studied his playbook. The problem with Trump is...well, I call him the Pussy Hitler. He loves what Hitler did, but he's too much of a pussy to ever do anything like it. Now, I hope none of you are offended, because I'm willing to bet a lot of you in this room voted for Trump. I know I did—because, hey, he was saying a lot of the right stuff, right? Unfortunately, this guy has no discipline, no self-control, no brains and I suspect, not even much of a bank account. Hitler knew how to be a Führer. Trump only knows how to be a fuck-up. Look, I'm sorry to speak so plainly. But...it's truth-telling time. We can't afford for him to fail and ruin it all for us in 2020. Am I wrong?

"Anyway, that's where we come in. By 2020, Trump will be dead as a doornail politically, if not in jail, trust me. There are going to be a lot of conservatives running around, feeling like the roof's caved in. And suddenly, our Senator Eddie di Pineda will be in position to be their conservative. While the media bangs on about Trump and Russians and Trump and racists, we will have quietly built a powerful organization that specializes in the right messaging without sacrificing our beliefs. That's key, right?"

Heads nodded. They were already liking this messaging.

"Senator Eddie is a Puerto Rican. Some of you have told me privately, you don't like that. Well, I'm going to push back. His race is not a negative. Instead, it's a firewall that will save our asses. People can vote for Senator Eddie and proudly brag that they're not racist...even though we're backing the same ideas as Trump. But we're arguing them more reasonably. In a more...more *muted* way. We're not insulting black people on Twitter every other day. Instead, we *look tolerant.* Nothing will be more important for a Republican candidate in 2020.

"And, by the way, in the meantime, we are not standing still. Far from it. The fact is, Trump, in spite of his blunders, has opened up some pathways, some very, very valuable pathways. And we're capitalizing on those pathways.

"We've now got an open line to the Russians. Because they want the same end game as us—to keep the culture from slipping out of our grasp. The Russian oligarchs are helping to back this project, because they understand its importance. Not only does it guarantee our survival in comfort during the worst days to come—but it also will reestablish our dominance in the new world to come.

"As for the trash that's threatening to overthrow us, the black, brown and yellow trash that's outbreeding us into oblivion? That trash is going to be taken out. But here's the beauty of our plan. *We're* not the ones who will take them out. *We're* not touching a hair on anybody's head. No, we are actually going to give those people what they want—the world. And, in return, the world is going to have them for breakfast. And while that happens, we'll be enjoying ourselves in our little underground resort."

An underground resort? What the fuck was he talking about? Was this going to be the world's biggest subterranean country club? Were they going to put in 18 holes down in one giant hole?

Then, suddenly, the lights lowered, Senator Eddie disappeared from the screen behind Duds and was replaced by an elegant logo. The logo consisted of two words I was already very familiar with— "WHITE RAIN."

"White Rain," Duds said with an ample amount of reverence. "That's what we've named our installation in Montana, the one you've all heard so much, which will be located right next to the headquarters of the Dark Sky main facility. Dark Sky's own Andrew Wright, the late Andrew Wright, God rest his soul, provided the land and the initial funding for this massive project...and I salute this patriot for his incredibly generous gift."

Applause. I joined in. If Andrew Wright was really dead, I had a lot to clap about. Maybe, instead, I should have felt bereaved by the loss of dead dear old Dad. Maybe I should've shed a tear or two—but I found my eyes to be conspicuously dry.

"Why did we name it White Rain? Because that's our metaphor for the self-cleansing the earth will soon be performing. It's going to rain, it's going to flood, everything's going to go haywire for a while...but in the end, we'll be left with a clean white planet. Sure, officially, we can claim climate change is a hoax—but, of course, we all know it's real. But we don't need to admit it. No, our job now is to make sure it happens as soon as possible. Because after the 'White Rain' falls...then comes the 'White Reign.' And that brand of rain is spelled R-E-I-G-N."

The motivated a loud murmur from the group, as the screen behind Duds began displaying video of a massive construction site on a massive area of dirt. But nothing was being built on top of the site. A convoy of construction vehicles and trucks were heading below the surface through huge cement entryways that took workers and equipment down, down, down into the ground.

"You won't believe what they've already built under there," Duds said, pointing to the screen. "A massive, luxury community is slowly taking shape. The best of everything and supplies to last a lifetime. They need to last that long. Because this is where you and your children and your grandchildren will be living once the storms become too powerful, ancient viruses get defrosted and the oceans rise too high.

"Every person in this room will be an important part of that community. Other purebred and heavily vetted individuals will also quietly migrate into White Rain in the years to come. Living there will be our finest minds and our most premium gene sets. And guess what? Even though I'm Italian, I still qualify!"

Another big wheezy laugh. One of the elderly headwaiters yelled out, "But who's going to clean the toilets?" An even BIGGER wheezy laugh.

"Hey, we got that covered," answered Duds in as reassuring a manner as possible. "We're going to establish a worker class to handle all our needs. Seriously."

Seriously. Seriously INSANE. This was what was being built in Montana? Or, should I say, *under* Montana? The whole preposterous plan was already the punchline of an old preposterous movie, *Dr. Strangelove*—and it was proposed by Peter Sellers, in a wheelchair, talking in a ridiculous German accent near the end of the film. Very near the end. Because, as he proposed it, the Russian ambassador who was listening in called back to the old country, where the order was given to nuke us all into oblivion. Cue the mushroom clouds.

But I guess that wouldn't be the ending this time. Because it turned out the Russians were in on it too. This was what tied the hard-right wingnuts to Putin—maintaining the last vestiges of a pure white heterosexual race.

"So, when the natural climate disasters start coming fast and furious, when all the other peoples are wiped out—not by our hands, but by God's—we will patiently wait. And, when it's all over, we'll come back up on the surface to rebuild in our own image. As we like to say around here, when the waters rise…white rain will pour down. And brother, let it pour."

One elderly headwaiter got up. Then another. Then another and another. Everyone was suddenly on their feet, clapping like Duds had just parted the Red Sea. I stayed seated and I shivered. *When the waters rise, white rain will pour down.* Another very familiar phrase, texted to my phone by the late Augustine Bravino with even more typos than a Trump tweet.

"Again, one last time, I want us all to acknowledge my mentor Andrew Wright's vision," Duds said over the lingering applause. His mentor. Oh Jesus. "Because of him, the funds and the means have been made available to begin to create our perfect society underneath the surface. I am also happy to report his superior bloodline will still be a vital part of that perfect society. Because, surprisingly, a previously unknown heir to Andrew Wright has been discovered…and will soon be revealed to all of you."

I looked at Duds in disbelief. Did he know? Was he about to out me?

As the old men clapped and cheered one more time, Duds did not look my way or acknowledge in any way I was that heir. Why hadn't he mentioned that he was going to say all this? Wouldn't he want to get me on board first? Was he thinking I was too mentally impaired to push back? I bent my neck back and looked at the ceiling, as if there was some help to be found above me somewhere. But there was nothing there but peeling paint.

After the applause died down, Duds went in for the final kill.

"So, yeah, we're off to a fantastic start with White Rain. But it's only a start. In order to bring it to completion, we will need more funds, more resources. A di Pineda presidency ensures that will happen. And we need it to happen. Because White Rain will guarantee that the immediate family of everyone in this room will be able to survive the coming global catastrophe. Only we will be able to thrive and reproduce with our own kind. Only then will we be able to create a higher level of being that should have been brought to fruition a hundred years ago. Now, we don't have to wait. Now, we can bring about the ultimate version of humanity."

I looked around at the old white men's faces. Most were still standing. All were transfixed by this idea of an underground utopia that would bring all their secret racist fantasies to life. It wasn't Reagan's shining city on a hill. No, it was a really, really nice basement below the dirt. But this group didn't see ugliness in any of it. They only saw pure pristine white beauty.

"That's why, gentlemen, tonight I'm asking for as much support as you can comfortably provide to our campaign. There are forces allied against us, as you know. And it will take all you can provide to combat those forces. I'm hoping you'll give us the ammunition we need to prevail."

One of the old men pulled out a checkbook from his tuxedo jacket pocket.

"You tell me how many zeroes to write down," he said. "And I will write them."

I had never seen Duds smile a more genuine smile.

Goodbye, Norma Jean

After the soiree was over, drink stations were rolled into the room for some final mix n' mingling. I remained seated, ignored by all.

Including Duds.

And that was bothering me. Not quite as much as the racism, white privilege and murdering for profit—but the fact that my existence had not been acknowledged at all during this fundraiser was curious, especially since Duds made sure to mention that Daddy Andy had a secret heir they didn't know about. I was not even asked to speak, which was the whole reason why I thought he wanted me there.

Maybe he was saving it for a big reveal. Or maybe he was bullshitting them. If Daddy Andy was dead, he could tell them anything he wanted, right? And I didn't care if he did, as long as I wasn't involved. Somebody else would have to stop this particular atrocity, I was done. After all, my involvement was supposed to be finished after the fundraiser. I just wanted to get my phone and get the hell out of there.

And that's when I realized things weren't going to go that smoothly.

Because, when I left the ballroom to go to the security station, Duds followed me. And when I asked the security officer for my phone, Duds said to him, "Not yet."

A little chill went down my spine.

"Duds," I said wearily in my idiot voice, "I am tired. My stomach hurts. I want to go to bed. Can't I go to bed, Duds?"

He smiled, patted me patronizingly on my shoulder and said, "Just want to wrap up our business, Max. Just want to tie everything up in a nice bow so we're all free and clear of each other. I assume you want the same thing, right?"

"Yes, that's right," I said, nodding slowly. I didn't mention the shit he said in the room about there being a secret heir to Andrew Wright. I wanted to pretend it never happened. And apparently, he was going to let me.

He led me down a nearby hallway. The guard who had sat next to Duds at the table, the one with the shaved head and the Glock on his hip, followed us. He didn't say a word, but he didn't have to. His whole aura screamed, "Don't fuck with me."

"Did Howard ever come back?" I asked Duds' back. "I wanted to say goodbye to Howard."

"No, Max," Duds said mildly. "Haven't seen him."

"Did anyone find Jeremy? Where is he?"

"I'm sure he'll be along."

We reached the end of the hallway, where there was one of those doors you're only supposed to use as an emergency exit. Duds pushed on its release bar, shoved it open and walked outside. He then held the door open for me and the guard.

We all walked out into a large and deserted grassy area, the kind of area where they'd hold an outdoor wedding or some other kind of event, because it had a perfect view of the beach. What it didn't have was a lot of visibility—the night sky was so cloudy; the moonlight never had a chance.

"I don't like it here, Duds," I said. Because I didn't.

"Just finishing things up, Max. I thought we should have some privacy." Duds pulled out his cell phone and opened an email. He showed the screen to me. The subject heading read: "DeCosta-Davidson Divorce Agreement: Please DocuSign."

I looked up from the phone. He still was sporting a warm smile. Holy shit, he was going to keep his promise.

"See, Max? I'm living up to our deal. Angela's already put her electronic signature on this—now I'm going to put in mine." He turned the phone back to himself, then clicked the email open, did a little scrawl with his finger, and did another click. He waited a moment. After a moment, he looked back down at the screen, clicked something open, and showed it to me. I looked at the screen. It said, "Document Complete."

Angela was actually free.

"See, Max? Divorce agreement finalized. Like I said when I met you, when I tell you something, you can take it to the bank."

I nodded. "Thank you, Duds. Thank you."

That's when he slapped me so hard, my teeth rattled and my legs gave out from under me. Oh Jesus, here we go again.

"You don't have to talk like a dolt anymore, Blowman. I know you've been faking."

Wrong, Duds, I wanted to say. I *was* a dolt. I should've known this was too easy. Duds had lived up to the bargain, I'd give him that. But it seemed like this was going to be like the other unpleasant talk we had outside stately Davidson manor—the one where he beat the shit out of me.

I sat up on the grass, I wiped my lip. A little blood.

"I paid off one of Angela's maids," he went on. "She's been telling me everything that's been going on. Including how you fucked the woman who was still my wife at the time."

I thought maybe he wouldn't be expecting it and I could get away with it—so I foolishly lunged for Duds' legs in an attempt to topple the Colossus of Rhodes. But I was way too slow and the guard standing by Duds was way too fast. The Glock was out of his holster before I made it an inch. I stopped myself but fast.

"You're old and tired, Blowman."

"And you're fat, Duds," I said, dropping my brain-damaged act. "Okay, you got me. But so what? What does it matter what happened with Angela? You were walking away from the marriage anyway."

Duds bent down so he could look me in the face.

"Yeah, asshole, I was. But I hadn't yet. And nobody turns me into a cuck." He turned to the guard. "Ashton, do me a favor and kick him in the head."

Before I knew it, Ashton did just that. Now I was on my left side down on the ground and my head was spinning. Duds straightened up again.

"Don't feel too bad. It was going to end this way anyway, Blowman."

"What way?" I groaned.

He said, in a wistful tone, "What d'ya think about Marilyn Monroe?"

"Marilyn Monroe? I don't know. She was hot?"

"I'm talking about her death, Blowman. I mean, it's still kind of a mystery. Some people think she was murdered, some people say suicide. I mean, if it was murder, it was the perfect set-up, what with her swallowing half a pharmacy every day. Even if Bobby Kennedy showed up to stuff a gazillion sleeping pills down her throat, who would be suspicious? She was just as likely to do it herself, right? When somebody's got emotional problems…"

He shrugged and I finally got it. Oh, fuck. Angela.

I knew better than to try, but emotions got the best of me. I moved to get up so I could come at Duds, but I was slow as a turtle on Ambien pudding and Ashton's boot quickly put me back down. And suddenly the Bananas Foster and a little of the fettucine alfredo was lying on the ground beside my mouth. I choked on the remainder in my throat, the part I hadn't vomited, then I barfed that up as well.

"Angela…" I said weakly, coughing on bile.

"Yeah, Angela. She's going to have an unfortunate overdose tonight. Murder or suicide? I'm sure people will think suicide. I mean, tonight she's gonna get the bad news."

"Bad news."

"About you dying."

"Dying. You just said in there…that the heir to Andrew Wright was…"

He bent down next to me again, being careful not to get grass stains on his tuxedo, and grabbed me by the shirt collar.

"I wasn't talking about you, Blowman."

"Then…who…?"

"The promised one," he said with a nasty chuckle.

The promised one. Another phrase Augustine had used. Who the fuck was the promised one?

I didn't have time to think much about it, because suddenly, Duds was shaking me by my shirt collar.

"Did you fucking think I was just going to let you walk? Did you fucking think I was just going to let Angela off the hook that easy? That's not how I do business, Blowman. I just wanted to get what I needed out of you. And, if you'll notice, I held up my end of the bargain. The divorce agreement is done. But so are you. And so is that whore."

"Jeremy…" I said.

"Oh, Jeremy Davidson is going to be fine. Colin just roofied him with a drink and now the punk is sleeping it off." He paused, so I could fully absorb how fucked my entire world has just become. "Okay, talk's over, Blowman. Ashton's gonna take you for a walk."

"Let's go," Ashton said in a voice that sounded like a demon whisper.

Duds straightened out his tie, jacket and pants, then gave me one last triumphant fuck-you grin. "Goodbye, Blowman. See ya on the other side."

He gave me one last punch to the gut, laughed and walked back towards the building.

Howard's End

Angela. He was going to have Angela killed. For what?

Spite. Miserable fucking spite.

Or was he really going to kill her? Maybe he was just mentally torturing me before he killed me. It would be the kind of thing he enjoyed doing, probably along with blowing up puppies in microwaves and running over orphans with lawnmowers. I had no way of knowing what he was really going to do. Meanwhile, my mouth was dry, my heart was racing and, yeah, my gut still ached, even more since Duds' last punch.

Duds' massive frame was lurching back towards the ballroom, leaving me alone with Ashton the demon whisperer. I stood up straight, but I could've just as easily fallen right back down if I let myself. I didn't know how much more physical and psychological torment I could take. Not that I had to worry about it dragging out much longer. From the look in Ashton's eyes, it seemed like I would be freed from my earthly chains in relatively short order.

"Put your hands in back of your head," Ashton said in his cold dead voice.

Really? Did he think I actually had a move to make? I had just thrown up and also had the shit kicked out of me. Jesus, I was 61. I should have been home in my boxers yelling at cable news or something. But this guy somehow saw me as a potential threat. Well, he was the boss. I put my hands behind my head.

"Towards the beach," he said, and he motioned for me to start walking across the large grassy area in the direction of the ocean. There wasn't much between us and the sand, just a few yards of manicured lawn and a line of palm trees and fencing marking the boundary between the beach resort and the actual beach.

I started walking.

"I'm really not worth killing," I said. "If you let me go, I'll send you a check in the mail. Promise."

No answer. Hard to talk someone out of something when they don't talk. Didn't matter. The check would have bounced anyway.

That's when I heard the whirr.

I was familiar with the whirr, it was ingrained in my brain. It was the whirr of a golf cart, the kind I had rode to freedom from the Community.

I didn't react to the noise. Instead, we kept walking, but I slowed it up a little, feigning stomach cramps. I heard the whirr coming closer and if that whirr meant a chance for life, I wanted to take it.

"Keep moving," said my new BFF Ashton.

I held my stomach and stumbled forward a few more steps. I knew he wanted to shoot me further away from the club, probably on the beach, so he couldn't do much about me slowing it down. I kept myself doubled over and dragged my feet.

"C'mon," he said impatiently.

The whirr came closer. I knew he had to hear it by then. I turned just as he did to see what it was.

Yep, it was a golf cart—coming straight at us. It flicked on its headlights.

"MOVE," Ashton barked at me, and I moved, but no way I could move, even at full throttle, as fast as that cart was coming at us. Not only that, it was turning directly towards us.

Ashton turned to face it down. "HALT!" he yelled, pointing his gun at the cart. "This is OFFICIAL BUSINESS!"

The cart kept coming.

Ashton didn't move, he remained standing with both hands on the Glock, Liam Neeson-style, aiming straight at the cart. But it still wasn't slowing down.

Ashton looked confused. In his mind, guns automatically won the day. But this cart was not swerving away from its target—him. He stood in place as if somebody had driven stakes through his feet into the ground. To him, the cart should stop. He was pointing a gun straight at it. The cart driver should've been able to see him by then. Continuing to drive was a death wish. Ashton didn't seem to understand death wishes.

"HALT!" Ashton yelled.

As the cart closed in, I squinted at it through the darkness. I finally managed to make out who was driving.

"Howard?" I said to myself.

"HALT! HALTHALTHALT!" screamed Ashton, *still* not moving.

He fired the Glock a split-second before the cart hit him head-on.

The Glock went flying in the air just as the cart rammed into Ashton. It ended up on its side and Howard, still clad in a tuxedo just like me, spilled out on the grass. Then, with the help of the cart's headlights, Howard quickly spotted where the Glock had landed in the grass and crawled over to get it. Ashton, shaking off the collision, cleared his head and saw what Howard was doing. He went for the gun too.

Too late.

Howard had the gun in hand and was aiming it at Ashton. Ashton went for a knife he had hanging from the other side of his belt. He raised it to a throwing position. Howard shot before Ashton could finish the move, and he and the knife fell to the ground.

Holy shit. Holy shit.

"Howard." I rushed over to him. "Are you okay?"

Howard looked up at me. I saw the blood spreading out over his white shirt's chest area. Ashton hadn't missed.

"No. No, I'm not. Fuck. Fuck fuck fuck."

"Jesus, what the hell were you thinking? Let me get you back in the cart, get you some help…"

Sirens were suddenly going off back at the club. Obviously, the shots had been heard. Howard turned to me.

"Max, get the fuck out of here. Duds will kill you."

"I can't leave. The kid…"

Howard was having trouble breathing. I ripped off Ashton's jacket and made a big ball out of it, stuffing it on top of Howard's wound to try and keep the bleeding to a minimum. I put his hand on top of it so he could keep pressure on it.

"If you're talking about Jeremy," said Howard, "He's okay. That Kevin guy you told me about. I found him and he went and found Jeremy. He's just been…been drugged…"

"So, Duds wasn't lying? But Angela…"

"Max! I can't account for everyone you fucking know! Just move! Go…go down to the beach! Duds will kill you one way or the…the other…"

He was fading.

I saw floodlights flash on back at the club. I heard voices murmuring. I knew Howard was right. They'd be down there soon.

"Max…go…" Howard said. "I'm…I'm fucking dying."

I looked at Howard. I hated him. I loved him. I needed to stay. I needed to leave.

"Okay," he said. "If you're gonna be a prick about this, then I'm…I'm gonna play the dying wish card and…and you have to grant somebody's…dying wish," he muttered.

"What is it, Howard?" I whispered.

"It's this. Promise me…you'll get…the fuck…out of here…now."

"I'll go, Howard," I said with tears in my eyes. "Scout's honor."

And goddamn me to hell, I left.

Beached

I got to the beach and, in my very, very rumpled tuxedo, I began stumbling my way down the sand in the dark, just as fast as I could, determined not to look back. I didn't see the point in turning around to see if anyone was coming after me. If they were, I wouldn't be able to do much in my condition.

As I wildly fled, I didn't know whether to scream in a panic or cry for a million years. Howard actually took the fall for me. I couldn't get over it. But I didn't know if he'd be the final sacrifice. Even though he said the kid was okay, I couldn't be sure. And then there was Angela. Again, was Duds' death threat real or a con?

Who knew? Not me.

The problem was I no longer had a cell phone—it was still back at the fundraiser. Sure, it was just a cheap piece of shit I bought at the gas station in Mayo when I was the guest of Glenda Schmidt, but I could still email and do internet and, besides that, it had all my phone numbers in it, none of which I knew by heart. Who remembered phone numbers anymore? I could still tell you the number of my aunt back in my hometown from 50 years ago, because I'd call every weekend to see if my cousin could hang out—but any phone number I'd gotten in the last couple of years? Forget about it.

I was shivering a little, even though it was in the upper 60's on this warm Florida autumn night. And as I was shivering, I was also sweating. My system was all screwed up, but at least I was pretty sure all the fettucine was out of my system. I slowed my frantic jogging. I was running out of breath and I had to pace myself.

I checked my inside jacket pocket. My slim wallet was still in there with my license and my running-on-empty debit card. That was reassuring. Finally, I took my speed down to a walk, a slow meandering walk, wandering down the coast in a tuxedo like a beach bum James Bond.

Every once in a while, a helicopter would whiz by overhead. Or I'd hear a strange noise that was probably nothing to worry about. And every time, I jumped a little. I stayed close to the underbrush that divided the beach from the mainland. I thought I could dive into it and hide if I spotted something or someone pursuing me. But, for the most part, it was just dark and quiet. And increasingly uncomfortable, because the sand was gathering in my black socks and Florsheims. The beach wasn't exactly designed for formalwear.

After a while, I realized I had no idea how long I had been walking or how much distance I'd put between me and the resort. So, I finally gathered up my courage and turned around to see what was behind me—which was exactly nothing. I couldn't even see the Hut-to-Peen any longer. That made me relax a bit—especially since, up ahead, I saw the outer edges of another resort, where maybe I could get some help.

But first, I needed a break.

I approached an area with a few small benches at the end of a path that came down from the resort I was approaching. I sat down on one of the benches, huffing and puffing, and stayed there for a few moments until I remembered I still had some smokes on me. What was a better cure for huffing and puffing than smoking? I pulled out a cigarette and lit it up. Not the best idea—a spymaster in the movies would certainly recommend against it, there could be snipers in the palm trees, after all. But, despite my panicked exhaustion, I didn't give a shit. Smoking that cigarette felt more important than my survival.

I took a couple drags on the cancer stick and thought a moment. I realized I was more scared for the kid and Angie than myself. I realized maybe part of the reason Howard was willing to die was because he felt he had nothing left to live for. And on that note, he and I were perilously in sync. My money was running out, my health was for shit, and I had to wonder what exactly I was fighting for. If the country was so fucked up that public funds were being directed to a white supremist hole in the ground, what the hell was the point of any of it?

Just then I heard footsteps coming towards me. My entire body tensed up. Maybe this was it. Maybe they had been tracking me the whole time. Didn't matter. Whoever was approaching and whatever they were intending…I couldn't do shit about. I saw where the footsteps were coming from—a figure was walking down the path from the resort to where I was sitting. I quickly turned away. Maybe it was just a guest. Maybe it was nothing to worry about. I looked at the waves and took another drag on my USA Menthol Light.

"Didn't expect to see anyone else. I'm usually down here by myself most nights," I heard a male voice say.

I turned. There was a man, around 50, a little dark-skinned, so maybe Latino, it was hard to tell in the middle of the night. He had a nice haircut, even though the hairline was in quick retreat, was in decent shape, and wore a polo shirt, shorts and sandals. His shirt wasn't tucked in, he got points for that.

He sat down on the next bench and looked me over, as if he was doing his own mental calculations about who I was and what I was doing there. After all, I was a guy in a tuxedo sitting on a bench by himself at the beach. The good news was, as far as I could tell, he was just some guy who had no idea who I was or why I was there.

"Kind of much for the beach, don't you think?" he finally asked, eyeing my monkey suit.

"Look, I know we don't know each other, but I'm kind of desperate," I said, a little too quickly. "Do you have a cell phone on you and can I use it to make a call? One call?"

His brow furrowed. I had just dumped a lot on him at once. "Uh…. sure. I guess so," he finally said. He looked me over again as he dug out his phone from the pocket of his shorts. "Coverage here might not be so great, but…" He handed me the phone.

"Thanks," I said. "I just have to find the number first, so…"

"Take your time." I hadn't noticed he had a cigar in his free hand. He lit it up. Guess that was what this nightly beach visit was all about for him. I smelled it. His stogie was a lot higher quality than a Dutch Masters. I opened the phone's browser and started doing some detective work to get the Davidsons' home number, the same way I had gotten it when I was at Glenda Schmidt's. I found it and called.

"Hello?" said a familiar, flat voice on the other end. Certainly not the voice I expected.

"Patrice?" I said in astonishment. "Patrice Plotkin?"

"Yeah, who's this?"

"Max. Max Bowman. What are you doing there?"

"Oh, Max, you're alive. Nice to keep us informed. Thanks."

"Patrice…"

"Kevin asked me to hang out here tonight and keep an eye on Angela Davidson. It turned out he was right to worry. Because I caught some dipwad trying to sneak in and I beat his ass down."

"Oh, thank God. Angela's okay?"

"Yeah, but the guy's not, trust me."

"I trust you. Did he happen to have a lot of pills on him?"

"Oh yeah. This lame-o could have started his own pharmacy. I'm thinking he wanted to make it look like the Davidson lady overdosed."

"You're absolutely right."

"How do you know? What the hell's going on? Where are you now?"

"Just tell Angela I'm glad she's okay and if you talk to Kevin, tell him the same. I'm assuming Jeremy's okay too?"

"Flying home tonight, both of them."

"Good. Let everyone know I'm okay."

A pause.

"So, wait. You're not coming back here?"

"No."

"Where the hell *are* you going?"

"Unfinished business."

"Unfinished business. What is this, Macho Dialogue 101? How about you talk like a person?"

"No."

"Well, can they reach you at this number?"

"No."

"Jesus, this is getting tiring. Is there any other goddam number they can call you at?"

"No."

"Fine. Go. Whatever."

Then she hung up on me. I had to laugh. Patrice Plotkin didn't play. I handed the phone back to my new friend, who was now staring at me with excited shock.

"You're Max Bowman?" he asked as he took the phone.

Oh, shit. I had said my name.

"What happened to your hair?" he asked.

Roberto

I had a new friend.

His name was Roberto Diaz and he had been closely following my exploits for the last couple of years. He had seen my *60 Minutes* interview, he was even a member of my Facebook page. He didn't trust what was going on with the government then and he certainly didn't like what was going on with it now.

As he told me all this, he walked me back to his suite and, thanks to the obnoxious and omnipresent signage, I saw exactly what resort I had arrived at—President Donald Trump's very own Mar-A-Lago. How the hell could he stay here, I asked, if he was so upset about the country?

"Well," he said, "I've been coming here a few years, I know all the people here…"

Then he shrugged.

I got it. He had been a Trumpie. But he saw the writing on the wall and he didn't like what it said.

Inside his suite, he let me take a shower, a shower that felt better than any other shower I had ever had, and he let me wear the bathrobe that came with the room. After I came out in said bathrobe, that's when he decided to tell me the story of his life.

His father had immigrated from Cuba, he himself had built up a huge real estate business, then sold it right before the 2008 housing crash because he saw the bubble was about to burst. After the crash, he reinvested his money in property that was suddenly an incredible bargain. That property quickly went back up in value as the recovery took hold. So, he made two fortunes.

But the rest of his life had kind of gone to shit.

He and his wife had raised two kids. Once those kids were both in college, she suddenly asked him to leave. She claimed he was addicted to porn and she didn't want any part of a life with a guy like that. He told me he wasn't addicted to porn, he just liked to watch it occasionally, like any guy, like me, right?

I wasn't getting involved in that discussion, but then he started talking about how you could watch porn anywhere, even on your phone and you didn't even have to pay for it, it was crazy. The downside for him was, they didn't even put any effort into it anymore, they'd throw two girls and a guy on a couch and that would be the whole thing. Where was the poetry? Where was the creativity? Where were the production values? I said I didn't know and he said it was because of the goddam internet, which had ruined everything. Then he went on about the specific thing he liked, a bunch of naked women sticking things into each other. I don't remember much, because that's when I started falling asleep in the chair.

He woke me up and graciously gave me the bedroom. There was a four-poster queen bed in it. He told me he'd have them bring him a rollaway bed and set it up in the living room for him.

"Thanks," I nodded.

"You're welcome," he said in return and added that it was the least he could do for an American hero.

I saw him booting up the laptop as I shut the bedroom door behind me and collapsed on the bed. Hey. I thought maybe the guy *was* a porn addict.

That was the last thing I remember before I slept. And slept.

The next morning, around 11, I woke up and he ordered us breakfast. That's when he peppered me with questions about everything. I answered them. I didn't care what I told him. I told him about Dark Sky, about Blue Fire, about the Community and how my hair had gone white, about Daddy Andy Wright and, finally, about how Senator Eddie di Pineda was a clueless puppet. Roberto said that was because di Pineda was a Puerto Rican, Cubans had an iron fist and Puerto Ricans had spines of jelly. Another discussion I didn't want to get into, so I ate my eggs and let Roberto rant and rave about the pros and cons of what island in the Greater Antilles you happened to come from.

Through it all, Roberto's phone buzzed and buzzed and buzzed. He ignored it, but I kept looking at it. He finally told me people had been calling for me all morning, which is why he had turned off the ringer. He knew I was trying to stay out of sight and he didn't want me to have to worry about everyone and their dog calling for me. I thanked him for that and told him I'd appreciate it if he stuck to that policy. I knew that Patrice must have passed Roberto's number on to all concerned parties after I called the night before, but I didn't want to deal with anyone else at that moment. I had confirmed everyone was okay except my dog, and I had to assume she was doing all right. And that was all I needed to know.

"So what the hell are you gonna do?" Roberto finally said. "You got no clothes, no car, no nothing."

"I got a little money. I'll rent a car and buy some clothes. I've got one more place to go."

"Where?"

"A little town in Maryland. One last thing I gotta find out about."

He looked at me a moment, then jumped up out of his chair.

"I'm gonna give you money." He grabbed his wallet off a nearby, opened it up and pulled out a wad of hundreds.

"Roberto…" I said with a shake of my head.

"After what you've been through? Man, you deserve this and more." He tossed the wad in my lap. "Clothes. Give your sizes, I'll go get you a wardrobe, there's a boutique here, I can get you everything you need, even some dock shoes, you don't want to be wearing those Oxfords. You stay here in the room in case they're out there looking for you."

"Roberto, seriously, you don't have to…"

He looked me up and down. "Never mind, I can guess your size. No arguments, I'm going to go get you clothes. And I know you're not going anywhere in the meantime, because you don't have anything to wear." He laughed a booming laugh. "And then, buddy? I'm going to get you a car, buy you the nicest car you ever drove in your life. You are going to Maryland in *style*."

He chuckled as he headed for the door.

"10 ½!" I yelled after him. If he was going to buy me shoes, they should at least be the right damn size.

As soon as he was gone, I closed his laptop, which was sitting on the desk. The image on the screen was of a couple of naked women and some…some instruments and some lubricants, and I wanted to finish eating without looking at any of it.

This Old House

So, there I was, speeding up I-95 in a brand-new Mercedes convertible, rocking my brand-new Mar-a-Lago baseball cap and polo shirt, both of which prominently displayed the resort logo. Boy, did I get a dirty look from a guy at a gas station in North Carolina. On the other hand, a woman applauded me at a McDonalds.

I was also wearing the new jeans and dock shoes Roberto bought me—those, fortunately, were unbranded. I'd rather drive around in my underwear than have Trump's name on my ass. Besides the new outfit and the new rental, I also had a new rollaway suitcase in the trunk, filled with other clothes and sundry items. Plus, I had about $1500 in my wallet that wasn't there before.

To be honest, Roberto got so much pleasure out of doing that for me, it would have been disrespectful to have turned it all away. Of course, there was also the fact that I was in no position to turn *any* of it away. This wasn't the first time I had found myself alone in a strange place with nothing but the clothes on my back. Luckily, Roberto found me and came to my aid. Why not be a little Blanche DuBois about it all and rely on the kindness of strangers?

Sure, I could have called for help from someone else—Angie, the kid, even Kev if I could have tracked him down. Probably not Patrice Plotkin. But I didn't want anyone else involved—I wanted to check out the last piece of the puzzle on my own. Because it involved family. I just wasn't sure how.

After my mom had died, my brother Alan had started digging, as he usually did. He loved to spend hours online searching our family shit. We already knew our father had cut us out of both of their wills, clearing the way for the oldest, Henry aka "Fuckface" (FF for short), to inherit what was left of our folks' retirement account.

But it made Alan wonder about the old family house, the one we had grown up in. Alan asked FF about it, since they still had some semblance of a relationship, as much of a relationship as you could have with FF. FF told him it was sold after Mom went into assisted living. But Alan was still curious, so when she kicked the bucket, he decided to see if he could find a record of the actual sale. He did. And he emailed me what he found.

That's where I got an unpleasant surprise—that it hadn't been a person or a couple that had bought the house. It was some foundation, a foundation called "The Eugene Group." Alan thought that was weird. Stranger still, he couldn't find out much about this particular organization in his online searching.

I didn't write back and tell him what I knew—that the Eugene Group was heavily backing the Senator Eddie campaign, as well as the underground White Rain facility. That its name was obviously an all-too-cute nod to eugenics. That it was undoubtedly another dark and dangerous shell group created by Daddy Andy before his death.

Instead, I asked myself a series of questions that didn't seem to have an answer. Why the hell did Andrew Wright invest in our old family home? It was a worthless old house in a worthless old steel town that had been ravaged by manufacturing fleeing overseas. What the hell were they doing with the place? Going through my old comic book collection in the attic?

They better not have fucked with my copy of *Spider-Man* #33.

After a couple of days of driving, I finally reached my old childhood haunts around the aging remains of the Sparrow Point Steel Plant, southeast of Baltimore, off the Patapsco River. I drove by the old plant, which I saw was rapidly falling apart and mostly tagged for demolition. The iconic giant steel star at the plant entrance still stood, however, as did most of the buildings. My grandfather had been foreman at that plant, which was owned by Bethlehem Steel when there was a Bethlehem Steel. But that had been a long time ago in a different America.

I steered back up towards the familiar streets of my hometown. Most of the neighborhoods were still intact. But when I got to our neck of the woods, the picture wasn't so cheery. Many of the homes on our street had been torn down and never replaced—and the ones that weren't were largely foreclosed and abandoned.

As I approached our old home, I saw one of the abandoned homes was right across the street from our house. That was where the Gerbers had lived. One of their children had some kind of mental disability—luckily, back then, other kids dealt with that kind of situation respectfully. FF, for example, had nailed him in the back of the head with a half-eaten pear one bright and sunny afternoon. The Gerbers moved soon after.

I stopped and parked a half a block away, so nobody would see me. I got out of the car and stood there, just staring at the old house. Seemed small. I guessed where you lived as a kid shrunk proportionally to how tall you had gotten as an adult and this basic, nondescript two-story clapboard home was no exception. My father had remodeled parts of it and added on to it over the years, but it was still a piece of shit house that he never bothered to move us out of. I realized at some point he was afraid to. Even though he hated his working-class roots, he never felt comfortable with those above his station in life. Result? An unhappy life spent purposely stuck in place.

Alan had been my ally in battling the unhappiness in that house. But it felt like Henry just soaked up all our parents' shit without ever finding an outlet for it. When he wasn't throwing fruit at the mentally-impaired, he was getting into fights in high school and hanging out with what were then called "JDs"—juvenile delinquents. He got busted once for underage drinking, and my dad saw him smoking one day and confronted him about it. FF lied about it and my dad punched him down to the ground, the only time he ever hit any of us.

Henry's pinnacle of happiness may have come right after high school, when he was still living at home and working a dumb job. When he had finally earned enough money, he went out and bought a Pontiac GTO, one of the hottest muscle cars of the late 60's. I had never seen him so filled with glee as the day he was waxing it in the driveway. He was even nice to me that day. Which was a rarity, because usually he was a complete dick.

The car, of course, never really changed anything about his life, but it took him a little while to figure it out. The progression was subtle but noticeable. He most resembled an inflated balloon sitting in a corner slowly losing air, even though there weren't any evident leaks. All personality seemed to recede from his being. He grew quieter. He started crossing his long, skinny legs like a preacher sitting at a church social and suddenly he was buttoning the top button on his shirts. Finally, he married a quiet neighbor girl and managed a local jewelry store where she worked for a while.

Then he decided he never wanted to work at a job again.

The first wife left him, but he was lucky enough to bag a lawyer for wife number two. She was a plain-looking woman who, many of us assumed, wanted Henry for the genetic material he offered, because it sure wasn't about his personality. I will say he was the best-looking of the three of us, so apparently it was more Bowman family eugenics at work. They moved to Vermont, where Henry built a house for them. The guy could do anything with his hands, I give him that. They had two kids and the family lived off her law practice.

Roberto's money bought me a new cell phone (at the gas station where I had gotten the dirty look) and I used it to email Alan another question—was Henry still married to the lawyer? Alan loved a new challenge so, by the time I had driven through a couple more states, he already had an answer for me. Henry and the lawyer had gotten divorced a few years before, not long before Mom went into assisted living. I sent Alan another question—who got the house that Henry built? Somehow, Alan found the divorce papers. She kept the house and paid him to go away.

So—where did he go to? He was seven years older than me, 68 to my 61, so he was already pushing 65 when all that other stuff happened. Was he actually living in our old family home, the home I was now staring at? I didn't know why, but I had a hunch he was. It was like I *felt* him. But that would mean he was involved with the Eugene Group. Which made no fucking sense to me.

I hadn't seen Henry in probably twenty years. We never had a close relationship. Twice, when I was still basically a kid and he was around 18, he had punched me in the stomach as hard as he could—once, just because I insisted on watching *Mr. Ed* when he didn't want me to. I had a feeling those incidents were more about my father's fist metaphorically punching down the family tree.

So who *was* this guy now? If he was in the house, what the hell was he doing in there?

I had driven all the way to Maryland to find out. I didn't want to. But I had to.

So, I started walking towards the front door.

Lockout

I walked up the narrow, cracked walkway, bordered by unkempt scraggly blades of grass on either side, all the way to the front stoop. The place had aged some since I bounced Superballs on that pavement and watched them fly up into the clouds. As I got to the door, I glanced to the right at the big window that looked into the living room—but, at the moment, the curtains were drawn and you couldn't really see inside. They were translucent, though. You could see shadows of things that might be moving.

And, after I rang the doorbell, some things definitely moved.

One shadow disappeared towards the back of the house, while the other shadow seemed to come up from a chair or a couch. It paused and then moved to come answer the door.

It opened. And there was Henry. His top button was still buttoned. I think he actually gasped without moving a muscle in his face.

I looked him over. His hair was just starting to go silver—I guessed we both had good hair genes, unlike Alan who was bald as a cue ball—and he had maintained his shape better than I had. That's because he was as OCD about food as he was about his top shirt button. I remembered him once speaking sharply to his daughter about how much mustard she was putting on her sandwich. Yes, mustard. Probably no body issues resulted from that condiment kerfuffle. Huh-uh. No way, no how.

I had goose pimples. The brother I never wanted to see again was standing right in front of me under very strange circumstances— circumstances that he had to know far more about than I did. He peered at me through the kind of glasses you would picture on a 19th century physician. His eyes were dazed, confused and a little frightened, all under a layer of false calm that attempted to mask all those other emotions. It was a layer he manufactured at some point in his early twenties.

He continued to look at me for another moment, uncomprehendingly, like I had projected my being to our childhood home from another dimension, as if it was impossible that I could be standing there on our old front stoop, which was just a small cement slab that had room for a couple of people to stand and maybe a small dog. A small dog like mine.

"Hi," I said evenly, realizing I was still wearing my Mar-a-Lago swag and wondering if he would notice.

"Max?" He looked on either side of me and all around the yard, as if maybe I had brought a SWAT team along for the ride.

"Can I come in?"

"Why...what...?"

I looked past him into the house to see what I could see. He didn't like me doing that.

"It's not a good time."

"Well, I just came back to see the old place. You living here now?" I asked. "Alone?"

"Look, it's good to see you...but it's not a good time. Sorry," he finally mumbled.

He shut the door. I looked back over to the right at the big window and saw his shadow move towards the back of the house, in the same direction the other shadow had gone. If I remembered right, the stairs to the basement were in that direction.

I rang the doorbell a couple more times. No more shadows through the window. That was it for our big brotherly reunion, apparently.

I walked around the corner to check out one side of the house, then the other. Around the corner was as far as I could go—there was high fencing blocking entry to the backyard on both sides of the house. The side windows had their shades drawn as well. And those shades were heavy-duty—you couldn't even make out shadows through them.

Finally, I tried the door on the side of the small one-car garage that was attached to the side of the house. Locked. I looked in through the garage window. I saw a well-worn pick-up inside along with some ancient tools hanging on the wall that were my father's. Nothing out of the ordinary.

So I turned and took in the entirety of the old Bowman homestead. I shook my head to clear the avalanche of memories the old place was triggering, like the time Alan and I launched a water rocket—did they still make those? —and it went through a neighbor's window. Alan told me to go get it. I didn't. After a half-hour or so, the neighbor girl came over with it and told us her mom said not to do that again. We didn't.

But I couldn't get lost in the past. The present was what had brought me there. Something was going on in that house, something that had to do with the whole dirty Andrew Wright business. I went back to the front stoop and rang the doorbell again. Nothing.

WTF, FF?

After a minute or two, I gave up. I walked the half-block back to the Mercedes and sat in it for a moment with the top down. It was late afternoon and autumn cool, but I didn't mind, because the sun was still up in the sky and it felt good on the back of my neck. I had a smoke and thought a bit, while I continued to watch the house to see if maybe Henry would peek his head out to make sure I was gone. But he didn't. No other movement.

That's when I saw a familiar Jeep Patriot coming down the street towards me.

I quickly backed the Mercedes another block or so away from the house, which took me around a curve. Once I got around it, once I knew we couldn't be seen from the house, I stopped. The kid pulled up next to me, so our two vehicles took up the whole street. That wasn't a big deal. It wasn't like there was any traffic to be blocked.

I rolled down my window. He rolled down his. I almost cried, it was that good to see the kid again. But the tears weren't going to flow. They rarely did, because one of the times Henry had punched me in the gut, I mentally resolved not to let him see me cry—ever. I didn't want to give him the satisfaction. Something shut down in me from then on. Sure, I cried. But not easy and not often.

"Max, thank God. What the hell are you doing here?"

"How about if I ask you the same thing?"

"Kevin tracked down the cell phone you called from. We found that Roberto guy. He said you said you were driving to Maryland. Kevin told me what you told him, about the Eugene Group buying your old family home. So, we put two and two together…"

"And it all added up to me being here."

He looked at me closely another moment. "Does it say 'Mar-a-Lago' on that hat?"

I sighed, then I took it off and threw it in the street. "Yeah. Long story. Feel free to run it over."

He looked around what was left of the neighborhood. "This is where you grew up?" he asked with all the distaste of a rich kid who didn't know any better.

"Yeah. Where's Kev?"

"Back in Hollywood. Emergency meeting on his…project." He frowned.

"And Colin the Bureau?"

More frowning. "Howard found Kevin at the resort, after you told him he was around. I don't know how, but Kevin found Colin's room. I was out cold on the bed, I guess he—they—put something in my drink. Anyway…Kevin did whatever to Colin, then had them picked up. Turns out he—they—were getting big money wired from some fake company linked to Russian oligarchs."

The kid stopped. Then he gave me the news I already knew.

"Howard's dead."

I had figured he wouldn't survive that shot. But getting it confirmed still hit me hard.

"The campaign says it's the terrorists that killed Howard," PMA went on. "And that they kidnapped you."

I nodded. It wasn't like I was surprised or anything. He told me Angela was okay and so was Eydie. I nodded some more. I was glad, very glad. The kid stared at the floor of his car.

"You're not gonna tell me 'I told you so?'" he finally asked. "About Colin?"

"Nope. As long as you drive me to the nearest big box sporting goods store. I'll just park this little beauty here for now. It's got a top-notch alarm system."

He gave me a questioning look as I pulled up closer to the curb to make it an official park job, then put up the top. Then I got out and walked back towards his Jeep.

"There's a Big 5 about six miles away," the kid said staring at his phone map app as I got in on the passenger side.

"You'd probably prefer Dick's, wouldn't you?" I said with a smile.

"Dicks. So now you're making gay jokes. About how I'd prefer a store named Dicks."

"Yes. Yes, I am."

He took a deep breath.

"By the way, did Roberto show you any of his porn?" I asked. "That stuff would be enough to turn me gay."

PMA stared at me. "Max, your skin is as white as your hair. I don't know what gave you the bright idea to come here, but I think we should go back to Virginia. That doctor still needs to check you out."

"I'm okay. I didn't push it driving up here from Florida, so I got some decent sleep at some indecent motels."

"But...why *are* you here? I mean, what the hell are you expecting to find?"

"I don't know what I'm expecting. But there's something. So drive."

The kid threw his head back as if he were the most disgusted twenty-year-old in the country. Which he might have been at that moment.

"*Drive,*" I said again with a little more authority and he did.

The kid and I got some dinner while we were out and had a much-needed conversation. I wanted to be sure Duds actually did sign the final divorce agreement from Angela. The kid confirmed. Then I told him about White Rain and eugenics and all the horrible shit that Duds laid down at that last fundraiser. The kid took it all in and then he made a couple of good points.

Point Number One: "So, just because my Mom said one stupid thing about Jews, you do understand she's not as bad as those white power guys."

"I know, she was raised with that shit. But she also needs to be called on that shit."

"Yeah," the kid nodded. "But...I mean...you and her..."

"Look, my brother is a borderline Nazi, so don't worry about it."

"Your brother? The one in the house?"

"No, the other one."

He gave me a horrified look.

"Are you trying to tell me you're the normal one?"

"I'll leave that judgment to others."

The kid went ahead to Point Number Two.

"You know, Duds only let you in that last fundraiser because he knew he was going to kill you afterwards. That means he's still going to kill you. And if your brother is really working with them, which I still think is a ridiculous idea, then…"

"Then he knows where I am," I said.

"Maybe this group bought your house for your brother just to keep him out of their hair?"

"Then why is it all locked up? Why is the backyard fenced off? Why are all the windows covered? Why the hell did he not even want me to look inside?"

"Because he's a freak?"

"That's a given." I glanced at my watch. "We better get to Big 5 before it closes."

I signaled the waiter for the check.

The Night Shift

When we got back, it was dark. I went and parked my Mercedes in a long-term parking garage a few miles away, then the kid drove us back to the old neighborhood, turning the headlights off as we got close to the old homestead.

We came down the street from the opposite direction from the way we left—and that's when I noticed a vacant lot a couple of doors down from my old house, where four cars were parked on top of what was left of the lawn. I wondered who those cars belonged to, because it was a little hard to believe there were even four other people living on the street besides my brother. I saw the kid noticed the impromptu parking lot as well.

"What do you think that's about?" he asked.

"Don't know."

"I bet the cars belong to squatters, living in some of the abandoned houses."

"You're out of your neighborhood, kid. People living in abandoned houses don't usually have cars."

He frowned. He didn't want to validate all my rotten feelings about my rotting old house. But if my gut had a mouth, it would have been screaming that shit was going on there in the extreme.

I asked the kid to park his Jeep behind the abandoned house across the street from my house—someone had already thoughtfully flattened the foreclosure fence around the place, so it wouldn't be hard to drive around the side. Henry wouldn't be able to spot the vehicle if it was parked behind the house.

After the kid parked the Jeep in the backyard, we entered the house through its busted back door and carried in our purchases from the sporting goods store—a couple of sleeping bags, inflatable mattresses to put them on, binoculars, a hunting knife, some water and snacks, and, at the kid's insistence, a small handgun, nothing fancy. I didn't have the stones to argue with him about getting the pistol after what went down at Putt-Putt Acres.

"So, this is it," he said as we set up our sleeping areas on the second floor in what was left of the master suite—basically walls with peeling paint and a very scuffed-up hardwood floor. "Guess we're going to go on stakeout."

"I'll be Richard Dreyfuss and you be Emilio Estevez."

He gave me a blank look.

"You never saw *Stakeout*, the hit comedy movie? Oh, that's right, you weren't born yet. Okay, let's blow up the mattresses."

Then I stopped because I realized something. I looked up and caught the kid staring at me. He had also realized that same something. The mattresses had electronic air pumps. There was no way the power was on in an abandoned house.

In other words, we were both idiots.

"Huh. Well, maybe we can catch a long nap at a Holiday Inn during the days?" I offered.

The kid sighed, walked over and opened the window. Then he stared out across the street at my old family home.

"Max, let's just stay one night, tonight. And if nothing happens, let's just go home." He took his phone out of his pocket and eyed it with disdain. "Signal here sucks." He put the phone on the windowsill, along with his wallet and keys, and resumed watching the house.

My exhaustion was catching up with me again, so I let him take the watch. Me, I sat on one of the very uninflated mattresses near the wall and leaned back for what I thought would be a short catnap.

When I woke up, I glanced at the time on my phone and was shocked to see it was around midnight. Some catnap. I looked over at the kid, who had found an old chair with most of the seat gone. He had draped part of the other uninflated mattress over it and was sitting on it and staring out the window.

"Anything?" I asked.

He jumped at little. "Jesus. I thought you were out for the night."

I got up, awkwardly. When you're 61, that's the only way you can get up from the floor. The kid got up from his chair and gave me a hand, which was much appreciated. My butt was sore, my back was sore and my essence was sore. I stood shoulder-to-shoulder with the kid as I looked out the window and shivered a little. The mercury had taken a dip while I slept.

"Anyway, to answer your question, nothing, Max. Nothing. At least nothing that I've seen. The lights are still on in the basement, that's pretty much it."

"The basement," I said ominously.

"Yes, the *basement*, Max," he said, mocking my tone. "Just what do you think your brother's up to?"

"Him? Nothing. It's other people I worry about."

"What other people?"

We stood there in silence a moment. He'd tear apart any of the many crazy things I was thinking, so I kept them to myself. Instead, I changed the subject to something I thought I should talk to him about. Not that he'd listen.

"I wanted to say something."

He turned to me. I rarely said something. Of substance anyway.

"I'm sorry about Kevin. I'm even sorry about Colin the Bureau. But love doesn't come easy. Especially when you're not even old enough to drink."

He shrugged and turned back to the window. I walked over to the corner and reached into a bag of random shit we had bought. I pulled out a bottle of water and opened it up. My throat was dry from the nap, so I took a big swig.

"I thought I was in love at 22. Boy, was I an idiot," I said, trying to keep the one-sided conversation going. Then I came back and stood next to him. "You're just too young to know anything."

"Well, now that you're so old and wise—how about my mom?" the kid asked, continuing to stare out the window.

"Hasn't been my focus."

"Love kinda makes you focus whether you want to or not." Then he looked at me. I liked Angie. But I was being honest. I had too much on my plate—and not enough at the same time.

"Kid, I literally have nothing left. Lost my apartment, my car, almost all my money. I've got nothing to offer anybody."

"Max, stop the bullshit, you can still make a living, we can do the detective agency and, yeah, maybe my Mom would have to put up the seed money, but so what? Your name is what's going to sell it, that's the thing people will…"

I interrupted with maybe a little too much anger. "Kid, I'm too tired to think about taking a dump, let alone starting a new career. Do it yourself. Use my name with my blessing. We'll do a licensing deal."

"What is this, 'Shark Tank?'"

"Look," I went on, "You don't need me. You don't need anyone. I don't have all the answers, nobody does. You have to find your own. Of course, first, you have to figure out what the fucking questions are."

"Well, I got a question. What do you need? Do you need my mom? If not, maybe you should get out of both of our lives."

He continued to look away. I stopped talking. I couldn't blame him for getting pissed. I was sleeping with his mother and that was some hardcore Oedipal shit. But I felt blocked about the relationship. It wasn't just me feeling lower than whale shit. It was also the fact that she and I were very different, and not just in our view of the Chosen People. She was part of the Washington D.C. moneyed class and I fit in there about as well as a monkey in a kayak. It was too much of a culture clash and I didn't think I'd end up making the cut in her world.

"Just…just give me some time," I said weakly.

He shrugged again. I sat down hard on the kid's makeshift chair. I was still a little woozy from the snooze. Or something. The kid turned when I started breathing heavily and looked down at me. And he kept looking, because it was obvious I was straining to keep it together. Things were starting to go upside down in my head again and I was putting everything into keeping them right-side up.

"Max," he said a little more softly, seeing me struggle. "Seriously. Let's get you home."

"I just told you. I don't have a home."

"You know what I mean."

"You're the one who should go home. Look, I do care about your mom. The only reason I pushed myself through all this was to free her from Duds. But that's over. Mission accomplished, as a great man once said. Now I just want to know what the hell's happening at my old house. If it's just a snipe hunt, I'll stay and search for snipe. But this is my thing now and when it's over, I'll come back. No reason for you to stick this out with me. Go home and get on with your life." I stopped. And then I let it come out. "Mine is pretty much over."

"Jesus, stop being a drama queen, it doesn't have to be like this."

"But it is. I haven't been right since Florida. I don't know if it was all the electroshocks I got on the way out or whether my brain's just fucked from all the benzo brickle they had me eating for months on end. I don't know, I just know my body and my brain feel like they're falling apart. So, let me do this. It doesn't matter what happens to me. Especially since I probably don't have much time left."

The kid was pissed again. "You don't want any more time, Max, just admit it, you *want* to fucking die. And that's not fair to me, my mom or even to your goddamn stupid dog."

"Eydie. My dog's name is Eydie."

"I just think you're depressed. I don't blame you, but…"

I doubled over in the chair. The pain was back to my chest. Burning pain. It was almost as if I summoned it.

"I'm getting you to a hospital."

"No, kid. No, you're not." I took a deep breath, slowly sat upright and put on a strained smile. "See? I'm fine."

"You need help, medical help."

I shook my head, took out a cigarette and lit it. I was beginning to realize that I usually felt the need to smoke when I was in a suicidal frame of mind. Maybe because smoking was like killing yourself in slow motion.

"You don't think somebody's gonna spot that?" the kid asked, eyeing my cig.

"Maybe they'll think it's a firefly."

Exasperated, the kid grabbed my arm and started to pull me up. "I mean it. That's it. Get up, we're…"

Then things started happening.

Lights outside. Headlights from a car. The kid turned back to the open window and I got up on my feet. The pain was subsiding. Cigarettes— nature's little helper.

We watched as an ordinary everyday car drove past the home and then parked in the vacant lot where the other vehicles were. When the headlights went out, we heard the sound of a car door opening and closing—then the "Bee-boop" that signaled it was being locked by a remote key.

The plug had been pulled on the neighborhood streetlights at some point, so it was hard to make out what the driver looked like in the darkness. What wasn't difficult to figure out was the person was heading right for the front door of my brother's house.

"It's a woman," the kid said, looking through the binoculars.

Then more headlights. Another car. And then another. They all parked in the same lot, leaving an exit path open for the cars that were already there.

"Feels like a shift change," I said. "Like when the sheepdog and the wolf would punch their timeclocks in the old Looney Tunes cartoons." The kid gave me an irritated glance, because I was talking Old Man again. "One of them was named Ralph," I added, just to sprinkle in some colorful detail.

We heard the front door open, so our eyes shot from the vacant lot back to my old family home. The light from inside illuminated the new arrival, an older woman. As she went in, another woman, wearing all white, greeted her and exited the home—she put on her coat as she went out in the cool night air.

The same process kept repeating—there was one more woman, and then two intimidating-looking men, all changing places with their counterparts. Four people coming and four people going in all.

"The guys look like security or something," I said. "And the women were all wearing white as far as I can tell."

"Nurses?" the kid guessed.

"Nurses," I said.

"Maybe your brother's wife is sick."

"She's very healthy. Mostly because she left him years ago."

"And you saw your brother yesterday and he was okay."

"Physically."

"Then what…"

I was about to interrupt his question in order to propose a theory. And that's when the explosion came.

Burning Down the House

The blast felt like it came from the back of the house.

But we couldn't see out back—the only window in the room looked out on the street, where there was no sign of anything. We began to smell fire and smoke. The kid stuck his head out the window and looked to the side.

"Smoke's coming from the back." He looked at me in a panic. "My Jeep!"

The kid ran over to grab our brand-new pistol, then bolted out of the bedroom and down the stairs. I followed, without the running part. That changed once I heard a couple of shots. Then I dialed my speed up to a respectable trot.

I got down to the backdoor and threw it open. The kid's Jeep Patriot was in flames, flames that illuminated a familiar figure, someone I thought was dead. It was Ashton the Demon Whisperer, looming behind the flames as if the Devil himself had given him a temporary work contract.

Apparently, he had blown up the kid's car to get our attention. His face was impassive but determined, and half of his shaved head was covered with a slightly blood-stained bandage. Howard's bullet must have just grazed Ashton's head back at the Hut-to-Peen and put him down temporarily. I'd seen the head graze happen in countless low-budget Westerns, but I never thought it was a real thing. Score one for all those shitty cowboy movies made for five bucks in the San Fernando Valley.

Ashton brought up his Glock and pointed it at me, as he furtively scanned the rest of the small patchy backyard. He had to be looking for the kid, which was good news—it meant the creep had missed PMA when they exchanged shots. Most likely, the kid was hiding in the overgrown shrubs and trees lining the boundaries of the yard and Ashton didn't know exactly where.

I looked at the weapon in Ashton's hand. The Glock. It was the same Glock that killed Howard. Ashton, keeping the weapon trained on me, marched quickly around the back of the burning Jeep chassis and came right towards me as his eyes continued to search the edges of the yard.

"DAVIDSON. JEREMY DAVIDSON. COME OUT OR I SHOOT BOWMAN!" he bellowed. Wow. This *was* a low-budget Western.

Ashton was steps away. I asked politely, "So. The bullet just nipped your scalp? Too bad you didn't have any hair to cushion the impact."

"I was a fucking Navy Seal, you goddamn pussy!"

With that, he slammed the pistol into the side of my head. I not only saw stars, I saw planets, comets and nebulas as I collapsed onto the crabgrass. Through my mental fog, I heard more bellowing from Ashton to the darkness around the fire. "COME OUT NOW, LITTLE BOY."

People make mistakes when they get angry. And, even in my condition, I knew Ashton had made a very big mistake by knocking me down. He had given the kid a clear shot—and the kid knew how to shoot.

Bang.

Ashton let out a yelp and I managed to open my eyes wide enough to see his bandaged bullethead hit the ground right next to me. He held his hip in pain—that's where the kid had shot him. Ashton grit his teeth. He was done fucking around. He let go of his bloody hip and turned to me, bringing up his Glock at the same time.

"Fuck you," he seethed as he aimed it at my face.

That lovely sentiment would be his last. The kid, who was already rushing over to where we were laying on the ground, saw Ashton's move and quickly fired again. The bullet hit Ashton's melon square in the forehead, no grazing this time around. He rolled over on his back and his hand fell limply but heavily on my balls. Ouch.

The kid approached. The Jeep fire was still raging and the light from the inferno made it so I could see just how shaken up he was. You shouldn't have to be killing people at his age. Actually, you shouldn't have to be killing people at any age. He knelt by me and felt the side of my head where Ashton had pistol-whipped me. I winced.

"You okay?"

"Better than him," I answered, eyeing what was left of the guy's cranium.

"Who was he?" the kid asked as he helped me up—but, before I could answer, we both noticed that part of the Jeep had flown into the side of the house, most likely during the initial explosion. And now, that part of the house, the second story where we had left all our shit, was on fire. And that cheap wood was going to flare up faster than a Christmas tree in February.

"Shit, my stuff's in there! I'm going in."

That felt like a very, very bad idea to me. I gripped his shirt as hard as I could. "No, that's crazy. What's in there, your car keys? You're not gonna need those!"

"No, but I need my phone and my wallet…look, don't sweat it, I can get in and out fast!"

"Kid!"

He broke away from me and ran into the house before I could say anything more. And I had plenty more to say—it just wasn't coming out very fast because the left side of my face was beginning to swell up. Then a thought hit me. If Ashton was there, that meant there was another shoe left to drop. A big fat shoe. A really big fat shoe. And it was going to drop hard.

And, as I felt my body suddenly being slammed into the side of the house, I realized that it had, in fact, dropped.

"Blowman. I knew you and that little cocksucker would be here."

Duds had his forearm pressed firmly against my back, keeping my swollen face against the side of the house, which was growing increasingly warm because, right above my head, flames were blazing.

"What's in the basement, Duds?" I mumbled into the wall. "Across the street. What's in the basement?"

He whirled me around and put his big beefy hand around my throat, then he pulled out his own gun with the other. "You fucking loser," was his only reply to my question.

"MAX!" The kid was yelling from inside the house. "CALL 911 IF YOU CAN GET A SIGNAL DOWN THERE! I DON'T KNOW IF I CAN MAKE IT BACK TO THE STAIRS! FIRE IN HERE IS BAD!"

Oh, God, I knew going in there was stupid—the house was going to be ashes in a few minutes. I couldn't answer him, since Duds was as close as possible to strangling me. As sparks started to rain down on us, he yanked me away from the house with such force, I almost went down to the ground again. I turned to check the house. The fire was out of control.

"You want to know what's in the basement?" Duds asked. "I think you deserve to see for yourself." He took his hand off my neck and motioned with the gun to take a walk with him. I kept staring at the house. "Say goodbye to Jeremy Davidson, Blowman. Say goodbye to everything, including yourself. C'mon, let's move."

"You're actually going to let him burn to death?"

"Like you guys wouldn't let me fry. Now, move your ass."

I took a breath. Jesus. I never felt so helpless. I never felt so hopeless.

"MOVE!" Duds yelled, a little spittle hitting my nose.

I didn't move. Instead, I sighed and said, "Just fucking shoot me."

Duds blinked. For once, he was speechless.

"Seriously. Just shoot me. I'm not moving. I think I already know what's in that basement. And if you're gonna let the kid burn, fuck it. I'm done."

But he wasn't. He balled up his left hand into a fist and plunged it into my gut. Third beating of the week. I bent over from the impact and then he hit me on the back of the head with the same fist. I went down on my belly. Suddenly my chest was burning again along with every other fucking thing that was wrong with me. I rolled over and the next thing I knew, Duds was dragging me by my arm across the ground and around the burning house.

I heard the kid yell "MAX!" one last time as Duds continued to drag me across the street towards my old home. I turned to look ahead at the house—and saw Henry standing impassively on the front stoop, staring at the fire, staring at Duds, staring at me.

"Yeah, there's big brother Henry." Duds cackled down at me. "He knew who your real daddy was all the time. That piece of shit who pretended to be your father let him in on the whole thing, because he wanted to recruit Henry to the CIA. Make him part of the team. And help indoctrinate you into our way of thinking. But look at his dead eyes. The lights went out inside him a while ago, huh, Blowman?"

As my back felt the street asphalt scraping my clothes, I took another look at Henry, who was still gawking at the whole macabre scene. Was Duds telling the truth? Did Henry actually know Andrew Wright was my father when I was growing up? Maybe that's why he tormented me as a kid. Because Mom and Dad thought I was better than him. Because I was made with Andrew Wright's specialness.

"That's why we thought this was the perfect safe house," Duds went on. "Nobody gives a shit about this neighborhood anymore. And nobody gives a shit about Henry."

I was pretty sure Henry was in earshot of that last declaration. But he still stood there, front door open behind him, acting as if he was nonchalantly watching a neighbor mow a lawn or kids play ball in the street, not witnessing the house across the street burn down with someone trapped inside it and not watching his youngest brother being dragged across the street by a 350-pound psychopath.

We reached the stoop. My back burned from the dragging and I could only wonder what was left of the jacket I was wearing. Duds yanked me up to my feet as Henry continued to non-react. Duds pushed me towards my biggest brother.

"A family reunion!" Duds exclaimed with evil glee. "You guys want to hug it out?"

"Maybe I should call the fire department," Henry finally said in an all-too-serious monotone.

"Yeah," said Duds with his usual thick frosting of sarcasm. "Yeah, that's what we want, the fire department here, asking questions. You dumb son of a bitch, just let it burn, nobody's going to care. There's nobody *to* care."

Then Duds pushed me into the house. As he did, I looked over my shoulder and saw Henry, calmly walking across the street towards the burning house.

The Basement

The inside of my old house looked remarkably unchanged. The same commemorative church plates were still hanging on the wall—did anybody make those anymore? Why did they make them in the first place? It just made me think about going to church every damn Sunday morning and that made me think about the Reverend Todd Mansfield, who liked two things too much—Kentucky Bourbon and the breasts of teenage girls. When he'd had too much of the former, he would lay his hands on the latter and ended up banished to a parish in Haiti, where I later heard he had taken up voodoo. Of course, that was also around the time I heard that Beaver Cleaver had died in Vietnam.

I looked around some more. I noticed the carpeting had been removed, exposing the hardwood floor. Nice move. HGTV loved that shit. There was even some new furniture, but it already looked old because I was so old. Then there were the framed family photos still sitting on the ancient credenza in the dining room—like the one with the three of us taken when we were boys, where we were wearing matching jackets and bowties and our hair was similarly slicked-down. The familiarity at this point bred more than contempt—it gave me the chills.

How the hell did so much go so wrong? We all looked the part back then, the same kind of lovely, clean-cut white folks you'd see on any family TV show circa 1959, but the reality was more Kierkegaard's *Fear and Trembling* than *Leave It to Beaver.*

"Home, sweet home, eh, Blowman?"

And with that, Duds took my arm and practically threw me down the stairs to the basement. I somehow got my footing towards the lower end of the stairway, but then lost it again and fell to the floor, all my weight coming down on my right wrist and giving me a probable sprain, because I really, really needed one more piece of my body to get bashed up.

I let out a little cry of pain as I gathered what was left of my wits and looked around. This cellar was very different than the one of my youth. It was not the same dank, dark hole in the ground where Alan set up his pellet gun shooting gallery with old cardboard boxes and shot up my GI Joe action figures when I wasn't looking. This was not where he and I sat on the floor and poured practically a whole bottle of vinegar in his Zorro lunchbox, then added a box of baking soda, and watched the concoction bubble up over and over the edges and spread into a big foamy puddle, panicking us into running upstairs and outside with the lunchbox, where we threw it into a nearby construction ditch, which undoubtedly became a Superfund cleanup site.

No, that half-finished cellar with a dirt floor was gone. I was inside a huge, spotless, grand underground palace, concrete walls all painted white, with bright overhead LED lighting. The area around me was at least double the size of the original basement. Not only that, but it looked to me like it had been extended in a different direction. There was a hallway that wasn't there before, and at the end of that hallway was a door to presumably yet another room, which meant the basement might have been bigger than the entire house on top of it.

By the hallway door were the two security men the kid and I had seen entering the house earlier. Wearing nondescript jumpsuits and caps and armed with automatic weapons, they were eyeing me in the same way an octopus might view a dead elephant it had come upon on the sea floor. What the hell was this and why the hell was it here?

As Duds' heavy footsteps came plodding down the stairs, I took the remaining moments I had left to desperately search for a way out, because I needed to find a way to save the kid. Unfortunately, I saw no exit strategy. What I saw was one corner filled with security monitors showing various angles on the outside of the house, a lot of locked steel cabinets lining the walls and some kind of medical machinery in another corner, next to a medical station, complete with hospital bed, supplies and curtains that could be drawn to ensure privacy.

"What's going on?" asked Security Guy #1, looking down at me as Duds stepped down into the room.

"We have a visitor is all." Duds motioned to the closed door. "How is he?"

Security Guy #2 shrugged. "Same as always. He's awake."

Duds lifted me to my feet. "Come on, Blowman."

Security Guy #2 opened the door for us and Duds, pulling me by the arm, took me inside.

This room wasn't as large as the one I had just been in. Nor was it nearly as bright. No, its dimmed lighting fixtures kept everything in it enveloped in semi-darkness. As we entered, I immediately saw the two nurses we had spotted entering the house seated on a couch near the door, playing with their cell phones. Duds looked at them with a cold fury.

"This is what we pay you cunts to do?"

They looked up at him in shock.

"Oh, Mr. DeCosta," one said, "he's asleep right now. We've gone over his vitals and…"

Duds cut her off with a curt "Get out." They jumped up and left the room and he slammed the door behind them.

I continued to look around. On one wall was a giant mounted LED TV screen tuned to the History Channel, which was showing one of its roughly three million documentaries on World War II. The sound was muted. Unwieldy piles of papers sat in a corner of the room on some steel shelving. There were sealed boxes stacked along another wall. Finally, there was another bank of security monitors set up just like the ones in the other room. However, these monitors were dark.

"They don't work?" I asked. I wanted to see what was going on across the street. I wanted to see if the kid had made it out of the house.

"We keep 'em off at night, so they don't disturb him," Duds answered.

"Disturb who?"

Then I saw the main attraction in the far corner. I had almost missed it, because that part of the room was completely in the shadows. I finally made out an oversized super-wheelchair of some sort, with IVs attached and some other layered complex electronics along the side of its base.

My heart dropped. It had to be what I suspected. It had to be.

The supersized wheelchair lit up with a buzzing sound and whirled around. Sitting in it was what was left of my Daddy Andy. And it wasn't a pretty sight.

The upper right quadrant of his head seemed to have been rebuilt and covered over with raw metal, making him look like the world's oldest cyborg. That metal extended over his right eye—I guessed that might have been where my shot had got him. He had some kind of keyboard/speaker combo set up on a tray in front of him—and what was left of his withered body was covered by a hospital gown. His left eye twitched and blinked as it stared at me, while the rest of what face you could see seemed twisted into a permanent grimace. Before, he was a monster on the inside. Now, his outsides made for a matching set.

"That's what you did to Andrew Wright," Duds whispered to me. "The night you shot him in the head. That's what you did to your own father. To a great patriot. But look at him. You couldn't fucking stop him. And now you never will."

I shuddered. It was the only appropriate reaction.

Daddy Andy touched a button on one of his armrests and, with a small joystick, he steered his super-wheelchair wheeled closer to me. With his other hand, he began typing quickly on the keyboard. As he typed, a robotic voice came out of the speaker—apparently, he had lost the ability to talk so a computer program took care of that end. Maybe I had only gotten one bullet in him, but that bullet must have passed through his eye and gone into his brain, where it jangled more than a few wires. Okay, so it didn't kill him, but it fucking sure came close. Kudos, bullet.

"Your hair…is white," said the programmed robotic voice through the speaker.

Man, I was tired of hearing that.

"Yeah. Thanks to the fine folks at the Community," I managed to answer.

A pause as his one eye studied me. There was a slight bit of sadness in it.

"You…could…have had the world," said the robotic voice as he typed. "The…new world…the one we are…creeping." A beat. Daddy Andy typed quickly to correct his techno-voice. "Creating."

Seeing this old freak again and knowing at last that he *had* managed to survive the shooting further unnerved me. My chest was aching, I was sweating and breathing once again came hard. I worked hard to conceal all of it—I needed to keep my symptoms under control and play it cool. Weakness was always a welcome target with these fuckwits.

"You mean, the great White Reign? Your final triumph?" I asked with all the power of an asthmatic mouse.

"Yes. It will…happen. We…will go undergrad."

"What?"

A beat. He retyped. "Underground. And when the stems are over…" A beat. More retyping. "…storms are over…we will rile." A beat. More retyping. "Rule."

He was trying to type too fast, that's how damn excited he was about his Brave New World.

"You can still jorp us." Beat, retype. "Join us."

"You couldn't fit an auto-correct in that software?" I asked. Duds grabbed my throat from the back. My voice choked and I got the message. Humor wasn't welcome around there.

After Duds removed his hand and I almost coughed up a lung, I stood silent a moment. Why was I still alive? Were they still counting on me to be Daddy Andy's heir? Why else was I still in mostly one piece? Duds had told me they didn't need me anymore. They had the "promised one." Ashton was supposed to kill me, that I knew for a fact.

So…???

"Henry knew you were my father the whole time?" I asked, after I coughed a little.

"Yes. Henry. Another…disappointming." A beat. He started retyping, but I told him I got the idea. Then I asked the question I really wanted answered—was Henry or even Alan the so-called promised one? Was he their father as well? Was one of them his ace—or alternate bastard child—in the hole?

"No. Obly you."

Just me. But Henry knew. Henry had to grow up keeping that secret. Maybe they even applied a little mind control to his boy brain, just as they had mine, in order to keep him on the path to righteousness, aka employment at the CIA. Maybe all that pressure and all that weirdness was what ultimately made Henry's soul collapse and transformed him into an unsalvageable burnout. I didn't have room to worry about him, though. I was too worried about the kid, not to mention the rest of humanity.

Maybe I was even worried about me.

Suddenly confronted with my immediate demise, I realized I wanted to live more than I thought I did. Maybe there were things worth sticking around for. Maybe Angie and I could be something once we got beyond the minor dollop of antisemitism, maybe I could be there for the kid and maybe Eydie wouldn't have to spend her remaining doggy years crying at my grave.

Or maybe she would. The pain inside me was unbearable. I felt more and more like I was going to pass out. And my wrist fucking hurt, and my head, and my leg and...

"You...do not look weck." A beat, retype. "Well."

"Well, Daddy Andy, I don't feel well. But at least I can take comfort in knowing your poisoned gene pool stops with me."

That's when Daddy Andy managed to screw up a semblance of a sinister sneer. I turned to Duds, who was chuckling to himself. I didn't think I had said anything particularly funny. But they did.

Of course, they were in on the joke. I wasn't.

The Promised One

"The promised one." The words Augustine Bravino had said to me. The words Duds had repeated to me. I couldn't imagine who the hell the poor son of a bitch might be if it wasn't me, the original poor son of a bitch.

Duds opened the door. I heard him quietly say something to one of the nurses in the other room, something I couldn't make out. I stopped trying to hear and leaned against the wall to keep up my strength. Then I turned back to Daddy Andy, who was watching me, studying me. I thought a moment. Another possibility came to me. But it seemed…impossible? But I said it anyway.

"You couldn't have made another kid."

"I have been stroller…" Beat. Retype. "…sterile for 20 years."

Behind me, Duds gave out with a laugh. "He didn't have to make another kid, Blowman. You did all the work for us."

I turned to Duds with a start. And that's when one of the nurses escorted her in. Someone I never expected to see again. Never. Never, ever, ever.

But there she was.

It was Lady Blue Eyes herself, Barbara, my personal ice cream delivery person from the Community.

She was wearing a bathrobe over a pair of pajamas and looked like she had just been woken up from a sound sleep. A part of me rejoiced at seeing her. I knew that was the part of me that had waited for ice cream every morning for ten months and was so happy to see it coming through the front door. It was the same part of me that felt we should all stop and appreciate the USA because whatever is done in the name of this great land is necessary and aligned with the life-affirming wishes of a great and benevolent God.

"Hello, Max." She looked at me more closely and felt my swollen face with such a delicate touch, I felt no pain. "What's happened to you?"

"You did fuck her, right, Blowman?" asked Duds in his usual discrete manner. "She said she did. Passed a lie detector test."

I nodded slowly, in shock. "I…I just didn't think that…" How could I put this? "…that I…I left that much in her?"

Lady Blue Eyes nodded and kissed me gently on my other cheek, the one that wasn't swollen. "I feel so honored to carry your child, Max. And they're taking such good care of me here. They treat me like a queen."

"You left enough, Blowman," said Duds.

What the hell. What the hell. *What the hell.*

Daddy Andy wheeled in closer and began to type again. "We already gnaw…." Beat, retype. "…know it's a boy from the ulvrgarch."

"Ultrasound," said Duds with a little impatience, stopping Daddy Andy from any more keyboard action. "Congratulations, Blowman."

"It smelled like smoke up there," Lady Blue Eyes said to Duds with some concern.

"The home across the street happens to be on fire, dear," Duds said, with surprising tenderness. "Let's get you back up to bed, so Mr. Wright and I can finish up our business here." He motioned for the nurse to take her away.

When the nurse opened the door to leave, however, one of the security guards ran in past her and Lady Blue Eyes. He was out of breath.

"Henry…"

"What about him?" demanded Duds. The security guy switched on the security monitors. And on one of the monitors, I very clearly saw Henry holding a flaming piece of wood, presumably from the house across the street…and slowly resting the burning end of it against the side of our house. As in, the house we were all in at the moment.

"WHAT THE FUCK!" Duds screamed. "GO STOP HIM!"

"What do we do? You said we weren't supposed to hurt him…" The security guard was freaked out. "SHIT, THE GARAGE!" yelled Duds. Everyone's eyes shot to the monitor that showed the garage, which was already on fire. Apparently, that had been Henry's first stop.

"JESUS! JUST STOP HIM! BOTH OF YOU!"

Duds turned to the nurse, still standing there. "Get Barbara out of here. Take her in your car. Drive her to a motel. Call me when she's safe. GO."

The nurse hurried out. I looked at the monitors again. One of the security guys had already made it outside and was carefully but quickly going after Henry. Henry reacted like a villager confronted with Frankenstein's monster—he turned and swung his makeshift torch right into the guy's face. The security guy screamed in agony and went down. Henry bent down and lit the guard's clothes on fire. More screaming. More flames. It wasn't a pleasant scene.

"Jesus, no," yelled Duds. "Jesus!"

Then we watched in shock as the other security guy entered the picture outside. But he stopped in his tracks when he spotted his co-worker burning on the ground, rolling around, shrieking. He took a lesson from that and went for his gun while keeping a safe distance from Henry.

Unfortunately, he had one of those holsters you had to unsnap in order to get to the pistol—which took a few seconds he would never get back. Henry simply threw the flaming piece of wood with dead aim straight at the guy's head. He yelped and quickly joined his blazing buddy on the lawn. And then Henry quietly walked over, picked up the burning piece of wood and lit *that* security guy's clothes on fire.

Through it all, my brother's expression remained strangely tranquil. He had the same impassive look on his face as when I saw him standing on the porch before. Obviously though, however serene he seemed, old FF had finally snapped. And he was determined to burn his decades of psychological pain all the way down to the ground.

Almost simultaneously, we all realized we weren't watching a horror movie, but real life. Duds shook his head in disbelief, then rushed into the other section of the basement and ordered the other nurse out of the house, he'd go with her and make sure she was safe. Then he slammed the door shut behind him. I heard a lock fall into place.

I looked back at the monitors, where I saw the first nurse running away from the house with Lady Blue Eyes. They'd be safe. Soon after, the next nurse exited through the front door, followed by Duds holding his gun, looking around anxiously for any sign of Henry. But Henry seemed to have vanished.

I watched as Duds pulled out his phone and tapped three numbers—9-1-1. Guess he had no choice but to call the fire department at this point. The flames on my old house weren't out of control yet, but it was old wood and it wouldn't be long before there were more ashes than house.

I turned to Daddy Andy. We were all alone. And he was once again furiously typing.

"That is a fire doob." Beat, retype. "Door. Ceiling is fireproof."

"So, we're safe. Great. Probably have your own air system down here. What was this whole basement reno, a test run for the compound in Montana?"

More typing. "There is still time, Max. You can rise your sin and..." He stopped and started to retype.

"I get it, I get it, I can raise my son and live to a ripe old age...as long as I commit to being all white and all right."

Daddy Andy didn't say—or type, I should say—anything. He stared at me through that weird twitchy eye of his. Maybe he was thinking survival trumped decency for me, as it did for most people. I wanted to disabuse him of that notion, even if it took my last breath.

"You think your blood's so special?" I asked. "So did Genghis Khan, Kublai Khan, Hitler, Mussolini, Ivan the Terrible and Trump the Moron. You're just another asshole, just like they were. You all presume genocide is the answer, but what the fuck is the question? What the fuck is the point? You think God's handpicked you to lead us all to some kind of ultimate victory? A victory over what?"

His eye glared at me. Everything went a little wobbly, so I leaned against the wall again.

"I mean, I don't get it. I really don't get it. You've built your whole fucking life on this crazy shit. Decades skulking around in the government, constantly trying to impose white rule on whatever country you wanted. All paid for by the American taxpayer. And you know what, it never works. It never works. Not...not for long, anyway."

I put my head back against the wall and stared at the ceiling, which seemed to be swirling. I could hear Daddy Andy start to type again and I could even somehow hear the anger in his keystrokes.

"Then you will dir." Beat, retype. "Die."

"I expect so. And then, lucky you...you get to pass your enchanted DNA through me to the baby...your...your precious DNA..."

I wiped my brow. I couldn't stay standing any longer. I sunk down to a sitting position against the wall, next to one of those stacks of papers. Next thing I knew I was vomiting on the floor next to me. At least there wasn't much in there, mostly just the water I drank across the street. Which reminded me of the kid. Which made me really pissed off.

"You fucker…" I gasped. "You've destroyed so much…so much…for nothing. For…*nothing*. You…"

I let out a groan. I couldn't finish. I eyed the monitors. Duds stood in the front yard, still eyeing the neighborhood for Henry, as a fire engine arrived. I turned back to Daddy Andy and shook my head. The bastard had taken everything I had. He made every day of my life a living nightmare for years. He had screwed me up in ways I couldn't even grasp, starting when he screwed my mother.

And then there was casualty list—Jules, Howard, Marco, and a lot of other innocents who tried to help but got cut down by Daddy Andy's tribe of followers. And now the kid, the closest thing to a son I'd ever have no matter what lived in the belly of Lady Blue Eyes, had probably joined that cursed list. A couple of tears oozed out the corners of my eyes despite my best efforts to keep them in.

Daddy Andy noticed and typed. "You are…weak."

Okay, he had me. I was definitely weak at that moment. But as I stared at his smug little twisted smile, I realized something. If I was going to go, I was going to take that triple-A slab of diseased meat with me. It wasn't cold-blooded murder in my book. Because, in my book, the sick bastard didn't qualify as a human being.

Determination trumped my pain and dizziness. I reached into my pocket and pulled out my cigarette lighter. Daddy Andy looked at it with some confusion reflected in his giant veined eye, as if he was having trouble making out what it was. I managed to flick it to a flame—then I reached over and lit the edge of the pile of papers that was near my head.

Then he knew what it was.

He started wheeling toward me, toward the small fire I had started. And he started weakly huffing and puffing, as if he actually thought he could blow it out from the seat of his super-duper-wheelchair. But he was simply too far away. He kept trying, however, and stayed completely focused on the flames.

So, while that kept him busy, I crawled down to the next pile of papers. I flicked the lighter on again. I set them on fire too.

Daddy Andy's big eye went ballistic. He quickly steered his chair over to the second fire and tried to blow that one out. Again, he couldn't do it. Again, he kept trying.

I got down on my hands and knees and slowly crawled behind the super-wheelchair. Once I got behind it, I scanned its back and found what I was looking for. The battery pack.

I reached up from the floor and tried to yank it open.

Daddy Andy didn't even take the time to type, "Whrt are you dbing?" Instead, the second he felt me pulling on the back, he used his controls to move the chair away from me. I found another place to grip the chair with my other hand, the one with the bad wrist, and clung on for dear life as he began to pull me behind him around the room. This was not a fun ride, especially since I had just been dragged across the street. The expensive wardrobe Roberto had gifted me was rapidly turning into rags.

I used my free hand to explore the back of the chair until I found it— the release button on the battery pack. I pushed it with all my might, which was just enough to instantly pop the battery out of its casing.

The chair came to an abrupt halt.

I threw the battery across the room, as far as I could. It must have only powered the chair, not Daddy Andy's communication hardware, because, as I lay there on the floor breathing heavily, I heard his fingers on the keyboard again, followed by the creepy robotic voice.

"Stop," it said. "You can have all the mammy you want…" Beat. Retype. "Money…"

Mammy. I had to laugh, because suddenly I thought of Al Jolson on his hands and knees. Which inspired me to pull myself up on my knees. I waddled forward on them and once again grabbed the back of the super-wheelchair for support. The chair lurched a bit from my weight and Andy tried to turn to see what I was up to.

"Don't worry, Pops," I said. "I'm gonna come around to you."

I then pulled myself around to the side of the chair, the side with the pole holding the IV bags and the tubes that traveled from those bags to the veins in his arm. The tubes were what I was after.

"What art yob doing?" asked the robotic voice.

My answer was to yank on the tubes. And yank again and again. But I was too weak to get the job done. I heard Daddy Andy shifting in his seat in discomfort, because he obviously felt the tug on his IVs.

"Stop," said the robotic voice. "Stop. Talk twy me, Max. We are…"

I threw myself to the ground, tubes in my hand, in order to create enough force to pull them out of his arm.

"…fambily…"

I hit the floor with their bloody ends in my hands. I had fallen forward, in front of the super-wheelchair, so I turned and looked up to see Daddy Andy's reaction. His face had gone white and his mouth was wide open, as if he was trying to let out a scream. Nothing came out, which was somehow more disturbing.

"Aklgarpalka!" said the robotic voice of his speaker. Or at least that's what it sounded like. Then it just began to go "AAAAAAAAAAAAAAAAAAAAA" in a droning, ear-splitting tone. I looked up at Daddy Andy and saw his finger was tapping repeatedly on the "A' key, like it was in some kind of spasm.

I wanted to be sure Andrew Wright never uttered another word, with or without electronic help. I got myself back up on my arms and crawled around the chair to the other side, where I could get to the tray where the keyboard rested.

"AAAAAAAAAAAAAAAAAAA"

Daddy Andy, completely helpless, watched me the whole time, but there was nothing he could do. Should his complete impotence have brought me so much pleasure? Or the fact that this all-powerful ghoul was finally, finally, fucking FINALLY stripped of any ability to act? No, it shouldn't have. But it did.

"AAAAAAAAAAAAAAAAAAA"

I reached up and weakly yanked on the keyboard and speaker wires. It wasn't enough. I had to let myself fall again to bring them down with me.

"AAA...AA!"

The drone quickly cut out. But I had done more damage than I had anticipated. Those wires were apparently connected to more than the keyboard and the speaker. Sparks flew. What was left of Andrew Wright began choking and convulsing. And I suddenly knew that I had short-circuited whatever was keeping his system operational.

I got myself up to a sitting position for the final show. There was more gagging. More strange and almost inhuman noises. His eye was fixed on me, not with anger and contempt, but more with a curious respect. The look seemed to indicate that he finally came to accept I was good enough to be his son, because I was somehow strong enough to destroy him.

The eye remained open as the machinery whirred to a stop. Then there was silence, complete silence and nothing else. Even the paper fires had fizzled out.

And then it was over. My Daddy Andy, a person I had never even heard of a few years before, was dead, just weeks after my mom. I was an official orphan at 61.

"Just another asshole," I murmured to myself.

My task complete, my brain allowed my body to completely collapse. I fell forward onto the floor, gasping for air, my entire body trembling. It felt like somebody had ripped out all my wires and I was shutting down too, just like dear old dad.

That's when the door flew open and some smoke billowed in. And emerging from that smoke was the massive, enraged figure of Duds. He took everything in, then glared down at me.

"What did you do? You motherfucker. You piece of shit."

"Still a saint compared to you," I weakly said with all the force of a bug with laryngitis.

He pulled out his gun as my vision doubled and my chest pain tripled.

"Have it your way, Saint Blowman. Maybe you earned your way into heaven. Let's find out."

My eyes closed as I steeled myself for what was to come. I heard a shot and instinctively flinched.

But I felt nothing.

I made the effort to push my eyelids back open. And immediately saw all 350 pounds of Duds come crashing to the floor, right on his big, fat, evil face. Blood leaked out the back of his head from a perfectly placed wound. I looked up to see who had done the good deed. Was it Kev? Had he come back from the West Coast to check up on us? Or was it maybe the kid? Maybe he had escaped from the burning house after all.

But...no and no. It wasn't Kev. It wasn't the kid. It was...well, in retrospect, I should have known who it was.

For the third time, Patrice Plotkin, Queen of the Last-Minute Rescue, had saved the day. Looking badass as hell, she strolled through the smoke clutching her gun with both hands, keeping it aimed directly at Duds' head. She was clearly ready to unload another round if the fat bastard moved a finger.

"Is this shit over now?" she asked me wearily.

I laughed a little, despite the fact there was nothing left in my tank. And then everything went black.

The End

I was hoping to see the tunnel.

You know, that tunnel of light you're supposed to travel through when you die? When all your friends and family (well, at least the dead ones) come to welcome you to the afterlife? Maybe give you some pointers?

But there was no tunnel when I felt myself go under. There was just darkness. And then there were some random dreams and floating images, nothing that made sense, just crazy shit like a turtle wearing a dress. I felt let down by the lack of organization. If I was dead, it seemed like somebody would have gone to the trouble of putting together some kind of welcoming committee, or at least a PowerPoint on "What to Expect When You're No Longer Alive."

But nothing. Just random dreams. Floating images.

And finally, my eyes opening to see…well, I was in a hospital.

I saw the kid sitting by the bed. Was that Angela standing nearby, sipping from a water bottle—and, suddenly spotting my open eyes, spitting out the water and running to get help?

My eyes closed again as I heard an official-sounding voice saying something like, "He's weak, let him sleep," and then I heard nothing. I went back to the randomness, but this time, with the knowledge that I had not, in fact, died. I was still around. And I actually felt all right about that.

I woke up again. I had no idea how much time had passed. The kid was still there in a chair, but asleep in a position that was bound to give him a stiff neck.

"Kid?" I asked.

He couldn't have been napping too hard, because his eyes flew open.

"Max!"

"How come you're still alive?"

"I could ask you the same question." And then he told me how he had escaped from the burning house. The flames between him and the stairs were too high, too hot, so he took the uninflated inflatable mattresses we had bought and wrapped them around himself—and then he threw himself through the flames and onto the stairway. He made it downstairs and outside, but he swallowed a lot of smoke—so much that he collapsed on the lawn. The paramedics found him there and took him to the hospital.

"Oh," I said. "So I guess buying those air mattresses…wasn't so stupid…" And then I went back under.

The next time I woke up, nobody was around. I looked at the window and saw it was the middle of the night. The nurse finally came by to clean up my shit and piss. When she saw I was awake, she got excited and went to get a doctor. When she found one and dragged him into the room, he began to review my chart with a trace of irritation.

"How bad was the heart attack?" I asked.

His answer: I didn't have one.

From what he could tell from the paperwork, I was suffering from a concussion (from Ashton's pistol-whipping) and some severe-yet-mysterious trauma (from my escape from the Community). The doctor also helpfully added something about the trauma being compounded by a nasty case of nervous exhaustion from ongoing stress.

Having said that, he told me they had checked my arteries to make sure they were okay. Turned out a couple of them were 70, 80% blocked. So, they were going to install some stents, just to be safe, when I was a little more rested. Better safe than sorry. I agreed. I was done with sorry. It was time to explore safe for a while.

The kid came back with Angie. I looked at her, really looked at her. I offered my hand. She took it. PMA smiled. All three of us had taken turns not expecting to see each other ever again. Each of us had been wonderfully wrong.

"I'm starting to think you're Superman," Angie finally said. "An old, decrepit Superman."

"I think that just makes me more impressive." I turned to the kid. "What happened to Henry?"

"They found him wandering around a few blocks away." The kid paused. "He's…in the asylum. They say he's not dangerous."

"As long as they keep him away from matches. And Duds? Daddy Andy?"

"Dead. Dead."

"Good. Good." I turned to Angela. "So, you're a widow now. You're available."

She smiled. "I was already available, idiot. Remember? You got me my divorce." Then she leaned over and gave me a soft kiss on my dry lips.

It was the best kiss of my life.

I gradually found a few things out.

Kevin had coerced Patrice Plotkin to go one last time, against her better judgment of course, to make sure the kid and I were safe. As always, her timing was impeccable.

As for my family home, the fire department had arrived in the nick of time. Most of it was still standing—only the garage was mostly gone. Patrice brought the authorities down to the basement, where they discovered all they needed to know about what was going on in Montana, as well as the very gross remains of Andrew Wright. A subsequent leak of the White Rain documents to a cable news outfit created a media frenzy that resulted in the complete shutdown of that little project, as well as many, many arrests.

And Lady Blue Eyes? Eight weeks into her pregnancy, she took a DNA blood test to determine parentage. Turned out it wasn't my baby. Apparently, Lady Blue Eyes had a thing for sedated old men and had screwed a sizable number of Community residents—mostly newbies who were still capable of doing the deed. The real daddy was determined to be Joe Lenius, an ex-CIA guy from Chicago who had tried to blow the whistle on Andrew Wright and found himself rewarded with his own Community townhouse. Once they rescued him and weaned him off the magic ice cream, he was excited to hear he was having another child. So excited he immediately died of a stroke. He was worth a fortune and had no family, so all his money went to whoever was in Lady Blue Eyes' belly.

When I was finally recovered and my stents had been installed, they said I could go home. Home. That meant stately Davidson Manor, at least for the time being. I wanted to take my new Mercedes back to Virginia and luckily, it was still in the parking garage where I left it. The kid drove while Angela and I sat in the backseat, holding hands like a couple of wrinkled teenagers. I told her if she bankrolled the office, I'd do the detective agency with the kid—but not to mention it to him for a few weeks. Otherwise, he'd start nagging me on a daily basis to get it going. First, I felt like I needed some rest, some real rest for a change, as opposed to losing consciousness between crises.

It was mid-afternoon when we reached Virginia Beach and drove through the gates of stately Davidson Manor. The kid parked the Mercedes in front and helped me out of the back seat. After I got out, I stood there for a moment, taking in the welcome sight and feeling real peace for the first time in years. I realized there would no longer be an Andrew Wright to torment me and everyone else left in my life. I was free. Sure, another asshole like him might come along—there was currently one in the White House. But that asshole and those that would inevitably follow him wouldn't be my problem. I had served my time.

Chef opened the front door and Eydie shot out past him. She stopped and stared at me a moment in disbelief. I teared up. Then the pooch came running at me and jumped up and down at me repeatedly. As usual, I covered my nuts in defense, then finally knelt and patted her little head as the kid and Angie approached.

I guess I did have a home after all.

"Max…" the kid said with some surprise as I was still kneeling and petting Eydie. I turned to him. "The top of your head."

Angela looked down at me and gasped.

"What?" I asked.

She laughed. "Your roots. They're coming in black. Your hair color is coming back."

I felt the top of my head, as if I could know the color by touch.

I had gone from feeling cursed to feeling blessed. A part of me finally let go and I cried. I couldn't control it and, for once, I didn't want to. I got to my feet and sobbed and sobbed and sobbed. Angie hugged me, the kid patted me on the back and Eydie jumped up and down in front of me.

Chef came down to join our little family reunion.

"You know what I'm going to make for you all? Some delicious ice cream sundaes! Who wants a delicious ice cream sundae?"

I smiled at him.

"I like ice cream," I said.

Joel Canfield

About the Author

A novelist, screenwriter and ghostwriter, Canfield has lived in New York City, Chicago, Detroit, Miami Beach, Auckland, New Zealand, and his own personal Pennsylvania trifecta, Pittsburgh, Wilkes-Barre and his hometown of Bethlehem. He now resides in Long Beach, California with his favorite blondes, writer-editor wife Lisa and dog Betsy, but he will undoubtedly move again, because that's just what he does.

Canfield's books include *Dark Sky, Blue Fire* and *Red Earth* (the first three books in the Max Bowman series); *What's Driving You???: How I Overcame Abuse and Learned to Lead in the NBA* (co-authored with Keyon Dooling and Lisa Canfield); *Pill Mill: My Years of Money, Madness, Sex and Drugs* (co-authored with Christian Valdes and Lisa Canfield); and *226: How I Became the First Blind Person to Kayak the Grand Canyon* (co-authored with Lonnie Bedwell. *Blue Fire* was a 2016 Silver Honoree in the Benjamin Franklin Digital Awards as well as a semi-finalist in the Book Life Prize in Fiction competition. *Red Earth* was a 2017 Gold Honoree in the Benjamin Franklin Digital Awards. He has also co-written two Hallmark movies, *Eat, Play, Love* and *Yes, I Do* with Lisa Canfield, and they contain no swearing or violence.

For more about Joel and his lovely wife, visit www.gethipcreative.com.